DESOLATION

To Alexandra
a wonderful
person that is
special to me

Dr. Wm F. Covey

DESOLATION

Dr. William F. Covey

ARPress
ILLUMINATING IDEAS.
EMPOWERING VOICES

ARPress
45 Dan Road Suite 5
Canton, MA 02021

Hotline: 1(888) 821-0229
Fax: 1(508) 545-7580

Ordering Information:

Quantity sales. Special discounts are available on quantity purchases by corporations, associations, and others. For details, contact the publisher at the address above.

Printed in the United States of America.

| ISBN-13: | Softcover | 979-8-89389-332-8 |
| | eBook | 979-8-89389-331-1 |

Library of Congress Control Number: 2024916057

TABLE OF CONTENTS

INTRODUCTION

DAY'S OF NOAH

Language of the first ancestors—alphabet on vertical left.

Illustrated by J. Harold Mallon

Translation of message from the language of the fi rst ancestors

"Before man, God ruled the planet in perfect harmony. Now that man has been awakened by the Creator, woe to Mother Earth for she will become an abomination of desolation because humans, animals that can talk, are selfi sh and greedy creatures"

LANGUAGE OF THE FIRST ANCIENTS

Illustrated by J. Harold Mallon

Hebrew script compared to that of the Ancients of the land of Noah before the 5th rebirth.

GOLDEN TEMPLE MESSAGE
OF THE ANCIENT EARTH DWELLERS

This is the message to all animals that can talk. We want you to learn about the terrible destruction of Mother Earth by the Great and Powerful Light from the Sky that washed the foundations of our ancestors away and left your forefathers with naught.

Illustrated by J. Harold Mallon

Will those survivors reading this message take it deep into their hearts as to know the truth of their predestination? Years after the burning fire that eradicated thousands of species a new global destruction is facing Humans. For months, our men of knowledge had told us to discern the warnings of the skies that indicate Mother Earth will forego changes. We were told Earth would be hit by a giant light cloud from the skies which would destroy the Earth as we know it and take away its evil and destructive forces so as to start anew. Leaders of the Ionians, my race, have left this message to those that are the descendents of the New

Man (Noah). For New Man was chosen to withstand the onslaught and replenish life on Earth with those remaining creatures that otherwise would have faced the same demise as us.

If humans, animals that can talk, are reading this, man has evolved to the state it was before the 'Great End' of the fourth civilization. The Fifth Purification will destroy most animals that walk about Mother Earth. This message is a warning to all future Humans living in the fifth generation of Mother Earth to never take life on this planet for granted. Life is a gift from the Great Spirit and Mother Earth is the place created to nourish life as the Great Spirit has designed her. Do not take this warning as mere nonsense. Believe our report. Mother Earth will eventually have a sixth purification and leave you in desolation. Will you survive? Time will tell all.

Beware, everyday is different and one day cannot be compared to another. We did and now we are no more. If you are reading this warning, you are now living in the Fifth Rebirth of Mother Earth. One day your demise will be at hand, too. Be ready.

Judge Methusos, known ruler of the fourth creation of Mother Earth.

This interpretation was derived from the original text using the Hebrew language as a guideline for a comparative study using computer generated decoding techniques.

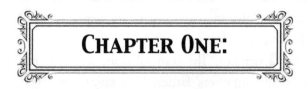

NEW HOPI MEHA

"Sarah, Sarah Meha, it is time to purify your heart," cried a voice from nowhere. The voice sounded like the wind whistling through the bristles of a pine tree.

It startled Sarah Begay, an elderly Hopi lady. She looked in all directions trying to see who or what called out her name. She saw no one and nothing for as far as her eyes could see across the vast landscapes of the Hopi plateau.

"Sarah, heed my call. Millions will die soon if not protected. It is the end of this age for Mother Earth," cried out the mystic voice.

Sarah stopped and picked up a stick to protect herself. "Sarah Meha, the time of purification has arrived," said the voice this time sounding like many winds.

"Who are you? What are you?" asked Sarah raising the ironwood branch to defend herself against the unknown that sent cold chills running up and down her spine.

"I am the Great Spirit Caretaker of the ancient wisdom," said the mysterious voice. This time it presented itself by making a breeze move across her face like being touched by a hand.

"This voice is not real. It is the wind howling. I must be hearing my own thoughts." she thought. She tightly squeezed the branch ready to fight for her life, "I feel like it is touching me. I must be going crazy."

Then out of thin air appeared a man dressed as an ancient Hopi warrior. Sarah froze in her footsteps when the Warrior spoke out vehemently.

"I am Maasaw. I am the one that left the instruction to your ancestors to know the future which instructs all Hopi to know the time of the times," said the ancient spirit Caretaker of the ancient wisdom that sounded like thunder.

"I am but a woman. The transmissions were left to "The Ones," which were my grandfathers' fathers," she said trembling.

"Sarah Meha, heed my warnings and prepare our people for what will be," said Maasaw this time with a voice of a thousand rivers.

"Please, choose another. I am too old and not important enough to guide the Hopi people," said Sarah petrified by the presence of the powerful Great Spirit of her ancestral fathers.

"It is I who decides to whom I will dispense the secret transmissions and reveal the truth about the Meha. I know your married name is Navajo, but you are of the ancient Hopi bloodline. For years Hopi elders have been corrupted by strangers that try to explain the time of the times with their feeble knowledge. I know the truth. Listen to me and learn the truth. Hear my voice and tell our people that this age is coming to an end," said Maasaw with such power that Sarah started to feel faint from the fear she was experiencing.

"No one knows the truth about the Meha. There are many different beliefs as to what the Meha really means," she cried out trying to argue with the Caretaker of the Hopi people.

"My child, weep not, for I will teach you the truth," said Maasaw speaking with compassion to Sarah as she wept.

"No one will believe what I would say. I am an old woman and not of the tribal elders. Why haven't you chosen our tribe's medicine man or my son to receive this great message?" asked Sarah, crying while pleading her case out of shock and despair.

"I have chosen who I have chosen. You have been favored because you are pure of heart. Your purity is known and revered in the hereafter. Heed my call," said Maasaw this time sounding like many waterfalls.

"It is the custom of our people that men are the spiritual leaders of the Hopi," responded Sarah.

"The Hopi men have been corrupted by those that do not know the truth. These strangers have insisted they are the Chosen Ones and prophets of the truth. They have not been told the truth, except for what has been revealed to the children of the Promised Land," said Maasaw vehemently sounding like a thunderhead exploding after an intense lightening strike.

"I am so scared that I cannot move my arms or legs," cried out Sarah, "Why do you keep calling me Sarah Meha when my name is Sarah Begay?" she asked trying to figure why the ancient spirit of her fathers was contacting her.

"You have been chosen to transmit thousands of years of knowledge to your people, so you will be called Sarah Meha," firmly replied Maasaw.

"I will be mocked, scorned, and laughed at," cried Sarah shaking from fear.

"I am Maasaw, little one, hear my voice. I have come to reveal the secrets of The Great Day of Purification to you. You will not be mocked and scorned by any Hopi. This day of visitation has been expected for thousands of years. Listen to me Meha, so the Hopi nation will be spared from a world that will be purified. Your nation must learn how to survive as this age of Mother Earth will soon end. You have been chosen to reveal the secrets of the great destruction that will engulf the entire world," said Maasaw this time sounding like a whirlwind.

"I will listen and do as you have commanded, Great Spirit of my ancestors, but it will be to no avail," pleaded Sarah hoping Maasaw would simply vanish back into the spirit world.

"Meha, I will give you the knowledge to establish the New Meha. I was the one that presented the instructions for the original Meha," said Maasaw speaking like the four great winds that encompass Mother Earth.

"How can an old woman be a Spiritual Leader at this magnitude for the Hopi people? I will be ridiculed and laughed at by my people," cried Sarah again, now being completely overtaken by fear.

"My little daughter, your spiritual ancestors know the truth. The knowledge of our people has been polluted with doctrines that are not of Hopi origins. Not only does 'The Sixth Purification' of Mother Earth need to be revealed, but the purification of the Hopi nation must be rekindled, too. You will have to complete a PA-MU-YA before you will be spiritually acceptable to understand the parables of the Meha. When you have completed your purification, the living human beings of the Hopi nation will depend on you. Heed my voice," said Maasaw now sounding like the strong winds of a hurricane.

As Maasaw spoke, three Hopi ancestral spirits appeared as Kachinas dancing while singing ancient Hopi songs and chants. The three pounded their drums as they sang out for the protection of the Hopi people from what would soon come over Mother Earth. The ancient spirit chants calmed her down enough that her body stopped shaking as much. Then the Kachina warriors started singing the same songs Sarah's grandfather had sung to her as a child over seventy years ago.

Sarah felt good thinking about the times she spent with her grandfather. He had taught her that the white strangers were wrong to condemn the Hopi ancient ancestral spirits. Now Sarah was listening to Maasaw tell her that she was the one chosen to rekindle the fire of the Hopi people and reveal the complete meaning of the 3500-year-old Meha.

Maasaw had made it clear to Sarah that she was the one chosen to receive the instructions needed to protect her tribe from the massive destruction that would occur during the Sixth Purification of Mother Earth. As the scattered sunrays broke over the eastern mountains, Maasaw disappeared as the bright morning sunrays blinded Sarah. She let go of the staff she had held so tightly in her left hand. Still transfixed by Maasaw's visitation, Sarah started looking to the east, west, south, and north, and then she looked straight up into the heavens to see if he was there. After Maasaw had vanished into the unknown, Sarah started thinking she had been hallucinating. From a distance Abel saw that his mother was having problems standing, so he ran over to assist her. He found her mumbling to herself and trembling terribly so he took her back to the Begay ranch house. Still shaking Sarah immediately sat down in her favorite chair on the front porch and said nothing for two hours.

"Danny, Maasaw visited me this morning before sun rise," said Sarah, trembling as she spoke thinking about what her husband might say about her experience.

"Oh, Sarah my darling are you sure? Maybe one the white stranger's diseases has attacked your mind. You are speaking with a forked tongue. A Black Ring Tail rattlesnake ready to strike with his deadly venom could not be as poisoned as your speech," cried out Danny, as he looked toward the heavens thinking his wife had lost her mind.

"I told Maasaw I would be scorned and laughed at by my people," she said, as she bent over and lowered her head in shame.

"Oh, my darling Sarah, please forgive me. I have known you since you were three years old and you have never lied to me one time. Now

I stand here insulting you. Please forgive me my darling," said Danny, the desert fire warrior regretting what he had said.

"I forgive you, but you must hear me out. After I finish telling you about my experience, if I am not worthy of your respect, then you can feed me to the dogs," replied Sarah.

"I could never hurt the love of my life. Please darling, tell me what happened so I will understand the burden weighing on your mind," said Danny humbly.

He had great respect for his wife of fifty years, but was still apprehensive to listen to her mystic experience, thinking she was starting to lose her mental faculties. Nevertheless, because he loved so he asked her to tell him what had happened.

"I was getting ready to lead the sheep to a new pasture when I heard a voice speaking to me from nowhere. Next thing, an ancient warrior appeared before my eyes in a cloud. I thought at first I was dreaming or seeing the image of a ghost. Then he started to speak to me openly, as if he had known me from my childhood. Fear started rushing up and down my body."

"What did he say?" asked Danny leaning toward her starting to become serious.

"He called me Sarah Meha and told me many will die from the purification coming upon Mother Earth. I was so scared that my body froze in place. Next, he told me his name was Maasaw. I told him my name is Sarah Begay, and then he told me I was Hopi and not Navajo. Then he called me Sarah Meha, agains," said Sarah, as tears started running down her cheeks.

"Oh, my Sarah, my sweet Sarah, the spirits of our fathers has come to warn us about the future. I am Navajo married to a Hopi that the Caretaker has chosen. My precious Sarah, what does this mean that the Great Spirits of the sky would take the time to visit you? Sarah the Gods of our fathers must angry with us," said Danny being confused with what had happened to Sarah.

While Danny and Sarah were growing up, Danny's family lived only a few miles away from Sarah's parent's home. Danny was Navajo and

Sarah was Hopi. For centuries the Navajo and Hopi Native Americans had disputes over land and water rights. To make matters worse, the government of the United States of America placed the Hopi Native American reservation on land encompassed by the Navajo reservation. Many Navajos and Hopis did not get along because they constantly disagreed over the boundaries set by the American government. Danny and Sarah had been ridiculed most of their life by various tribesmen on both side due to the tribal disputes.

"Nonsense, Danny, I say that is nonsense. We love one another and we have already been persecuted enough by our own people. Why would the Spirit of our fathers wait this long to approach us? There has to be another reason for this visitation," said Sarah, being upset with Danny's comments.

"Sarah, we must talk to the Hopi elders at once and tell them about your visitation from Maasaw. They must be told what has happened to you this morning. It will be for the good of the Hopi people," said Danny, trying to appease his wife.

"No, I will not humiliate myself in front of my elders," replied Sarah.

"Sarah, my darling, we must let the elders know what you have seen," pleaded Danny.

"Call the elders then, but tell them they will have to come to our house for me to speak about this. I will tell them all that I have seen and heard," she said reluctantly.

Danny got into his new dark blue pickup truck and sped away to speak with Sarah's Hopi tribal leaders. After Danny had left, Sarah decided to return to the pasture to tend to her precious sheep. When Sarah arrived at the pastor where Maasaw had appeared to her, she noticed that Abel had already moved her precious sheep to a new pastor. As she walked over to the new pastor she decided to tell her son what had happened to her and what his father had decided to do. He immediately went to the east side of the barn and gathered some firewood for a bonfire. The bonfire would be necessary for a traditional Hopi open-pit campfire meeting if the tribal elders decided to meet with his mother.

Sarah returned to the Begay ranch house to cook a meal for her potential guest. In her kitchen she mixed up some batter for her unique 'Indian fry bread'. She then called Abel's wife to ask her if she would bring over some of her Prickly Pear cactus jelly. Sarah felt the jelly would make the fry bread even more special for her guests. Sarah then made a large pot of fresh lamb stew using the same recipe her mother had taught her over sixty years ago. Time seemed to vanish that day for Sarah being so deeply engrossed in her thoughts about her experience. Danny returned with the Hopi tribal chief just before dusk to discuss Sarah's mysterious spiritual visitation from Maasaw. He wanted to see if Sarah was mentally stable.

"Chief, it is a pleasure to have you to visit my humble home," said Danny to his long time friend, the tribal leader of the Hopi native American tribe.

"Where is Sarah?" asked Chief Blackcloud.

"I think she is tending the animals with my son," replied Danny.

"The others should be here any minute, but I would like to talk to Sarah alone before they arrive," said Chief Blackcloud requesting a private meeting to check out Sarah.

Danny called for Sarah. She came at his beckoning along with her two sons, Abel and Ronnie. As they entered the house, Chief Steven Blackcloud motioned for Sarah to speak with him alone. She nodded her head yes, so they went outside.

"Sarah, if what you have heard or seen is real, the elders will not condemn you, but they will be very interested in wanting to know everything you experienced in detail," said the Chief in a very pleasant tone of voice.

"I fear they will mock me and ridicule me since I have married a Navajo. Why would Maasaw visit a Hopi with half-breed sons and daughter," said Sarah lowering her head and being frank about her beliefs.

"I am not a spiritual man. I do not claim to be the one that knows much about the spirits of our fathers, but I do know that Maasaw has not visited our people for thousands of years until now. Sarah, they are not coming here to ridicule you but to hear the words of our ancestral spirits. I am not talking to you as the chief of the Hopi people, but as your friend. I want to let you know that after speaking to your husband about your fears, I will ask everyone attending this gathering to honor and respect you. I promise you, our tribal leaders will not ignore, scorned, or mock you. You have my word," said the chief, concerned for Sarah's welfare.

"Thank you, for your respect and honor," replied Sarah softly.

"It is my duty to serve my people the best way I can," he replied.

"I will do my best Chief Blackcloud, to accurately account for every word spoken by Maasaw," said Sarah, feeling comfortable that her leaders would not shame her in any fashion. About ten minutes later the elders arrived. Sarah started cooking the Indian fry bread that she planned to serve her guests. The elders sat down and ate the meal to honor Danny and his household. One elder liked the food so much he had a second serving of the lamb stew.

He then complimented Sarah by telling her this excellent food was one of the best gifts a woman could give a man, save love and beautiful children. Sarah smiled as all of the elders agreed with elder Joseph. After the light meal, the group congregated outside where Abel had started the bonfire. As they all gathered around the newly kindled fire, it started burning hotter shooting up bright orange, yellow and red flames several feet high up into the air. You could hear the wood crackle and snap as the blazing fire lit up the night. "Sarah, it would be an honor if you would tell everyone here, in your own words, what you saw and heard this morning," said the chief politely.

Everyone became so quiet you could hear the coyotes howling in the distant hills. The fire crackled louder as it grew larger creating gigantic wild flames that swirled about. As Sarah started to speak in a flash Maasaw appeared. All of the Hopi elders froze in place. Everyone was so startled and frightened they started trembling. You could hear their knees knocking and their teeth rattling so hard they sounded like a den of diamondback rattlesnakes ready to make a strike.

"My children and children's children, The day of purification draws neigh. Listen to Sarah for she has been chosen to be the living Meha representing the spirits of your ancestors. She must be purified first, and then you will have to be purified to understand the message of the Meha," said the mystical and terrifying ancestral Spirit.

All of the elders were now petrified. They hardly breathed keeping their eyes fixed on Maasaw. Then, instantly, there appeared three ancient warrior ancestral spirits dressed as Kachinas pounding on Native American ceremonial drums. Two of the Kachina dancers started singing Hopi war cries that had been handed down from generation to generation for thousands of years.

This brought soothing calmness to the elders that eased their fears. One of the elders started singing along with the ancient warriors and two others started to dance around. Then the Kachina spirits started performing the ancient Tawa ceremonial war dance taught to the Hopi by their generations of grandfathers. The traditional ceremonial war cries uplifted the elders' spirits. Then the Kachina dancers suddenly stopped as Maasaw started to speak.

"After Sarah Meha is purified, all Hopi will need their souls purified to understand the secrets of the new Meha," said Maasaw sounding like a thousand rumbling thunderclouds.

Maasaw and the ancient Kachina warriors then vanished as fast as one can blink an eye. The elders slowly turned, and looked at Sarah, not saying a word. No doubt remained in anyone's heart, mind, or soul that what she had experienced that morning was real.

After everyone calmed down Sarah began to tell them what Maasaw had told her. None of the elders questioned a single word that she spoke. They all listened with both eyes and ears wide open and their mouths tightly shut staring at her in awe.

It did not take long for Sarah to tell them everything that she had previously experienced. When she finished, the Chief forbid anyone to approach Sarah. He told the elders with authority she needed to rest her weary body. He then instructed them that they should keep quiet about

Maasaw's visitation this evening since it was sacred to the Hopi Nation. All agreed.

One Hopi tribal elder still managed to ask Sarah if she would reveal what they must do to purify themselves. He wanted to prepare himself to be worthy to receive Maasaw's instructions. Sarah told all of them that she did not know much about the PA-MU-YA (the Hopi Native American word for the purification process). Taking a deep breath she told them that they would be the first to know if Maasaw contacted her again.

Miguel burst out, "I know the ways of purification." Everyone gave him a grim look so he did not make any more comments as the tribal leaders left the Begay ranch.

For a two week period from the time the tribal leaders experienced Maasaw, a different elder would stop by every day to ask Sarah if Maasaw had returned. Chief Blackcloud's warning to keep the visitation of Maasaw secret did not stop the tribal leaders from telling everyone what happened. It started a rumor mill propelled Sarah into the spotlight. Her fame spread like a wildfire as she rapidly became a living legend among the Hopi people. As the weeks passed, Sarah became restless and depressed since Maasaw had not returned to reveal the instructions as to when she should start her purification.

Danny constantly comforted Sarah with words of wisdom. Sarah's heart melted every time Danny poured out his love and kindness to soothe her troubled soul, but it did not calm her down. He tried everyday to reasoned with her without any success. He kept explaining that the Hopi spiritual ancestors live differently than human beings. Sarah understood Danny's reasoning that humans, created from the elements of Mother Earth, live in different deminsion that those of the spirit world. But this did not satisfy her desire and anxiety to speak to Maasaw. She felt is was vital to hear from Maasaw before she started her purification process.

After three months had passed without any spiritual ancestral visitations some of the elders slowed their frequency of visits to once a week, while others opted not to visit at all. They started to doubt what they had seen with their own eyes and heard with their own ears. Some felt it was a hallucination others a vision. It did not take long for the gossip mill to start hatany new rumors to spread across the Hopi lands like a wildfire. Many started to believe that Sarah's Maasaw visitations were a figment of her imagination.

Danny did not give in to Sarah's depression and reassured her every morning to be patient and strong as she waited for Maasaw's instructions. With Danny by her side, Sarah held on to her hope to see Maasaw. After a few months she stop thinking about her PA-MU-YA and returned to tending to her precious sheep. Finally, Sarah stopped laying awake night after night emotionally stressed out what she was suppose to do and sleep peacefully.

The winter season ended and the task of trimming her sheep's long wooly coats had arrived. She carefully prepared the barnyard to sheer her precious sheep. Every year Abel would do most of the sheering since Sarah was far too old for such a hard task. Sarah would argue with Abel every year to let her help hold down the sheep.

This made him crazy listening to her reasons to help. He tried to resist her arguments but all he could do was shake his head as she would not relent her desires to help. Every year she would calmly explained to him that it provided good mental therapy and physical exercise for her to help trim her precious sheep's winter coat. He reluctantly agreed every year.

From previous arguments that he had lost with his mother he learned to laugh within his heart and let her do as she pleased. Abel knew his mother was a powerful lady that did not take kindly to being told what to do. From his childhood days he learned that his mother's stubbornness was impossible to break. Although she was ridiculously hard headed, Abel knew her intentions were the best to treat everyone with the utmost respect, love and kindness.

Later that year on a cool, windy spring morning near daybreak, Sarah walked out her front door as usual to move her sheep to a new holding pasture. On this particular spring morning the sky was crystal blue free of any clouds or pollution. Sarah looked to the east and could see the mountain tops of second mesa break up the early morning sunrays.

Then a few moments later she looked away so that the full power of the sun did not blind her. Sarah set her tea cup down and picked up her iron wood staff. Along the way she stopped at the well and got a drink of fresh water. The early morning sunlight had now engulfed the entire eastern horizon. At the very moment when Sarah lifted up her right hand to shade her eyes from the brilliant morning sun Maasaw appeared.

"Sarah Meha, when are going to start your PA-MU-YA?" asked the ancient warrior sounding like a thousand waterfalls.

"I have already been cleansing my body with pure soap and water from the creek," replied Sarah stunned by Maasaw's sudden appearance.

She want to tell Maasaw she was waiting for his instruction was but was lost for words. Bowing her head she tightly grasped the iron wood staff she holding in her left hand. Once again Maasaw had scared the living daylights out of her. Realizing what was happening many emotions overcame her body from fear to joy in a matter of seconds. She then took a deep breath and slow breathed out tyring to regain control of her emotions.

"Sarah Meha, you must cleanse your conscience—spirit, soul, and mind—not your body. Your body is connected to the world of flesh, but your conscience is what is connected to the spirit world. Your purification must be done in a way that connects you to the spirit of all that lives on Mother Earth. Mother Earth's celestial material at the original creation was a spiritual thought first. These thoughts consisted of the creation of wind, earth, fire, and water. Spiritual life forces are what has sustained life since time began, not those of material origins. With this in mind, you must be cleansed spiritually to understand life," explained Maasaw.

"How must I do that, Caretaker of the Hopi people?" asked Sarah being confused.

"You must listen to the crackling fire sing out to you and observe the red hot rocks glow from the energy they have received by the burning wood. Listen to Mother Earth's creeks filled with pristine water sing many different songs as they nourish all that lives. You must let the four winds blow against your face and listen to their many different stories. They will speak to your heart and soul with their whistles and howls," said Maasaw enlightening Sarah.

"I can feel your words grip my spirit as you speak," replied Sarah.

"Sarah Meha, you must observe the four winds as they stir up many different dust clouds from natal Mother Earth to move them from one location to another. Listen with your heart and soul to gain the knowledge, wisdom, and understanding of what they are telling you. As you become closer to them, they will reveal their mysteries as they move about to and fro. Listen to them carefully, since they have much to tell your spirit," said Maasaw, this time speaking like a powerful waterfall rumbling down the mountain.

"I have listened to the wind tell me stories since I was a child," she responded.

"Sarah Meha, you must do as your forefathers have done for thousands of years and live off of those things natural to the land. You must thank the animals, water, and plants for giving up their spirit of life, so you will live another day. This is how you must purify yourself.," said Maasaw still sounding like a powerful waterfall.

"How long will it take to complete my PA-MU-YA?" asked Sarah.

Sarah Meha, your PA-MU-YA will be complete after twenty-one consecutive days of being one with Mother Earth. After your purification is complete, then the New Meha message will be revealed to you in its pure state. At that time you will be able to understand the spiritual words of life," said Maasaw, as he vanished into the invisible four winds that encompass Mother Earth.

Sarah stood there motionless staring at the distant mountains of the second mesa thinking about Maasaw's instructions. She thought about her visitation that many Hopis had been waiting centuries to receive. As Abel drove up that morning, he noticed his mother standing like a statue, so he jumped out of the truck and ran over to her as fast as he could, yelling every step of the way.

"Mother, mother, are you alright?" asked Abel concerned about his mother.

Sarah slowly turned and smiled at him.

"Yes, I am fine. Maasaw has just visited me. He gave me the instructions how I must purify myself," said Sarah, emotionally relieved that Maasaw had finally reappeared to her.

"Mother, I think you need to celebrate. You need to prepare yourself a cup tea," replied Abel relieved his mother had finally been redeemed.

"Yes, I think you're right. I will. Can you manage the sheep without me this morning?" asked Sarah very calmly.

"Mother, I can, and will, manage them just fine. Let me walk you to the house first," requested Abel, putting forth his right hand to help his mother cross a small mud puddle.

"No, my son, I can manage. I want to walk it alone so I can think about what has just happened to me this morning and what may happen next," she replied, turning her head to look away from the glaring rays of the morning sun.

Sarah slowly walked back to her home smiling all the way. After she arrived she told her husband all that had transpired. "Sarah, I must tell our spiritual and reservation leaders about this," exclaimed Danny.

"I do not think they will have time for me. Can we wait until another time?" she asked.

"My darling, you do not understand this is the other time. This is what our people have been waiting thousands of years for," said Danny more convincingly.

"If you think it is that important, go ahead but I am still a bit weakened by the experience," said Sarah standing in front of the stove preparing a cup of Mormon Tea.

Since Danny convinced Sarah to tell her experience to the tribal leaders. He immediately drove to town to talk to Chief Blackcloud and the tribal medicine man, Since Miguel had convinced Danny they should be the first ones to here about Sarah's instructions from Maasaw. Danny explained to the Hopi leaders that Sarah had reluctantly promised to tell anyone after all of the rumors spread about her. Chief Blackcloud assured Danny he would take every measure needed to ensure his wife would be well received. Even with the Chief's word it did not take long after the meeting before many were spreading gossip about Sarah again. The rumor mills started boiling with outlandish misinformation about Sarah recent visitation. The news about Sarah spread throughout the reservation faster than a lightening strike.

As the sun set over the top of the sacred San Francisco Peaks, Chief Blackcloud and ten traditional Hopi elders stood at Danny and Sarah Begay's doorstep. Sarah hesitated for a moment but then slowly opened the door. After a few moments she began to tell the group about her brief encounter with Maasaw. She did her best to explain what Maasaw had told her about how to purify her spirit for twenty-one consecutive days before a New Meha would be revealed to the Hopi Nation.

"Sarah, did you ask Maasaw who 'The Ones' of the original Meha were?" asked one of the Elders of the Hopi people.

"I did not ask Maasaw a single word. I only listened since I was too terrified of it all. His message was brief and thorough about how the entire Hopi nation needed to be purified," replied Sarah.

"It appears to me Sarah's forefathers must have been 'The Ones' to receive the first Meha" remarked Chief Blackcloud. "That was over 3500 years ago. It would be impossible for anyone to argue with your statement. How can you make that decision?" questioned Miguel.

"Of course, you can disagree with me today, but Maasaw has chosen whom he has chosen," replied Chief Blackcloud attacking Miguel's disbelief.

"It would be pointless to discuss this any further or make any logical decisions about the original Meha. Since Maasaw has called Sarah the New Meha, what are we to think?" asked Miguel directing his question toward the Hopi traditionalist.

"Although, I am the Chief of the Hopi people, it does not mean you must believe my statement. But do not forget what you personally saw with your own eyes and then you turned your back on Sarah," said Chief Blackcloud reminding them about their prior encounter with the Caretaker and then denied what they had seen.

Everyone kept their comments to themselves being ashamed of their past statements about Sarah. After a few moments of silence it was decided by the council that what Sarah had told the tribal elders was authentic.

Since time began, Native Americans had always respected the earth, wind, fire and water, and considered them to be the sacred elements of life. It was an accepted fact, that since the beginning of time most Native Americans respected and gave thanks to the plants and animals for giving up their living spirits, so their people could survive. The Hopi elders agreed a twenty-one-day purification (PA-MU-YA) would be the appropriate thing to do.

Sarah agreed to inform the Chief and tribal elders about any future visitations. Strong Arrow, one of the elder's, wrote down every word Sarah said about her Maasaw experience. He felt that what had been spoken to her must be recorded and kept preserved because it was sacred and exclusive to the Hopi nation. Although many of the elders felt that this message was directed to all human beings they still agreed with Strong Arrow. The group gave their respects to the Begay family and left.

When heat of the summer months had subsided, Sarah felt it was a good time to start purifying her spirit, soul, and mind. Danny agreed with his 77 year-old wife's decision that it would be easier to complete her twenty-one-day purification during the cooler months.

Being early autumn, Sarah started her first day of the twenty-one day purification cleansing. She asked her two sons to build an authentic ceremonial campfire the way her ancestors would have done thousands of years ago. This way she could meditate by the fire and thinking about what Maasaw instructed her to do. She carefully listened to the fire make its crackling and wind noises as it burned into red hot coals. To help her get in the mood she had prepared some sacred Hopi corn cobs, still in their husks, to be burned on the open pit fire. Her plan was for the entire family to eat the freshly roasted corn as her ancestors had done for millennia. Sarah instructed everyone to eat the corn slowly, tasting every kernel, to give respect to the sacred corn plant that gave its life, so that her Hopi family could prosper another day. Everyone responded to her wishes with respect and honor. No one asked any questions, except the five year old Dugan. He wanted grandma to tell him the vanishing coyote story, again.

As the fire burned into red hot coals around ten o'clock at night, Sarah sat there quietly looking at an innumer amount of stars that laced the sky that evening. Everyone sat quietly staring into the night sky observing the billions and billions of brilliant stars that magnificently lit up the heavens. It was dead calm that evening on the Arizona high plateau. The tranquil evening ended instantly when the night sky lit up like daytime. The children burst out as they were awed by a falling star that blinded them as it burned brighter than the sun. Everyone looked at Sarah thinking it was Maasaw visiting their grandmother.

"Mother, is that Maasaw?" asked one the children.

"No, that was a spirit of one of your ancestors racing across the sky," she replied.

"Mother why are you telling my children these stories when you are the person receiving new spiritual knowledge, wisdom, understanding, and hope for the Hopi people," remarked Abel's wife sarcastically.

"Being chosen by Maasaw is an honor that the white, black, brown, and yellow strangers would never be able to understand. But telling my grandchildren Hopi stories carried down from generation to generation is something they need to hear so they will understand the ways of the Hopi," said Sarah calmly.

Sarah explained to her family that she must not be disturbed for twenty-one days so that she could accomplish her PA-MU-YA the way Maasaw had instructed her to. Her family didn't ask any questions, except her eldest son. He wanted to know if she still would like to help with the sheep during her purification. She hid her true feelings from Abel by telling him she would be too busy. The Begay family gathering ended so their mother could rest up to begin her quest.

The next morning, Sarah prepared her husband some hot coffee along with his usual breakfast. Sarah then boiled some water to make herself a locally grown herbal drink. Sarah thought Maasaw would approve of her making a drinking out of a native plant to begin her purification.

The local herb grew wild in the plateaus and higher elevations of the Arizona wilderness. Since the wild herbal tea lost its potency quickly, it had to be picked fresh, and then boiled, while still green to obtain the best flavor. To Sarah, this was the tastiest drink in the world. Sarah was blessed because she could have this special, rare, arid tea often because it grew abundantly on her land.After having her cup of tea she cleaned her house and then sat down in her wooden rocker on the left side of the front porch. She rocked back and forth thinking about the history of her people and how her ancestors might have accomplished their PA-MU-YA.

After a few hours of meditation, she got up and went back in the house, "Danny, my Hopi nation has been a peaceful, nomadic people successfully living on this land for thousands of years," said Sarah still thinking about her PA-MUYA.

"Yes, my darling," responded Danny while taking a sip of his coffee.

"I feel my people have been lied to, corrupted, and bullied around by the white strangers for nearly two hundred years. It appears to me our present lives depend on their beliefs, cultures, and animals introduced by them. They do not know anything about what our ancestral fathers had to do to survive and live in harmony with Mother Earth. I know the invasion of the white stranger had been known to our Hopi forefathers because the Meha had foretold them that it would happen thousands of years ago," said Sarah, expressing her feelings.

Surprised by Sarah's comments, Danny didn't know how to respond.

"Sarah, I have never heard you talk like this before. Are you angry or bitter about something?" he asked.

"No, my great warrior, I am not bitter. I am scared to death, knowing I am about to receive the new Meha instructions from the Caretaker Spirit of my ancestors. The Hopi people has had to adapt to the white strangers new religion about the spirit world that is contrary to ours. They not only condemn us, but have tried to forbid us to practice our ancient Hopi beliefs. It is a mixed blessing that our ancestors knew thousands of years beforehand that the white strangers would invade our lands. The Meha has forewarned all Hopis about the white strangers' invasion, but no one believe the instructions left by 'The Ones'. Why are the whites so arrogant and always belittling us?" asked Sarah, airing out her inner emotions.

"My darling, Sarah, I am a simple man of simple ways. I do not know why the white strangers first tried to starve us out and then outright kill us. They have put our people through hell and back. I think most of them still speak with a forked tongue, but not all of them," responded Danny calmly. Sarah put her head down and returned to her favorite spot on the porch. Sarah started rocking again as she thought about the promise guaranteed by the Hopi Chief. Sarah did not want anyone to start anymore rumors about her spiritual experiences because she had been emotionally drained by all of the previous ridiculous stories.

Since Sarah worst fear was being ridiculed she didn't really plan on telling anyone what occurred during her purification. Separating herself from all negative thoughts, she started concentrating on what she would do on her first day, in regards to her purification. She deeply thought about visulizing what had existed on the land during the days of the original Hopi peoples. She felt she would have to act and live the way her ancestors did before the corruption caused by white strangers. After walking about the farm for awhile she realized she could not imagine her forefather's lifestyle so she decided that was enough for one day.

The next morning she felt mentally and emotionally ready to begin her quest to purify herself to be presentable to the Great Spirit in the sky. After drinking a cup of Mormon Tea, she started her trek. She walked around observing every little thing, trying to understand the reason for its existence. She studied every rock, bird, and plant until she walked upon a small pool of water that her precious sheep occasionally drank from. Being extremely silent, she could hear the hawks cry out as they let the four winds guide them above Mother Earth. She could feel the wind blowing as they blew against the scrub bushes that made some whispering sounds. She pondered for awhile wondering what they were saying. She continued to wander around aimlessly for a few hours the second day, trying to get in touch with nature.

By listening to the water, the wind, and the hawk spirits she felt like she was starting to get closer to Mother Earth. This day she decided that all life on Mother Earth was an extremely special gift. She rejoiced within her soul for all the unique living creatures the Great Spirit had created for the Hopi people. She then picked up a small juniper tree branch and studied it very carefully trying to understand its importance to Mother Earth. The rest of the day she walked along the bank of a small dry wash exploring the different facets of life that it nourished without any visible water.

On the third day during her purification trek, Sarah found a young hawk that could not fly because it had a severely injured wing. Sarah decided to take the young bird home to nurse until it was well enough to fend for itself. While gently picking up the young hawk she was surprise, that the young hawk attached itself to Sarah as if it were her mother. That day she made a vow to take care of the injured young bird until it would be able to fly high among the four winds of the heavens.

After getting home, she made a nest for it in her barn and fed it some red worms. Later that evening, Sarah decided to call her youngest son, Ronnie, to come over and discuss a river rafting trip down the mighty Colorado River.

"Ronnie, I want to take a white water rafting adventure down the Colorado River," said Sarah talking to him over the phone.

"Mother, have you gone crazy? Those trips are not for the elderly, especially you, mother. You could get hurt or drown," burst out Ronnie.

"Son, I must get in touch with Mother Earth to purify myself, and this would be a fantastic way for me to do so. I want you to take me. Will you do that?" asked Sarah.

"Mother, are you serious?" asked Ronnie.

"Yes, and I want you to go with me. You know Dad is too old," she replied.

"Dad is too old. You are too old," replied Ronnie.

"Ronnie, I need this to complete my PA-MU-YA," she explained.

Reluctantly, Ronnie scheduled a three-day rafting adventure down the Colorado River. Danny chuckled but agreed with Sarah. He knew if he didn't agree with her she would do it anyway.

On the morning of the fifth day, Sarah was going to have her chance to experience the mighty Colorado River, and ride it right down to the middle of the Grand Canyon.

"Ma'am, you need to put on a life vest and choose a place near the back of the raft," ordered the crew captain of the Colorado River Raft Adventures.

"I will put on the life vest, but I want to ride in the front of the raft so I can get close to the river and get in touch with Mother Earth," she replied.

"Mother, I think it would be better for you to get in the back of the raft. In the front of the raft, you will get extremely wet and tossed about. At your age, riding in the front is not a safe thing for you to do," said Ronnie, pleading with his mother.

"The answer is no. I have paid hundreds of dollars for this experience, and I want my money's worth," she argued back.

"If your mother wants to ride in the front, you will have to sit next to her and make sure that she does not get hurt," said the skipper.

When all of the bickering was over, Sarah was sitting in the front of the ten-man river raft next to her youngest son. Sarah's raft was one of five rafts of this particular river adventure group. Three others carried eight passengers each, and the fifth carried food and supplies for the entire trip down the mighty Colorado River. The trip started from the famous Marble Canyon, a few miles south of Glenn Canyon Dam that created the man-made Lake Powel.

All of the rafters had to walk down a steep cliff of the magnificent Marble Canyon to board the rafts to start the journey. The main oarsman gave the raft a shove to dislodge it from the river bank. He then jumped on board and started rowing. The rafting adventure had begun.

At the beginning of the trip, the water looked like a mirror because it was so calm. As Sarah studied the wild reeds growing along the river bank, she noticed a five-point mule deer getting a drink of the reddish

Colorado River water. Then she saw a Bald Eagle swoop down and swipe a large rainbow trout out of the river within fifty feet of the raft. She, as were the other passengers, were awed by the natural wonder. Sarah was elated floating down the river her forefathers had conquered thousands of years ago.

After a few hours, the rafters could hear a rumbling that grew louder by the minute. Then they could see some white water foaming and churning up every drop of water in the mighty Colorado. Sarah fixed her eyes on the roaring white water.

"Hang on tight, everyone. This is a category three white water rapid. It is going to be a wet and wild ride," yelled out the oarsman. About that moment, the raft started twisting, turning and bobbing up and down. The skipper and oarsman battled the swift currents to keep the raft from capsizing. Sarah bounced in every direction as the ice cold Colorado River water splashed about her body, giving her a good drenching. Ronnie hung on for dear life as Sarah enjoyed Mother Earth's life-giving liquid splashing all over her. Being soaked from head to toe made her feel like a little girl playing in a pool of water.

After a few minutes, the wild white water ride was behind them, as the currents of the Colorado River became calm. It was a special moment for Sarah as she saw a pair of chuckwallas nesting along the river bank. She looked all around as she was getting spiritually involved with Mother Earth closer than ever before. Her emotions ran high as she day dreamed about her first white water experience.

As they traveled farther down the Colorado River the multicolored sheer cliffs of the Grand Canyon started to grow upward. Sarah felt like she was sinking into Mother Earth deeper and deeper by the minute. The smooth ride was about to end as they could hear a distant roar echo off of the steep canyon walls. Sarah and Ronnie looked at one another as the roar became louder and louder. Ronnie started bracing himself and practicing holding his breath before the oarsman gave out any instructions.

"Everyone, this is a category two white water rapid. That means it is less intense than the first we encountered this morning but it is still dangerous. Hang on tight," barked out the skipper.

Sarah started smiling as the roar became deafening. She felt like she was finally in oneness with Mother Earth for the first time in her life. As they entered the rapids the raft started twisting and bending up and down. The oarsman yelled at the skipper to push left as to not run over a large sharp boulder sticking out of the middle of the river. The raft hit the bolder, which gashed a hole in the left side. The oarsman frantically tried to fix the damaged raft as the skipper could barely control it. Ronnie turned white as a ghost while Sarah laughed out loud at all of the excitement.

The raft washed ashore, so the passengers scurried out of it as fast as possible onto the silky sand deposits of the Colorado River bank. The other four rafts landed near them. The crew captain decided it was enough for one day so the crew hastily set up camp and repaired the damaged raft. Ronnie and Sarah got to have a tent of their own since one crew decided to sleep under the stars. Dinner was served which consisted of fresh rainbow trout fillets, pinto beans, fried potatoes, and a crispy mixed salad. Sarah loved the meal, especially since she didn't have to prepare it or clean up the mess.

"Lights out!" yelled the crew captain, "Rafting tomorrow will be even more exciting."

Lights out meant the campfire would soon be extinguished so everyone would need to get into their assigned tents. Sarah and Ronnie retired to their tent and, in minutes, were sound asleep. Sarah was used to getting up before dawn, so she awakened about four o'clock the next morning. She got dressed and went to the camp mess area to get a cup of hot tea, but none was available.

Since it was moments before sunrise, Sarah walked down to the river's edge to get in touch with nature. After she had sat down and studied the plants, insects and landscape for a few minutes a wild Arizona mountain lion came down to the river's edge to get a drink of water. The cougar stopped only twenty feet away from Sarah. She stared at the mountain lion observing every move it made. She watched it nourish itself by taking a long drink of the muddy Colorado River. The wild cat then lifted its head and stared at Sarah as if it knew her. Sarah smiled back at the wild creature studying its every move. Then Ronnie yelled out.

"Mother, watch out! There is a dangerous animal very close to you. Mother, don't move. I will protect you!" cried out Ronnie.

"Son, son, son! What are you trying to do, ruin my purification process?" asked Sarah scolding him.

Ronnie shook his head, throwing a rock at the wild cat to scare it off. The giant cat ran up the hill to the edge of a cave and stopped to view the humans argue. Sarah turned away from Ronnie to see where the lion had dashed off to. The large beige cat starred at Sarah for moment and then proceeded into the cave. Then to Sarah and Ronnie's surprise the cat showed them one of her kittens as if to say, stay away from my den. Ronnie persuaded his mother to return back to the camp where it was safe.

At the camp Ronnie and Sarah sat down and enjoyed the gourmet breakfast prepared by the crew. After everyone had finished eating they wrapped up the camp and pushed off to start the second day of the river rafting adventure. Sarah couldn't wait to strap herself into the front seat again to continue her journey down the mighty Colorado. Ronnie shook his head looking at his mother. He then peered at the giant reddish cliffs, wondering how he ever let his mother talk him into such a danger adventure.

After a few hours of mild currents the river took a serpentine bend to the left and then to the right. The river twisted back and forth six more times throughout the canyon walls until they came to an open area where everyone could see the top of the mile high Grand Canyon. Sarah was thrilled by the sight as she turned her head first to the left and then to the right, up and down, then back and forth many times. The cliffs that made up the Grand Canyon basin was an awesome site for her. She smiled when a desert hawk came swooping down from high above and instantly adjusted its flight to skim the surface of the river.

Then a familiar sound started getting louder and louder, but no one could see the rapid because it was around a river bend hidden behind a massive cliff.

"Everyone, this is the world famous Lava Falls which is a category four white water rapid. What makes this rapids so famous is that it is the fastest drop of any rapids on earth. Please check your safety ropes to see if they are attached to your vests and the raft. Hang on with both hands at all times. This will be the wildest ride of all and the toughest rapid we will face during the entire trip. Please keep low and hang on tight," yelled out the skipper his final instructions as he positioned the raft to best place to navigate the churning rapids. Ronnie held his breath as Sarah braced herself for the ride of their lifetime. The raft began to shake and twist out of shape as it spun around up and down the rapids. The oarsman and skipper fought the current with all of their strength. The raft was continually filling with water from dipping down into the river swells. The skipper stood up, grabbed a large pole and started frantically pushing the raft in many different directions trying to keep his ship away from any life-threatening situations. Then, all of a sudden, the skipper disappeared. The oarsman did not notice him missing because he was too busy fighting to keep the raft afloat. In a few minutes they had made it through the wildest rapids on Mother Earth.

At that point, everyone noticed the skipper hanging on to a life rope attached to his life vest and the raft. Being half drowned and hypothermic, the skipper cried out for the oarsman to steer the raft to the shore right away. Everyone pitched in to help the oarsman bring the raft to a golden red sandbank. After the skipper was rescued the Oarsman immediately wrapped him in some thick flannel blankets.

"Did anyone see who that Indian was that knocked me out the boat?" screamed the skipper.

"What Indian? Do mean a Native American or a person from India?" yelled back the oarsman questioning him.

"I am serious. A savage, I mean, a Native American, knocked me out of the raft. Did anyone see him?" asked the skipper.

"Skipper, I think you must have hit your head on a rock when you were tossed out of the raft. There wasn't anyone, Indian or otherwise knocking you out of the raft," laughed the oarsman.

Sarah smiled because she knew the skipper got a glimpse of Maasaw while he was watching over her as she purified herself. Ronnie became offended and a little disturbed by the skipper using an ethnic derogatory term. Sarah looked at her son and nodded her head, nonverbally telling to him to ignore the white stranger's abusive vocabulary. Ronnie honored his mother's request.

The skipper recovered quickly, so the river adventure continued until they reached a beautiful, breathtaking, arched cliff made out of windswept, red sandstone. Sarah looked at the unique designs and dimensions etched into the cliff. She rubbed her hands along the picturesque walls to touch Mother Earth. She then praised the Good Spirit that had formed the cliffs through thousands of years of erosion. Ronnie and Sarah then went back to the river camp because it was time for dinner to be served. This would be the last evening meal for Sarah and Ronnie because tomorrow would be the final day of their river rafting excursion.

Since Sarah knew it was her last chance to experience the mighty Colorado River basin she rose early to watch the sunrise. When the sun peak over the mile high scenic cliffs of the mystic Grand Canyon it turned its bluish walls bright orange. The Colorado River water started to sparkle like it was made of millions of diamonds. She noticed a few native fish jumping for the bugs flying close to the water's edge. It was a majestic feeling for her to experience the river that had carved out the Grand Canyon.

The skipper shoved off the raft yelling at the oarsman to take the lead. The oarsman stirred the raft to the center of the river so the rafters could get the best view of the magnificent Grand Canyon gorge fingering out in many directions. Sarah looked at one cliff, following it up to the top of the canyon where she noticed some pine trees that looked like tiny green shrubs. The different layers of the canyon walls were purple, grey, orange, red, brown, and misty blue. Even Ronnie enjoyed the awesome sight of the Grand Canyon viewed from the Colorado River basin over a mile below the canyon walls.

The trip ended in an area where a helicopter lifted Sarah, Ronnie, and two others out of the worlds largest and grandest of all canyons on Mother Earth. Sarah twisted her head in all directions, looking at the marvelous canyon walls as the helicopter started lifting them up to the southern rim of the canyon. On their way up out of the canyon the helicopter sped past three vultures soaring high above the canyon walls floating amongst the four winds. To Sarah it felt like she was soaring in the heavens like a bird of prey. When they reached the top of the south rim, the helicopter made a spinning move before landing safely. Ronnie and Sarah were met by Ronnie's wife and Danny at the southern entrance of the Grand Canyon National Park.

Sarah embraced her husband. Ronnie could not stop talking about the trip. His continuous yapping irritated everyone as they traveled back to the Hopi Native American Reservation. They drove along the southern Grand Canyon National Park road to the park's East gate. This exit from the park, also served as the entrance gate to the Navajo Native American Reservation.

When they arrived home, Sarah went to her favorite spot on the front porch and sat down. She rocked back and forth thinking about her fantastic voyage down the spectacular Colorado River. Being exhausted from the experience Sarah decided to rest her weary body for awhile.

After two days of rest, Sarah decided to visit her favorite creek bed. She was excited to find that the creek was flowing over its banks with thick reddish-brown muddy water. The water swirled about as it rushed down the often dry creek bed carrying debris of all sorts in its swift current. Sarah studied the power of the water spirit thinking how it gave life and took life with the same energy. The overflowing creek was not as magnificent as the Colorado River, but it still captivated her attention. She sat there for a few hours, watching the intensity of the rushing water until it diminished to a harmless trickle.

The flood was caused by a cloud burst pounded Mother Earth with such massive rain drops it was hard for Sarah and Danny to hear one another talk inside of the house. The thunderstorm had raced across the land that evening producing hundreds of lightning strikes. It was a miracle the massive lightening bolts did not started any forest fires. Her little house on the plateau shook every time a thunder bolt cracked, flashed, and rumbled.

After observing the creek flood waters reside, she got up and walked back to her home to rest. At home, rocking to and fro, she thought about how fast she had grown old, as if it had only taken moments. She walked over to the mirror, stared at the wrinkles in her face, and then snapped her fingers.

"It feels like my life has passed by like the snap of my fingers," she said slowly staring at herself in the mirror, "My, oh, my, where have the years gone? Life is like that thunderstorm that raced across my little piece of land last night, here then gone," said Sarah, still speaking into the mirror as tears started running down her cheeks.

The time that she spent by the creek bed was an awakening for her. Sarah spent the next six days walking around the Painted Desert and Petrified Forest National Monuments. She marveled at the arrays of endless colors that appeared to be painted on every hill and the trees that had turned into stone. She enjoyed observing the many different species of wildlife and landscapes designed by the Good Spirit to live in harmony with Mother Earth.

On the seventeenth day of her quest, the young hawk she had rescued earlier appeared ready to be set free and take care of himself the way the Great Creator Spirit had intended.

"Goodbye, my mighty winged friend. Today you must live your life as God has intended," said Sarah to the desert hawk. She immediately gave thanks to the Great Spirit for giving her a chance to be close to one of the creatures that flew among the heavens.

On the twentieth day, while Sarah was staring out her front window she noticed the hawk that she had nursed to health screech out as it had tried to lift a large jackrabbit from the ground. It had lifted the rabbit about twenty feet into the air before it had to let it go. Sarah ran out of her home to see what had happened to the rabbit.

As she approached the area where the jackrabbit had fallen, she could hear some high pitched screams. There lay the jackrabbit, crying out from its injuries. Its hind legs had been broken from the fall. Sarah got her son Abel to capture the severely traumatized animal in the hope she could nurse it back to health. The hawk Sarah had earlier set free was watched from a nearby tree as Sarah took the crippled jackrabbit to her barn. As they entered the barn, the hawk left his perch and was carried away by the four winds to never be seen again.

"Mother, I don't think this rabbit will survive the night," said her son.

"Yes, Abel , you may be correct, but I am purifying myself, and this creature needs my care as long as it is alive in the world of flesh, I will tend to it. You must learn to have mercy on the weak, Abel," replied Sarah.

"Yes, mother," replied Abel, refraining from making any further comments.

Sarah stayed up all night with the jackrabbit, trying to soothe its spirit by tending to its wounds. She slept in the barn right next to the injured rodent until the next morning. As the sun rose, Sarah realized this began her twentyfirst day, which would complete her PA-MU-YA. Sarah was sure Maasaw would instantly appear to her, but nothing happened. Sarah retired that evening greatly disappointed.

Three weeks passed since she had completed her purification and no Maasaw. As six more weeks passed by the jackrabbit was completely healed but still no sign of Maasaw. Sarah started to doubt if Maasaw would ever return.

After six months, Sarah had totally given up any hope that Maasaw would ever return. She got up late one cold autumn morning to help her son tend the sheep as she had done for many years. Arriving at the old pasture she saw Abel try to jump a ravine, but failed and severely sprain his right ankle. He got up and started jumping around like a Mexican Jumping Bean and howling a few choice Hopi words. Sarah helped her traumatized son limp back to the house. Danny got some fresh crushed ice and packed Abel's ankle the way his grandfather had done over seventy years ago with snow for his older brother. At that very moment, Maasaw appeared.

Everyone froze in their place.

"Sarah Meha your 'PA-MU-YA' is acceptable. Gather up the men of your house and Miguel. Miguel will need his naturally-colored sand to make the most important sand painting of his life. Have your sons bring some earth paint and chisels. Go to the rising rocks of the sacred mountain of the North tomorrow morning. Tell no one about this, except Miguel," said Maasaw.

It happened so fast, Abel completely forgot about his ankle pain. Sarah shouted for joy, and Danny danced his favorite ancient Navajo warrior dance taught to him by his grandfather. Abel just sat there as if he had seen a ghost. Danny hugged Sarah wondering what was going to happen next.

Sarah, her husband, two sons, and Elder Miguel put all that Maasaw had requested into the back of their new pickup and set off for the rising rocks near the Second Mesa. It was a peaceful morning, all of the four winds were quiet as the sun crested the eastern mountains. Abel noticed that the early morning rays were broken into a pattern like the Arizona State flag. Elder Miguel laughed while telling Abel that the Arizona flag design was stolen from a southern Native American artist many moons ago. Abel looked at Miguel wondering what he was talking about.

After a couple of hours of driving around, they arrived at the very site Maasaw had described to Sarah. They unloaded the truck and put up a tent to shelter Sarah from the cool breeze generated by the sacred Great Mountain of the Ancient Spirits. They sat around for almost four hours, waiting patiently for some sort of supernatural experience to take place. Sarah became tired and fell asleep. The others let her sleep because they figured if Maasaw ever showed up she would be awakened.

"Sarah Meha, listen to me and record what is to come upon all of the Earth. It will be purified to clean it from man's many destructive ways," said Maasaw to Sarah in her dreams.

"Am I dreaming or have I been taken into the spirit world of my fathers?" asked Sarah.

"My Little Beautiful Butterfly, you are the only one worthy of this message. The others are not acceptable to be in my presence and hear my instructions about Mother Earth's future" replied Maasaw gently.

"What do you want me to do?" asked Sarah.

"Remember what you will be shown. The Earth will rock and reel for twelve years before it comes to rest. Many will be taken away to cleanse her of the corruption man has brought upon himself. Listen to my instructions," said Maasaw.

"Yes, Great Spirit of my ancestors," replied Sarah.

"Draw an Earth broken in pieces, then draw an Earth covered with smoke turning the skies orange and the sun blood red, and then chisel America broken up into three parts. Next, draw a city of gold rising out of the great waters to the west," commanded Maasaw, as several Hopi ancestor spirits dressed as Kachinas appeared.. The Kachina spirits constantly sang chants while dancing rhythmically to some distant sounding drums.

One ancient ancestor spirit carved out a flat stone from the mountain and then the second spirit painted four parallel lines connected to four large circles. The first circle had cracks all through it, and the second circle was covered with clouds, and the third circle had a man with a broken leg drawn in it, and the fourth circle had an eagle with its wings spread completely out.

"What does this mean?" asked Sarah.

"It shall be revealed, Sarah Meha, when it is time. What man has done to the Earth, he has done to himself which has compromised his very right to exist. Man's interdependency with the earth, wind, fire, and water has been ignored and now he is compromised. Mother Earth is going to turn her back on man's destructive ways and purify herself," said Maasaw.

A third ancient warrior took colored sand and formed a large round circle of white stone and then put black stone next to it. He used crushed turquoise stone to divide the circle into four equal parts. The upper right part portrayed a drop of water, the lower right part portrayed black clouds.

The upper left part portrayed foot steps walking about the land. The lower left part showed a green tree leaf divided into three parts: green to represent life of an age, yellow to represent the end of an age, and brown to represent the death of an age.

"What am I to do with these images and inscriptions?" asked Sarah.

"Remember what you have seen. Trace each drawing in your mind so isn't polluted with the stranger's ways. The interpretation will follow when the time of times is determined," said Maasaw.

Maasaw vanished, and Sarah woke up suddenly, sweating blood.

"Oh my darling, your nose is bleeding," said Danny frantically.

"Pinch her nose for a few minutes and the bleeding should stop," ordered Miguel. After a few moments Sarah's nose stopped bleeding so she decided to tell everyone what she had just experienced. She tried to speak, but the men kept interrupting her with many questions about how she felt. She finally told everyone to be quiet because she had something important to say about what Maasaw had shown her while she was sleeping.

"Maasaw has visited this time while I was sleeping," said Sarah.

"I think this is a hoax," said Elder Miguel.

"How do you know that she didn't see saw Maasaw while she was asleep?" asked Abel

"What do you know, half-breed?" replied Elder Miguel.

"That's not right to call my son a half-breed!" yelled Danny at the top of his lungs.

"Why is everyone acting so crazy with words," said Sarah, crying.

"Why did Maasaw choose you, Sarah, since you are married to a Navajo?" asked Elder Miguel, yelling and carrying on like an idiot.

"Elder Miguel, I didn't ask you to come on this mission. Maasaw told me to bring you along. Why are you acting like a mad dog?" asked Sarah.

"I was expecting to see the Caretaker, to ask him some questions that have plagued the Hopi nation for centuries. When I think I will get the chance, he visits you in a dream. This seems like a hoax to me," replied Elder Miguel.

"Elder, it has been the way of the Hopi people to be kind and accept anyone into our tribe. Chief Blackcloud would have a fit if he knew you were acting this way. Now, settle down and let us complete Maasaw's instructions," commanded Sarah.

"Danny, Abel, Ronnie, and Sarah, I apologize for being emotionally out of control. Here we are, two half-breeds, two Hopis and one Navajo, embarking on an assignment the Hopi people have been waiting thousands of years for. It is obvious the Great Spirit chooses the time and place to appear," said Elder Miguel realizing he had made a fool out of himself.

"If there are no other words to utter, can my mother give us Maasaw's instructions?" asked Ronnie wanting to know what Maasaw had told his mother to do.

"Mother, I think everyone is fine. We are just a little bit weary by such an important event that has been placed on your shoulders," said Abel.

"Abel and Ronnie, get your chisels and hammers out. We must find an open cave with a clean wall for Danny to paint what Maasaw has shown me. Elder Miguel, you will need your colored sands," said Sarah calmly.

The five set out looking for an area to construct the new Meha. After about twenty minutes of searching, Abel found the perfect location. It was an arched cave about twenty feet in diameter, the floor covered with fine sand. Sarah had Ronnie and Abel hoe the sandstone rock until it had a semi-smooth surface. Next, she asked Danny and Elder Miguel to prepare the sand to make a ten foot diameter, circular sand painting.

They immediately started carving the sandstone by the specific instructions that Sarah had told them. Elder Miguel and Danny looked on in awe, listening to Sarah give such unique instructions to her sons. Elder Miguel had changed his attitude since he had displayed his unruliness at the sacred site chosen to draw the new Meha. The men worked hard for several hours, not stopping for a minute to rest until the task had been completed. When the task had finally been completed, it was late afternoon so everyone decided to go back to the Begay house.

Sarah prepared some venison stew mixed with some grilled onions that she placed on top of the fry bread.

Weeks later many traditional Hopi studied the New Meha trying to figure out what Maasaw's instructions meant. Chief Blackcloud and the other Hopi leaders decided to build a fence around the area to keep it safe from the public until the message could be interpreted.

"Sarah, I love you and always will. But can I ask you a personal question?" asked Danny, trying to figure out what was happening to his wife.

"Why are you asking me to ask me a question, my desert warrior?" asked Sarah puzzled by Danny's unusual behavior.

"I wanted to ask you what it was like talking to the Caretaker," replied Danny, "but I was not sure how or when to ask you."

"No different than talking to you, except he did not ask me any questions. In contrary, he simply gave me instructions. It was a shocking experience but, most of all, it was quite comforting to find out that there really is life after death," she replied.

"Many of the white stranger's religious leaders say they have been visited by the Great Spirit, but they have never shown any Hopi their proof. I am glad the elders, the Chief, our sons, and even I, have seen the messenger from the Great Spirit of our ancestors. I feel as you do, dear, that there must be some form of life after we enter into the spirit world of our forefathers," he replied kissing her good night as they went to sleep When Sarah and Danny were fast asleep, Sarah was awakened by a voice that sounded like ocean waves crashing ashore.

"Sarah, hear my voice," said Maasaw.

"Is that you calling me?" asked Sarah still half asleep.

"Heed my words. You must instruct those that are chosen to become the remnants of mankind," said Maasaw, as he vanished into the spiritual ream.

Sarah opened her eyes looked around the room, smiled and then went back to sleep.

CHAPTER TWO:

ABORIGINE DREAMTIME

Yirawala kept the beliefs of his ancestors that man's life on earth is simply a preparation for entering the spirit world to live for eternity. He was taught by his grandfather that the Dreamtime was, and is, the correct way for a man of the flesh to be contacted by those that lived in the spirit world. Aborigines believe that spiritual beings live and move about faster than the physical speed of light. Many times deep in the Outback of Australia an Aborigine elder spiritual leader Yirawala painted himself with red and yellow ochre before entering the Dreamtime. Yirawala had several Dreamtime experiences, but nothing extraordinary.

He was told many things about his children and how the seasonal rains would bring a renewed life to his people. He was as spiritual as any other Aborigine but was somewhat disappointed by the lack of information the Dreamtime offered him throughout his life.

Now a very old man, Yirawala rested very often and seldom would try to enter the Dreamtime. Being bored one day, he decided to join the younger elders during an evening ritual at the upper caves. He entered into the Dreamtime this evening without any expectations, and just like that, his life changed forever. He had visited the Dreamtime for over seventy years before this first contact occurred with the Dreamtime messenger called the Rainbow Serpent. "Yirawala, the corruption of Earth's natal mother will rebel soon because man has destroyed thousands of her living plant and animal species, so it is time for the Sixth Rebirth," said the messenger of Ngaljod, the Rainbow Serpent.

"Why have you finally come to me?" asked Yirawala, the senior elder of the Aborigine tribes.

It was not like him to question Ngaljod because he had been taught to obey every word spoken by the Dreamtime messengers without any questions. But here sat Yirawala asking questions. His family had lived in this part of the Outback for over fifty thousand years and no one had ever questioned a Dreamtime messenger. Yirawala being left without during his entire life did not trust this messenger, so he decided question this Dreamtime message. Even being more defiant he was addressing the Rainbow Serpent. A human questioning those that lived at the speed of light, especially the top messenger, was something an Aborigine did not do during a Dreamtime experience.

"It is time to awaken your people as to what will come upon Mother Earth. I have been the messenger to all of your ancestors. I have contacted you today because I am going to take you deep within the caves of the Dreamtime. I will teach you what must be told to the inhabitants of Mother Earth," said the messenger of Ngaljod.

Yirawala was carried away into the Dreamtime by the spirits of Ngaljod. He was taken to the land of decisions and times to come. Upon arriving, Yirawala heard the sweet sound of several Didgeridoo flutes, which calmed his worried spirit. He was then whisked away by the Rainbow Serpent to the Nullabor Plains, deep within the caves of his ancestral creators. He was taken there to view rock cravings of the future. The carvings represented the Sixth Rebirth of Mother Earth.

There he met his ancestral mother as she danced for the joy and then the sadness that would soon come upon the lands of her children. She was dancing for the propagation of the Aborigine race. Marayka rubbed her body against the phallus-shaped stones that lined the cave to intensify the earthly magnetism and fertility for the future children of the Aborigine people.

After watching Marayka perform many dances of the fertility ritual, he was then taken even deeper into the caves. There Ngaljod once again showed Yirawala the future of Mother Earth. He had been exposed twice to the Sixth Rebirth secret cave carvings. Yirawala looked around wondering what he was looking at. He was told that the secrets of the cave carvings must be painted for the Aborigine people. His instructions were to educate the Aborigine so they could tell the rest of the living world what was going to happen to Mother Earth.

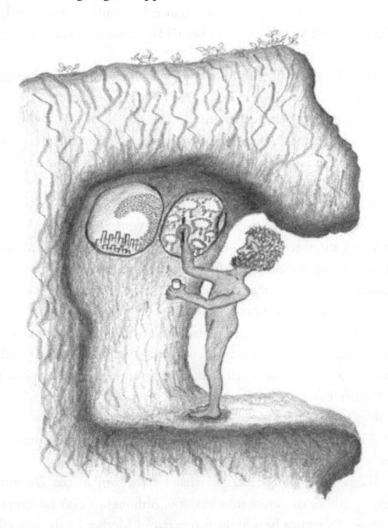

He was taken deeper into the Dreamtime to an empty cave and given some white paint to practice painting the secret cave carvings. He was told to do this over and over so he would remember how to paint them when he left the Dreamtime. After a few sketches, the Dreamtime messenger suddenly reunited him to his body. It seemed to Yirawala, he had been in a trance for a time before time before being returned to his flesh state of being. Being back among the living, his fellow living inhabitants of Mother Earth, he was awaked by a powerful, unrelenting voice.

"Yirawala, you have been in a trance for hours. Are you with us? Where are you? Where have you been?" asked Kunmanara of Aberdeen Rock.

Yirawala slowly opened his eyes to view the world of the living. He then turned and addressed Kunmanara. "I am not exactly sure, but I will tell you what I have experienced."

"Grandfather, this is not one of your many Dreamtime stories of the past to teach us about our ceremonies and rituals?" asked his youngest grandson.

Yirawala had always been disgusted with his grandson, who was thirty-nine years old because he never once respected Aborigine rituals. He wasn't disgusted with him because he woke him up but, rather, because he had crossed over to live with the white invaders. Kunmanara's decision not to live on the ancestral lands given to the Aborigines by the ancients irritated Yirawala to no end.

"My son's son, you need to learn about your forefather's knowledge that has been handed down for thousands of years. Instead, you believe what the white invaders tell you. Their information about our part of Mother Earth is only two hundred years old," explained Yirawala harshly.

"Grandfather, we have discussed this already," said Kunmanara gently.

"Regardless of my feelings, what I have seen in the Dreamtime must be told to the white invaders, too. Although, I can't tolerate their arrogance they must be told the future fate of Mother Earth. You will be the chosen one to do such a thing," replied Yirawala.

Reluctantly, he spoke to his grandson that had left the traditional ways of the Aborigine people to follow the ways of the white invaders. Yirawala really loved his grandson since he performed his circumcision twenty-seven years ago, but he couldn't understand Kunmanara's decision to join the white invaders. It angered Yirawala that Kunmanara didn't marry and protect the lady and her family betrothed to him during his circumcision ceremony.

"Grandfather, what have you seen?" insisted his grandson. As he spoke to his grandson, the other elders listened without interrupting. This highly aroused their interest because Yirawala generally had nothing to say or do with the white invaders.

"When the Dreamtime message has been explained to me, I will tell you what I have seen. Go your way my child and return when you have learned to respect the ways of your ancestors. You wouldn't understand what is coming upon the world anyway. I am the one that performed your initiation, but you did not want to live as your ancestors and reach the higher levels of the Dreamtime. Now you want to know all about it," replied Yirawala.

Everyone laid down to rest for the evening, except Yirawala. He sat up all night meditating about his Dreamtime experience wondering what it was all about.

The next morning the sun broke over the horizon, blinding Yirawala so much he couldn't open his eyes, so he decided it would be a good time to go to sleep. After a few hours of rest, he started walking about the land naked and barefoot as his ancestors had done for thousands of years. He wanted to get in touch with the original Aborigine people's way of life that had been shunned by the new ways of the white invaders. He took a boomerang, a flint knife, and a spear made from the rocks of his ancestral Outback sacred mountains. He knew his journey must be pure and simple, excluding any material item the white invaders had brought into his ancestral lands. Any object that was not made by the traditional Aborigine people was unacceptable to Yirawala because it disrupted his Aboriginal way of life. After a full day of meditation, he returned to his outstation in the northern region of the Australian Outback.

The next day he wanted to walk the Outback alone. Yirawala did not get to travel by himself because his eldest son and three other tribesmen wanted to walk and talk with Yirawala about his remarkable experience.

41

After walking about for a few hours in the Outback, they came upon a wallaby drinking water from a bottomless pond. Nothing seemed to disturb the wallaby as she kept drinking not paying any attention to them.

One of the elders wanted to use his boomerang to kill the wallaby for dinner, but Yirawala stopped him, although everyone's stomachs were beginning to growl from hunger. Yirawala forbade anyone to harm this creature, fearing it was one of his ancestors watching over him. To eat this creature was a temptation that Yirawala had to erase from their minds.

They walked up to the opposite side of the pool of water and got a drink, at the same time watching the wallaby. The wallaby stopped drinking and waved its right paw at Yirawala. Yirawala had never seen this happen before. He told his colleagues that this must be an ancestor disguised as a wallaby sent to watch them. The other tribesmen did not comment about what Yirawala had to say about the wallaby. After a brief rest, the group ventured deep into the Outback until they came upon a rocky formation that had some cave paintings composed of white and black dots. Every elder knew exactly what the unusual cave drawing portrayed, except Yirawala's grandson. He pleaded with the elders to explain what the paintings meant. Each painting had to be explained to him in detail because he had forgotten his Aborigine teachings about these figures. After resting for awhile the elders decided to gather some firewood and hunt some food to eat.

As they were gathering the wood, two birds flew close to Yirawala. He took two large boomerangs and threw them at the same time. With absolute accuracy, he knocked both birds down. Kunmanara ran and gathered up the birds for the first meal of the day. One of the other elders found a plant to boil to make a traditional Aborigine drink. The evening approached quickly, so the group decided to set the giant wood pile a blaze they had built earlier. Yirawala decided to fast that day so as the other ate he sat down next to the giant bonfire to meditate. He slowly drifted into a trance as the elders started playing two different sizes of Didgeridoo flutes.

"Yirawala, why haven't you painted the message given to you?" asked the messenger of the Rainbow Serpent.

"I will not exhibit these carvings or tell my people the Dreamtime visitation until I am sure it is true and not of my own imagination," replied the wise Yirawala.

"That is a very good answer but not an acceptable one. Time is short and the world must be warned what will suddenly come upon them," said the spirit with authority.

Without warning, one of the spiritual Aborigine ancestors whisked Yirawala away into a dimension he had never seen before during any of his prior Dreamtime experiences. He was carried away into a special realm to enhance his knowledge about the pending Sixth Rebirth. There he was shown what must be done to ensure future generations of Aborigine people. Yirawala was stunned by what he shown.

Yirawala always believed those living in the Dreamtime were accurate and truthful, but this seemed unrealistic to him. Being extremely conservative, he believed the traditional ways of his ancestors were the best lifestyle for all Aborigines. Being ashamed of the new generation of Aborigines, that ignored their roots, propelled him to continuously preach about his fifty-thousand-year-old ancestral roots.

He mourned daily because his precious holy place to live was being constantly destroyed by the white invaders. Now being asked by those of the Dreamtime to give the white invaders information to survive the Sixth Rebirth was too much to ask of him. He felt his message was to help those that were trying to destroy his beloved land, people and culture. He truly had a hard time finding a place in his heart to do such a horrible command.

"Yirawala, what the Great Spirit of your ancestor's commands must be done. The rock where you are camped is the perfect place to paint the future of the world," said the messenger of Ngaljod.

Still in the Dreamtime, Yirawala was taken even deeper into the scared caves of his natal ancestors far below Mother Earth's surface. Yirawala saw Marayka again rubbing herself upon the phallus rocks again, but this time she started rubbing her body against his. The

Rainbow messenger watched as Yirawala started sweating throughout his body. Marayka continued to rub the phallus stones and then rub up against him. Yirawala rapidly became weakened by Marayka's actions. She could not help noticing he was standing in a pool of sweat, so she backed off as Ngaljod carefully observed how he reacted.

"Why are you sweating so much, Yirawala?" asked the Rainbow Serpent messenger facetiously.

"My ancestral spirit mother, Marayka, has placed my body into a state that has excited me so sexually that I have become weakened. She has aroused me like the first time I enjoyed the company of my wife, except a thousand times more intense. This is the strongest desire I have ever experienced with a woman. I know she is a spirit, but she gave me such a strong feeling that my body started to overheat to the point that I am now exhausted. It felt like I was making love to a thousand women at once," replied Yirawala.

"Your ancestors were glad to be seduced by Marayka. This ritual has brought many generations of fertility to the Aborigine people. It is sad for me to say, that today many have followed after the white invaders style of regeneration. Your people will soon melt away into nothingness. The ways of your ancestors will be forever lost, and then the Aborigine people will become extinct," said the messenger.

"How old is Marayka?" asked Yirawala.

"Yirawala, time doesn't begin or end in the spirit world, so the age of one spirit is irrelevant. We spirits are of one age since time has no beginning or ending, so time and age only apply to those that live slower than the speed of light. You are in the Dreamtime; your age is not a factor here either. Those that live in the spirit world don't grow older or younger. You are what you are and that you will always be," said the messenger.

Yirawala stood there in a pool of sweat for a few minutes trying to regain his composure. Moments later, a third messenger took him even deeper into the caves where he was first shown cave carvings. Yirawala observed giant waves washing away city after city around the world. Then he was shown a cave carving that illustrated many mushroom sprouting up all over China and India. The mushrooms produced black clouds of smoke and debris that turned the sun blood red and hid the stars and moon.

The thick clouds blanketed the night sky so much they blocked out the Spiritual Ancestor's view of Mother Earth. After a few moments, he was taken to an inner chamber where he was shown three circles. One circle depicted the Earth as it stands, the second showed the Earth's land changing places with its great seas, and the third circle shocked Yirawala. He saw an Earth indescribable by words.

Then, he was taken deeper and deeper down into the caves where the darkness was so thick that he could feel it with his hands. Yirawala saw men screaming and running in all directions from fear of the unknown. What they were running from had gripped them with so much fear their eyes bulged out of their heads.

"Do you understand what these cave carvings represent, Yirawala?" asked the messenger.

"I do not understand them. The only way I will know is if you will teach me," he replied.

"I will teach you when the moon is ripe with its power," said the messenger.

"Please teach me now, so I can tell my people what will befall them during the Sixth Rebirth. I promise to tell the white invaders, too, even after what they have done to my people and the land of my ancestors. I will tell what will befall them during the Sixth Rebirth of Mother Earth," remarked Yirawala.

"In due time, I know you will, but at the moment I want you to paint these carvings. They must be painted on the caves where you are now camped. After they have been completed, I will send another messenger to explain what they mean," said the messenger of Ngaljod.

"I am willing to instruct all human beings," pleaded Yirawala.

"In due time, in due time," said the messenger as he vanished.

Without any further conversation, Yirawala was whisked away. He opened his eyes to look around to see where he was. He could see the others of his group were fast asleep. The bonfire was still blazing over twenty feet high, throwing millions of sacred sparks miles into the night sky. Yirawala was confounded to find that everyone had fallen asleep since the stars had been awake for only two hours. Then he tried to get up but couldn't. He struggled again and again but couldn't get up on his feet. This started to worry Yirawala. He could not help by wonder what exceedingly strange force had overcome his physical body.

"Kunmanara, wake up and help me! Kunmanara, wake up and help your grandfather," yelled out Yirawala.

No one moved a muscle. Now Yirawala was afraid they were all dead from some poison in the water or the food they had indulged before the sun closed its eyes for the day.

"Kunmanara, Kunmanara! Kunmanara!" yelled out Yirawala vehemently.

All of a sudden he heard the drums of his grandfather pounding his favorite beat. Fear overtook his entire body. He looked in all directions and couldn't see any image of anyone or anything. The drums started pounding louder and louder. The sound became so loud that Yirawala felt those sleeping should have had their teeth rattling against one another.

"Kunmanara, Manandjiwala, Jarinyanu wake up! Have you left the flesh world for the Dreamtime? Return and join me in the world of the living," he cried out loud, and then started talking to himself, "They must be in the Dreamtime while I have returned to the land of the flesh. I will have to patiently wait until the Rainbow Serpent returns them to me," said Yirawala trying to ease his wariness.

"Ngaljod, what have you done to my people? Where have you taken them? Bring them back to me!" said Yirawala not being sure of his thoughts.

Then Marayka appeared to him once more. She danced around him constantly, in rhythmic patterns, to the drums that were pounding in perfect unison. Yirawala sat there watching her every move while listening and wondering if his ancestral spirits were playing the drums.

All of sudden, a massive Didgeridoo was being played by a little boy about six years old. Yirawala stared at the young warrior as he watched

Marayka dance to the music that drowned out all other sounds that filled the night air. Yirawala then realized something rather peculiar about the cave where the bonfire was blazing high into the evening sky. The sparks from the bonfire were all dancing a particular ceremonial dance of the ancients. Yirawala rubbed his eyes over and over looking at the sparks created by the bonfire. He watched the sparks change positions as if they were dancing with one another. As the music started to soften, it appeared to Yirawala that the sparks stopped dancing.

At that point Yirawala decided he must be dead, and this was the ancestral way of welcoming him home to the eternal Dreamtime. He closed his eyes and laid his head on a soft rock and let go of his walking stick. To Yirawala's surprise, the Rainbow Serpent woke him and then brilliantly displayed its colors and ferocity. Yirawala hid his face from the burst of blinding rainbow colored lights.

"What have I done to be frightened this way?" cried out Yirawala thinking he was dead.

"My child, whom I created before there was, and will be after, there is no more. I have come to protect those to be created before they are. You have been on a journey to learn the secrets of the Dreamtime. I am here to help you remember what you have seen," said Ngaljod.

"Why have you chosen me to tell the world what is coming upon mankind during the Sixth Rebirth? Will this change the present time and the times to come?" asked Yirawala.

"Yirawala, awaken and tell those that will listen. Those that survive will need to rebuild what was because what is will be no more," said Ngaljod, as he disappeared back into the Dreamtime realm.

Yirawala suddenly woke up sitting in a chair lined with golden lambskin his grandson had given him for his eightieth birthday. Kunmanara had purchased the chair in Perth two years before his four-score birthday. Yirawala, being extremely rebellious about any white-invader-made device, had to be fooled into believing Kunmanara had made it himself. It was filled with soft goose down and covered with silk, so the elder could be extremely comfortable while he relaxed his weary body. Yirawala looked around wondering if he was still in the

Dreamtime with Ngaljod. His daughterin-law brought him a hot cup of Outback tea and placed it on the small hand carved wooden table with a stone top taken from the valley of scared rocks.

"Drink your hot herbs, Yirawala. It will be dinner time soon and you will need to be fully awake. Tonight we will have your favorite meal— baked lizard with honey ants," commanded the lady of the house.

"Where am I!" burst out Yirawala.

"You are home," replied Molly, his favorite daughter.

"What day is it!" asked Yirawala vehemently.

"It is the same day you asked me about this morning!" rudely remarked his daughter-in-law.

"What day would that be?" asked Yirawala realizing he was in the world of the living.

"Father, are you alright? You're speaking like you have lost your mind. Do you know what time it is and where you are at?" said his sixty-year-old favorite daughter.

"Please call Kunmanara for me," pleaded Yirawala.

"He will be home in a few minutes. You will have to wait to talk to him," replied his daughter-in-law.

"Yes, I can wait, but those living in the world can't wait?" he said thinking out loud.

About ten minutes passed before a well used Land Rover pulled into the dirt driveway. Kunmanara got out of the car and brought several items into the house. He had gone to Alice Rock and Aberdeen to purchase some white invader items, as Yirawala would call his family needed. Yirawala sat there motionless for a few moments.

He finally decided to get up and help his grandson unload the vehicle. Later that night, Yirawala took Kunmanara outside and told him about his experience in the Dreamtime. Kunmanara unquestionably accepted what his grandfather had told him as fact since he had always respected his grandfather. Being concerned about the vision, Kunmanara called some tribal elders from a few nearby tribes for a meeting to discuss his grandfather's experience.

It took a couple of days before everyone could attend the special meeting. After a few leaders heard Yirawala's it was decided to invite every leader to a meeting to discuss Yirawala's Dreamtime experience at the Outstation near the Aborigine ancestral sacred caves. Over a hundred elders and spiritual leaders came to hear what happened to Yirawala during his Dreamtime visitation with Ngaljod. Some opened their eyes wide while others thought it was an old man dreaming dreams during an afternoon nap. A certain group of seven elders decided to have a ceremonial bonfire in the Outback by the northern sacred caves. This was to decide if Yirawala's Dreamtime was real or an old man's aging fantasy.

"Yirawala, we will build three bonfires. This is so Wandjuk can help you paint the cave carvings that Ngaljod revealed to you deep within the caves of the Nullabor Plains," said one of the northwestern outstation elders.

"I will do the best I can to remember cave carvings," replied Yirawala.

At that precise moment, it became crystal clear in Yirawala's mind what he had seen and experienced. He looked up into the sky and then down at Mother Earth. Then he smiled at everyone, knowing it was not a fantasy but a real experience.

"What are we going to do?" asked Wandjuk.

"We will be able to replicate exactly what was shown to me," replied Yirawala.

Yirawala explained in detail to Wandjuk what must be done. Working feverishly, it took them two weeks to complete the dot paintings of what Yirawala had been shown. Yirawala concentrate on completing the dot paintings without trying to interpret them.

They artistically constructed three ocean waves washing several worldwide coastal cities away on one cave wall. On an adjacent wall of the ocean waves, they carved eastern Asia filled with mushroom clouds. They were of various sizes, spewing out black clouds that turned the sun red. Underneath the upper caves, Yirawala painted men of all nations running in many different directions with eyes bulging from their sockets from the fear that had surrounded them. Yirawala painted the men's faces so you could feel the fear that had gripped their souls from the horrible disasters taking place.

On a third cave wall, they painted three large circles. One depicted a normal Earth. The second circle had Earth experiencing her seas and land changing places. The Earth spun wildly out of control, ninety degrees off of its axis. The southern hemisphere's glaciers were melting, and the northern hemisphere was turning into one giant ice sheet. The third circle displayed a new Earth that did not look anything like the original Earth. Yirawala had studied world maps made by the white invaders many years of his life so he knew Earth was radically altered. Ancient lands had disappeared as new land appeared that hadn't existed before the mushroom clouds.

After they finished all of the paintings, the elders were returned to the sight to see what Ngaljod, the Rainbow Serpent, of the Dreamtime had shown Yirawala. He did not paint any scenes of Marayka dancing around the phallus stones, fearing it was too powerful of an aphrodisiac. Yirawala feared many men might become as aroused he did when she danced for him. After studying the dot configurations for awhile, many arguments broke out a their true meanings. Decipher these carvings was far too perplexing for even the most experienced elder tribesmen. Since no one could actually interpret the Dreamtime message since it had been given to Yirawala. They all agreed Yirawala would have to be the one to interpret the meanings of the cave carvings.

After many days of discussions among themselves, the elders of the various tribes decided Yirawala would have to return to the Dreamtime and seek more wisdom, understanding, and knowledge from those that traveled at the speed of light. Yirawala resisted their plea to reenter the Dreamtime to seek information about the drawings meanings, but for the Aborigine people sake agreed to do so. During the Dreamtime, the Rainbow Serpent praised Yirawala and the Aborigine people for keeping Mother Earth pure and potent for life. The serpent explained how this was necessary for the spirits to exist within the magnetic realms of Mother Earth's power.

"Yirawala, the Aborigine have kept the trees, animals, and mountains pure throughout the thousands of years of while living on the land. Mother Earth had been kept in pristine shape as your ancestors first seen her from the beginning of the time of the times," said the Dreamtime ancestral spirit as the messenger took him deep inside Mother Earth.

"Where are you taking me?" asked Yirawala.

"This is the deepest cave below the Nullabor Plains where the beautiful women were first awakened. The Great Father Spirit gave men beautiful women to replenish Mother Earth so life would continue," said the spirit of the Dreamtime, "I am taking you there since life will have to be replenished after the Sixth Rebirth."

"Why do we need the Sixth Rebirth?" asked Yirawala.

"The Sixth Rebirth is the solution," cried the Rainbow messenger.

"What do our people need to know to survive this great and terrible age called the Sixth Rebirth? Will it come gradually or suddenly upon Mother Earth?"

"Yirawala, you must paint yourself with red and yellow ochre and then fast so you will be permitted to journey again into the deep plains of Nullabor. It will take many days of fasting to prepare your body to understand what the carvings mean," said the ancestral voice sounding like torrential rains during a powerful monsoon storm.

"I will fast as my Ancestral Spirits have asked," said Yirawala humbly.

"Yirawala, the plants and animals all sing songs as they reproduce, which brings joy in creating life. Now they will cry out for safety as Mother Earth will rebel from the constant abuse by man. Soon you shall receive the knowledge necessary for the protection of the chosen remnant," said the messenger of Ngaljod.

"What remnant?" asked Yirawala.

"That has been decided by the Father of Creation. There is only one spirit that is good, the creator of all living flesh and spirits," said the Rainbow spirit.

"How will I know these remnants? I am regulated by the white invaders that carved up Mother Earth that have tried to commit genocide against my people, will they be the ones to inherit Mother Earth?" asked Yirawala worrying what will happen to the Aborigine people.

"Too many questions, Yirawala, about these people. You must find it in your heart to warn your brothers and the white invaders, too. Yirawala, you must learn to love everyone," said the spirit speaking so intensely it rattled the very ground where Yirawala sat.

"Why does Mother Earth have to be so violent during her Sixth Rebirth?" asked Yirawala worrying over what was about to come upon Mother Earth.

"What man does to the Earth, he does to himself. His very right to exist has been compromised by his neglectful ways of constantly destroying Mother Earth. Man's interdependency with Mother Earth—wind, earth, fire, and water—has been lost. Mother Earth is now dieing from man's abuse. The time has come for Mother Earth to turn her back on man and his neglectful acts. The Sixth Rebirth is at hand. Many events will occur shortly, so prepare your people. The Ancestral Ceremony that created life from the dust of Mother Earth at the beginning must be performed again," said the Spirit, as Yirawala drifted about in the Dreamtime.

"I will do as you have commanded since all humans have come from the dust of Mother Earth," replied Yirawala.

"From dust, man has risen to take his part among the living on Mother Earth and to dust he will return, when this age ends," said the messenger spirit.

"What will happen to the plants and animals during the Rebirth?" asked Yirawala.

"The Great Spirit knows how to take care of his creations. He loves all of the lesser and greater creations the same. The end of this age has been planned from the beginning of time," said the messenger vanishing as Yirawala returned from the Dreamtime.

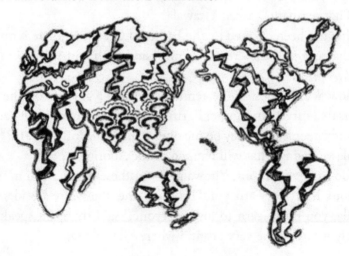

CHAPTER THREE:

ANCIENT HEBREWS

At the same time of the Hopi and Aborigine visitations, an ultra-orthodox Jewish Rabbi named David Raboy was contacted by a holy messenger to warn the people of Earth's pending doom.

"Rabbi Raboy, fear not, for I come in peace. It is time to reveal the mysteries of the prophecies as to the fate of all living flesh. I come to proclaim the word of knowledge, wisdom and understanding," said the Angelic messenger of light. The Rabbi was spellbound by a voice resonating from nowhere.

"Who are you? Where have you come from?" asked the Rabbi. Then he had to cover his face with both of his hands as the messenger appeared to protect himself from a radiant brilliant golden light.

"I am who I am. Record what shall be revealed to all mankind. The Red Heifer shall be sacrificed so the new temple can be built at the appropriate Holy site in the new city. The new city shall be called Yahweh Shammah," said the messenger sounding like a hundred Shofars blasting out.

"How can we build on the soil of the Holy site when we are not exactly sure where the location is?" asked Raboy, trembling. The Rabbi cowered away from the messenger by first hiding his face, and then curled up into the fetal position, as he ducked to the floor. Being totally surprised, Rabbi Raboy started shaking wondering what was happening. He first thought it was a surreal dream, but changed his mind to believe he had a neurological disorder or brain dysfunction. He slowly opened his eyes, and still was blinded by the golden brilliant light emanating from the angelic messenger.

"After the earth turns upside down the Holy site shall be revealed. Knowledge has already been given but not the understanding or wisdom to know how this will come upon all mankind, beasts of the field, and all that lives," said the messenger with authority.

"How will I know this?" asked the Rabbi.

"You will know by the words already spoken," said the messenger.

"We have a plan to build the Holy Temple," remarked the Rabbi looking at the hind side of the messenger.

"The design of the Temple has already been revealed to you thoroughly by the Lord through the faithful servant Ezekiel. Do not change Ezekiel's instructions, for it is the Holy Creators' inspired word. The area and dimensions shall be exact without any deviations. If anyone says they have already built the Holy Temple or states it will be built in any other place than Israel, they are liars and thieves. The New Jerusalem shall be built by the Messiah and no other. If anyone states any other information, they are enemies of the Creator of all things, the Holy of Holies, Yahweh. He is the only true and Good Lord of all creation. All others are liars, murders, and thieves," boldly said the messenger.

"Oh mighty one, messenger of the God of my fathers, there are no Red Heifers left in the world. How can we sacrifice a Red Heifer to dedicate the temple to the Holy Creator of all life?" earnestly asked Rabbi Raboy.

"The Red Heifer exists on the most holy of hidden scrolls handed down from Moses created during the days of Mount Sinai. The original Red Heifer was sacrificed and its skin was saved. It was hidden among the seventh sacred scroll by being dowsed with the blood of the original altars. When it is burned, it will represent the Red Heifer sacrifice. This sacrifice will be used to dedicate the temple that Ezekiel foretold to your people," said the messenger..

"When will we start to build the temple that Ezekiel has prophesied?" asked Raboy.

"That will be revealed when it is time. Today, write down the message set before you."

Being scared beyond comprehension, Raboy took out a pen and notepad and prepared to write down the message.

"Write quickly, the time draws near that the light will not shine where it ought. The passages from the prophets will start to unravel. Fear the only Holy Spirit. The passages of Isaiah, Jeremiah, Zephaniah, Ezekiel and Habakkuk are now upon you. The Dead Sea Scrolls have revealed that God is the same yesterday, today, and forever—the only Holy God of truth. Hear my words for they are the words of your Almighty Creator," said the messenger earnestly.

"I will do as you have commanded," said Raboy trembling. His disbelief hindered him, as he wrote down the passages verse by verse.

"My servant of the chosen people that have deserted me many times, this is your final message. Until the time of the times has been completed and the abomination of desolation stands where it ought not, as Daniel has told you, the Messiah will hide his face from this overbearing people. You will mourn for the Messiah, when your eyes are opened, and then you will be ashamed when you understand the truth," warned the messenger of light.

"We already mourn, as we wait for the Messiah," replied Raboy.

"You do not know what manner you speak. This message is not only for your people to hear. No one will be able to understand this divine message without divine intervention," said the messenger, as he disappeared.

In a flash, the messenger vanished into where he had come from, into a dimension Rabbi Raboy could not comprehend. Rabbi Raboy sat there quivering like a leaf blowing in the wind, wondering what had just happened to him. Barely being in control of his emotions and body functions, Raboy struggled over to look out his east chamber window. He had to find out if anyone else had noticed the blinding, brilliant light that filled his office. Everyone on the streets walked about as if nothing had ever taken place.

Being rattled to the point he could not think straight, he decided to have a cup of coffee. Never having experienced a single sip of coffee in his life, Raboy decided this was a good day to make some changes in his life. Raboy figured that drinking a fresh brewed cup coffee would help him calm down. He was shaking so much that he could not study the cup enough with both hands. He decided to set the coffe cup down under coffee pot spout before he took the initative to get his first cup of coffee. After the cup was full he grabbed with both hands.

Everyone started looking at him as he shook uncontrollably while holding his cup of coffee. The coffee spilt on the floor, his shoes, and cloke. He decided to forget having a cup of coffee. Quickly he set the cup of coffee down on table, and then pulled out a chair and sat down at the round mosaic table. No matter how much he tried, he could not stop shaking.

"Rabbi, what is the matter with you? You look like you have just seen a ghost," said the Russian seminar student.

"I have seen something far worrisome than a ghost and more powerful," said Raboy.

"What did you see?" asked the student in his native Hebrew tongue.

"I am not at liberty to tell you at this moment, but, if and when the time comes I will explain to you what has happened to me. I have no idea why I've been chosen for this assignment," said Rabbi Raboy. Raboy realized he was not making much sense so he got up and left the room immediately to avoid any more confrontations or questions.

After a few days, Rabbi Raboy, a Cohen ultra orthodox caretaker of the secret Hebrew scrolls, went to his friend and colleague. He wanted to tell him about his mysterious experience but decided it would be too scandalous to mention. Who would believe his report that he was the first Rabbi in over two thousand years to a receive a visitation from a cherubim. Then he figured he should tell his friends because is was astonishing news that a 'Cohen' Rabbi in modern times had been contacted by the spirit world. Not sharing a word of his supernatural experience with his friend made him realize that he was too scared to speak out he left his friends house. The next morning he traveled to the Mea Shar'im section of Jerusalem. He slowly entered the great study hall of enlightenment.

"Rabbi," said one of the younger students.

"Rabbi," said another student.

"Rabbi," said Rabbi Goldberg.

"Rabbi this, Rabbi that. What is all of this Rabbi nonsense about?" asked Rabbi Raboy.

"Rabbi Raboy, are you feeling well?" asked Rabbi Goldberg.

"I had a visitation from an angelic messenger. When he appeared, I was blinded from the brilliant glow of his presence," said Raboy.

"Were you dreaming? Did anyone else see this vision?" asked Rabbi Klein laughing out loud thinking Raboy was making a joke.

"No, I was all alone working on the secret scrolls when, instantly out of nowhere, an overpowering voice spoke directly to me. The doors were locked on both sides. Then, out of nowhere, a bright light blinded me. This nine foot tall being of light told me to write down these scriptures and then read the Dead Sea Scrolls to postulate their pure interpretation," said Rabbi Raboy being serious with Goldberg.

"Maybe it was a dream when you dosed off for a moment?" said Rabbi Goldberg still thinking Raboy was making up a story.

"Yes, it could have been that. I dosed off and dreamed this all up. Now, can you look up these scriptures, and then, if it isn't too much trouble, write them down. Please, would you compare them to any of the Dead Sea Scrolls available for any type of a direct interpretation?" asked Rabbi Raboy wearisome about exposing himself.

"We would be more than glad to," said Rabbi Klein, rolling his eyes, unconvinced Raboy was telling him the truth.

Three days later, the student assigned to research the Dead Sea Scrolls went to the Tel Aviv Cohen artifact chambers to knock on Rabbi Raboy's office door. Raboy did not answer because he was at a meeting with his peers discussing the safety of the Ark of Covenant, which had been relocated in the Mea Shar'im section of Jerusalem. The student decided to leave the blue folder under his door with the exact interpretation of the scriptures Rabbi Raboy had requested. The Dead Sea Scrolls research team had worked very hard to meticulously interpret the complete message because they were curious about Raboy's choice of scriptures.

Rabbi Raboy returned later that afternoon and found the blue folder at the foot of his door. He picked it up and opened it right after he entered the secure room. He sat down and read it through a few times. Then he carefully read every note the research team attached to each verse. One note explained how the research team tried to find every verse of Isaiah in the Dead Sea Scrolls, but they had to use the books of the prophets to complete meaning of the scripture.

"Dear Rabbi, we were able to find every scripture you requested in the book of Isaiah using the Dead Sea Scrolls as our only source. Unfortunately to compare and interpret them verbatim, the books of the prophets were used as an alternative. We are amazed what the message had to say since it suggests the earth will be compromised. At one point, several students felt it was a sign that the end of this age is now upon us. We really do not understand the meaning of this message. If you can give us some more verses, maybe we can give a better interpretation. Please, let us know, "Sincerely, Rabbi Goldberg"

Rabbi Raboy now felt he would get ridiculed if he continued to ask Goldberg for any more assistance. Being alarmed with what the messages said he took a deep breath before reading it one more time:

"What will you do on the day of visitation and desolation that shall come from afar? Desolation shall come upon you suddenly and the whole land shall be a desolation and an astonishment, fear and a snare is come upon us, desolation and destruction. That day is a day of wrath, a day of trouble and distress, a day of waste and desolation, a day of darkness and gloominess, a day of clouds and thick darkness therefore shall all hands be faint, and every man's heart shall melt, and they shall be afraid: pangs and sorrows shall take hold of them; they shall be in pain as a woman that travails; they shall be amazed one at another; their faces shall be as flames for the stars of heaven, and the constellations shall not give their light; the sun shall be darkened in his going forth, the moon shall not shine her light, and the foundations of the Earth will move exceedingly. The Earth shall reel to and fro like a drunk and shall be removed like a cottage from the mountains shall be thrown down; the steep places shall fall, and every wall shall fall to the ground when the everlasting mountains are scattered and the Earth is turned upside down and the inhabitants scattered abroad, a few men left on Earth."

Raboy was disturbed by this message, so he sat there quietly gathering his thoughts. He slowly lifted a glass of seltzer water to his mouth and drank it in one gulp. Raboy interpreted the message that God was getting ready to disrupt the entire universe.

Two months had passed since the great and terrible message was revealed to Raboy. During this period, there were not any cosmic or earthly disturbances so Raboy became complacent. Feeling like he had completed all that was requested of him, he graciously pinned the message to his agenda wall.

"Now that you know what is coming upon the Earth, and what mankind will face in the future, what are you going to do about it? The Dead Sea Scrolls were preserved to prove the skeptics and disbelievers that the scriptures cannot be broken. The Holy Creator has told the truth since the beginning of time and what He has said will be done," said a voice from nowhere that sounded like thunder.

"Who are you?" exclaimed Raboy out loud.

"I am who I am," replied the powerful voice.

"I give up. I must be going crazy," said Rabbi Raboy looking around the room in all directions desperately trying to get a glimpse of someone or something.

"You have been chosen to proclaim this report. The knowledge you have of the future must be revealed so those that believe will be saved by their obedience. Those that hide the truth are cowards, liars, and an abomination to the Holy Creator of all things that were, that are, and are to come," said the voice appearing as a brilliant, tall column of golden purple light.

Rabbi Raboy fell to the ground cowering away from the messenger. He hid his face, afraid to look upon this creature of great stature and power. His entire body started shaking and his heart grew faint from fear. Then the spiritual messenger lifted up Raboy and set him in one of the office chairs.

"Why have you chosen a coward like me to tell the world these things? My colleagues will call me a crazy man. Telling the public the end of the world is near will land me in a mental institution. Besides, who do I reveal these prophecies of the future, too?" asked Rabbi Raboy.

"Oh, you stiff-necked people of Abraham that was chosen but refused to obey the original covenant of the Lord. You hid the truth from the world and concealed His messages like they only belonged to you. Stop asking me questions. Do as it is required of you," said the being of light as he vanished.

Twenty minutes later, Rabbi Raboy got up and reread the original message he had pinned to his agenda board. He sat there all day wondering what was happening. Then he started worrying about his health. He decided to make an appointment with the local Neurologist thinking his mind was being attacked by some neurological disease.

Two weeks later he sat patiently waiting in a quaint neurological examination room for the doctor to exam. After an hour wait Dr. Steinman finally entered the room with his female assistant. He took out the appropriate medical examination equipment to check out Rabbi Raboy's subjective complaint. The doctor first looked at his eyes, ears, and tongue and wrote down his objective findings. The doctor then asked the nurse to take Raboy's vital readings again. She put the blood pressure cuff on his left arm as the doctor placed his stethoscope to Raboy's chest to examine his heart and lungs. At that very moment, a brilliant light blinded the doctor and nurse. They dropped everything and ducked down while Raboy sat there staring at the entity.

"It's nice for you to show up at the doctor's office so I can be immediately committed to an insane asylum and locked away for good in my own padded cell," said Rabbi Raboy.

"David, why are you so stiff-necked and rebellious?" said the voice with great authority.

"Because you are figment of my imagination, and hopefully, you will be gone, as soon as, the doctor finds a cure for me," said Raboy calmly. About that time, Rabbi Raboy looked around the room and saw the doctor and nurse lying on the floor with their heads covered up. Raboy thought he had scared them by talking to himself that they hid from him. Then he noticed them on the floor.

"Doctor, what are you doing on the floor?" asked Raboy.

"I, ah, I, ah, don't know. I thought, I saw an explosion or flash of light that was something, ah. I am not really sure," responded the doctor, as he and his assistant rose up off the floor and suspiciously looked about the room.

"Doctor, what are looking for?" asked Raboy.

"I was looking, ah, looking for ahhh, nothing especially," replied the doctor.

Then, a voice that sounded like thunder blasted out. It told everyone to stop what they were doing and listen. The doctor's and nurse's eyes got as big as full moons. All at once, a brilliant golden radiant light with deep shades of purple burst into the room. Everyone froze in place except Raboy, who calmly looked at the entity.

"Doctor, can you see this image surrounded by the brilliant, golden purple, radiant light, too?" asked Raboy addressing his doctor and the assistant frozen in place.

"Raboy, why are you mocking me?" asked the messenger with a thunderous voice, "Doctor, answer me! Can you see and hear what I am hearing?" cried out Raboy.

"Be not afraid, I come in peace to warn the world as what is to come," said the messenger.

The doctor and nurse were lifted off of the floor by the power of the messenger and set them upright on the bed. The doctor shook as he stared straight ahead not believing he faced a nine-foot-tall being of light.. The nurse closed her eyes, fearing for her life. Raboy looked around the room and realized finally he was not dreaming or having a neurological dysfunction. Raboy noticed that the nurse had her hands over her eyes.

"Warn the people with the message that has been given to you. The end of this ages in now at hand," said the entity, as it vanished.

"Doctor Steinman, Rachel, did you hear what I heard?" asked Raboy reluctantly.

"Rabbi, I think you are healthy as anyone your age can be. Your examination is over," said the doctor as he looked around the room.

"Doctor Steinman, did you see and hear what I saw?" asked Raboy again.

"Rabbi, what we saw or heard will not be included in your evaluation notes. I know we saw something, but if I included what I thought I saw and heard we would both be called quacks. Let's keep this experience our little secret," demanded Dr. Steinman.

"How can we keep such information a secret?" asked Raboy.

"Rabbi, please trust me on this one. We do not know what we heard or saw. As far as I am concerned, the message that you have received is a private matter. I am a professional doctor, and you are a well respected spiritual leader so we must keep quiet to protect reputations. My reputation is all I have to assure my creditability as a physician," said the doctor frankly.

"Doctor, I would like to ask you and your assistant one small itsy bitsy question if I may."

"One question and that's the end of this conversation," replied the doctor.

"You did see the messenger and heard what was said?" asked Raboy.

"We saw and heard something. That is my final comment about this subject. Have a good-day, Rabbi," said the doctor, hastily leaving the room.

Rabbi Raboy took off the gown and put his ultra orthodox attire on and left the doctor's office. On his way out, he stopped by the front office to settle up his account for the doctor visit. After he asked for the total charges for the day, the back office nurse spoke quietly into the ear of the front office receptionist.

"There is no charge for today's services and the doctor said you will not need a follow-up visit," stated the lady at the front desk sternly, looking at the Rabbi.

Rabbi Raboy nodded his head and politely left the office. He knew what the doctor and nurse had seen would not be reported to anyone for any reason. This eased the Rabbi's conscience but worried his spirit. Here he had two witnesses who knew what he saw was real, but they would deny anything they saw that day. This is something he would have to accept as the way it would be, rather than living with the way it ought to be.

Being quite possibly the most confused man on Earth that crispy winter morning Raboy walked about in the Beni Brak, (Hundred Gates district of Tel Aviv, Israel), dazed at what to do next. He was in a peculiar and perplexing situation since he had told to convince the people that the end of the world would happen soon. How would he answer if they asked when and how?

Rabbi Raboy had studied many scientific theories about how the sun could burn out, an ice age would eventually develop and how the green house gases are devastating the earth, but telling everyone the world is going to end from information he got out of the Old Testament would bring ridicule. He figured by telling everyone his information was from a messenger of light would cause the people to laugh at him. The problem now rested on his shoulders to speak out and be scorned or keep quiet and disobey the Lord. He put his head down and tried to figure out what was happening in the spirit world that would allow physical Earth to be destroyed.

"What type of cataclysmic event is this going to be that angels are visiting me?" thought the Rabbi.

It was time to close shop and head home for the day so Rabbi Raboy carefully wrote down his experience on a small red tablet and then placed it in his right pocket. Since his wife had asked that he stop by the market and purchase a few things for his future daughter-in-law's announcement party he drove back to Tel Aviv.

"How can I help you?" asked the deli counter help.

"I would like two pounds of fresh smoked fish, one pound of cream cheese and a dozen Matzo pieces," he replied.

"Ahh, sir did you want Atlantic or Mediterranean smoked fish?" asked the counter help.

"What is the difference?" Raboy asked.

"About two dollars a pound," replied the fair, eighteenyear-young lady.

"Other than two dollars a pound, what is the difference between the smoked fish?" asked Raboy again.

"Well, the Atlantic smoked fish comes from the Atlantic Ocean and the Mediterranean smoked fish comes from the Mediterranean Sea," replied the deli counter help.

"Alright, alright, which one costs two dollars a pound less?" asked Raboy.

"The Atlantic smoked fish costs two dollars a pound less," replied the beautiful young lady.

"Why does the Mediterranean Sea smoked fish cost more?" asked the Rabbi.

"Well, it is Mediterranean Sea natural grown, and the cheaper Atlantic smoked fish is Atlantic Ocean farm grown," she replied.

"Where is the manager?" asked Raboy, frustrated with her answers.

"I am the manager. Good afternoon Rabbi, how can I help you?" he asked with a very friendly smile.

"I am trying to buy some fresh smoked fish for my son's engagement introduction gathering tonight. I have been asking for ten minutes now what is the difference between Pacific smoked fish and Atlantic smoked fish," said the Rabbi.

"Oh, that is a simple question to answer. The Mediterranean Sea is two dollars a pound more," replied the deli manager.

"Are you people stupid or what? I want to know, physically, what is the difference between the two different smoked fish. Aren't they both grown and gathered from oceans? If so, then why does one cost two dollars a pound more than the other one?" asked Rabbi Raboy wondering if the two mental midgets were missing some brain cells.

"I know what you want to know. Rabbi, the farm raised smoked Kippers do not have as much flavor as the Atlantic so the smoked Herring is tastier," she replied.

"Alright, which smoked fish would you serve at you daughter-in-laws engagement party?" asked Raboy.

"Neither," said the manager and young lady at the same time.

"We have the catch of the day for those types of special events," replied the manager.

"Please give me two pounds and don't tell me what it is or where it came from, as long as it is the best you have," said the Rabbi.

"That would be fresh Pacific Salmon. It is expensive, but . . .," said the young lady, as Rabbi Raboy interrupted her.

"I do not care. My family always gets the best," said the Rabbi boisterously.

The young lady quickly finished up his order and included a dozen kosher dill pickle slices for his trouble. Rabbi Raboy went home and sat down in his favorite chair and opened up a new book called 'What Do You Expect from Your In-Laws—Nothing but Grief'. No sooner than he started to read, he snoozed off until he heard someone knocking at the door.

"Deborah, would you get that?" he barked out.

"Are your arms and legs broken, dear? You get it, I'm busy," she replied.

He slowly got up out of the chair and proceeded to the door. As he opened the door, his jaw dropped when the first new in-law he saw was the young lady from the deli shop. Everyone politely introduced themselves.

"Our guests are here," yelled out Rabbi Raboy.

His future daughter-in-law and son rushed in from the back porch after hearing the announcement.

"Mr. Silverman, it is a pleasure to see you. Please, come in and make yourself at home," suggested the Rabbi.

"Rabbi, give me a hug since we are soon to become family," replied Mrs. Silverman.

"Mrs. Silverman, it is my pleasure to have you over for this engagement party," said Rabbi Raboy.

"Cut all of the formal introductions, David. We are family now," interjected Mrs. Deborah Raboy.

While they were eating smoked Pacific Salmon with cream cheese and talking about the upcoming wedding, Rabbi Raboy got up and proceeded to the bathroom. When he got there, the door was locked, so he patiently waited his turn. After about few minutes, he decided to knock on the door to see what was taking the person in the bathroom so long. No one answered his knock, so he knocked again, this time harder, asking if someone was inside. But there was only silence.

He decided to push on the door to see if it would open and to his surprise, it did. The bathroom was empty, so he proceeded into the room. After relieving himself, he started to freshen up when the young girl from the deli came rushing in. She lowered her panties from under her brightly colored dress and sat down to urinate right in front of him.

"Ahh, Miss Silverman, what are you doing?" asked Raboy in shock.

"What does it look like I am doing, future father-in-law?" she replied answering his question, giggling.

"Miss Silverman, my son is not marrying you. You are not supposed to come in the bathroom when someone is still using it," he responded in shock.

"Well, I had to go, and you have been in here a very long time," she replied.

"When you do something wrong, what does your mother call you?" asked the Rabbi.

"Abigail," she answered.

"Well, Abigail, if someone where to come here now, we would both be in big trouble." Rabbi Raboy wondered if this young, beautiful fair skinned, blue eyed blond was an idiot.

"Rabbi David, or Rabbi Raboy, or Daddy David, I only had to use the bathroom in an emergency situation, so why are you so upset?" she asked in soft, sexy voice.

"Abigail, does your family practice this at your home?" he asked wondering what her answer might be.

"Of course not, because we have more than one bathroom. One of them is my private bathroom," she said with a smartalecky tone of voice.

"You spoiled little brat. I think I ought to place you over my knee and give you a spanking right here and now," he said scolding her.

"I would like that Rabbi because my father has never spanked me or even paid attention to me one minute during my life. His favorite is Hanna, your son's future wife. Your son Eyal will have his hands full because he is marrying my father and mother, too," she replied, laughing.

"You know it is the custom for the daughter-in-law to live at her mother's home for the first year of marriage, so that will not be a problem," Rabbi Raboy replied.

"What about my spanking? I am ready to receive my punishment now," she said, giggling.

Rabbi Raboy gave up trying to carry on a sensible conversation with a young lady with soft big blue eyes that sparkled with innocence. He wondered if he should open the bathroom door and leave while she was using the toilet. Then she got up off of the stool and adjusted her clothing right in front of him with a big smile. Rabbi Raboy shook his head again in disbelief as the two left the room at the same time. He felt this young lady had a screw loose, but he liked her personality for some strange reason, which puzzled Raboy. Although somewhat distraught over the ordeal, he kept his mouth shut and lips sealed about what had happened.

The engagement party went smoothly and ended on a joyful note. When it was time to say good-bye for the evening, Abigail hugged David and gave him a big kiss on the cheek calling him Daddy Raboy. Mrs. Raboy smiled when Abigail did this because she was thrilled that Abigail accepted the Raboy family as her own. David looked at his wife and shrugged his shoulders, not understanding either woman's thinking.

Mrs. Raboy smiled at him as to say it was alright. She accepted Abigail as family too because this gave her the feeling of having the daughter she never had. Exhausted from the week of wild and unusual experiences, Rabbi Raboy sat down and crossed his legs, thought about nothing. Abigail Silverman's unusual attraction to him added to his list of confusion, he was at the point that his last brain cell was about to melting down.

Several months later, the Raboy/Silverman wedding took place at the Beni Bark synagogue, situated on a hill overlooking a small valley. A slight breeze kept everyone cool in the olive garden where wedding was held at two o'clock in the afternoon. The Sanhedrin Garden was full of new olive trees because one was planted every time a child was born among the Cohen's ultra-orthodox community.

Rabbi Raboy watched Mr. Silverman give his daughter's hand to his son to begin the ceremony. At the end of the ceremony, a glass was given to the groom, who, in his all black attire, hastily put the glass under his shoe and crushed it to mourn the destruction of the Temple. It was customary among the Cohen's to make sure their children would never forget to build a Temple to the Lord of Hosts when the opportunity came about.

A line was formed so the bride and groom could be displayed one last time before the groom whisked her away to a secret place to consummate their marriage. As the bride was being abducted by the groom, Abigail ran over to Rabbi Raboy and gave him a big hug and kiss on the lips.

He was so upset that he tried to fight back with the same tactics. He kissed her back and called her his daughter in front of the crowd in which everyone cheered thinking he had accepted her as his daughter. His mind went blank as she kissed him again. His only protective reaction was to repeat the words my new daughter over and over. His wife looked at him and the young damsel for one moment, and then she rejoiced figuring David had finally given her the daughter she so desired from the first day of their engagement.

"David, I am glad you like this young lady because I have asked her to help me around the house. She will not be a maid or anything like that. She will be my substitute daughter. Since you two get along so delightfully, this will be a wonderful time for the Raboy household," said Mrs. Raboy joyfully.

Rabbi Raboy was ready to jump off of the high balcony to end the insanity of it all, but he decided it would be easier to accept Abigail as his daughter, for his wife's sake. Figuring he would be at work during most of the time that she would be at his house, he would be safe from her craziness. Later that month, in the morning, Abigail came over to help Mrs. Raboy with her chores. About noon, Mrs. Raboy asked Abigail if she would take the Rabbi a surprise hot lunch to his office. Of course, Abigail said she would love to.

"Hello. Hello," yelled out Abigail.

Rabbi Raboy hesitantly opened the inner chamber door to see who was calling.

"Rabbi, your wife sent me here to bring you this special hot lunch."

"Abigail, I thought that was your voice but I was not sure."

"Here is your lunch. It is a hot lunch, so you will need to eat it right away," she said.

Abigail opened the containers and laid the lunch out for the Rabbi. She put a white cloth napkin around his neck. She then filled the spoon with a scoop of lentil soup and started to feed the Rabbi like he was a baby.

"Abigail, I am quiet capable of feeding myself," said the Rabbi.

"Oh, you're no fun at all. Here, take a taste to see if you even like it or not," she insisted.

The two started arguing over how the Rabbi was to eat the hot lunch. They argued and argued until the hot soup was finished. Abigail gently wiped off his cheeks with a towel.

"What do you want from me, Abigail? I am a married man, and you are a very young, beautiful lady. What do you want from me?" he repeatedly asked her, as she started kissing him all over.

"No, this is not right, Abigail. Please, stop at once and go back home, or to my house, or wherever you want to go, as long as it is away from here," he said firmly.

"Alright, if that is the way you want it. I am just trying to make you feel loved by the daughter you never had," she replied.

"Abigail, I do not know what game you are playing but you have to stop it before you destroy my marriage of thirty years. After all, I am a man of God doing Godly duties," he said frankly.

"Doesn't the Holy Book say be fruitful and multiply?" she asked.

"It also says that you are not to commit adultery," he replied.

At that moment a brilliant golden light appeared so the two of them fell to the floor to hide out of fear from the messenger's radiance that blinded them.

"Arise, I come in peace. Abigail, you have been chosen to assist the Rabbi. The two of you shall be married to complete the Lord's Will. Your son will help restore the world to a peaceful and safe place to live," said the messenger, as he vanished.

Astonished Abigail and Rabbi Raboy stared at one another. Abigail was stunned by the mysterious messenger of light being told she would marry Raboy and have his child . Rabbi Raboy put his arms around Abigail to help soothe her spirits. Abigail was so shocked she could not utter a word.

"Abigail, please do not speak about this to anyone. I beg you to keep your silence."

She just looked at him not moving, except for her body still quivered from fear.

"Abigail, speak to me," he demanded.

"Keep silent about the brilliant messenger of light or that we are to get married and have a special son?" she asked.

"Keep everything quiet because the world will think we are both crazy."

"Yes, nothing happened today. This was all a misunderstanding or something. It was a mirage," she replied. Abigail left the office not speaking or looking back. She was so shook up that she stopped visiting the Raboys after the incident. She did call Mrs. Raboy from time to time telling her she was very busy and would come by soon to see her.

A few months later, Abigail approached Rabbi Raboy and asked him if he would be the high priest that would oversee the vows at her wedding and counsel her fiancé. Of course, he said yes.

The wedding was to be held at the same place where her sister had married the Rabbi's son. Abigail was going to marry Samuel Niv Frazen, a young soldier doing his eighteen months of compulsory military duty. He had stolen Abigail's heart only two weeks after meeting her. Rabbi

Raboy was relieved to know Abigail had finally found someone of her own age to marry and live out her life with.

Three months had passed since Abigail asked Rabbi Raboy to conduct her marriage ceremonies when she showed up at the Rabbi's door step, crying and out of control.

"Abigail, my little daughter what is wrong?" he asked.

"It's my fiancé. It's my mother and father. It's my sister and your son," she cried out. Raboy could sense something was seriously wrong by the tone of Abigail's voice.

"Yes, your fiancé and family, what about them?" asked the Rabbi ever so gently.

"They all were killed by a suicide bomber a few minutes ago," she cried out. Raboy then understood that her heart had been shattered into a thousand pieces.

"Oh, my God, oh, my God, oh, my God," he cried out repeatedly shocked by the news.

Still being grief stricken, two months after the funeral, Mrs. Raboy suffered a massive heart attack and died. The entire Beni Bark neighborhood attended the ceremonies along with hundreds of others from the Jerusalem Mea Shar'im. Rabbi Raboy was left emotionally and physically empty because his lovely wife left and son died so suddenly. His heart kept sinking deeper and deeper into his chest from grief as he stared at the coffin that was trimmed with gold and pink satin. Abigail went over and picked a red carnation, from one of the floral arrangements, and then gave it to Raboy since it was his wife's favorite flower.

As time went by, Abigail would stop by the Raboy house and cook the Rabbi dinner, clean the house, and wash his clothes. The two grew very close to one another, talking about the angelic visitations the Rabbi and Abigail had experienced. With Abigail being twenty-one and the Rabbi being fifty-two years old they appeared to be father and daughter when they would go shopping together for household items.

One evening, Abigail felt emotionally low moping around the Raboy house, quietly keeping to herself. When Raboy returned from a meeting in Jerusalem about the rights and rituals of the Torah he noticed her listlessness. He walked over and sat down in his favorite chair not to disturb Abigail. She walked over to him and sat down on his lap.

"Make love to me right now so I can remember my husband," she commanded.

"Abigail, you were not married. I think your grief has affected your thinking. I do not think making love is the answer," he replied tenderly, thinking she had become extremely depressed thinking about the needless destruction of her family.

"Rabbi, every time I think of making love, you are always on my mind. You are the man I fell in love with when I first saw you at the deli shop. Please, let me make love to you so I can clear my mind of the past," she whispered in his ear.

Rabbi Raboy got up and explicitly explained to her he could make love only to a wife. Plus, he could only marry a virgin of the Cohen background. The two shared a platonic relationship for quite awhile then one morning the President of the Hebrew University of Israel requested Rabbi Raboy to visit the Jewish synagogue in Australia. Abigail's heart was crushed because Raboy did not ask her to come along. He tried to explain to her several different ways that an unmarried young female traveling by his side would not be sanctioned by the Cohen's of the Hebrew University. She became agitated with Raboy's strict dedication to the doctrine of the Cohen Ultra Orthodox Jews because she could not be with him.

"Marry me, David Orr Raboy. Please, marry me. I want you to be your wife, not a Rabbi friend. I want to be by your side for the rest of my life and especially during your travels," she said telling him how she really felt about him.

"I must call my colleagues to discuss this situation," he said.

"Why? It is not their life or their concern. It is only our concern and our life," she replied.

"Do you really want to marry a man twice your age? Plus, you must be a virgin and of a good Cohen family. Your entire family history must be checked out which may reveal any unknown secrets you have," he explained to her with a gentle voice.

"That is not how you ask a beautiful to take your hand in marriage, but I still accept. I am a virgin, and I am from a good Cohen family," she replied, as she started kissing him all over, showing her deep passion for him. The flames of love made her glow.

"Abigail, please get control yourself!" pleaded Rabbi Raboy.

"I'm in love with the sexiest man on Mother Earth. God Almighty, you have blessed me with overwhelming joy. Your visitation was true. Praise the Lord for His everlasting mercy and goodness. I just love the Lord and I love you," she sang out like being in love for the first time.

After a brief investigation, the Beni Bark and Mea Shar'im Cohen Rabbi groups sanctioned the marriage. The two were married with the blessings by both of the Cohen Rabbi Orthodox communities. Mr. and Mrs. Silverman would have been proud of their daughter's choice to marry such a respectable man. The two now had permission from the University to travel together and spend an extra two weeks in Australia for a honeymoon. They boarded an A670 super ramjet and left for the Outback to visit an orthodox Jewish synagogue.

"Sweetie, what is your assignment in Australia anyway? That is, if you can disclose the Ultra Orthodox Judean secret information?" asked Abigail, being facetious.

"Sweetheart, this is not an Israeli secret intelligence gathering mission. I am simply going to be present at a circumcision of an Aborigine Aberdeen Tribal leader's grandson. We now have Aborigine conversions in the Outback of Australia," remarked Rabbi Raboy.

"Why are they sending you and not a Rabbi from an Australian Synagogue?" she asked.

"I am of the order of the sixteen keepers of the holy pronunciation of the Lord's Holy name. They wanted to have one of the Cohen Ultra Orthodox Rabbis of the secret sect make sure the newly chosen people are acting according to the Order of the Cohen Judean Torah counsel," he said without any hesitation.

The Airliner flew from Tel Aviv to Perth by way of the Red Sea corridor and then across the Indian Ocean directly to Western Australia in three hours. They laughed and talked every nautical mile until they landed to start Rabbi Raboy's mission.

"Sweetheart, how long have the Aborigines been circumcising their young men?" asked Abigail.

"I am not sure, but I think they have been circumcising their boys as long as, ahh . . . I think before our patriarch Abraham performed the first circumcision on his son Isaac thousands of years ago," replied Rabbi Raboy.

"This will be a very interesting mission since the customs of the Aborigines are like night and day compared to Hebrew history and culture," remarked Abigail.

"People are people. God created all of us, which brings me to the point of Noah's Ark. The Aborigine original ancestor had to have been one of Noah's offspring," said the Rabbi.

"So, they are Jewish, as well as everyone on Earth?" asked Abigail.

"Ah, no they are not Jewish, but they are the grandchildren of Noah, as we are. There are many differences between the Aborigine and the Jews. Their food supply and eating standards is nothing like ours. We wear clothes, and they do not like to. I think it is due to their geographical climate," replied the Rabbi.

"What do you mean by saying they do not like to wear clothes?" she asked, stunned by his comment.

"Traditional Aborigines view wearing clothes optional since it has been their custom for thousands of years," he stated.

"After all, I feel that is the natural way God made man to live in the first place. We were created in his own image so maybe he does not wear any clothes. That's how they lived in the Garden of Eden until Adam and Eve disobeyed," he replied.

"Why did man break the rules of the Garden of Eden in the first place by disobeying the Lord? Is that why we wear clothes to cover our shame?" she asked.

"That is what the Torah states in Genesis," he replied.

"Why haven't the Aborigines abided by the same rules?" she asked him frankly.

"My dear, not everyone wears the same garments due to the geographical regions of earth. Adam and Eve wore fig leaves over certain portions of their bodies. Since I was not there, I cannot answer your question completely or correctly. Since they respect one another's spirit as the most important part of living on Mother Earth, their reproduction is a spiritual act more than a physical act so they do not wear clothes to hide their shame," he muttered quickly.

"Do Aborigine men and women become more spiritual as they grow older?" she asked.

"I am not sure how to answer your question, except to say their belief is that the older the ladies become, the more desirable and beautiful they become," he answered.

"This seems like an interesting culture to love the person's core, rather than lusting after their flesh. What a good way to love and live," she replied.

Not one minute after they had checked into the hotel, Abigail started her little girl act.

"Let's make some Australian love, so I can sleep like a baby tonight," she replied.

Rabbi Raboy looked into her sweet baby blue eyes that sparkled like diamonds that made his heart melt. He did not say a word as they enjoyed the first evening of their honeymoon in Australia. After three hours of making passionate love, Raboy passed out in the arms of his beautiful special wife.

He entered into a deep sleep and started to dream the same dream, over and, over and over. He was talking to a man called Yirawala that explained the Aborigine ways and mysteries of the Dreamtime. He yelled out in his sleep "Yirawala" several times, awakening Abigail to the point she was shaking. She thought her husband was suffering from an unknown Australian illness.

"Wake up Honey, wake up Honey," she yelled out as she shook him.

"What, what is wrong, what is wrong?" he asked sluggishly.

"You keep calling out for Yirawala over and over to tell you the truth," she said.

"Oh, my dearest sweet little angel, the trip must have rattled my brain waves," he remarked to Abigail, half conscious.

"You kept calling out the name Yirawala. Is that someone you know?" she asked.

"No, I do not know any one that is called by that name," he replied slowly.

"Well, let's write it down. Maybe the locals may know what it means," she said softly as she put her husband's head on her bosom.

A week later, they asked a local that owned the general store at Ayers Rock about the name. He told the Raboy's it sounded like an Aborigine name. They were directed to an Aborigine rock shop at the edge of town. After eating lunch, they decided to visit the rock shop.

"Ah, sir, have you ever heard the name Yirawala before?" asked Rabbi Raboy.

"Yes, he is my great-grandfather," replied the shop keeper, "Why are you asking about him or his name?" asked the shopkeeper.

Abigail and Rabbi Raboy looked at one another and then turned to reply.

"I had a dream repeatedly in which I met with this elderly gentleman that talked about a specific Dreamtime message," replied Raboy.

The shopkeeper stopped immediately to question Raboy.

"Are you Middle Eastern?" asked the shopkeeper.

"Yes, I am of the Cohen Ultra Orthodox Jewish sect from Tel Aviv," replied Raboy.

"I will tell my great-grandfather of this. Where can you be reached?" asked the shopkeeper.

"We are going to the North central Aborigine Tribal ceremony to watch the elders perform some circumcisions," replied Raboy.

"Oh, you want to see the initiation of the young boys to become young, unmarried men," replied the shopkeeper.

"Well, something like that, I suppose," replied Raboy.

"I will find you after I talk with the elders. They must give me permission," replied the shopkeeper.

"We will be in Australia for a few weeks, so I will be looking forward to meet your great-grandfather, Yirawala," said Raboy.

The conversation ended with the Raboys leaving to continue their honeymoon itinerary. Rabbi Raboy left the name of his motel with the Aborigine in charge of the rock shop. The two Raboys went about their business as if nothing spectacular had happened to them.

Raboy and his wife decided to do some shopping in the little desert town of Alice Springs and climb Ayers Rock along with many other tourists from around the world.

"Sweetheart, do you really want to climb to the top of this giant monolith during the afternoon heat? Can't we wait until morning when it will be less of a challenge?" asked Raboy trying to get out of the climb.

"Sweetie, you do not have to climb the world's largest rock with me. Save your energy for tonight because there will be full moon and I would love to have a kosher meal with moonlight love for dessert," she replied smiling at her husband.

"Is that all you ever think about—making love?" he asked.

"That is why I married you, sweetheart, to make love, and love, and love," she replied.

"Why don't you climb the mountain with that group of German tourists? Oh, can you please take the camera? I'd love to bring home some pictures for our memoirs and friends," he asked, as she prepared to climb Ayers Rock.

She packed the camera and took off for her journey. He patiently waited at the beginning of the Ayers Rock trail gazebo that created shade to protect everyone from the intense heat. Abigail made it to the top of Ayers Rock and back down safely. The two ate a late lunch and started to go back to their motel when Manandjiwala approached them.

"Yirawala says that you may attend our tribal initiation of circumcision of our young boys to become unmarried men, too. Our Dreamtime messenger has also told Yirawala that you would come to explain his Dreamtime experience. I will tell you later when and where the ceremony will take place," said Manandjiwala.

CHAPTER FOUR:

REBIRTH PROPHECY

"**A**bigail, are you ready yet? Are you excited I will be the first Israeli to participate in an Aborigine tribal circumcision ceremony?" asked David being excited for a new experience. "Isn't this a caveman initiation of young children that will be chopped up to become unmarried men? These boys are thirteen years old. Should not they have been circumcised when they were babies?" she asked harshly not wanting to be hurried by Raboy.

"Sweetheart, this is their custom. Besides at this initiation, the ones that get circumcised also have a young girl betrothed to them that is usually five years old," he added.

"These people still have betrothals? That is silly. Are we going back into the dark ages when women were traded like cattle?"

"Abigail, Abigail, this is their tribal custom that has been handed down from millennium to millennium. If we are to learn anything about their tribal circumcision customs, we must attend and accept what is put before us. It is a privilege and honor to be an invited guest, and besides our circumcision customs are remarkably similar. Now, do you want to come or not?"

"Of course, I will attend and participate. I would not want to miss any cultural event that you will need to learn about. After all, education is very important no matter what the source is," she replied, rolling her eyes still being upset that Raboy was pushing her to get ready faster.

The two were driven by Manandjiwala to Nandjiwarra a tribal elder and grandfather that would be performing one of the circumcisions. Raboy knew it was going to be an honor to witness Nandjiwarra's grandson become an unmarried man which would be accomplished right after the circumcision initiation of the tribe's young males. Since it was a fivehour drive they had to leave at three in the morning to reach the ceremonial grounds so Rabbi would not miss the event. Manandjiwala told him he would make it in plenty of time to be informed and prepared for the ceremony.

"Yirawala, this is Rabbi David Raboy of the Ultra Orthodox Judean tribe from Israel called the Jews. He is here to witness the young men initiation ceremony," said Nandjiwarra explaining to his brother why an outsider was at the sacred ceremonial grounds.

"These Jews cannot attend our ceremony. They are not dressed properly and do they understand the reason for our ceremony?" asked Yirawala, being the one that invited Raboy.

"Elder, it will not be a problem because we are fully prepared to accept your customs and ways without questioning them," said Raboy telling a little white lie to be able to attend.

"Do we really want to go through with this?" asked Abigail.

"We will dress and conduct ourselves appropriately for this very important initiation ceremony," replied Rabbi Raboy not knowing what he had just agreed to.

"That will be acceptable. Lead him to the place of the elders and prepare him. Take his wife to our beautiful women so they can prepare her for the ceremony," replied Yirawala. Rabbi Raboy was shocked when he found out that he was required to completely undress. He was left with nothing on, except his hat which was acceptable to the Aborigines since it was an important ceremonial custom of his Cohen Ultra Orthodox Jewish sect. He sat there patiently while his body was painted and then feathered for the event. He was honored by being placed next to Nandjiwarra on the ceremonial grounds.

Abigail was undressed by the beautiful Aborigine women until she was stark naked. The ceremonial mothers dressed her according to Aborigine customs using yellow ochre with black dots. Due to Abigail's extreme fair complexion, the ladies preparing her for the ceremony felt the white dots weren't appropriate for her. The women were meticulous while painting and dressing Abigail because they wanted to make sure she would fit into the sacred ceremony not creating any disruptions.

The circumcision ceremony began with all of the tribal members singing ancestral songs followed by traditional ceremonial dancing. The young boys were kept off of the ceremonial grounds as custom demanded. Hidden in the distance, they could hear the Didgeridoo flutes echoing off the cliffs playing the same sounds that their ancestors had created thousands of years ago. The young boys were nervous, trying to meditate while hearing the ceremonial songs and dancing increase in intensity. Some of the young boys were scared while others were excited. Their hearts pounded faster and their eyes opened wider as the ceremony celebration became more and more intense.

The young women grievously cried out for the young boys. David watched Abigail being pulled into the ring of female dancers. Abigail paraded with the young, married ladies being totally naked, except for a few dots of paint on her face, breasts, stomach, and legs. Raboy was stunned watching her dance with the young ladies that wailed, singing songs while they danced around the center of the ceremonial grounds.

The Aborigine men accepted Abigail as a beautiful white lady that danced and sang along as if she was part of their tribe. Rabbi Raboy opened his eyes wider and wider every as he held his breath watching his wife dance and sing as if she were a native Aborigine.

"Rabbi, your wife has been accepted into the tribe by our women. It is your turn to participate in the initiation of young men," said Nandjiwarra.

"Thank you," replied Rabbi Raboy. Being stunned, those were the only words he could muster.

The ceremonial circumcisers, the boy's grandfathers, were fiercely painted with yellow ochre and fresh human blood. They kept fueling the fire to blaze higher and higher.

The moment had arrived for the young boys to be brought to the center of the ceremonial grounds. Nandjiwarra took his grandson, who had been painted with the elder's blood, and laid him on a mat made of the men. He sat on top of him and took out a sharp quartz stone tool freshly cut just days before the ceremony.

A boomerang was placed in the boy's mouth to bite down to maintain his trance. He had been taught from an early age how to put his body into a trance so as not to feel any pain or to act like he did not feel any pain The razor sharp stone tool was held in the grandfather's right hand as he took the young man's penis with his left hand. He twisted the penis's foreskin away from the rest of the organ. After singing and crying out very loud to the ancestors he quickly sliced off the foreskin. Very little blood spewed out while the young man kept quiet showing his tribal members he had a strong spirit and the strength needed to protect and provide for his future family.

The young man was then placed on the ground in the middle of the ceremony as three other young men that following him had to endure the same circumcision custom. Rabbi Raboy, not wanting to miss a single action, watched carefully without blinking his eyes to make sure he saw every procedure. Right after the last circumcision, four young girls were paraded into the center of the ceremonial grounds by their mothers.

Each mother gave their five-year-old daughter to the respected grandfather of the circumcised boy. Each young girl then was betrothed to a specific circumcised young man who had been chosen by the elders years prior to the ceremony. There would be no sex between the couple for about fifteen years because this would create 'bad magic' for the entire tribe. Usually the young men would reach the age of twenty seven and the betrothed young girl would be twenty before they would consummate their marriage.

This explicit ceremonial ritual was enacted to let the tribe members know that each young man would dedicate his life to protect and hunt for the young lady and her parents for the rest of his natural life. After the betrothal ceremony, each young lady was given back to her mother. The circumcised boy was taken from his grandfather and placed under the care of his mother. This ended the ritual part of the ceremony, so the tribal families started setting out dishes of food gathered and prepared that same day. As everyone started to eat, drink, and be merry. Abigail slowly walked over to Rabbi Raboy.

"Are we going to eat with them or wait until we get back to the mote?" she asked, still being totally nude in front of the other elder men.

"I suppose we can taste some of their food that looks kosher," he replied.

"Shall we dress or continue in our Adam and Eve outfits?" Abigail laughed.

"I suppose it does not really matter at this point," he said, rolling his eyes to imitate some of Abigail's actions when he would say something she that thought was stupid.

The Rabbi took some freshly cooked chicken and fresh spring water, as did Abigail. The two ate as if they had been among the Aborigine all of their lives. After mingling with the crowd for a few minutes and meeting several different tribal members, Abigail and David decided to get dressed and leave. They put their clothes over the ceremonial decorations not wanting to offend or disrespect the Aborigine tribal leaders and their families.

"Guanjila, this is the man I told you about," said Manandjiwala.

"Rabbi, we must meet again alone by the caves of my ancestors," said Guanjila, as the Raboys got into the Land Rover to head back to their motel.

"Yes, that would be nice. Please, inform Manandjiwala to tell us when and where you would like to meet," he replied, as he shut the door.

Abigail and David said their good-byes, and then waved to everyone as they drove off. They constantly smiled at one another during the entire five-hour return trip.

It was late at night when they arrived back at their motel, when Abigail noticed a tall lanky Aborigine man looking at them very strangely. The Rabbi figured it was because he could see the ceremonial paints still on their faces.

"Thank you, Manandjiwala, for your valuable assistance today," said Raboy, as he shook his hand good-bye.

"Sweetheart that was quite an exquisite event. I cannot believe you undressed and paraded around with the young married women as you did," he said waiting for her response.

"I did what needed to be done, so my loving husband could complete his research," she remarked politely, as if it were the right thing to do.

"Abigail, if you are angry with me for insisting you come to the ceremony, I am truly sorry," he said apologetically.

"David, I love you, and whatever it takes to help or please you, I have no problem with that. These people did not have any cameras to take photos. They were as naked as I was, so I did not have a problem participating by their customs. I did stand out a bit having a fair complexion, sky blue eyes, and long blond hair contrary to their black hair and skin but that is the way God created them and me. I am alright with the situation, are you?" she asked smiling.

"Well, can we keep this private from the rest of the world?" he asked.

"Of course," she replied.

"It looks like we need to take a shower for an hour and then eat some normal food," he said, smiling.

"No, we do not need to take a shower and then eat," she replied.

"Aren't you hungry and feel a little bit unclean, my love?" he asked.

"Yes, I am a bit soiled, and tired, and hungry, but I want to make love to you in this condition first. This may be the day God blesses me with a child. What a story we would have to tell him about the day he was conceived." She said kissing the Rabbi on the neck.

"If you put it that way, alright."

"If the Aborigines do not have any problems with sexual situations, why should we?" she asked, waiting to hear the answer she wanted David to give.

"Yes, they do not. I think you like their sexual ways and customs," he replied.

"They made sex so free without any restrictions like you are not doing something wrong every time your body cries out for love," she said.

"Is that so?" he replied.

"One of the elderly ladies told me, according to their customs, she was actually more beautiful and desirable at 73 years old than the twenty year olds are. She said she demanded sex with the older and younger single men to satisfy her needs to keep her from becoming frustrated," she continued.

"I think maybe that is what is wrong with the Middle East?" he replied.

"What the women are frustrated," she replied.

"No, the men are," he replied trying agree with her earlier statement.

"Men of industrialized nations need to listen to the Aborigine about sex issues. The elder Aborigine women believe that a sexually dissatisfied wife generates unimaginable disharmony," she explained, laughing, "Those evil businessmen promote young women in their advertisements as the only desirable women available. Where do they get their statistics? I know for a fact that young and old women need the same amount of attention, including sex, as far as I am concerned. They should not promote their products to such a limited age group. Are you going to end my frustration so I can be a satisfied woman?" she asked softly, as she undressed and caressed her husband.

The two made love, showered, ate, and then prayed to the Lord thanking Him for his sweet blessing and asking for His tender loving mercy before calling it a night. They decided to sleep-in the next morning, but before daybreak they received an urgent message from the Sydney Orthodox Jewish society requesting that Raboy to visit their synagogue. They had found out about his angelic visitations and wanted him to address their congregation , but in reality they wanted him to reveal some of the sealed information that was contained in the secret scrolls.

The Australian Orthodox Jewish group heard rumors that he eaten the flesh of unclean animals, dined with infidels, and ate meals that were not kosher. They were planning to scorn and pressure him by any means possible even using dirty tactics if necessary to gain access to information they were not privileged to receive. A few of them wanted to know which secret pronunciation of Yahweh's Holy name he held. The Orthodox Jews knew there were sixteen different ways to pronounce the Holy name of Yahweh but had no idea what they were. They figured Raboy would cave in and tell them his secret pronunciation because if they, in turn, kept quiet about the unclean acts he had committed while observing the Aborigines.

"Rabbi, how are you, my brother? Is this your daughter?" asked the elder Rabbi Cohen.

"Rabbi, I am glad to find you in good health today. I would like to introduce my wife to you. Rabbi Cohen, this is Abigail," replied Raboy politely.

"Glad to meet you. I will ask my wife if she can prepare a kosher feast tonight, for you and David," he replied.

As Rabbi Raboy walked through the Synagogue, he noticed a seating area to the left had high glass walls that enclosed the entire area. He compared the left to the right side of the synagogue but did not make any comments. Abigail kept quiet as David scrutinized the synagogue in every detail. Raboy noticed that there were eight candle sticks burning throughout the synagogue for the celebration of lights.

Being astonished at what he saw, he closely observed that their candles were made of very expensive beeswax. He had seen these candles before in the Middle East that were very expensive. He was amused that they used wooden vessels to gather offerings that had the names of Abraham the patriarch and Melchizedek the prince of Salem carved into them. He was fascinated by the several golden vessels designed to sacrifice various animals for anointment for their member's sins.

He wondered if the Australian Jewish brothers were practicing atonement sacrifices. His curiosity reached its pinnacle when he saw copies of Moses' and King Solomon's ceremonial vessels lying about. He could not hold back any longer so he asked the senior Rabbi if they were vessels created for future use in the New Jerusalem Temple.

He choked when he saw a replica of the Ark of Covenant that housed the original Ten Commandments etched in stone by Yahweh. After catching his breath, he was awed to see copies of the exact golden cherubs placed on the lid of the Ark of Covenant that were made with pure gold. Glancing up into the rafters he could not help but notice several giant chandeliers made of fine laden brass etched with the holy Hebrew Torah laws.

"Rabbi, welcome to our humble synagogue. I know you are accustomed to much more lavishness, but we make out the best we can down under. That is, in Australia," said Rabbi Weise.

"Yes, this is a lovely synagogue to worship the Lord," replied Rabbi Raboy.

"I notice your cloak is somewhat different than other Cohen Ultra Orthodox Rabbis," said Rabbi Weise.

"My cloak represents is no different from you," said Raboy think that they were trying to get him to admit he was the seventh of the sixteen holy keepers of the Lord's holy name, "Why would you remark that my cloak is different from yours when we are wearing the same over coat Rabbi Cohen?" asked Rabbi Raboy knowing what he was asking between the lines.

"My pardon Rabbi, I just wanted to know the truth about why you are here," replied Rabbi Weise.

"Rabbi, I will never reveal why I am here. I will only reveal what I know to the one that takes my place, which will not be decided by me," said Rabbi Raboy, knowing what Rabbi Weise was trying to do.

"Oh no, I would never ask you to tell me what you know. That is the Ultra Orthodox law handed down by the Maccabees hundreds of years ago," said Rabbi Weise.

"Rabbi, not to be rude, but you are an Orthodox Jew aren't you? You are not a Reformed or Conservative Jew that abolishes and obliterates the laws of the Torah, are you?" asked Raboy harshly.

"His answer is yes and no, Rabbi, but that is not why we have asked you to come here. We have other issues to discuss with you. We want to know about the sacrifice of the Red Heifer to dedicate the new Temple," said Rabbi Cohen.

"What I was told about the dedication of the new Temple and the Red Heifer is only for the ears of Cohen Ultra Orthodox Jews living in Israel. The information you seek is not intended for anyone else's ears until that day arrives," replied Rabbi Raboy.

"Why are you associating with the Aborigines? Is something about to happen we need to know about?" asked Rabbi Weise.

"Rabbi Weise, Rabbi Cohen, I was sent down here to observe and study the Aborigine. Since they are the only other people that have ancient tribal laws pertaining to circumcision. I was merely comparing their traditions and laws to the Hebrew eight-day circumcision law given to us by Abraham. My report will be available soon. As to the other fifteen that are keepers of the holy pronunciation of God Almighty's holy name, I do not know rightfully who they are. If that is all, I will head back to the Outback to complete my research," sternly replied Raboy.

"Why are you Israeli Cohen Ultra Orthodox Jews so secretive?" asked Weise.

"Do you know where the Ark of the Covenant is? Do you know where the stones that contain the original Ten Commandments are? Do you know where the new Temple will be built and who will construct it? Do you know the right pronunciation of the name of the God of our Fathers? Do you know what it is like to hold on to the ways that Moses has taught our forefathers?" asked Rabbi Raboy.

"We have some idea because we are not marooned on some desert island," replied Rabbi Weise sarcastically.

"Why does your synagogue have high windows on the left side and no windows on the right side? Is this to separate the women and children from the men during the Sabbath meetings?" asked Raboy.

"It is our custom to keep the women and children quiet during the holy hour. The best way to do that in Australia was to build large barriers to keep the noise makers quiet. No offense, Mrs. Raboy," said Rabbi Cohen.

"None taken. After what I had to endure with the Aborigine women during their ceremonies, this is quite amusing," she replied.

After spending two days with the Australian Orthodox Jews, Raboy was disgusted by their behavior. He knew they did not have the commitment and knowledge of the Israeli Cohen Ultra Orthodox Jews to possess God's sacred secrets. He felt the way they dressed was pitifully painful. In his eyes, according to the scared laws of the Torah, their attire was completely wrong.

The Raboy's decided to leave Sydney without saying good-bye to anyone associated with the synagogue at Sydney. He was extremely irritated by them pushing him for information that was too sacred for them to have. Figuring they would just cause him more grief, asking for unspoken information about Yahweh, he got out of harms way. They decided to take the train from Sydney Alice Springs so they could see Australia at ground level. It was an experience they both would never forget. Some of the landscapes reminded the Raboy family of their homeland. After many hours of relaxing and enjoying the sites they could see on the train the made it safely to Alice Springs. They left the train station and headed to Yirawala's grandson's rock shop. Now they could hopefully taken to Yirawala so they could speak with him one last time before leaving for Israel.

"Manandjiwala, I would like to spend some time with your great-grandfather, Yirawala. Would that be possible?" asked Rabbi Raboy.

"He told me when you are ready to reveal the secrets of our ancestors he would be ready to listen to you," replied Manandjiwala.

"I would like to talk to one more time before we leave Australia for good I know very little about the Dreamtime, so interpret his spiritual experiences maybe something impossible for me to do," remarked Raboy.

"Tomorrow my shop will be closed, so let's leave tomorrow morning for my tribal outstation?" suggested the tall, thin, bearded Manandjiwala.

Abigail, David, and Manandjiwala set out for the deep Outback early in the morning before the sun woke up. They were about by a dust devil when the sun started to rise. Abigail immediately put on her designer Sinai Desert sunglasses to block out the sun's early morning blinding glare. Later that morning she noticed a peculiar bird fly down and grab a snake lying in the middle of the road. She asked Manandjiwala to stop so she could take a picture. After stopping and letting Abigail take several pictures, Manandjiwala explained to them that this was the highly revered Kookaburra bird. To the Aborigine, it was the most important and honored creature given to Aborigine people by their Dreamtime ancestors. He explained to the Raboys that it was so very important to the Aborigine tribes because it ate Australia's poisonous snakes keeping the lands free from evil ancestors that would bring harm to the Aborigine people.

Abigail took several pictures of the landscapes and animals while traveling along the dusty outback road. The fivehour trip down the dusty road ended when they reached the sacred mountain caves the ancestors had given to the Aborigine thousands of years ago to make tools. Yirawala was there in a trance meditation in the Dreamtime. Getting out of the vehicle, they noticed he sat next to a bonfire burning up its last coals. All of a sudden, ten fiercely painted Aborigine tribesmen surrounded them with spears and boomerangs ready to chase off any intruders.

Manandjiwala yelled out at his fellow tribesmen in their native tongue. "It is I. What are you doing?" he cried out like a warrior ready for battle.

"We are stopping these white demons from entering the ancestral caves during Yirawala's Dreamtime," replied his older brother.

"This is Rabbi Raboy and his wife. They were invited by Yirawala to meet him here to discuss his Dreamtime experience that was before the time of the times," yelled Manandjiwala.

All of the tribesmen lowered their weapons once they recognized who they were.

"You know Yirawala cannot be disturbed during his meditations," replied Gulpiuji, one of the elders.

"Yes, I know. We will wait until my grandfather receives us," replied Manandjiwala.

After about twenty minutes, Yirawala came to the vehicle where Raboy waited patiently. He asked Manandjiwala to leave the Rabbi and take his wife to be with the other women of the tribe. Raboy asked Abigail to give him some space while he spoke to Yirawala privately.

"Come with me Rabbi, and learn some of the ways of my ancestors. Our ancestors that travel at the speed of light made our present tribal laws over fifty thousand years ago. This was so we would know how to take care of Mother Earth, and in return she would take care of us. When the white invaders came into the land of our ancestors, nothing had changed for thousands of years. The white invaders have carved Mother Earth into pieces, drained her water, and have brought in new animal species that are killing off many of Australia's precious natural animals," explained Yirawala, softly and slowly.

"Yes, the world is getting polluted daily, and it seems everyone is complacent about the problem," replied Raboy.

"Look at our world today. It has been paved over to the point Mother Earth cannot breathe properly. They have carved it up to the point many plants and animals have been obliterated from existence," said Yirawala being overtaken by his emotions.

"I agree, but is that why I dreamed about you?" asked Raboy.

"I do not know the answer to your question, but the Dreamtime is very important to Aborigines so maybe our ancestors felt it is the only way they could contact you," uttered Yirawala looking for answers to his own dreamtime experiences.

"So be it," replied Raboy being confused about his dream. He knew from his studies of the Bible his forefather Jacob wrestled an angel and through his hip out of joint, and Joseph interpreted the Pharos's dream to become a leader of the Egyptian people, so he knew dreams were very important.

"I have been given some extremely unique Dreamtime messages that I do not understand and feel those that travel at the speed of light wanted you and I to meet. Since you knew my name before you had ever met me, I know you are here for a divine reason that we will eventually understand," said Yirawala.

"It would be my pleasure to discuss what you experienced," replied Raboy, dusting off his black attire.

They hiked about a quarter mile into the land of the stones and caves that were created by the ancestors of the Aborigine people. They ended up at a wind swept cave with an overhanging ledge that extended fifteen feet and was about twenty feet high. After discussing each other's spiritual encounters, they headed back to the sacred caves where Yirawala experienced his Dreamtime messages.

Gulpiuji, along with the other tribesmen, had gathered up some firewood for another bonfire, if needed, later that night.

This was done so Rabbi Raboy could experience an Aborigine Dreamtime ritual.

As Manandjiwala drove Abigail to Yirawala's Outstation, he almost ran over a kangaroo. He was to drop her off to be with the beautiful women of Yirawala's tribe about two miles away from the ancient ancestors caves. Abigail observed several women hunting and gathering food. She waved at a young lady she had met at the circumcision ceremony named Maradjika. The young lady was not able to wave back because she was carrying her six-month-old child in her left hand and a spear in the right hand. Both ladies smiled at one another as Manandjiwala drove to the edge of the tribal outstation, parked the vehicle, and presented Abigail to Yirawala's wife.

"How are you doing today?" asked Abigail.

"I cannot gather food today because my granddaughter is having her time," replied Lene.

"Maybe I could watch her while you gather the day's needs?" asked Abigail.

"That would be a nice thing for you to do. You must call me if she has pain, so I can help her meditate it away," she replied.

"How can I call you when you do not have a cell phone?"

"All you have to do is think my name. I will hear you telepathically. We have been talking to one another like this for thousands of years."

"I do not understand how you can do that?"

"Just call out my name when she needs a midwife, I will come."

"Of course, I will," replied Abigail being confused as what to say.

After Abigail was instructed what to do, the grandmother and her five-year-old great-granddaughter picked up their spears and Coolamons to gather up the day's meal. Despite the heat generated by the blazing sun, she patiently waited for Yirawala's wife and her granddaughter to return. About four hours later, they returned with the little five-year-old girl totting some lily roots and three little lizards in her left hand.

"Abigail, my great-granddaughter has caught you some food to eat since you took care of her mother," said Lene.

"Oh, that is so thoughtful of her, but I have already eaten today," replied Abigail.

"You will still have to eat some of her catch because it will diminish her ability to hunt if she is rejected," replied Lene.

"You mean I must eat the skewered lizards and burnt lily roots mixed with honey ants?" gasped Abigail.

"If you just taste them and smile for the little hunter, I am sure her mother will be grateful," remarked Lene.

Abigail held her breath and took a bit of everything offered to her. Afterwards, she thanked the little girl for taking care of her. Later, Lene told Abigail she had eaten pieces of the white invaders' chicken, wild lily roots, and some Aberdeen bee honey. Lene explained to Abigail the deception was allowed to happen, so the little female hunter and gatherer would learn to survive in the Outback. Lene laughed as she told Abigail it was prepared to look like she had eaten the lizard meat.

Abigail was a little upset and relieved at the same time. Lene explained how the Aborigine children were taught to survive on their own, starting as early as three years old. After listening to Lene, Abigail now understood the honor and necessity of this custom for the child's future survival.

After eating their afternoon meal, the women immediately started preparing for the evening dinner. Abigail helped since she wanted to learn how to cook Aborigine foods so she could share her Outback experience with her friends back home. Later that day the food was served in wooded dishes along with some fresh water because fresh spring water was the Aborigine's preferred drink.

Abigail learned much from Lene about how the Aborigine depended so much on fresh, natural food. Lene explained how the white invader's alcohol, drugs, and tobacco products went against the natural way the Creator had intended man to live on Mother Earth. Lene implied that the white invaders evil tonic was killing the spirits of the Aborigine people. Abigail got to hear the other side of the Australian history that day from the Aborigine point of view.

During the same period, Rabbi Raboy viewed the new cave drawings that the messenger of Ngaljod had shown Yirawala.

"Yirawala, I have been visited by spirit beings as well but not in a dream. I was visited by an angelic being while I was awake that gave me specific instructions as to the future of Mother Earth. I will read what was commanded of me to proclaim to the world if you would like. Maybe you will understand its meaning," said Raboy wanting to share his supernatural experience.

"It would be inspiring to learn about your spiritual ancestors," he replied.

"Yirawala, it appears there is more to the spirit world than mortal man will ever know."

Raboy read the message in English since it was the only common language that Yirawala and Raboy could converse in. Yirawala listened quietly to Raboy. Raboy was fascinated with Yirawala's nonverbal response, a simple head nod of acknowledgement of what Raboy had said.

"I must tell you, as a keeper of the Holy of Holies ancient holy scriptures, I must keep many secrets from my Cohen Rabbi brothers. Those that are interested in the antique artifacts of our last Temple are misled on purpose. They must be lead to believe nothing exists," said Raboy exposing forbidden knowledge about the hidden Temple sacred instruments.

"Why do you keep your tribesmen in the dark?"

"To protect our culture and sacred vessels from all of those that would like to destroy our links to the past. Our temple's most coveted property, handed down from Moses, has been safely hidden from the world for many generations from those that would have stolen and destroyed them. They will not be revealed until the new Temple has been built," said Raboy.

"I understand exactly what you are saying. It sounds to me that your race has been on the same list as ours, targeted for genocide. After Mother Earth has completed her Sixth Rebirth, maybe everyone will be accepted for who they are and not as others would like them to be," replied Yirawala.

"That would be world peace—an environment that humans have or will not ever evolve to. A level where humans were more than animals that could talk, animals that could think and respect others as they are. Not what they think they ought to be," said Raboy.

After a couple of hours of exchanging experiences, Raboy, and Yirawala stopped to drink some fresh creek water. Raboy opened up a container and shared some fresh kosher sandwiches and vegetables with Yirawala that Abigail had packed that morning for the trip. Yirawala ate the kosher food without asking any questions since he did not want to offend the Rabbi. They continued their discussions as they ate.

"This was my first Dreamtime message that scared me. These dot paintings represent what I was shown. It was unnerving to see the great waters creating giant waves that engulfed the mountains and destroyed city after city. I painted India and China covered with mushrooms sprouting up everywhere, thick clouds that turned the sun blood red, while hiding the stars and moon from the night skies," explained Yirawala.

He did not allow Raboy to take pictures of his work but did let him make drawings and take notes of each Dreamtime message painted on the sacred cave walls. Yirawala felt the white invader's camera would upset his Dreamtime ancestors. Raboy understood and respected Yirawala's beliefs. He was concerned that Yirawala felt he could decipher the true meaning about his Dreamtime message about the Sixth Rebirth.

"I will do my best to decipher the paintings' meanings," said Raboy.

"It's time to go now. I can hear my tribesmen calling me," said Yirawala.

"Isn't your tribe two miles from here?"

"Yes, but Aborigine can talk mind to mind over thousands of miles. Let's go to the place where the bonfire is being prepared."

"Can we please wait until I finish my notes, Yirawala?"

"Rabbi, hurry, but please copy them correctly because they are sacred. I will tell you about another Dreamtime message at the bonfire."

Raboy hastily sketched the drawings and walked with Yirawala to another area where an enormous bonfire could be seen blazing in the distance. When the reached the stone caves, Yirawala rested for a few moments before he continued to talk about another spiritual experience.

"My next Dreamtime took me into unexplored regions of the Dreamtime, deep into the caves of my ancestors. I was shown four circles that represented Mother Earth. The first one appeared as the Earth looks today, the second one represented a future Mother Earth with its water and land changing places, and the third was indescribable. I had no idea what I was looking at. Mother Earth did not appear to be like any of the white invader's pictures and maps. The last circle scared me. Men, women, and children were running in all directions crying for the rocks to fall on them so they could die to ease their fears of what was coming upon them," said Yirawala.

"I cannot explain your Dreamtime message by what I have heard and seen today. If you are willing, I can have it compared by my colleagues. Many of the books of the prophets have recorded that an abomination of desolation from afar will destroy Mother Earth. It will be a day of wrath, trouble, and waste that Mother Earth has never seen before. Thick black clouds shall encompass the entire Earth leaving it in total darkness. Men will be so scared they will die just thinking about what is coming upon them. The stars and moon shall not give their light, and the sun will turn blood red. The Earth will rock and reel and eventually turn upside down, as the mountains will become flat and every tall building shall be destroyed," said Rabbi Raboy.

"Will that be the end of Mother Earth?" asked Yirawala.

"No, but I think most of the Earth's population will be killed or displaced due to the destruction."

"I have been told that my spiritual experience reveals what will happen during the Sixth Rebirth. Our legends tell us that Mother Earth has had five rebirths during the ages of my ancestors and nothing can stop her once she starts to cleanse herself. It will be a terrible time for humans, plants, and animals that live on Earth. I hope the Good Ancestral Spirits of the Dreamtime protects some of the Aborigine people because we have not harmed Mother Earth," said Yirawala.

"Yes, I hope you are right and there is a remnant left on Earth. I hope the God of our father, Abraham, will have mercy on us like he did for Noah during the great flood," replied Raboy, wondering what the Lord would allow to happen to mankind because of their evilness.

"Marayka has rubbed herself on me so the Aborigine people will be fertile during these times to come."

"Who is Marayka?" asked Raboy.

"She is the first mother of all the children that walk on the Earth."

"It sounds as though she is equivalent to Eve which is recorded in our Torah as the mother of all mankind."

Raboy compiled many pages of notes as Yirawala spoke. Raboy told him that he would try to interpret his Dreamtime message. Yirawala and Rabbi Raboy bonded that day by both cutting the tip of their first finger and then rubbing it onto the others forehead. Both supernatural messages were shared and sealed in the minds of Raboy and Yirawala respectively. They both agreed that, until they understood what they had been shown, it would continue to be a secret between them. If that left the general populous in utter darkness, so be it until it was time to unveil the secrets of the abomination of desolation. A time that would destroy much of Mother Earth. Their lips were sealed until the time of times was revealed.

The group of elders remained at the bonfire as Manandjiwala brought Abigail back to pick up the Rabbi. It was ten o'clock at night when they started packing up the Land Rover. Yirawala was dropped off at his encampment where he and Raboy said their good-byes by embracing and shaking hands. During the five-hour road trip back to Alice Springs, Raboy decided his Australian assignment had been accomplished. Raboy called his Cohen Rabbi colleagues at Tel Aviv and told them that three months in Australia was long enough to be away from his homeland. David then called his University colleagues in Israel and told them he felt that he had finished his assignment and would submit his report of findings after he returned home.

Upon boarding the super Jumbo jet Airliner to go home to Tel Aviv, Israel, they were told that they had to sit in the economy class because the first class section had been over sold. Abigail told the flight attendant she did not care if she had to ride in the luggage section, she wanted to go home. The flight attended laughed and then apologized for the company's errors.

They were seated next to a Dr. Simon Hal Einstein, Ph.D., an anthropologist from the Jerusalem University. The seating assignment was a terrible experience for Abigail because the man next to her was so fat that she had to squirm and wiggle in order to find comfort a zone. David smiled as he politely changed seats with Abigail. He sat next to the burly man with a long curly black beard. Raboy had to crunch his shoulders together and crossed his arms so tight that it made it hard for him to breath.

"Sir, are you Jewish?" asked Rabbi Raboy.

"Yes, I am an Orthodox Jew, but not an Ultra Orthodox like you, Rabbi," replied the man laughing as he spoke.

"How was your visit in Australia?" asked Raboy. "It was nice, and yours?" asked the man.

"I had to meet with the Southern Cross Rabbis at the Sydney Synagogue to discuss some of the artifacts they had pertaining to the collection of tithes."

"Yes, I have seen their collection vessels," commented the fat man.

"It was a very stressful event."

"Did you do anything interesting during your visit to Australia?" asked the doctor.

The two talked for hours as Abigail cat napped during the long flight home. As they were talking, the doctor happened to mention he was an anthropologist, so Rabbi Raboy took the opportunity to converse about the Aborigine Dreamtime carvings. The doctor explained how the Aborigine's respected them as historical fact as recorded by their ancestors during the thousands of years of their existence.

"What do you think, Doc?" asked Raboy.

"Well, anyone can interpret any drawing anyway they like, as they can call it a prophecy or whatever. I think there is some divine truth to what these people have recorded but to understand exactly what it means, I cannot explain. I do know we can carbon date them to check out the time period they were created."

"Are there any other people that have any ancient prophecies not taken seriously around the world?" asked Raboy.

"Rabbi, every nation on earth has ancestral drawings, carvings, dwellings, or such that depicts some sort of history, mystery, or future prophecies. My job is to find the differences, with respect to the Torah and secular books about our history, and then compare it with the ancient texts of the many different civilizations.

"That appears to be a complicated task. Have you learned about prophecies other than those in the books of the prophets? I feel these Aborigine's carvings about the Sixth Rebirth foretells a message that the Earth will self-destruct like in the days of Noah." Said Raboy wondering if Einstein had compared prophecies about the end of the present age.

"I have studied several papers that indicate that there are several tribes around the world that have carvings and drawings that forecast the end of the world that are thousands of years old. The Hopi American Meha is supposed to be an ancient prophecy dating back thirty-five hundred years ago," he replied.

"Hopi, what is that?"

"These are a rare group of Native American people that have lived on the same land for tens of thousands of years. Of course, we know the Earth is only about six thousands years old from creation, so let's say since Noah. These people have prophecies that are unique to the North and South American continents," explained Dr. Einstein.

"Dr. Einstein, are you related to Albert?" asked Raboy. "Ahh, no, he was a genius and I am a student. Now to continue, you can find these people in Northern Arizona on a reservation in the middle of a larger Native American reservation."

Rabbi Raboy took many notes of the interesting comments made by the anthropologist. While Raboy was taking notes, the fasten seat belt light came on. The plane landed safely and Abigail and David Raboy were picked up at the airport by their Cohen colleagues. They were driven straight home without anyone asking them any questions. They knew Raboy would need to rest for a week before returning to work.

Three weeks after the trip, Abigail started feeling queasy and threw up her breakfast. Rabbi Raboy was heart sick because he though she had contracted a disease during their adventures in the Outback or that some tainted food she had eaten during the return flight had poisoned her. He called the doctor to come over at once. The doctor hesitated at first but decided it would be wise to keep her isolated from the general public and his patients after what Raboy told him about their assignment in the Outback.

The doctor arrived within the hour. After a few minutes of discussion, he took down Abigail's history. Within minutes he decided his diagnosis, prognosis, and treatment protocol. He left Abigail's bedside and walked out to talk to Raboy. Raboy lowered his head and remained silent knowing it would be bad news about his second wife. The fear and pain gripped him so hard his heart pounded and stomach twisted out of shape. He felt it was the end for Abigail so he rushed past the doctor to Abigail's side.

"How long do you have to live? I'm sorry I have taken you to death's doors," he cried.

"Sweetheart, I am not dying," she said softly. "Then what is wrong with you?"

"I am pregnant with our child," she said with sweet smile on her face.

"I'm pregnant again," he said, jumping up and down in relief.

"David, you are not pregnant. I am," she said running to the toilet to vomit.

Abigail stayed home during her pregnancy, being the perfect housewife preparing herself to become a mother. Rabbi Raboy did not do much at work because he was too engrossed by thinking about his future child. He did his job of protecting the seventh of the sixteen secret pronunciations of the Lord's Holy name and studied the secret scrolls, but little else. The beings that were nine feet tall appearing as a brilliant light did not reappear during Abigail's pregnancy. Many months passed so Raboy felt his supernatural experiences were over.

David and Abigail enjoyed raising their son in a peaceful, loving environment for two years. David periodically looked at the prophecy he had pinned to his bulletin board. The Raboys lived a relatively quiet life. Abigail decided to have a gathering at their home for their son's second birthday.

"Our son is going to be two years old. His big blue eyes, and blondish red wavy hair makes him the dreamboat of dreamboats," said Abigail.

"I like his strong will and quiet demeanor," replied David. The party lasted until young Daniel Jeremiah Raboy fell asleep. Family and friends left because the guest of honor had fallen asleep with a beautiful smile on his face. The next day the most prominent elder of the Cohen Ultra-Orthodox Synagogue in Tele Aviv, Israel relayed as message that the American Ambassador for Israel wanted to visit with him. David Raboy agreed to the meeting without asking any questions.

"Ambassador Wilcox, it is my pleasure to meet you. Why have you asked me here?"

"It is rather embarrassing for me to explain but the United States of America keeps track of all prophecies and religious activities. They monitor spiritual groups to see if there is any validity to what they have said or seen regarding future world events. I know this is rather odd, but we have heard from the Australian and Israeli governments that you have had quite an experience lately. I would like to hear what you have to say. It will be taken seriously without one word, sentence, or paragraph being revealed to the public. If you could tell me about your experiences with the occult and/or the spiritual side of life, the US government would be much obliged," said the Ambassador not revealing his true intentions.

"I will tell you everything I have experienced, but my visions, or visitations, are a mystery to me. The time I spent in Australia with Yirawala is an experience I will never forget," replied Raboy. Rabbi David Orr Raboy told the American Ambassador the outline of his travels and experiences. The Ambassador's staff recorded every word he spoke, taking it seriously, so the United States government could analyze the information and compare it to other supernatural phenomenon. Raboy did not mention one word of the secrets Yirawala and he agreed upon in the Outback.

"Rabbi, I understand that Jeremiah Raboy, the Israeli Ambassador to the United States, is related to you." said Wilcox.

"Sir, you must know Jedi is my brother."

"Yes we do, but I wanted to find out if you are in good graces with him or not," replied Wilcox, as he took a drink of his Earl Gray tea.

"What does Jeri have to do with me?"

"Well, the President and Jeri are pretty close and Jeri mentioned to the President about your angelic visitations, so the President would like to meet you. He is curious."

"Mr. Wilcox, cut to the chase. What do you want or better yet, what does the United States government want from me?"

"As I told you, the United States is always interested in unusual encounters, be it aliens from other planets, the demons from the dark lagoon, or Bible prophecies," replied Wilcox sipping his tea.

"How does the United States classify my experience?"

"Your experience has been classified as a supernatural, angelic visitation," replied the sly Wilcox.

"How can they classify my experience from what others have told you?"

"It's not what we have been told, on the contrary, it's what we have gathered from your government, the Australian government, and your friends and family," replied Wilcox.

"You people have been investigating me without me knowing about it?" asked Raboy, alarmed.

"Yes, if you want to put it that way."

"Why are people like you so sneaky? What is the point?"

"Rabbi, I assure you we have kept this quiet because you are a Cohen Ultra-Orthodox Jewish Rabbi. You are one of sixteen that keeps the secret scrolls hidden from the rest of the world, plus you have had quite a super natural experience. Since Pearl Harbor and the Twin Towers heinous attacks on our land we don't trust any one or any nation. Your recent prophecy is an outright scary scenario to us if it is what the world will look like sometime in the near future," replied Wilcox.

"Ambassador, I do not even know what I saw or experienced, yet your secret spying groups are already analyzing information that is vague at its best."

"Sir, if the United States is to keep control of the world, we must know everything before it happens, not after it happens," he replied.

"If I were to ever go to the United States of America, I would be glad to meet with your President," replied Rabbi Raboy.

"Glad to hear it. We can set up a meeting with the President immediately. While you are there you can stop by and visit your brother at the Israeli Embassy."

Wilcox had already received orders to send Raboy to Washington, D.C., before his meeting with the Rabbi Raboy. "I am not ready to go right away, Ambassador," replied Raboy.

"I will make arrangements for you to fly on a private jet to Washington."

"Is that necessary?"

"For your safety, yes, it will be. I will make arrangements with your government so you can visit the US in, say about, a day from now."

"More like a month from now," replied Raboy.

Raboy agreed to visit the President of the United States of America. Rabbi Raboy added Arizona to his agenda hoping to visit the Hopi Meha that Dr. Einstein told him about. Arrangements were made with White House staff to have Abigail and Raboy meet secretly with the President. To keep all secret parties confused they scheduled Raboy to address an Orthodox convention in Arizona regarding the sanctity of the Ultra Orthodox Jews to control the operations of the newly proposed Temple. With Rabbi Raboy being the keeper of the secret sacred scrolls, it was easy to convince some Arizona and California Rabbis to have a mini convention to discuss the future possibilities of the temple's special dedication ceremonies.

The plan was set so Raboy would first go to Arizona and meet with certain committees dealing with Jewish religion issues, and then later visit the President. His arrangements were to be in Arizona for about a month, and then on his way back to Israel he would visit his brother Jerry, the Israeli Ambassador to the United States, and the American President. Raboy was excited because this would be an opportunity of a lifetime to visit the Hopi Native American that may give him some information about his supernatural experiences. He could visit and study the ancient Meha carvings and drawings that Dr. Einstein had told him about. He would be able to compare his personal experience with the Aborigine and Hopi cultures. He figured this would be the perfect opportunity for him to study the Hopi cultural prophetic history.

Abigail always wanted to visit the Grand Canyon National Park, so she was excited as Raboy to visit Arizona. She had wanted to see the Red Rocks of Sedona and the giant Saguaro cacti. This would also get her close to Disneyland, which was a childhood dream to meet Mickey Mouse in person.

Plans were set in motion so Raboy and his beautiful wife and son went to America. They landed in New York City, New York for two days where Rabbi Raboy visited many wealthy Jews that offered monies needed to build the new Temple. After many discussions about the new Temple, he left New York City on a hot August day and headed for Arizona. Minutes after they landed in Phoenix, a monsoon summer storm composed of thick dust, ear deafening thunder, and blinding lightning hit the Valley of the Sun. The wall of dust was a thousand feet high and fifty miles long, pushed by a ninety mile an hour wind. The Rabbi wore his official attire that made him melt in the Arizona 115 degree dry heat.

After gathering their luggage, they were greeted by the elder Rabbi of Temple Beth Israel and taken to their hotel. Later, the next evening, Raboy was to appear at a large gathering to honor his visit. Some of the Conservative and Reformed Jewish Rabbis thought everyone was going overboard until they heard about the Rabbi's angelic visitations.

"Rabbi David Orr Raboy, your son wants to kiss you good night and his mother wants to make American love to you, and maybe since we are in the desert, let's make Arizona Desert love, too," said Abigail, as she handed Daniel to David.

"Sweetheart, why don't we make Arizona rest tonight and American love tomorrow night?" asked the weary Rabbi.

"Sweetie, you do not have to have sex with me for me to make love to you," she replied.

"Abigail, what I really need right now is a small glass of kosher wine and a chair to relax my weary body," he said softly.

"I am your slave to fulfill your desires, so your every wish is my command!" she shouted, unhappy that his requests did not include her love.

"Sweetheart, the flight has really exhausted me. Why aren't you tired?"

"Sweetie, I am exhausted too, but I have reserved energy to make love to my hero," she replied quietly.

"Maybe after a couple glasses of wine I will be in the mood," he said..

Abigail had room service bring up a wine holder filled with ice and a new bottle of California kosher wine for the occasion. The evening ended with the two cuddled up on the sofa. The next morning before daybreak Abigail and David were woke up by Daniel who wanted something to eat.

It was an ironic situation—the Rabbi was in America to see the President, but he really wanted to be in Arizona to see the Hopi Meha. Even crazier, the Arizona Rabbis thought he was there to visit their Synagogue and speak about the building of the new Temple. To have a Rabbi that was an Israeli Ultra-Orthodox visit the Jewish synagogue in Arizona seemed somewhat peculiar to the Conservative Jews, but they said nothing. It was an honor for the Jewish conservative contingency to meet the first Rabbi in thousands of years to be visited by an angel. Even more outlandish to the Reformed Jews, he was not given any new prophecy about the Jewish people.

The only thing Raboy knew for sure was that every Jew living on Mother Earth was ready for the New Temple to be built. He also knew that no one knew how, when, or where to build it. Even the Cohen Rabbis argued as to the exact location and dimensions of the structure of the Lord's House of Prayer for all people. Raboy knew a few ex-Cohen orthodox members who turned coat and joined the Conservative sects there to question him. He prepared a speech that would confuse them about the real agenda of the Cohen's.

Rabbi Raboy had been battered with so much nonsense in Australia from the Reformed Jews that he was not about to take any abuse from the Americans who had no idea what was really happening within the Cohen Ultra Orthodox sect. He felt most of these new fangled Jews customized the Torah to fit their needs, disregarded what the Lord told them to do. With all of this in mind, he proceeded to the meeting to address the Jewish delegates from the United States.

CHAPTER FIVE:

PURIFICATION PROPHECY

"**D**oes anyone here know where the Hopi Indian Reservation is located? Does anyone have any idea where the Hopi Meha is located?" asked Rabbi Raboy, directing his question to the populous of the consortium assembled at the Temple Beth Israel synagogue in Phoenix, Arizona.

"Rabbi Fellerman has visited several ruins in the southwest's Native American civilizations. He would be the one to call on," said Rabbi Strom.

"How do I get in touch with him?" asked Rabbi Raboy.

"You could call him," said Rabbi Max Strom.

"Yes, I could call him if I knew what his phone number was," replied Rabbi Raboy.

"All you had to do is ask," remarked Rabbi Strom.

"I thought I did ask," replied Raboy.

"Don't make a fuss over it. I'll call him right now on my cell phone. I'll let you talk to him directly," said Strom, dialing his colleague's number.

"Hello, is this Rabbi Fellerman?" asked Strom.

"Yes, it is. This is Rabbi Strom, I presume," replied Rabbi Eric Fellerman.

"Yes, it is. I have a request that I hope you may be able or willing to help me with," replied Strom.

"What can I do for you?" asked Fellerman.

As Rabbi Fellerman was still talking, Rabbi Strom handed his cell phone over to Raboy.

"Ahh, hello," said Raboy with his Israeli-English accent.

"And to whom am I talking with?" asked Fellerman.

"I am Rabbi Raboy from Israel. Rabbi Strom told me you know something about the history of the Native Americans in Arizona."

"Yes, I know a thing or two about the native, ancient civilizations."

"That is good to hear. I would like to know where to find the Hopi Native American's Meha."

"Yeah, that should not be too hard to do. They have a reservation in Northeastern Arizona. Go up to Northern Arizona and ask around."

"Rabbi Fellerman, I know that much. Don't you have some contacts or information that would lead me to the exact area?"

"Rabbi, I live in Omaha, Nebraska and presently I am on vacation in Hawaii."

"Alright, I see, well thank you very much for your help, Rabbi Fellerman," said Raboy, as he handed the phone back to Rabbi Strom.

"Did he help?" asked Rabbi Strom.

"Yes, he did and thank you very much for your explicit assistance," responded Raboy returning his attention to the special gathering that basically was about nothing.

The meeting ended with more questions having been raised than answered. Everyone agreed nothing had been accomplished that couldn't have been done without the meeting. Knowing the Cohen Rabbis had complete control of when and where the New Temple would be built, the Arizona Jewish contingency thought Raboy would actually tell them some valuable information as to when and where the building process would begin. The secrets of the Cohen's could not be pried out of the Raboy. After six days of private meetings and public appearances, the meetings were adjourned leaving the Southwest American Jewish society still in the dark about the New Temple.

Raboy knew his time was running out in Arizona, so he prepared to visit the Hopi Meha. The conversation he had with Dr. Einstein while on his return trip from Australia haunted his spirit and gave him the burning desire to find out what the Hopi Meha was all about. He returned to the hotel and told Abigail he had not found out much from the Arizona Jewish consortium about the whereabouts of the Hopi Meha, except that it was in Northeastern Arizona.

"Sweetheart, it appears that no one knows anything about anything. We are going to have to do it ourselves," he said, disgusted with the Arizona Rabbis' lack of knowledge about Arizona Native American cultures.

"What do you want to do?" she asked, caressing his neck.

"I want to see the Hopi Meha and compare it with Yirawala's and my personal super natural experiences." he replied.

"Sweetie, I do, too."

"Sweetheart, let's pack up, rent a car, and explore Arizona like we did in Australia," he said.

They decided to rent a four-wheel drive utility vehicle which came with a complete tourist package titled "Everywhere possible to use this vehicle in Arizona." After studying the Arizona tourist road maps, they decided to visit the Grand Canyon first since it was on the way to the Hopi reservation. They ate, packed, and took off to explore Arizona.

The Raboys decided to visit Sedona and Oak Creek Canyon, too since it was on the way to the Grand Canyon National Park. Sedona was scenic with its red monoliths towering over the pine and oak trees that laced the valley below. Abigail got a thrill watching the vacationers slide down the slippery rocks called Slide Rock, filled with the icy cold waters of Oak Creek. This stone creek bed formed a natural water slide surrounded by thousand foot canyon walls. After taking many pictures of the scenic cliffs, they left Sedona and headed for Flagstaff, Arizona.

Flagstaff was a beautiful city indeed covered with giant Ponderosa pine trees overlooked by the snow capped San Francisco Peaks of the Arizona Rocky Mountains,. Because Flagstaff was around seven thousand feet in elevation, it was cold compared to the dry heat of the Phoenix valley of the sun. They decided to purchasing some light jackets in a small clothing store. As they exited the store they were pelted by some pea size hail stones created by an Arizona summer monsoon thunderstorm. The thunderstorm also produced a mixture of massive rain drops and sleet that was mixed with the hail stones. The loud thunder and massive lightening bolts scared Abigail and little Daniel, so the Rabbi decided to wait out the storm. Abigail suggested they have lunch until the storm passed.

Of course, a Cohen Rabbi could not eat at just any restaurant; it has to be kosher. Abigail noticed a little deli store next to the clothing store called King David's Deli. The two smiled at one another thinking it was a nice Jewish establishment that offered Jewish style kosher food. When they entered the deli, it was a shock for them to see a Native American preparing sandwiches, so they requested to speak to the manager. Mr. Kaufman approached the Rabbi.

"What's the matter? Is my food not to your liking? Are my prices too expensive for your tastes? This is a Kosher Deli and things do cost more to make. My kosher food is fit for a Jewish Rabbi," said Mr. Kaufman.

"Mr. Kaufman, my husband is a Jewish Rabbi from Israel that deciphers the secret scrolls handed down by our forefather. He is a Cohen Ultra Orthodox Rabbi that is tired and hungry. Can you please give him a little respect?" demanded Abigail, staring down the overweight deli owner.

"Rabbi, my apology to you and my most humble apologies to your family. How can I assist your daughter, and grandson and of course, you?" he asked.

"This is my husband, and this is his son Daniel Jeremiah Raboy," burst out Abigail.

"Sir, we want to purchase some food that is prepared by Orthodox Jewish kosher standards. You have this lady working here that appears to be a Native American. Does she have any idea what it takes to prepare and serve a kosher meal?" asked Raboy gently.

"She most certainly does. Her mother is my wife, and I am a kosher Jew. She is a Native American of the Navajo tribe, which has a very large reservation near here," he replied.

"Good, then make me a kosher sandwich with pickles and give me a fresh glass of water to drink. May I ask this Native American a question or two, that is, if you do not mind," asked Raboy hoping she could give him the directions to the Hopi Meha. The deli owner nodded his head and shrugged his shoulders indicating it was alright with him.

"Young lady, do you know where the Hopi Meha is located?" he asked her politely.

"I have nothing to do with the Hopi people because they steal our water and land," she replied.

"I thought the white strangers stole your land," replied Abigail.

"You white people just do not get it. The world was not created just for you. There are many types of peoples running through the forest and living off of the land. You think God Almighty created Mother Earth just for the white man. How arrogant and selfish," she replied.

"Miss, I apologize if we insulted you about being Abel to prepare kosher food," remarked Abigail trying to calm the young lady down.

"I do not know anything about Hopi culture. Sorry," she replied.

After finishing their meal at the deli, the Raboys got in their vehicle and headed toward the Grand Canyon National Park. Along the way they saw many billboard signs that offered helicopter, plane, river rafting, and mule rides to get a bird's eye view of the world's most spectacular canyon. It seemed like they were approaching an amusement park instead of one of the most majestic natural land formations ever created by God Almighty. They slowly drove down the highway taking in all of the sites until they approached the park's south entrance.

Upon arriving at the park entrance, they paid the entry fee and drove slowly to the first vista. David parked the car close to the canyon in a small parking lot. Without realizing it Abigail walked right up to the railing which was the edge of the five thousand feet deep canyon. David carried his son right up to the canyon railing and was awed by the surreal view. He then turned around to check on Abigail and saw her frozen in her footsteps.

"Abigail, are you afraid of heights?" he asked her slowly.

"I do not know. How can someone tell if they are afraid of heights?" she asked, turning her head away from the eight mile wide and over one mile deep canyon. She was shaking while holding a death grip on a small canyon walkway railing with both hands.

"My legs feel shaky to some degree, sweetheart. How are you feeling?" he asked her gently trying distract her to ease her fear.

"Of course, sweetie, you have been traveling for seven hours today. You do need some rest. Let's see if we can rent a room in that beautiful log cabin hotel over there that is a ways back from the canyon wall. Is that motel alright?" she said, struggling to breathe while looking down and away from the vast expanse of the canyon. Abigail wanted desperately to view the magnificent canyon, but she had passed her comfort zone by getting too close to the canyon's edge. She knew at that point she would have to view the magnificent canyon from a distance.

At first, David thought she was weary from the trip but then realized she was panic stricken, so he wanted to get her away from the canyon wall immediately. She was frozen in place. Knowing she had succumbed to her fear, he knew he had to step in immediately to resolve her situation. Quickly he picked up his son with one arm and grabbed his wife with the other as he hastily pulled her away from the majestic canyon's edge. He led them toward the entrance of a beautiful massive log cabin motel that Abigail had pointed to. He did not stop moving away from the canyon wall until they were at a comfortable distance for Abigail to regain her composure. He could see the relief on her face when they reached the motel steps where she released her death grip on his hand.

They entered the hundred-year-old hotel built by the Grand Canyon Railroad to entice tourists to visit the canyon. Raboy approached the desk where a man wore a hat resembling his, so he figured that he was an Ultra Orthodox Jew.

"Sir, I would like to get a room for tonight," he asked the clerk that wore the hat.

"Do you have a confirmation number for your reservation?"

"No, I did not know I needed a room until my wife informed me a few minutes ago."

"Sorry sir, no room if you do not have a confirmed reservation."

"I only need a small room for tonight."

"Sir, we are booked up for the next two years." Then the hotel manager walked up to the desk clerk.

"Rabbi, how are you doing today?" asked a tall, dark haired, nicely groomed gentleman.

"Well, not too good. My wife needs to rest from our travels, and there are not any rooms available."

"Rabbi, where are you from?" asked the gentleman.

"I am from Tele Aviv, Israel on vacation with my wife and son."

Raboy pointed to a beautiful young lady with big blue eyes that sparkling like diamonds. The gentleman and young clerk looked at one another, and then looked at the lady again, and then looked again at Rabbi Raboy.

"Rabbi, let me take a second look at our reservation list," said the manager taking a few moments to look at this reservation book, "Today is your lucky day because only a moment ago we received a cancellation for one of our premiere suites. I will have the bell hop take up your belongings right away," said the manager.

Later that evening, the gentleman that managed the hotel being from Israel called the Raboy and invited them to join him for a kosher meal. Raboy was delighted to meet with a fellow countryman, so he accepted the invitation.

"Mr. Yosef Frank, do you know where we can find the Hopi Meha?" asked Rabbi Raboy.

"I have no idea what a Meha is, but I do know who the Hopi Indians are," replied Mr. Frank.

"Good, maybe the Hopi Indians know where their Meha is," replied Raboy.

"Sweetie, they are called Hopi Native Americans," interrupted Abigail.

The next morning the Raboy family packed up the rented vehicle drove along the southern rim of the Grand Canyon National Park road to the eastern park exit. At the eastern park exit/entrance, they climbed the original park lookout tower constructed from the park's natural surrounding sandstone. It had been designed by an architect that wanted to give the maximum view of the canyon. When they finally left the National Park, Abigail remembered she did not buy any souvenirs. She asked David to turn around immediately so she could buy a keepsake to remember her visit.

The first place where they could turn around was a point on the road located on a piece of land where a Navajo lady was selling her handmade wares. Abigail decided to shop at the lady's open air shop where she bought a beautiful sterling silver squash blossom necklace inlaid with turquoise that had been handcrafted by a Navajo craftsman. Her face light up like the sun when she adorned the necklace. At that moment her beautiful smile would have melted any man's heart.

"Do you still want me to go back to the park?" asked Raboy.

"No sweetie, I love you so much. Hey, maybe this lady knows where the Hopi Meha is," she said.

"Ms., do you know where the Hopi Meha is?" asked the Rabbi.

"I am Navajo, sorry I cannot help you," she replied.

"Wow, this Hopi Meha must be the best kept secret in the world," he replied.

The Navajo lady just looked at him and smiled. The dry desert air had dried out Abigail and Daniel's mouth so they both complained about being thirsty. David stopped at a small Native American convenience market to buy the Raboy family some fresh water to drink. He bought some fresh fruit, too to quench their parched lips caused by the dry Arizona climate. The Native American told them they were suffering from cottonmouth.

After being refreshed, they continued to drive through the Navajo Reservation until they came to a little town called Cameron, Arizona. They decided to stop and get some gasoline at a small convenient store. While David was filling up the vehicle's gas tank Abigail noticed a little elderly Native American lady having a hard time cleaning the window on her dark blue pickup truck.

"Ma'am, let me assist you," said Abigail.

"Thank you, but I can do it by myself," she replied.

"It would be my pleasure to assist you, since you remind me of my mother."

The elderly Native American lady gave way to Abigail's request. She took the window cleaner and started to scrub the bugs off of their vehicle's windshield. She then decided to scrub the bugs off of the Raboy's vehicle, too. Out of the corner of his eye Raboy watched his wife assist the elderly lady without interrupting her. David knew better than to disturb Abigail because during the time she had served in the Israeli Army as a tank driver she resented being constantly told what to do.

After filling the tank, he went inside. As he stood in line to pay for his gasoline, he started talking to an elderly man that appeared to be a Native American to him. Since Raboy was becoming desperate to find the Hopi Meha, he decided to start asking everyone and anyone that might be able to help him find the Hopi Meha.

"Does anyone here know where I can find the Hopi Meha?" asked Raboy.

Daniel, Sarah's husband, froze in his footsteps.

"I am Navajo, but I know how you can find out," Dan replied.

"Wow, a Navajo that knows something about the Hopi Native Americans," he blurted out.

"My wife knows much about this Meha," replied Danny.

"I have traveled from Israel to find the Hopi Meha. I really hope she can help me."

David Raboy and Danny Begay walked out of the convenience gas station toward the same gas pump. To Raboy's surprise, it was the same truck his wife had cleaned the windshield of earlier. After the two talked for a few minutes, Sarah Begay and Abigail got out of their respective vehicles. Sarah and Danny's eyes opened wide when the Rabbi told Danny he had been visited by a spirit being. He explained that it was an angelic messenger sent by the Lord to warn the people about pending earth changes. He then briefly told them of his experience while visiting Australia where he met Yirawala, an Aborigine that visited his spirit realm called The Dreamtime. Danny told the Raboys that they would need to go to a Navajo town called Tuba City, Arizona. This was a city located on the Navajo reservation which was adjacent to the Hopi reservation close to the rocks that had the ancient Meha painted on a stone. David and Abigail Raboy rented a motel room in Tuba city to rest for the evening. Danny and Sarah Begay offered to escort them to the Hopi Mesa where the Meha had been created over 3500 years ago. Raboy had finally found what he had come to Arizona in the first place for. He was emotionally satisfied because he would get a personal look at the Hopi Meha. But the chance meeting came with a twist because he did not know Sarah Begay was the third person of the triangle of spiritual enlightenment. Meeting Sarah was the final factor that would change his life forever. "Sweetheart, it appears our journey is about to end. What do you think we'll do now? Go home and live out our lives peacefully in Israel?" asked David.

"Sweetie, isn't your life more fulfilling with these wild adventures we have shared?"

"Yes, but this is the last mission necessary to accomplish what the messenger of light declared to us," he said frankly.

"If it is our destiny to go home and raise a family in a secure environment, that would be fine with me, as long as you are by my side," she replied, looking at the man she truly loved. A love that was still burning as strong as the first day she fell in love.

"Maybe you are right. My destiny does seem somewhat different than that of most Orthodox Rabbis. Then again, they have not been visited by the blinding light," he said chuckling, gently rocking his son in his arms.

"Let's give thanks to the Lord for making this trip not only successful but exciting, as well. His tender mercies have blessed us immensely," said Abigail.

As David and Abigail lifted their head and hands toward heaven an eight foot tall beam of golden light appeared. The golden light was transparent and too magnificent to be described with any earthly comparison. The light radiated glory and power throughout the room. Rabbi Raboy and Abigail stood motionless.

"I come in peace. Today your son has been chosen to help rule the New Jerusalem as one of the judges of the entire world. He is one of many thousands that will live to see his children live a hundred years. The world, as you presently know it, will change. The end of this age that the Prophets of your forefather's have foretold will soon begin. This world shall be judged," said the spiritual messenger. Tears began to stream down Abigail's cheeks.

Although Rabbi Raboy was confused by the message, he felt an inner peace as he had never felt before in his life. He looked at Abigail and smiled as they hugged their son. It was impossible for them to go to sleep realizing the Creator had plans for their offspring that was beyond any dream a mother or father could have for their children.

"Well, that changes my mind about going home and settling down and living out a normal, peaceful life," said Raboy.

"About the time you think things are coming to closure, it gets even more intense. When I thought the door was closing on my life, puff just like that it opens even wider to let more in," said Abigail.

"Ever since I have met you my life has been anything, but ahh, ahh—I cannot really think of a word for it—ahh, uhmm, ahh, yes average," replied David.

"You are not an average human being, my love," she replied.

They rose early the next morning and impatiently waited for Danny and Sarah Begay to guide them to the Meha. David noticed a truck that was parked next to their truck that looked like the Begay's so he decided to investigate to see if it was the Begay's new truck. Raboy trying to dress western put on some black denim pants, black leather western boots, an American western blue and white stripped shirt, and his black orthodox hat. Abigail put on a pair of light blue, prewashed denim pants, a western blouse, lizard skin boots, an Arizonan cowboy hat, and her new turquoise squash blossom necklace.

This was the Raboy's attempt to dress similar to the Arizona Native Americans, except for the Rabbi's top hat which did not match any western American era fashion. They were dressed somewhere between a tourist and local resident. Thankfully in Arizona it did not matter to the Native Americans how you dressed, as long as you were comfortable.

"Danny! Sarah! Good-morning, I pray that you rested well last night?" asked Rabbi Raboy.

"Yes, we did," replied Danny.

The Begays had brought their son Abel to meet the Israelis since he wanted to visit the Meha, too. Everyone sat there silently drinking coffee, tea, water, and eating muffins until Abel spoke up and suggested it was time to visit the Black Mesa home of the Meha.

The Begays got in their pickup and the Raboys got in their utility vehicle to drive to the ancient Hopi hieroglyphs. After viewing the Meha for a couple of hours, Rabbi Raboy was confused how this could be related to the Aborigines' cave paintings. Sarah saw David talking to himself, so she decided to sit down and tell him what had happened to her over the last three years.

"Rabbi Raboy, do you believe that the Good Great Spirit of our ancestors visit their children with messengers on occasion?" asked Sarah.

"I am not sure what you are asking me," replied the Rabbi.

"Yes, you do, sweetie, because just last night a spiritual messenger of light revealed our sons future to us," interrupted Abigail. The Hopi men slowly turned and looked at her.

"You have seen Maasaw?" asked Sarah.

"I have seen a being of light that has not revealed his name but implies that he was created by the same creator as all of us that exist on Mother Earth," said the Rabbi reluctantly.

"Then I will tell you what has happened to me, so you will understand why my family has taken the time to show you our ancient Meha. Our ancient messenger of the Good Great Spirit, who we call Maasaw, has visited me several times. He has shown me many visions and has called me the New Meha. He said I am to be the chosen one to warn my people about the Sixth Purification of Mother Earth," Sarah replied. Sarah told the Raboys about her experience with Maasaw.

She explained how he was the Hopi spiritual caretaker of the Hopi nation that gave the original Meha message to her ancestors. She explained how Maasaw's ancient message forewarned her ancestors what the future of the Hopi people would be. The Rabbi took out his drawings of the Aborigine paintings and showed them to the Begays. After talking to David for an hour, Danny Begay took his son to the side and spoke in Navajo, so the Raboys would not understand their speech.

"My father has told me that you will need to see the New Meha given to my mother, but you must promise to keep it secret and you must promise to help our people interpret the message," commanded Abel.

"I will do what I can, my American friend, but I am not a prophet or one that deciphers dreams, visions, and prophecies. I am not really sure what the correct interpretations are of our ancestral prophecies that were given directly to my people by the Creator," replied Raboy.

Danny convinced Raboy to join him to speak to their Chief. They went to the Chief's house and Danny told him that David needed to see the New Meha and take notes. The Chief did not question Danny or Sarah Begay's request since Maasaw gave her the new message in the first place. He joined them as they drove to the site of the New Meha. The Hopi Chief had a fence to keep the general population from pilfering it. Chief Blackcloud unlocked the gate so Raboy could closely examine the work and take notes.

Raboy did not have any idea what he was looking at, but figured someone could decipher the message. After the meeting with the Hopi Chief, they decided to accept Danny and Sarah's invitation to visit their humble country house. The Begays lived near the center of the Hopi reservation, which was about fifty miles from Tuba City, Arizona. They filled the utility vehicle with their belongings and followed the Begays along a well traveled dusty Hopi reservation country road. The Chief told the Raboys he would personally tell the motel owner, who was related to him, to reserve a room for them that evening.

Ronnie and Abel, Sarah's sons, brought their families over to meet the visitors from Israel. They brought along some firewood to build a campfire to keep warm after the sun had set, because it cooled off rapidly on the Arizona high plateau. Abel knew his mother's home was too small for everyone to be inside and eat all at once, so he set up an area near the side porch to accommodate every one.

"Rabbi, this is fresh beef cooked with onions, corn, cayenne chili pepper powder, and garlic. This is pinto beans made with onions, garlic, salt, and pepper. And this is the world's number one Indian Frye Bread, said Ronnie Begay."

"It looks very good," said Raboy.

"The chili smells delicious. I bet it tastes fantastic. It is very different from our cultural foods and those of the Aborigine," said Abigail.

The Begay family looked at her, wondering what type of native food she was comparing Sarah's cooking to.

"Rabbi would you like some fresh goats milk with your meal?" asked Abel's wife.

"No, thank you, water would be fine," he replied. He knew that the Hopi Native

Americans did not know what foods were fitting for an Ultra Orthodox Rabbi to eat at the same time. David had to think fast to figure out which foods he could eat and not insult the Begay family by turning down certain food groups, but he was committed to abide by the rules that governed all Cohen Jews in regards to keeping their meals kosher.

"We have some fresh Mormon herbal tea that I am sure you will like," said Sarah.

"That sounds delightful," replied Abigail.

"I picked it yesterday morning, so it is very fresh," she continued.

After eating the delicious meal, the southwestern Native American family went outside and sat down on some Ponderosa Pine tree stumps that Ronnie had picked up in Heber, Arizona a few years prior. The little ones were given some Hopi candy corn to roast. Abigail roasted one for Daniel Jeremiah to enjoy the moment. As they sat around the campfire, Rabbi Raboy explained his supernatural message that included information from the copper Dead Sea Scrolls. Next, he told them about Yirawala's Dreamtime message concerning the Sixth Rebirth. He was asked several questions he could not answer. Everyone agreed that

God obviously must be trying to warn mankind about an impending danger that soon would come upon Mother Earth.

As the Raboys left the gathering to return to their motel, David told the Begays he would stay for a week to study the New Meha. Raboy did not expose his real intentions of comparing the New Meha to Yirawala's Dreamtime message and his message about the future.

"Sweetie, this is getting more intense by the day. I wonder what is really going to happen to our planet. Do you have any idea why we have been chosen to participate in this worldwide spiritual awakening?" asked Abigail.

"Sweetheart, nothing makes sense to me anymore. I have no idea what is going on either. My life as an Israeli Cohen Ultra-Orthodox Jewish Rabbi used to be far less complicated. Now I am some sort of receptacle for spiritual messages" replied David.

"What does that mean?" she asked.

"Sweetheart, I have no idea what I am trying to say. The God of our Fathers must want us to do something for the people that dwell on Mother Earth. What, I just don't know."

"I am so happy, tired, and scared at the same time," she replied.

He then wrapped his arms around her tenderly to comfort her.

"Maybe some Hopi Native American Reservation love making would relax you?" he jokingly whispered in her ear. She immediately stripped down, throwing her clothes on the floor. Being totally naked, she started undressing David as he stood there smiling. After a few hours of making Native American Reservation Love, the two cuddled up together and fell asleep on the small motel bed.

Late the next morning, the Raboys left the motel and drove about ninety miles deep into Hopi reservation to visit a dinosaur museum. The natural historic museum displayed some million year old fossilized dinosaur bones and foot prints. This time it was David that wanted to see the dinosaur foots prints not Abigail. A brochure at the motel described the tracks as being created over a hundred million years ago in an ancient lake bed, according to an Arizona State University paleontologist.

Rabbi Raboy particularly wanted to see these footprints because he was opposed to any notion that life on Earth was any older than six thousand years. He believed the Torah was correct which recorded the beginning of Earth time from the first day of creation. Raboy had studied the Torah for years trying to figure out where the extinct dinosaurs fit into the creation phase of earth.

Raboy thought about his belief, "According to Yahweh's Holy Word, Mother Earth was created less than seven thousand years ago. I believe that the Lord created the bones to test mankind's belief regarding the creation story, according to the Torah. After meeting Yirawala and Sarah, I am having second thoughts about the elapsed time during the creation. Maybe there may have been several creation periods. Before Noah, man's life was different in many ways. Adam was able to speak God's language, communicate with Eve, and name every animal on earth. Plus, Adam lived hundreds of years longer than any present day man. If Adam lived in the first creation of Mother Earth, and then after the flood Noah started the second creation of humans on Mother Earth. What is one to believe?" Raboy kept his thoughts to himself thinking about the extreme differences in man's existence between Adam, Noah, and modern man. Adam was a vegetarian and water drinker, Noah was a flesh eater and wine drinker, and modern man is a consumer of synthetic chemicals. Now he was being exposed to Native American and Aborigine beliefs that there were three creation periods before Adam.

Since he became educated about the Aborigine's Sixth Rebirth and Hopi Sixth Purification beliefs, he felt their beliefs might have some validity and merit and must rethink his present belief without contradicting the Torah. He wanted to investigate on his own to see if the Torah did not stipulate that there were three previous periods of creation before Yahweh created man. There had to be some sort of an explanation as to why man was created six thousand years ago and dinosaur's fossils were believed to have been created six hundred million years ago. Raboy could never tell any other Cohen Ultra Orthodox Rabbi his thoughts because it would mean immediate dismissal, and then he would be ostracized by the Cohen's.

"Sweetheart, these footprints are over two feet long," said Raboy.

"Yes, and they were made over sixty-five millions years ago."

"I don't think so. The Torah, which has always been exactly correct, contradicts the theory that earth is millions and billions of years old."

"How can you believe that when scientists can date objects on earth that are billions of years old?"

"I cannot argue with a time measuring theory that has no records to prove it, as with the Torah we can prove our beliefs. The known scrolls have recorded that Noah took pairs of all the known animals aboard the Ark to withstand the great flood. Now, hear me out before you interrupt. The secret scrolls have been interpreted to indicate that Noah only took the animals that man could deal with on such a small ship," replied Raboy wondering about it all.

"Yes, I believe that with all my heart, but—" interrupted Abigail.

"Abigail here me out. I personally feel millions of species of plants and animals succumbed to the great flood and became extinct. Before the flood there were saber tooth tigers, giant reptiles, mammoths, and other large animals that our forefathers did not choose to put aboard the floating zoo. We have evidence that the Mammoths had food in their mouths when they were suddenly overcome by some force that killed them in their tracks. And therefore, only the animals living on earth today are those that were allowed to board the Ark," he said trying to explain his beliefs without exposing his real thoughts to Abigail.

"I believe what you are saying is correct, but . . ." interrupted Abigail again.

"Sweetheart, let me finish. And in conclusion, the animals that were put aboard the Ark were put to sleep by the Lord's mighty angels. I believe that the Lord's angels, the Lord's most loyal servants, controlled the animals' thoughts so animals would not eat each other. Noah could not have stored up enough food for millions of species of animals to be fed for the time he was floating around on Mother Earth. It is obvious that God Almighty took care of the vessel that our forefather prepared, and that is why man is still alive today," explained David being firm in his beliefs.

"I still think it's exciting to see that there were very large animals running around on the earth when Adam and Eve had to fend for themselves in the wild," replied Abigail not telling the truth about how she believed.

"Now that is a statement that no one can argue with because there are no records to confirm or deny your statement. The Dead Sea Scrolls saved the Torah's authenticity and Jewish history from the skeptics ridicule and disbelief. The Dead Sea Scrolls is the undisputed proof that the Israelites have kept accurate records for thousands of years. The Dead Seas Scrolls proved our Book of the Prophets has been recorded accurately since they were first written down. The book of Isaiah has been analyzed to prove our modern Isaiah text is word for word the same manuscript written over two thousands years ago."

"Didn't you say that the Aborigine said their existence started over fifty thousand years ago?"

"I will address that problem later," he replied.

After the dinosaur museum visit they had to drive fifty miles on dirt back roads to return to the Begays ranch house. When they drove up, they saw Sarah out tending to her precious sheep and Danny whittling out a Kachina Doll called 'Kwahu' in the Hopi language and Eagle Dancer in English. The Kachina would stand about two feet tall after being completely carved from a single cottonwood tree root.

"Good morning Danny, when will Sarah be finished with her sheep?" asked Abigail.

"She will be finished soon," he replied.

Abigail took Jeremiah over to see the little lambs and goats that the Begays had in a wooden pen. Abigail noticed that Hopi corn fields were planted in strange pattern. Ronnie had driven up after the Raboys and offered to take them on a tour of his family's ranch. He proudly showed them the family farm that had been handed down from generation to generation for centuries. Ronnie explained how his Hopi family had cared for this land millenniums before the white strangers came and made them prisoners in their own land.

"This corn seems to be very important to the Hopi tribe," remarked the Rabbi.

"Yes, it is the food that our ancestors gave the Hopi people to survive on. The corn planted this way gives good luck for the entire Hopi nation. It has mystical powers to remove evil spirits and blesses our house at the same time. We traditional Hopi keep a corn plant growing in our house all of the time for that very reason. We believe the white strangers have not removed or relocated the Hopi nation like so many other Native American tribes. We believe the Great Spirit has protected his sacred Hopi people," said Ronnie.

"Our ancestors gave us the Ark of the Covenant which housed the Ten Commandments carved on stones by God Almighty himself. The God of our fathers has protected the chosen children of Abraham from totally being destroyed by many different nations that have attacked our lands," said Raboy, exposing a Cohen ultra orthodox Jewish secret.

"My cousin is Mormon. He says that they have the new prophesy and covenant that reveals Native Americans are the lost ten tribes of Israel," said Ronnie.

"Well, that makes us cousins if you are truly of the lost tribes of my brothers," replied Raboy.

"I am not a Mormon. I do not know if this story is fact or a fictional tale to promote the white stranger's reason for destroying my people and taking their land without any remorse. The Mexican government gave our land to the Mormons to populate their northern empire. At least the Mormons did not try to kill us outright. They rather tried to absorb us by promoting their religion, telling us to get rid of what was originally ours. I've read their book and it specifically states God Almighty will be creating a ruling force of a hundred and forty four thousand people. This ruling class of leaders will be assembled from the original twelve tribes of Israel. If we are indeed of the lost tribes of Israel, we will be the majority of the hundred and forty four thousand that will rule Mother Earth. But I personally think, it was a plot to keep us from killing them while they stole our land," replied Ronnie.

"Well, now, that is quite a summation. With the new DNA techniques used in Israeli laboratories we can identify those that are our offspring. I will ask the Hebrew University in Tele Aviv, Israel, to investigate this unusual belief since your tribal roots appear to be older than our tribal father, Isaac. Our secret scrolls have recorded that the lost tribes of Israel are not lost at all. Contrary to your statement, it is a fact that the displaced twelve tribes of Israel are deeply rooted among the Europeans and Middle-easterners. Our secret scrolls have recorded that most of the European's root father was Jacob, the son of Abraham. That is why we believe they readily accepted the Torah or Bible as being the inspired word of the Lord, the creator, and have shunned all other religions. Regardless of what is believed, this will be an interesting thesis to study," replied Raboy.

"Can I get a copy of the study?, That is, of course, if it can be made readily available for me to review?" asked Ronnie.

"I promise to make it available to you. I will tell you a few secrets that would make the rest of world cringe with disbelief. The Palestinians are our half brothers and the Jordanians are our cousins. We are not related to the Syrians, but the Iraqis are direct descendents of our father Abraham's cousin and brothers those born in Ur near the Tigress River. He left his relatives in Ur to find new lands for his offspring. Abraham had one son by Sarah, our matriarch mother, but had several wives and sons after she died that are our half brothers. Our secret scrolls have recorded all of the facts. I really do not think you are children of Abraham but rather are children of Noah, which means we are cousins. This Mormon leader must have gotten their information mixed up to indicate you are one of the lost ten tribes of Israel," stated Raboy.

Later that morning, Sarah and Abel returned from attending the sheep. Sarah freshened up, and then Raboy told the Begays he must leave because he had some other business to take care of. He explained that it would be an honor to return soon and study the New Meha further with Sarah. The Begays left an open invitation to the Raboys to visit them anytime. The Raboys said their good-byes and left for Sky Harbor International Airport located in Phoenix, Arizona so they could fly back to Washington, D.C. There they would finally get to accomplish why they had originally came to America in the first place.

"Can we stop at that giant meteor crater, so I can look at it? Can we, it's only a few miles out of the way?" Abigail asked.

"That we can do, but only for a few minutes," he replied.

"That's all the time I will need."

They were both awed by the size of the meteor crater. Raboy got down on his knees and prayed that God Almighty would spare Mother Earth from anymore of these types of cosmic collisions. They left the crater and traveled along Interstate 40 to Flagstaff, and then drove south on Interstate 17 until they reached Phoenix, Arizona. At Phoenix Sky Harbor International Airport, they boarded their plane without saying good-bye to any of the local Jewish rabbis.

Arriving in Washington, D.C., Ambassador Jeremiah Raboy, David's brother, picked them up at the National Airport accompanied by his wife and three daughters. The Ambassadors' entire Raboy family went to the airport because they were excited to meet their new aunt and cousin for the first time.

It was a cold rainy days as the raindrops were being twisted into many shapes by the wind gusts. No one could escape getting wet by hiding under an umbrella because the rain was swirling in all directions. Lightening struck a nearby power pole. setting it ablaze. As the crack, flash and rumble of the thunder rattled the air, the Raboys quickly jumped into the Embassy's Black Limousine to avoid being struck by the next strike. Heavy rain began pelting the car as the Raboy contingent left the airport.

Later that evening at the embassy, a large, Charter Oak table was set for a king's feast. There were sparkling crystal glasses ready to be filled with kosher wine, water, and drink. Four forks, two knives, and three spoons were placed next to each dinner plate along with three different types of blue and white striped silk napkins. The three traditional embassy napkins were specifically placed for the lap, hands, and collar. Bread, salad bowls, soup, dinner plates, fine crystal, and an array of beautiful flowers adorned the table.

Abigail laughed as she told Elizabeth that she gone from eating on the ground to this lavish dining room. She explained the regardless, of whether she ate her meals at hotel, in the humble surroundings of her Native American Hopi friends, or at royalty she felt at home.

"Oh, Mother, isn't Abigail the most beautiful woman you've ever seen?" remarked sixteen-year-old Sheila Raboy.

"Yes, she is an eyeful and appears to be the perfect match for your uncle David."

"How can she be in such perfect shape after having a child?" asked Sheila.

"Hush up, they are coming down the stairs," said Elizabeth Raboy.

The dignitaries had so many questions to ask Rabbi Raboy that he felt a bit claustrophobic. At midnight, Ambassador Raboy told everyone the Rabbi had a busy schedule tomorrow that included a meeting with the President of the United States. Everyone departed so Abigail and David could retire to their rooms and rest for the morrow.

The next morning breakfast was served with the same kosher setup but not as elaborate as the dinner tableware had been. It was a scenic breakfast since they were served at a table that set near a window that faced the Washington monument. Abigail looked about the vaulted room that was filled with many large golden chandeliers and pleasantly decorated with expensive blue and white satin curtains. Breakfast was over and it was time to run.

"Well, sweetheart, it appears they have given us these cell phones so we can contact one another throughout the day. It appears we will be apart until this evening. Hugs and kisses until tonight, my love," said David romantically.

"All my love and good wishes for the day, David. I will have Elizabeth help me get in touch with you if need be, sweetie," she said with a smile.

This would be the first time David and Abigail would be separated from one another in four years. David Raboy enjoyed being with his brother for the first time in many years. The Israeli limousine drove up the White House main gate and was admitted to enter by the Capitol police and Secret Service. They drove up to the White House entrance and parked the car. As they exited the vehicle they were escorted to a special Presidential office used for top secret briefings.

"Mr. President, it is my pleasure to meet you," said Raboy.

"Rabbi, I have heard that you have been visited by some angelic beings or such. Is that true or is everyone exaggerating?" asked the President.

"I am not sure what you have heard with all of the rumor mills adding to and subtracting from my account. Of course, my experiences were to have been kept quiet," he replied in a gentlemanly manner.

"We have heard many exciting tales about you, but that is not why I wanted to see you in person," said President Cleghorn.

"Then what exactly did you want with me?" asked the Rabbi.

"We have a special group of investigators called pisonic interpreters that have been following you around in Israel, Australia, and America. We have secretly gathered information about you and think you can help us make some future decisions about Asia and the far-east crisis that is developing," said the President.

"Wow, I am stunned. My life is so important that the United States government has assigned a surveillance squad to watch me. I do not know anything about any far east crisis," he replied.

"We are worried they were planning something detrimental to the entire planet. We feel the USA is out of harm's way, but we are hoping that your information may help us keep the rest of the world safe," replied the President.

"Who is planning a war? The Aborigine? The Hopi are not going to war," said Raboy being confused with what the White House was telling him.

Another man stepped forward. "Mr. Raboy, pardon me, I mean Rabbi. Our pisonic group has been involved with telekinetic communication research for years. We know the Aborigine somehow can accomplish what we can barely get off the ground. But again, that is still not the reason we asked you to come here," said Dr. Rothskiller of the CIA.

"Alright boys, what is going on here? What do you really want from me?" he asked impatiently.

"It's like this. We know you have had many angelic visitations and know you have been told to tell the general public about certain prophecies foretold thousands of years ago by Torah prophets concerning the end of the world. Why did we start to follow you? You went to Australia and gathered some data from an Aborigine that had a Dreamtime message in which you drew maps about certain earth changes. What made us even more curious was the fact that you visited the Hopi Reservation and met a Hopi lady named Sarah Begay. She was visited too, by supernatural spirit beings that gave her information called the New Meha that depicted the end of this generation. We would like to see and hear what your conclusions are," explained Dr. Rothskiller.

"Why would you want that? Do you think I have made some sense out of my notes?" asked Raboy.

"Rabbi, if there is going to be some cataclysmic earth changes coming up in the near or distant future, we would really like to be ready to deal with them," said General McIntire.

"I will tell you what I know, but I am not sure it will make any sense. Of course, you may have more knowledge to come up with some type of conclusive interpretations," he said frankly.

"We want to see your notes and listen to your personal experience, so we can figure out what to do for the defense and safety of the world at large, not just the United States or Israel," said Harry the Secretary of Defense.

"I will have to sort them out at the Embassy and then bring them to you later," replied Raboy.

"That will not be necessary," said his brother.

Ambassador Raboy had his bags gathered and put in the security vehicle that had accompanied the embassy limousine to the White House. Rabbi Raboy looked at his brother as if he were a thief. They all proceeded to the White House secret map room constructed of charter oak beams with white marble walls, and black and white checkered marble floors.

The room was created to keep track of the American expansion territories during the continental settlement years. Every time a new state was created and joined the Union a new geographical map was drawn up to specify the new lines of demarcation. When land was bought or annexed from territorial gained from a war, new maps were constantly updated by government surveyors.

Rabbi Raboy's book of notes and maps was brought in and handed to him. Rabbi Raboy looked around the room and studied the ten men that were carefully watching him wondering what was really going on here in this secret place.

"Here are the maps and notes from Yirawala the Aborigine and Sarah Begay the Hopi. Yirawala told me this represents the Sixth Rebirth and Sarah Begay, told me this would be the Sixth Purification of Mother Earth," explained Rabbi Raboy.

Dr. Rothskiller assisted the Rabbi in laying out the maps and notes to organize them in some sort of pattern. The linguistic scientists were already trying to interpret a hidden message. Mr. Kent placed a white board with pens of various colors and erasers in the middle of the room. The Aborigine, Hopi, and Torah prophecies were compared and labeled:

Hebrew 'Bible Prophecy'	Hopi 'Purification'	Aborigine 'Rebirth'
1. Earth turns upside down	Earth spinning off axis	shaken for 12 years
2. desolation and destruction	destruction and cleansing	destruction and rebirth
3. darkness and dust clouds	dark thick clouds	Earth spewing out clouds
4. knocked out of orbit	Earth broken in pieces	land and earth changing place
5. desolation from afar	purified earth	new Earth is formed
6. Earth will shatter	Earth cracked world wide	giant waves hitting cities
7. mountains scattered	golden city rises up	mushrooms India and China
8. sun turning blood red	sun turning blood red	sun turning blood red
9. men hearts failed from fear	men running for safety	men in panic and fear

"Mr. President, this will be enough information for us to investigate further on our own. It would be nice to have a copy of the Rabbi's notes, if he does not mind, so we can have our pisonic group work with them. Maybe we can find out when, where, and how this will occur," remarked Dr. Rothskiller.

"That will not be a problem," replied Rabbi Raboy.

"Wait a minute! The Israeli Prime Minister might have a problem with that," interjected Ambassador Raboy.

"Why would you say something like that, Ambassador Raboy? This message is for everyone living on the planet, not just for one group of people, so let's let the world know about it," said the Rabbi.

"Ahh, no, we cannot do that," said Mr. Kent.

"Why not?" asked Rabbi Raboy.

"The general public would panic, and we would have a security problem," replied Harry, the secretary of defense.

"We cannot tell the world population that the world is going to be changed or destroyed. Even worse, we do not know when, or why, or by whom, or how. It would only make us look like a bunch of idiots because, well, you know how the public would react. So, we would rather keep them and the news media in the dark," explained Dr. Rothskiller.

"We need time to study these messages and make sure we understand them ourselves before we speak of such things," said Mr. Kent.

"Rabbi Raboy, will you continue to study this topic? There will not be any restrictions placed on you from the United States government. We sorely would like you to inform us if there are any new developments," requested the President.

"Well, that about sums it up. You know less than I even with your professional analysts," said Rabbi Raboy.

"That is why you are here. We know that the Aborigine and Hopi prophecies were given to you for a specific reason. We are mystified, that our pisonic groups are not picking up anything that there is a spiritual awakening taking place. We are worried and hope that we can defuse the problem before any massive destruction takes place," said Dr. Rothskiller.

"Oh, by the way, Dr. Rothskiller, why are you using a different name than you did in Australia. Please, do not deny it was you. I distinctly remember talking to you at Ayers Rock while my wife was exploring the monolith," remarked Raboy.

"It is a CIA thing, so we can go undetected and such," he replied.

Everyone looked at Rabbi Raboy as he looked back at the astonished gentlemen and then smiled as he tipped his hat at them. As Raboy gathered up his notes, a top National Security agent entered the room

"President, we need to send an agent to Thailand for the conference of the Asian nations. We really need to find out about what sort of trouble is brewing between India and China. They are doing things we do not understand or know much about," said Harry, Secretary of Defense.

"Who do you have in mind?" asked the President.

"Send Huppenthal. Although he is not very trustworthy or have any leadership qualities, he is an excellent liar that talks up a good story, politically speaking. He basically is the right man to infiltrate the area," remarked Mr. Kent.

"We'll soon find out, or, to the contrary, we'll soon find out that we will not find out until it is too late," remarked Harry.

"Regardless of what we think, Huppenthal is the slime we need to send," stated Kent sarcastically.

CHAPTER SIX:

THE DAY OF WARNING

"Geneneral Rashin, this is Commander Lao Ling," said the British United Nations Commander, as he introduced the two generals.

"I say ole' chap, why are we meeting at this ghastly place?" asked General Wentworth.

"Security and secrecy," uttered Bin Mattsu of the far-east contingency.

"Why is this meeting so bloody secret? What is so privy between China and India that we must meet at a Bangkok brothel?" asked General Wentworth.

"You really don't know, do you?" asked Commander Ling.

"I do! You damn well know I do! These Chinese and Indians want to cover their assets if something goes awry. You bloody well know our negotiation tactics will get the blame. The rest of the world will receive bullshit press releases that will say something far from the truth," said Bin Mattsu, a Pakistani United Nations peace negotiator.

"What can possibly go wrong? We have counted and recounted the Indians and Chinese thermonuclear arsenal supply. Together they have a mere five thousand nukes total," stated General Wentworth with authority.

"General please, five thousand nukes can destroy most of the inhabitants of Earth," said Huppenthal, boldly calling General Wentworth an idiot.

"Not every one of them has a delivery system yet," remarked General Rashin, lying with every word he spoke.

"There are those that would carry them on their backs to deliver them to your targets if persuaded to do so," replied an angry Huppenthal.

"Ole' Chap, you must be realistic with your abstract thinking. I mean these indigents are not going to blow up the Himalayan mountain range with thermo nukes," Wentworth touted back.

"I do not think their nukes are aimed at the Himalayas. They are pointed toward—" said Huppenthal as he was interrupted by Wentworth.

"Mr. Huppenthal, are you an idiot or what? Do you need everything spelled out for you?" asked General Wentworth.

"I take that as an insult," replied Huppenthal.

"What sort of negotiation is this? We don't need the Brits and Yanks fighting about how we are going to annihilate ourselves. Can you gentlemen please refrain from expressing your personal assumptions?" asked Bin Mattsu telling the Brits and Yanks to keep their personal feelings out of the conversation.

"Gentlemen, it is obvious China and India both has enough thermonuclear devices to obliterate one another within an hour. You need not worry. We will not resort to the use of such weapons to settle a dispute over a few acres of land that are inhabited by ancient Indian indigents. Our negotiations will be successful because it is in the best interest of China and India to trade freely on the international market; whereas, a nuclear battle over a few square miles of land is absolutely foolish. We will resolve this issue in due time," said General Rashin, the military delegate from India.

"Gentlemen, Gentlemen, please we are so sorry this dispute had to come to this. A special meeting to resolve such simple matters is really uncalled for. A little piece of land that has been inhabited by ancient Chinese Maoist indigents from the time of the Ming dynasty is not worth risking human lives for. We know these indigent people do not care who their leader is or what country they are part of. We Chinese feel the land is so desolate it is not worth the loss of human lives. We also feel are not worth battling over. It would be absolutely foolish to battle over a few square miles of land," argued General Ling.

The meeting ended so Huppenthal and Wentworth left the meeting together since they were staying at the same hotel.

"Well, it looks like this issue has been resolved," remarked Huppenthal.

"Are all Americans as stupid as you, mate?" remarked General Wentworth.

"One more insult and we are going to be fighting," said Huppenthal.

"Ole' Chap, don't you realize the Indians and Chinese have just declared war on one another? These Asians boys always talk around what the truth is or whatever they would call the truth. You see chap, these Asians have this hidden honor and pride that we westerners do not understand. You must not only read between the lines, but you must add lines to complete their real intentions and hidden motives," said Wentworth.

"How did you gather that much information from the Indian and Chinese delegate's statements?" asked Huppenthal, not understanding the seriousness of the matter.

"They both silently said that the indigent people of the Himalayan area live in an area that belongs to them. They are going to fight for this territory for the natural resources. Really, they do not care about the Himalayan people," explained Wentworth.

"You snobby British always think you know it all. I think your whole government is filled with bunch of know-it-alls that are full of nonsensical ideas," said Huppenthal.

"Think what you want, mate, but I am telling you, get ready for something ugly and nasty. Their differences will not be addressed with bows and arrows," asked Wentworth, trying to get Huppenthal to understand the problem.

Huppenthal shook hands with the British General as he left the lobby of the hotel. The next morning Huppenthal left for Washington, D.C. to give his report to the Pentagon. After he had returned to the United States, Huppenthal called General Freetag to immediately inform the secretary of defense. Harry was urged by the Pentagon to contact the President.

"Hello, Mr. President. This is Harry. I must meet with you at once," he demanded.

"What's the matter? What's the rush?"

"No time for questions over the phone."

About three hours later, General Freetag, Harry, and Huppenthal entered the Presidential Oval Office. President Cleghorn sat there looking out the window.

"What is the emergency?" asked the President.

"Tell him, Huppenthal, tell him what you told me this morning," demanded Freetag.

"Both nations want exclusive rights to the Himalayan Glacier Milk source. Sir, they are willing to fight for control of the area. The British intelligence thinks this situation is so serious that war is imminent," replied Huppenthal.

"Do you mean to tell me this emergency meeting is about two nations fighting over Glacier Milk! What is so important about Glacier Milk?" asked the President.

"O.K. The Himalayan nomads, who live like prehistoric people, drink Himalayan melted glacier ice. Supposedly they live around one hundred and eighty years. Not one of the nomads has a birth certificate to prove their age, but the Indian and Chinese governments do not care about that fact. They are selling one liter of the Glacier Milk for a thousand U.S. dollars," explained Huppenthal.

"What concerns me is why India and China would fight over this mountain of ice." remarked the President.

"The demand is over one million bottles per day. That adds up to over four hundred billion dollars profit per year for the country that controls the Glacier Milk," explained Huppenthal.

"So let them fight it out," replied Harry.

"That is exactly what we cannot do. The British think they will resort to thermonuclear warfare to resolve their differences," remarked Huppenthal.

"Harry, get the ambassadors of Britain, China, and India on the blue phone so we can schedule a conference to discuss this issue sometime later next month," requested the President.

President Cleghorn shook his head after hearing about the Glacier Milk dispute. He did not think such a commodity would be worth fighting over. He proceeded to continue his daily chores and ignored Huppenthal's concerns as nonsense. Two days later after Huppenthal had called Wentworth he asked General Freetag to request another meeting with the President and Harry again regarding his warning.

"What did General Wentworth specifically have to say about the impasse over the Glacier Milk between India and China?" asked Harry.

"He told me the Indians and Chinese do not come right out and clearly state what they are thinking. Then he told me one must add up what has been said and then read between the lines to get the real gist of their statements," replied Huppenthal.

"Mr. President, this does not make any sense to me, but it would be best if we carefully watch any new developments. In reality, I don't think these Asian nations are going to selfdestruct over a few gallons of melted ice mixed with prehistoric dirt," advised Harry.

"Thank you, Mr. Huppenthal. Now, why in God's Green Earth did you call this an emergency? There does not appear to be any serious concerns for America regarding this conflict. I will take the time to talk to the Prime Minister of England. Hopefully, he will have some information to clarify your statement about this Asian conflict," said the President.

"But Mr. President, these people are crazy," replied Huppenthal.

"Aren't we all. Have a nice day and keep me posted, Mr. Huppenthal," replied the President. When Huppenthal exited the room, Joshua turned to Harry.

"Can you get in contact with that prophetic Jew from Israel?" asked Joshua.

"Do you mean Rabbi Raboy?" asked Harry, being unsure of whom the President was talking about. Being very religious he felt the pisonic groups were more evil than good, but now he had been ask to rely on a

Rabbi to do his job. He was upset with President Cleghorn at this point wondering if the President was getting away from protocol handling such a world crisis in this manner.

"Yes. Find him through his brother, that Israeli Ambassador, Jeremiah Raboy. I'd like to talk with him and pick his brain. I'd like to find out what he really knows about this Glacier Milk nonsense," said the President.

"Mr. President, I do not see the need, but I will get on it immediately," replied Harry.

Harry reluctantly instructed President Cleghorn's pisonic group to clandestinely monitor the Rabbi. He felt their intrusions were not necessary to uncover any secrets the Rabbi might be concealing, but he had orders to obey, so he carried out his assignment. The pisonic group's attempts were blocked because Rabbi Raboy was being protected by an impenetrable supernatural shield placed around him. During this period Raboy had no idea he was being probed by a US government psychic experiment.

Harry was informed by the pisonic leader that Raboy had some mysterious shield that blocked all psychic contact. They instructed Harry that he if had to gather any information from Raboy it would have to be in person. Harry made several plans to get Raboy into his arena to coax him into exposing any knowledge he had about the Indo-China conflict. Back in Arizona before dawn, Abigail woke up upset because she felt she had been totally ignored by Raboy. She insisted that they needed to take Daniel to Disneyland to celebrate his third birthday. Abigail told David she was tired of the tribal life and wanted to live a little before the Earth disappeared. In reality, Abigail had wanted to visit the theme park herself because she had always dreamed of meeting Mickey Mouse. Her son's birthday was the perfect excuse to make her dreams come true. Raboy heeded Abigail's demands and told the Begay family they planned to spend a few days visiting Disneyland. Danny told Raboy about the time he had taken his wife and sons there many years ago and loved the place. Down the road went the Raboys trekking across the reservation lands and off to Anaheim, California—Disneyland.

After the high desert, they entered Flagstaff's seven thousand feet alpine environment covered with giant Ponderosa pines and snow capped mountain peaks. David Raboy was once again fascinated by the beauty of Flagstaff, Arizona. He loved the giant, orange-colored bark of the Ponderosa pine trees that filled the air with a unique, fragrance. After driving about fifty miles west of Flagstaff Raboy was surprised by the dramatic change in landscapes. Of course, he expected some geographical changes, but he was not prepared for the type Arizona offered. As they entered Kingman they observed the land covered with high grass, juniper pines, and variety of cacti. They stopped at Kingman and studied the road maps. Abigail talked David into turning north off the planned route so she could see the Hoover Dam and experience the massive lighted signs of Las Vegas Strip. After crossing a desert covered with an array of beautiful desert plants, they encountered the Black Gorge where the mighty Colorado River was tamed by the massive Hoover Dam. They stopped and took many pictures looking over the seven hundred foot drop if the dam wall. They got to Las Vegas right after nightfall where Raboy was overwhelmed by the casino's architecture and gigantic lighting displays. Abigail did not allow Raboy to spend one penny gambling. They left Las Vegas the next morning and drove through Death

Valley so they might compare it to the Dead Sea.

It was one hundred and thirty five degrees when the Raboys drove through Death Valley the lowest place in North America. After visiting Stove Pipe Wells in the heart of Death Valley the drove until they reached Los Angeles, California. Abigail was amazed by the size of the California super highways. The traffic made her a little bit depressed, but she burst out with joy when she saw the peaks of Disneyland's Matter horn touching the sky. She told David she could hear the people scream as the Bobsleds raced through the Matter horn's caverns.

Raboy wanted to find some frugal lodgings but Abigail insisted they stay at the Disneyland Hotel. For Abigail, this was beyond a dream coming true. Inside of the park she was living in her own fantasyland. As they stood in line for over an hour to board Abigail's dream ride an Israeli Secret Police and a Central Intelligence Agent approached them.

"Rabbi Raboy, we are representatives from the American and Israeli governments. We are here to officially ask you and your family to step aside. The President of the United States and Ambassador of Israel needs to converse with you," said the agents dressed in black.

"Yes, we could do that, but right now we have two more days to spend at Disneyland. I am telling you that my wife will not budge from this place until we finish our trip."

The secret agents simultaneously phoned the White House and Israeli Embassy. They explained that they had located Rabbi Raboy, but he wanted to finish his vacation first. The White House and Israeli governments respected the Raboys' wishes so they sent six more special agents from American and Israeli governments to protect them. Rabbi Raboy wondered what on earth was going on but kept his lips and thoughts sealed so Abigail could enjoy the time of her life.

His decision to honor his wife's wishes by celebrating their son's third birthday at Disneyland was difficult task to enjoy with twelve agents following them everywhere. After Abigail had done everything she wanted to do at the theme park, they boarded a private jet that was flown directly to Washington, D.C.

Upon arriving they were immediately escorted to the White House. Every step he took Raboy wondered what was so serious to warrant this bizarre treatment. He kept quiet as he listened patiently to his brother carried on about this and that, but never mentioned one word what was so urgent he be rushed to the American Capitol. His wife was entertained by the First Lady in a sitting room while Raboy was lead to a special meeting room filled with several dignitaries representing several nations.

"Rabbi, we have a development that does not look good for the world in general," said the President. He then introduced the Rabbi to the Russian President, the British Prime Minister, and the German, French, Japanese, and Australian diplomats. They all shook hands.

"Mr. President, What developments are you referring, too?" asked Raboy.

"It appears that India and China are arguing over some special water called Glacier Milk. We cannot seem to get either of them to budge one inch to settle this disagreement peacefully."

"Water. I knew it," said Raboy.

"What do you mean by the comment 'I knew it'?" asked Mr. Kent.

"Israel needs water. Yes, water. Every nation near the Saudi Arabia peninsula needs water. I knew man would eventually forget about their battles over oil and land and fight for water as they had done for thousands of years," he replied.

"Rabbi, it isn't over the quantity of water, but a certain type of water that sells for a very high price. A price that generates over four hundred billions dollars profit per year," said the President.

"What kind of water costs that much?" asked Raboy.

"A type of water that helps you stay alive until you reach about 180 years old," replied Mr. Kent.

"I have never heard of such a thing. How can I be able to help you with an Indian and Chinese water problem?" asked Rabbi Raboy.

"Well, you can't," said the President.

"Then why have you brought me all the way to Washington, D.C. on a special Air Force jet? Are you telling me you have a problem with some issue that I cannot help you with but you brought me here anyway. Why would you do that?" he asked frantically.

"Brother, calm down. We have even asked the worldwide King Solomon Financial Network to intervene. They could not even make a deal with these hard headed Asians. We understand that their leaders have decided to use their respective militaries to fight it out. These people are even more stiff-necked about policy than the Israeli and Palestinian leaders are. We want you to ask you angelic messenger friend how to solve the problem," explained Jeremiah.

"You people are crazy, and I mean real crazy. You want me to ask my "angelic friend" to help resolve these matters? That is such a ridiculous statement that even the Lord Almighty is laughing at you," replied Raboy.

"Brother, we are serious. This is a very dangerous situation," said Jeremiah.

"How will my notes and maps be used to accomplish a resolution if a small war breaks out over water?" asked Rabbi Raboy.

"Sir, keep this top secret, but they are talking thermonuclear war," said Mr. Kent.

"You could have told me that over the phone," said the Rabbi.

"We wanted to know firsthand, in person, if you have received any more supernatural messages or visitations that may help us solve this potential disaster," said Harry.

"I was not given any specific time frame or specific information as to when or why any disaster would take place on earth," said the Rabbi.

"Brother, do you want to go home and be with your family?" asked the Ambassador.

"Now, what are you implying?" asked Raboy.

"Rabbi, this is a grave situation that needs an immediate resolution," said the President.

"I would like to consult with my Aborigine friends, and Hopi cousins. Maybe they can help," he said plainly.

"The Hopi Indians are not our cousins," said an ISP agent.

"According to the Mormon religious belief, it is written in some obscure secret scrolls they are of the lost ten tribes of Jacob. They have these golden plates stored in a secret place that proclaims that they are our cousins," replied the Rabbi. "No one on earth has ever seen them, but the Mormons stake their entire religious belief on them. I asked to see them, but they failed to exhibit them or prove their validity."

"I am confused about their claim because years ago our scientists have proven that there are only three different races that exist on earth. We know that the three races are those that have round hair, flat hair, and oval hair based on the differences of the hair follicles. Native Americans have flat hair and we have oval hair which excludes them from the Hebrew race. It is physically impossible for them to be ancestors of Jacob," said the Israeli ISP scientist.

"I believe as you because the Hopis do not have any cultural similarities to our Jewish historic culture," replied the Rabbi.

"They are humans, like us, that are made out of dirt by the creator and all humans originated from the same grandfather, Noah, but I am afraid they are not of the same father, Abraham. We know where the twelve, I mean the thirteen Israeli tribes are located at this very day. You should know this," said the Israeli ISP secret agent.

"I know what the truth is. I told them they were direct descendents of our father Noah but not Abraham. The forbidden books of the New Testament states that Christians are the Lord's sheep called by another name," he replied.

"These Christians just keep making up stories as if they were the truth. The problem with most Christians is that they believe that their opinions as fact," said the ISP agent.

"Regardless, as to what we believe about our ancestors, the Hopi and Aborigine have been forewarned about an impending danger just as we have been by the books of the prophets," replied Raboy.

"Gentlemen, we need to get back on track here," said the President.

The meeting ended when Rabbi Raboy agreed to do what he could to find out about the pending doom. Having no clue where to start, he contacted the Cohen Hebrew Rabbi high priest to request a private meeting of the Cohen Ultra-Orthodox Jewish Rabbis. Rabbi Raboy decided to explain to his fellow brothers that his visitation may be the warning that this was the beginning of the end of the present age.

It was ironic that he could not tell the government the truth about some of his religious secrets, and the Cohen brotherhood about several government secrets. So he had to warn his Cohen brotherhood about the impending dangers to their society to protect the Ark of the Covenant that housed the original Ten Commandment stones. Raboy was educated with the secret knowledge as to how the Ark of Covenant was hidden to keep Babylon from destroying it when the destroyed the first Temple in Judea, and when Rome sent Titus to destroy the second

Temple tearing it down to its foundation. From the beginning of the Philistines to present day the Cohen's had kept the Ark of Covenant hidden from those that would possibly destroy it.

As the keeper of the secret scrolls and the bearer of the seventh of the sixteen secret pronunciations of Yahweh's Holy name, he knew he stood in the middle of the entire scenario.. Raboy looked at himself in the mirror for a couple of moments trying to comprehend what the Lord had intended for him to do from the beginning. After meeting with his brotherhood he was ordered to return to Israel at once. Raboy rebelled and ignored everything he had ever been taught and returned to Arizona. He had no idea why he felt lead to return to his Hopi friends but did as his heart commanded him to do so.

CHAPTER SEVEN

ASIAN T-WAR

"It is good to see you again, Rabbi," said Sarah.

"Danny and Sarah, it is sure a pleasure to visit friends like you again," replied Abigail.

"What brings you back so soon?" asked Danny.

"I was requested to attend a very strange meeting in Washington, D.C. I'm here to discuss the meeting with Sarah. I wanted to consult with her and explain to her what the government knows about the supernatural message she received about the sixth purification of Mother Earth," replied Raboy.

"In the past, the great white fathers in Washington were only interested in us when they wanted to take some more of our land to make our prison smaller," said Ronnie.

"This time they need your help in an entirely different manner."

"The only time Washington D.C. is interested in Native Americans is when they want us to fight in their wars against tribes we don't have a quarrel with. It has always bothered me that they ignore us until they want our children to fight for American land we don't even own," said Ronnie Begay frustrated with American government policies concerning reservations.

"Ronnie, it was nothing like that at all."

"What type of help do they need from our small tribe?" asked Ronnie not as negative.

"As you know Ronnie, your mother has been given a supernatural message similar to the one received by both the Aborigine elder and me. The US government made some comparisons between the three messages that pertained to the future of Mother Earth. Some of the US secret agents are convinced that India and China are on the brink of a thermonuclear war. Our supernatural experiences maybe warnings as to what lies ahead for mankind. Such a war would cause massive worldwide nuclear waste fallout killings possibly millions of people."

"Are you and the government trying to use us for some dark plot?" asked Ronnie.

"No, Ronnie that is not what is going on here. I have come back to warn my friends about a possible war that will cause some major earth changes."

"What kind of changes?"

"Mr. Begay, does your son have a mental defect and does not understand what your wife has told him or what I am trying to tell him?" asked the Rabbi.

"This one has been stubborn even during my wife's time before he was born," replied Danny Begay, as he patted Ronnie on the left shoulder.

"Father, I am not difficult. I just know that we are going to have to fight forever if we want to keep our independent ways and customs. The Mormons have many of us believing we came from some of the same tribes as this man. Now he informs us that we most likely are not one of the tribes or generations of his father—Israel," said Ronnie.

"There isn't any record of Hebrews ever migrating to America" replied Raboy.

"We have writings that are four thousand years old and none of them resemble Hebrew. Now, you say that the world is going to end and only three people on Mother Earth know about it!" exclaimed Ronnie.

"To answer you question about our ancestral back grounds, our records do reveal that we are our cousins, of sorts. That would be according to our records of Noah and his Ark. See during the first global desolation caused by the great worldwide flood nearly everyone on Mother Earth died. Your history is older than the twelve tribes of Isaac, but our history concludes that we have a common grandfather in Noah." replied Raboy.

"You have told me that the Israelites started their tribe around four thousand years ago and that they still have the same style of writing. Does that mean we became stupid when we traveled ten thousand miles on foot, ending up on our sacred Hopi land? Our ancestors have been here for ten thousand years, but this Jacob is less than four thousand years old. None of these white stranger's stories have any merit or truth to them. They all speak with forked tongues, as far as I am concerned." Ronnie crossed his arms and turned away.

"Ronnie, if my family and I have offended you, then I will leave your land," said Raboy.

"No, you have been one of the few white strangers that have taken the time to learn about our ancestral history. You have not tried to change us but have taken the time to try to get to know our past," he muttered.

"Well, Ronnie, your mother's message might be what your tribe has been waiting to hear for millenniums. Now, I am here to find out if your mother's and my supernatural messages are somehow related to Yirawala's Dreamtime experience. It appears that the entire world is on the brink of a sudden cataclysmic change, hopefully we have some answers about man's future."

"My ancestors gave us the Meha over thirty-five hundred years ago. Is that about the time of Noah?" asked Ronnie.

"Ronnie, Ronnie you intrigue me. From the first man Adam's exit from the Garden of Eden to now is about six thousand years. Noah came about sixteen hundred years after Adam. That means Noah lived about four thousand four hundred years ago. Mathematically that would have your ancestors writing the Meha eight hundred years after Noah. The Tower of Babel was built between Noah's time and the Meha's, and all men were dispersed throughout the world. I think your people came to this land around that era. Jacob was born after that era so that is why we are cousins, not tribal brothers. It is apparent there is some historical misunderstanding," explained Raboy.

Rabbi Raboy then took the time to show the Begay family the government charts and their comparisons of the three spiritual messages. Danny asked Raboy if he could call the Hopi Chief and elders to look at the comparisons of the supernatural messages. Rabbi Raboy hesitated to show others but decided it was necessary to resolve the puzzle. Raboy already had his Cohen brothers in Israel trying to decipher the complex information.

For three months, Rabbi Raboy worked with the Hopi elders and the Tel Aviv Torah code breakers trying to decipher the messages. He periodically he sent reports to his brother at the Israeli Embassy in Washington, D.C., but it was difficult for Raboy to directly communicate with Yirawala because of his customs, so he sent letters to his great-grandson in Ayers Rock, Australia. Manandjiwala would deliver Raboy's personal messages by driving out to the tribal outstation where Yirawala dwelt. Yirawala responded by having Manandjiwala write back to the Rabbi. Through him, Yirawala explained to Raboy that he had been able to hear his thoughts so he knew what was going on in his life. Even with his knowledgeYirawala still informed Raboy with letters he kept seeing the same vision of mushroom clouds sprouting up out of the ground in India and China.

Manandjiwala told Raboy that the Australian government was monitoring Yirawala. He kept the Rabbi abreast of the situation that an elite Australian military commando kept in touch with Yirawala on a daily basis. They wanted to know immediately if Yirawala had received any more information during any of his Dreamtime experiences. Manandjiwala expressed to Raboy that he was confused about Yirawala. This was because Yirawala was extremely pleased that the Australian government was finally taking the time to seriously listen to what the Aborigine ancestral knowledge about the Dreamtime messages about the Sixth Rebirth.

In Arizona, the Hopi elders met and accepted the Rabbi's plea to build a shelter to keep them safe from any destruction that may occur during Mother Earth's purification, or rebirth process. Of course, Raboy emphasized this would only be a precautionary measure since he didn't really know if or when anything would really happen. Miguel, the Hopi medicine man believed that if the world were to be purified, the Hopi people would be protected by Maasaw. He also believed that several sacred Hopi caves should be prepared into shelters to protect his fellow tribesmen from Mother Earth's fury during her purification.

The American federal government and the Hopi tribal people worked in unison constructing several sacred caves to accommodate their tribal members. Since the Begays and Raboys received the prophecies, a special shelter was built for their group by the Army Corps of Engineers. The federal government wanted the separate cave outfitted with top secret communication devices because Sarah and Raboy were placed at the top of the priority list on the USA government's essential survivors list. Several top NSA and BLM agents used covert tactics to keep the construction of the shelters secret from the news media and public.

While the shelters were being built, Abigail decided to celebrate Little Daniel's fourth birthday with a once in a lifetime birthday party. She invited everyone she knew in Arizona so the birthday party would be a grandiose event. Ronnie suggested they should have the party at Lake Powel. Abigail thought about the idea for two days and then decided it as a wonderful idea. Abigail and Ronnie convinced Raboy that Lake Powel would be perfect for its rare beauty and tranquility. Abigail became more excited about seeing the scenic beauty of Glen Canyon stretched out over one hundred and eighty miles between the Arizona and Utah borders than her son's birthday. Abigail had seen pictures of the area in the Arizona Highways magazine and in the American National Park travel guide. Her heart melted from the thought of seeing another majestic natural wonder of Mother Earth.

"A sixty-five foot houseboat stocked with food and equipped with jet skis and fishing poles would be best," suggested Ronnie.

"I think that is a grand idea," replied Abigail.

"You will not believe how beautiful Lake Powell is. Whiteman's words really cannot describe what the Glenn Canyon mean to Native Americans," said Ronnie.

"Is it different than the Grand Canyon?" asked Abigail.

"This land is sacred to us. To the white strangers, it is just another recreation area. To Native Americans, this is the sacred land of our ancestors," he replied.

"I cannot wait to see this place," replied Abigail.

Twenty of the Raboy's Native American friends boarded the sixty foot houseboat at daybreak ready to travel up the lake for about fifty miles. Abigail had asked Ronnie to find the perfect area up the lake to camp at during their two day adventure. As they traveled up the mighty Colorado River the Raboy's were marveled by the crystal blue water making up the hundred and eighty mile long lake. The orange and red cliffs that made up the canyon walls were so spectacular that Abigail did not leave the observation deck during the entire trip. After traveling up the lake for forty miles, they found the perfect spot with white sandy beaches. You could see over fifty feet into the crystal clear waters that reflected the reddish-orange cliffs that over hung the beach area. Abigail shouted out to the Lord praising Him for creating such a beautiful place so she could celebrate Daniel's his fourth birthday party.

Ronnie handed Raboy a fishing pole and immediately they began catching fish. Raboy caught a five pound large mouth bass on the first cast. Later that day Abigail grilled the large mouth bass, several blue gill, and crappie that Ronnie and Raboy caught that day. She prepared and cooked the fish the way her mother had done using her ultra-orthodox Jewish kosher cooking standards. Miguel decorated the cake using his Native American sand painting skills. Abigail was speechless and Raboy was awed by the breath taking Hopi artwork. The day turned out to be a most memorial event filled with love and laughter.

The next morning everyone fished and water skied until they were exhausted. The final day of the celebration ended as the sun sat over the orange sandstone of the awesome Rainbow Bridge national monument. Abigail enjoyed Lake Powell so much that she didn't want to leave.

That night Abigail was awaken by a coyote howl she tossed and turned thinking about her homeland. The next morning she got the burning desire to go back to Israel.

"Sweetie, I have just realized that we need to go home to Israel and pick the figs before they become a nuisance."

"Sweetheart, that's already been taken care of. Let's relax and enjoy the trip," replied David.

"I could not sleep thinking about our home in Israel."

"Abigail, what is wrong?" asked Raboy.

"The world is getting ready to end and we have not made any plans about how we are going to cope with the situation." Raboy looked at Abigail wondering what she was thinking.

"David, we really need to go home and protect our friends."

"Protect our friends from what?" asked Raboy.

"The world is coming to an end," responded Abigail.

"Abigail, no one ever said the world was going to end. We really do not understand what will happen. But if you want to go home, that is fine. We have accomplished our mission here."

After returning to the Begay's ranch from Lake Powell, Abigail began packing to return to Israel, but little did she know what was happening in Washington, D.C. The Raboys soon found out something alarming was rapidly developing. Raboy was stunned when he received an urgent phone call from the Pentagon at the Begays' home. He listened to a few words and then hung up the phone and stared at the floor without uttering a word. Everyone waited for him to comment about the call.

"Sweetheart, a serious situation has developed, and the government needs my help right away. They would not explain the entire situation over the phone."

The Raboys left the reservation and was flown by an American government, private jet to Washington, D. C. President Cleghorn discussed American defenses with his Pentagon members as Raboy was briefed while in route to the American White House.

"Major McCord, with all of our computerized weapons, shouldn't we have a sufficient defense?" asked Joshua

"Mr. President, our most sophisticated weapons cannot read human minds yet. I know you have not forgotten that other nations are trying to figure out ways to circumvent our military industrial complex war machinery. One thing is for certain; there is no real sure way to stop multiple warheads when they have reached the critical zone of their targets. Second, third, and subsequent strikes mean more destruction, but who gets in the first whack is officially the aggressor and usually the winner," said Major Thomas McCord.

"Why don't I tell the American people the truth about our defense plans?" asked Joshua.

"I am surprised with you, Mr. President. That would be the first time any President has ever told the general public the truth about any war. The bottom line would be disaster and panic. Then the complete distrust of our government would follow, and then our spending on defenses would decrease by billions. You cannot have fear and strength at the same time; not even for one second if you are going to win the mental battles of trust and obedience," said Harry.

"So you are saying war is a mental battle?" asked the President.

"Joshua, there is a time to cry and a time to die but right now this is the time to run for the hills," said Harry.

"Wait a second. Like I was saying, I guess I was feeling sorry for my fellow man. I realize the negative impact by telling the public the truth. Would it really demoralize their spirit, hopes, and dreams?" asked the President.

"Sir, I am counting on our technology now," remarked Harry.

"First-strike capabilities create so many problems," replied Major McCord.

"You are damn right, because if they bomb us first, our public would not try to find out why. They would be wondering why we did not strike back," said Harry.

"Harry, let's play the watch and see game, but get our military ready to defend the American homeland," said Joshua.

"I would not have it any other way," replied Harry.

"Harry, our forefathers must have known this would eventually happen," said Joshua, uttering empty thoughts.

"Nothing personal, Mr. President, but what the hell are you saying?" asked Harry.

As the President discussed defensive tactical and strategically commands, Huppenthal and General Wentworth went to see Mr. Kent about the Asian conflict. Mr. Kent was told that India and China were past the breaking point. Wentworth explained how neither China or India were going to budge one way or the other about the disputed land. He disclosed British military intelligence information that a local military scrimmage had taken place over a one square mile area where the Glacier Milk stream bifurcated into each nation's respective waterways. The Brits knew the war had begun, but kept quiet figuring that one of the nations would eventually back down. Mr. Kent told General Wentworth that he felt nuclear maybe the only resolution.

As Mr. Kent had suspected it began to escalate to the point of no return for either nation. Mr. Kent immediately went to the White House to discuss the problem at hand. When he got there he tried to interrupt the meeting in progress but was told to wait.

"Mr. President, Captain Rex Billingsley, Commander Daniel Comer, and General Bill Gilkey will command Air Force One for the next twenty four hours. I will be moving Major McCord to command the Looking Glass. As you know, we must rotate crews between the 797 Jumbo jet twins," said the Pentagon Air Force Commander General David Bree.

"It is my pleasure to be working with you again Mr. Bree. As you know, every President has been given two secret markings to rule out any imposters. You will be given the new codes so your position cannot be overrun by zealots or radicals that would try to destroy our nation," said the President.

After talking to the Pentagon commander the President turned to address Mr. Kent. Harry left the room to make a phone call over his cell phone. A few moments later he rushed into the Oval Office and looked and sounded like a man that had the holy hell scared out of him.

"Get your family and get on board Air Force One. This time it is for real!" yelled Harry.

"What is for real?" asked the President.

"The Indians and Chinese have armed their nukes, and I mean all five thousand of them!"

"Are the Indians and Chinese going to attack the United States?" he asked calmly thinking Harry was over reacting.

"No sir, they are at the brink of thermonuclear war. Thermonuclear means they will use hydrogen nuclear bombs. We need to get your family into a nuclear fallout safe zone because it appears that a nuclear war is imminent. Sir, I do mean now!" screamed Harry.

As they talked, the Presidential helicopter made a quick landing bouncing up and down as it landed on the White House lawn. Six Marines jumped out of an escort Blackhawk helicopter that had landed next to the Presidential helicopter. Joshua grabbed his wife and two daughters and ran for the ramjet chopper. As they jumped aboard, the chopper took off and flew to Andrews AFB. Immediately, they boarded Air Force One that already had its turbines spinning, and was cleared for departure. They rushed aboard with five other prominent governmental staff members. The flight was accompanied by a four F-35 super attack jets until they landed at Black Mountain II three hours later. As they rushed off the plane they were protected by several armed guards that guided them into a special personal carrier to be taken to the control center of the Black Mountain II secret installation. After being briefed for thirty minutes, they were flown to a Rocky Mountain command center called Trinity subterranean safe zone.

"Harry, this better not be one of your tests. Has the general public been alerted yet?" the President asked.

"No, sir. We are not in a state of war yet, so it is against the law to alert the public until the act is taking place," said the General in command of NORAD IV.

"What the hell kind of nation do we have?" asked the President.

"Sir, we are a nation that stands for freedom, but we are not free. We are a nation governed by laws that eradicate many of our freedoms while the rest of the laws limit our freedom. Ironically, 'The Privacy Act' passed by the US Congress years ago actually took our privacy away and no one gets to know military secrets because it may put our troops in harms way. So there it is our government in action, of course secretly."

"What the hell are you saying? Everyone is in harms way, including our troops."

"Mr. President, this is a precautionary measure, so please relax, and wait until we have conformation," said the General handing the President a set of instructions in case of nuclear intrusion of American territorial of homeland areas.

"Harry, can you immediately get in touch with Rabbi Raboy for me. Please bring his brother along, as well," ordered the President.

"I suppose I can do that, sir." replied Harry.

"No sir, ahh, yes sir. I mean you can request their presence in a state of emergency but we cannot make them come," said the General.

"Well, arrest them, or whatever it takes, but get them here and I mean now!"

"Joshua, what in God's name, are you doing by bringing those Israelis to our secret Presidential safe zone? Are you a mental midget or what?" asked Harry.

"I want to know if he knows about this situation. Better yet, it would be nice to know what will come of this. Have you forgotten about those crazy maps and notes he had directly related to India and China only a few months ago?" The NORAD IV commander looked on, confused.

"I'll get it done immediately," replied Harry.

Ambassador Raboy was taken to Andrew's military base and put on board a USAF supersonic F-35 twin rotar-turbin jet that landed only two hours after takeoff from Washington, D.C. in Colorado. At the same time a Golden Eagle Marine unit out of Yuma, Arizona was immediately routed to the Hopi reservation. Their orders were to peacefully bring Rabbi Raboy to Cheyenne Mountain II without his family. The Marines landed in Tuba City, Arizona to start their mission to find Rabbi Raboy.

Strange as it was, the Raboys happened to be shopping in Tube City, Arizona that morning to buy some souvenirs to take back home to their Israeli friends. Abigail figured since she would not be coming back to Arizona for a very long time, if ever, she wanted some mementos. As they shopped, Raboy noticed several Navajo policemen talking to some Bureau of Land Management federal officers standing next to his vehicle. Raboy wanted to confront the officers, but Abigail asked David to wait and see what they were up to before confronting them.

After ten minutes of hiding in the shadows observing the officers, Raboy's curiosity ended his patients. Since he couldn't wait any longer, he approached the tribal policemen and federal officers. When he got near the truck, the officers confronted him. They were sent to inform him that the President of the United States wanted to see him right away. Raboy did not say a word as he stared at the tall lanky BLM officer. Turning toward Abigail he yelled at her to come to where he was at once and bring their son. The Colonel told Raboy his specific orders were to bring him alone. David dropped his him and looked at the ground for a moment. "Abigail, I don't know what is going on here, but the President of the United States has issued orders for the American military to pick me up and take me directly to a secret location somewhere around here," he said.

"Did we do something wrong? Can I come with you?" she asked.

"No to both questions. I have already asked and was denied. I want you to return to Sarah and Danny Begay's ranch and please wait there patiently until I return. I have asked the federal officers to escort you, so that you will be safe," he said with a worried look on his face.

Abigail kissed David good-bye just before he went with the commanders to board the Golden Eagle ramjet helicopter that whisked him away. As soon as Raboy took off the tall lanky BLM federal officer offered to escort Abigail back to the Begays farm. Being frightened and worried about what was going on she accepted the offer.

"Sir, ahh, Rabbi, we are taking you to the Winslow Airport where a US Air Force F-35 ramjet will take you to the Cheyenne Mountain II landing strip located somewhere in Colorado. We should arrive there any minute. The trip will take about an hour. I have been ordered to assist you anyway I can with your maps and notes. I am not sure what that means. I hope you do," said the Marine Colonel in charge of the Marine nuclear rescue team.

"Yes, I know what they are talking about," he replied.

After boarding the F-35 it took about thirty five minutes for the craft to reach the Cheyenne Mountain II. He was hastily escorted to a secret meeting room dug deep within the mountain's core that made it a thermonuclear safe house. Many humongous digital screens were lit up on every side of the room displaying the entire earth. He could hear the hum of the 35 mega watt laser optic beam receive and send stellar transmissions.

As he ventured further into the complex he heard Russian, English, German, Chinese, Indian, Spanish, and French being spoken simultaneously as he walked down the corridor to a top secret electronic map room. At the doorway of the room Raboy read a sign that stated in large red letters FOR YOUR EYES ONLY. Raboy was told that this meant no information left this room and if anyone does happened to mention one word of what they saw, they will be terminated. Raboy wanted to close his eyes at that point.

"Rabbi Raboy, we meet again. Sorry we had to meet under such extreme circumstances," said the President.

"What is all the fuss about?" asked the Rabbi. Then he noticed his brother standing on the other side of table.

"David, we have a world situation just as the Aborigine, Hopi, and you have warned us about," said the Israeli Ambassador speaking in Hebrew.

"What do you need me for?" asked the Rabbi, "You have all of my notes and maps. Is there something else I am supposed to know?" he asked.

"We were hoping that you might have something else to present, like a vision or an angelic visitation telling us when, or why, or how, or what is going to happen," said the President.

"How what is going to happen?" asked the Rabbi. The President explained the situation.

"I warned Yirawala to prepare a place among the sacred caves for his people. He believes the world is ready for the Sixth Rebirth. As you may be aware, the Army Corps of Engineers have built several shelters carved into base of the San Francisco Peaks for the Hopi. Some were built on the Hopi Reservation for what the Meha describes as the Sixth Purification. Has anyone done anything to prepare those living in Israel or the Middle East for nuclear fallout?" he asked softly, speaking in Hebrew with his brother. No one, in the room, understood a single word he said, except his brother.

"David, I have had some of our immediate family taken to the Masada and Jericho Israeli nuclear fallout shelters built during the 1980's," replied Ambassador Raboy in Hebrew.

"How soon will this nuclear war begin?" asked the Rabbi in English.

"Anytime, or any minute, or never," responded the President.

"Has anyone taken the time to alert the general public around the world or even in America for that matter?" asked the Rabbi, wondering what was happening.

"According to the 'Privacy Act' it is against the law to notify the public, unless there is immediate danger to the United States, and there isn't at this point. If your prophecies, maps, and notes are accurate, the world is in for hellfire," replied President Cleghorn.

"Do you really need me here anymore? If this war begins, I want to return to the Hopi reservation to my wife and child. It appears that there is not enough time for me to return to Israel. I want, at least, to warn my Hopi Native American friends," said Raboy looking up toward the heavens wondering what the Lord thought about man's evilness.

Rabbi Raboy was taken to a FS-35A jet and flown at mach 5 back to Winslow. The Marine nuclear rescue team was waiting there to fly him back to the Begay's ranch.

"May I ask you a question, Rabbi? Who do you think you are that the military has to personally escort you to the President, and then back to this little farm house over and over again?" said the US Army Colonel complaining about his orders.

"I don't know, but it appears India and China are about to have a thermonuclear war. I was called in to converse with the President about the situation since it was prophesied to me over five years ago," retorted the Rabbi.

"Why in the hell aren't we told about this?" asked the Colonel.

"I am told it is against your law to alert the people about any threat of a thermonuclear war, unless it is about to happen and it is directly aimed at your nation," said Raboy.

"Well, that's dumber than hell! Who in the hell puts these idiots into office in the first damn place?" asked the Colonel, not apologizing to Rabbi for his language.

"Those that take the time to vote," replied the Rabbi.

"Well, that leaves me out! Regardless of what I think, I have orders to stay with you, in case the President needs you during the next three days. Where are you staying?" asked the Colonel.

"We will have to stay in Tuba City, Arizona, or at Sarah and Danny Begay's ranch, or at the specially designed nuclear fallout shelter. Really, I don't know where I will be living during the next few days. Your men are free to join us, but you will have to supply your own food," replied the Rabbi being confused with the situation at hand.

The Airborne Helicopter Nuclear Rescue Squad stormed into Tuba City with the Rabbi and Ambassador aboard. They met with Danny, the Hopi police chief, two BLM police officers, and several National Security Agents. Everyone decided that Begay's ranch would be the best place to drop off Raboy since Abigail was there. The Marines, the Rabbi, Jeremiah Raboy, and three agents boarded the helicopter and took off toward the Begay's ranch.

Upon arriving at the ranch, several federal Native American police, three reservation police, and many family and friends of the Begays looked on in awe as three Marine helicopters landed in formation stirring up a giant dust storm. As the Rabbi got out of the helicopter

Danny Begay grabbed his hand and greeted him while saying "Yatehay" which in the Navajo native tongue meant hello.

The Rabbi was inundated with questions as everyone shouted from every direction all at once. The chaos didn't stop until the Hopi Chief, Daniel, pulled out his weapon and fired several rounds into the air. The Marine Colonel looked at him and laughed as everyone froze in place. Several specialized Marines grabbed their rifles and ran for cover due to the commotion the chieftain had caused.

"People, what are you doing?" yelled the Hopi Chief.

Ambassador Raboy nonverbally indicated, by waving his hands high, that he would explain everything to the people.

"Everyone, I am Ambassador Raboy, David's brother; that is, the Rabbi's brother. I will let him explain what the President told us," said Jeremiah Raboy, as he turned toward David.

"What I have to say concerns the entire population of Mother Earth. At this moment, a serious war may start in India and China that will affect the entire world. The President wanted to know if Sarah, Yirawala, or I had any information that may help curtail the current crisis. That is all I know. Time is short so we need to prepare for whatever may come upon us," explained Raboy.

"Why are you here and not headed back to Israel?" asked a federal officer.

"It is a very volatile situation that has restricted me from traveling. I am sure your government will be able to inform you more about the situation than I can," said Raboy as he turned and hugged his wife, and then Sarah Begay. The crowd started murmuring among themselves. After a couple of hours, the Hopi Chief sent everyone away so that the Begays and Raboys could have some peace and privacy. After about two hours the dust had settled from the dispersing crowd's vehicles.

The next morning the Colonel of the Golden Eagle Nuclear Fallout Helicopter Crew received another order to pick up the Ambassador's family. The colonel fired up the chopper engines, lifted the craft off of the ground, and screamed over to the Begay ranch. Later that evening the Marines brought the Ambassador's family to the small Northern Arizona ranch house.

"Officer, can your men relax long enough to have a cup of coffee? You are welcome, if you so desire," said Abel Begay.

"It would be my pleasure to join you," replied the colonel.

Ronnie Begay walked back and forth, studying one of the US Marines helicopter perched on his father's driveway.

"Can you give me a ride in this bird of prey?" asked Ronnie, directing his question to the Colonel.

"I see no reason not to, since it appears that our present mission has turned our military chopper into a civilian passenger craft," replied the Colonel smartly.

"I would get a kick out of flying to Tuba City and landing right in the middle of the grocery store parking lot and do some shopping for my mother. We don't have enough food for everyone tonight, so it would be a two fold mission," remarked Ronnie.

To his surprise the colonel agreed to the mission. He got at food list together and asked Abigail to assist him since she knew what foods were kosher. When they landed, the Navajo and Hopi people stared without saying a word. The Colonel, Ronnie, and Abigail got a grocery basket and started shopping while the pilot and crew member stayed with the gunship.

It was quite an unfamiliar site to see a beautiful Israeli lady, a Hopi Native American, and US Marine Colonel dressed in his combat uniform with a 45 caliper automatic weapon strapped to his side grocery shopping. Everyone stared but not a soul uttered a sound as they filled two grocery carts to the top. When they went to check out, Ronnie tried to pay, but the Colonel pushed him aside. He pulled out a federal credit card from his wallet and handed it to the cashier to pay the $921.87 tab. Ronnie, upset with the Colonel's tactics, stood back and watched the clerk bag the food and load it into the grocery cart.

"Colonel, why did you pay for our food?" asked Ronnie. "I didn't. Our government did. This is your tax dollars at work. The new military gives its command officers a credit card to buy whatever is needed from the local stores. We are stationed in so many different countries these days that when it is necessary to buy what the crew needs I just charge it to Uncle Sam. Of course, we do not go on shopping sprees, but we use it if we only need something immediately. This way we do not have to worry about carrying a multitude of the various currencies from around the world during our in country tours of duty," replied the officer.

"That is an awesome idea," remarked Abigail.

"How do you account for the charges? How does the government keep track of this?" asked Ronnie.

"Mr. Begay, the government has been monitoring the general public credit card purchases for years. When you buy something using your credit card, Washington, D.C. has computers that track and categorizes your transactions into different purchaser groups. This way they can keep track of who is buying what from whom. They know more about you than you do."

"I knew there was a reason why those credit card sharks keep sending me all those credit card opportunities," remarked Ronnie.

"It is a good thing and a bad thing. You see the government keeps track of everything everyone buys from the manufactures to the retail markets," remarked the colonel.

After returning, the food was placed into the kitchen where the women started preparing dinner. The men gathered around an open pit fireplace made of the Little Colorado round river rocks. The pit was constructed about one foot high, encompassing a circle about five feet in diameter. Some Ponderosa Pine tree stumps were used as stools. The main topic of conversation was being protected from a possible thermonuclear war. Everyone talked about what to do when Rabbi Raboy suggested that Tuba City, Cameron, Holbrook, Page, various other native American townships should be warned. He wanted to propose an open invitation to any Americans that would possibly want a safe shelter from any fallout.

Later the next day, a message was spread by radio in the Hopi and Navajo Native American traditional languages. After three days of broadcasting the message, only a few hundred people from various races, religions, and groups contacted the Hopi Chief for more information. He told them to contact Sarah Begay and Rabbi Raboy at the Begay ranch.

The Begays and Raboys watched the national and international newscasts over the digital radio and television stations everyday to seek out information about Asia. The news only mentioned that there had been some minor military battles in the Himalaya Mountains. Five days later, the Golden Eagle crew came to immediately escort and protect the Raboy and Begay groups to their respective fallout shelters.

"Rabbi, everybody, my orders are to take everyone to the fallout shelters because India and China have launched thermonuclear devices toward each other's borders. I understand the targets were purely military. That is all of the information I have. I must immediately take everyone to the subterranean shelters the government built for you," said the nervous Colonel.

"Colonel, what about your families and friends?" asked Abigail.

"Ma'am, that is part of this job you learn to deal with," replied the Colonel. It took about five minutes to pack up the Raboys' and Begays' personal items. Phone calls were made to other groups as they proceeded to the shelters that were designed to protect two hundred people at each location for about sixty days. Before the groups could get settled in the shelters, the Colonel was ordered by this base commander to take the Raboy and Begay group back home.

The Colonel explained to Raboy it was a horrible military decision by India and China to allow two small non-thermo nuclear devices to be discharged before a truce was negotiated. After an all clear was given to the Colonel escorted the group back to the Begay's ranch house. Once the Begays and Raboys had been safely taken back to the ranch house the Marine nuclear rescue squad departed back to the Yuma, Arizona US Marine base.

"Well, it appears the worst is over," said Raboy.

"Let's thank the Lord with Psalms for keeping the world safe for one more day," said Abigail.

It was near evening so the Begays and Raboys decided to build a large bonfire so they could relax from the intense experience. Little

Daniel Jeremiah, his three nieces and several Begay children roasted pinion nuts while the adults talked about the close call. David dosed off while listening to Abel talk about the sheep and corn that he needed to attended, too.

"Rabbi, Rabbi," a familiar voice kept calling him while he was fast asleep sitting in Danny's favorite Kennedy rocker, "Rabbi, this is only the beginning. We have taken shelter in the deep caves of the sacred mountains only a few miles from our out station," said the faint voice, "Rabbi, it is I. Talk to me Rabbi because I can hear you," said the voice over, and over very softly.

Raboy jumped to his feet and looked around for a second and then returned to the rocker and closed his eyes. Abigail noticed David talking in his sleep, asking questions, and then answering his own questions. She listened as he said that he understood that preparation must be made for the worst because a major battle between two Asian nations would be the beginning of Mother Earth's sorrows. He was only out for about five to ten minutes when he jumped to his feet again, this time startling Abigail.

"I must talk to the President right away," said Raboy.

"I will try to call him," said his brother.

"How are you going to call him when he is buried under a billion tons of earth?" asked Abigail.

"What are you thinking, Rabbi? We can't possibly do that," burst out Ronnie.

"We have no choice in the matter. This is the most urgent message I have ever received. If I have to drive to Colorado, I am going. This is the information the President has been seeking. I am going, so whoever is going, load up," said Raboy.

The entire Raboy families drove off that night. Insane as it may have been, they were Colorado-bound to speak directly to the President. They drove all night and arrived the next morning at the Cheyenne Mountain main gate. They were halted by two heavily armed military police. The guards gave Raboy a difficult time and even threatened to shoot the entire family if they did not leave the facility at once. Raboy jumped up and down yelling until one guard pointed his rifle at him. Raboy was distraught and ready to leave when the Colonel of the

Marine nuclear rescue squad recognized him on the security system. He decided to come topside and see what the Rabbi wanted. After a brief conversation with the Rabbi, the Colonel hastily escorted the Raboys down to the inner chambers where the President could be contacted at the S.T.B.

"Mr. President, I have received a message from Yirawala," said the Rabbi.

"Rabbi, we already know what you are going to say. Both nations are prepared to launch over five thousand thermonuclear weapons at one another. All of the Russian commanders have been ordered to move their military personnel out of harms way. Some of the Russian citizens in Siberia living close the China borders are being evacuated as we speak. This will totally rock the world. May God help mankind now," said the President.

The Rabbi was taken to a briefing room to watch the destruction that may take place which would be displayed on a digital crystal screen. He watched the enormous screen display a HD tape provided by the International Space Link. He learned from the director that the Space Link had been ordered to send signals directly to Britain, Australia, France, Russia, and the United States STB simultaneously. Being permitted to watch the giant screens in the top secret chambers the Raboys could see the computer lights flash and record hit, after hit, after hit throughout eastern Asia.

The United States military was on full nuclear military defense mode. They started to constantly communicate with the British, German, Japanese, French, Russian, Chinese, Indian, and Australian governments. Raboy was informed that Israel and many other Middle-eastern nations were stunned by the Asian nations' actions. Radical Moslems quickly realized how idiotic and futile their terrorist's actions had been. Some Muslim groups in Pakistan called for all out peace, but instead were hit by some of the Indian thermonuclear devices, which destroyed many of their cities. In China and India, city after city collapsed from the massive destructive force generated by the multi-megaton hydrogen bombs. NORAD IV knew every nation around the world would soon be shocked and confused as to what to do, including the United States of America.

"Ambassador, your Prime Minister is on the B-line," said the three-star Air Force General.

"Minister, this is Jeremiah Raboy," he responded with dignity, "Yes, minister. Yes, minister. Yes, minister. I can and will do that, Sir. Good-bye Sir, Shalom," said the Ambassador in Hebrew, as he hung up the phone.

"What was that all about?" asked the General.

"He told me to stay put. He told me that I will be the supreme commander of the Israeli military if our leadership succumbs to any nuclear fallout or war against my nation," he replied.

"Mankind has finally done it. We have finally done it. We have finally managed to destroy ourselves because of our greed," said the General over, and over, as he and the others watched flash after flash on the monitors.

Many foreign voices talked faster and faster as fear overcame them. The sorrow in their voices deepened as the thermonuclear exchanges hit some of their own cities. The people that were destroyed in the days of the Noah, and Sodom and Gomorrah must have had experienced a similar horror—total destruction of the land, people, and environment. "When the ice comet broke open and hit Earth, the flood gates from hell destroyed every human being, plant, and animal not aboard the Ark. When the fire and brimstone rained down on Sodom and Gomorrah, all things were destroyed. Now India and China had started the end of the present age of the entire Mother Earth," thought Raboy.

"It is written that man's flesh will burn off their body and the eyes will melt in their sockets. It is a horrible thing for those experiencing the mini solar explosions that are raining down terror upon their cities, families and friends," cried out Raboy.

Abigail fell to her knees and started crying out of control. "Abigail, this is not the time to break down. Please be strong because the world needs your precious help," said the general with tears bursting out from his eyes.

"Mr. President, we must leave to protect our American family," said Abigail over the intercom system between the Cheyenne Mountain and the STB.

"Go with Godspeed. I will send a military squad to protect you. Please, keep in contact with us. A military crew assigned to protect you will have a phone that will contact me directly," said President Cleghorn, bowing his head in disbelief.

"Mr. President, not to be factious, but I beg your pardon, but how can your military protect us from thermonuclear explosions and their fallout? Really, if a hydrogen nuclear bomb is overhead and ready to explode, we are in dire straights. What will they be protecting us from?" asked Raboy.

"Rabbi, there are many things that could happen to you besides being blasted to undistinguishable bits and pieces. Please, let me handle my job and take care of you. Why do you keep asking me foolish questions? We may need your help in the future. Now go do what you need to do and pray the Lord will protect you," remarked President Cleghorn.

Mr. Kent persuaded Raboy to wait around to see the first nuclear exchange results. Raboy explained how it was something he would rather not do, but after thinking about his family's safety, he realized this time Mr. Kent was telling the truth and hung around for awhile longer to see what would happen next.

CHAPTER EIGHT:

KILLER RAIN

Quietly sitting in a large oval dimly lit projection room, surrounded by twelve digital screens, Mr. Norton waited for conformation from the ISL (International Space Link). Being a reticent man, Mr. Norton did not make a sound as he studied the incoming data. The insipid signals blinked on and off repetitively on each screen first red then green. Mr. Norton turned his head to the number seven screen as it started playing an ungodly site.

"Mr. President," yelled Michael Norton, "We have the latest video tapes of the nuclear theater's devastation. As you know the ISL has been sending updates every eighty-nine minutes, but this time we are really receiving horrible news. This is man at his worst," said Mr. Norton.

Joshua sat there pondering what had happened, unknowingly biting his fingernails to the quick. He stared at the walls looking into the unknown. He could only imagine the extent of collateral damage caused by the Asian nuclear holocaust. As he walked in the room the five minutes of film appeared surreal to him. He was unable to fathom what could have possibly gone wrong to cause this Asian T-War in the first place. Josh's spirit cried out for the innocent victims but was too physically stunned to outwardly expose his emotions. He kept quiet and thought about how greedy and evil man is.

Rabbi David Raboy walked into the projection room. He stopped when he noticed the President of the United States fixed in a catatonic state. Raboy started to say something but hesitated, wondering what caused the flamboyant President to freeze up. Then Raboy's son, Daniel Jeremiah ran into the room toward his father and yelling that startled everyone. The group started gossiping among themselves, breaking the cold silence that gripped everyone that had been concentrating on the surreal videos. Raboy embraced his son by putting his arms around him and hugged him very gently.

"Daddy, when are we going home? Why I we go outside? I want to go hiking on the reservation with grandma Sarah like you promised me," demanded the five year old.

"We cannot at the moment, son, because we have to meet with some very special people," replied Rabbi Raboy trying to answer his son's question and at the same time avoiding telling him the awful truth. He stared at his son thinking about his innocence and wondered what kind of future he would have to grow up and live in.

"Daddy, I thought Grandpa Danny was special people," replied little Daniel innocently.

"He is very special and we will see him very soon but at the moment you must be quiet while I meet with the President of America."

"Okay, Daddy. Oh, look Daddy, they are playing some movies," yelled out Danny.

Raboy looked about and saw everyone in the subterranean shelter staring at him, which made him uncomfortable. Looking over his left shoulder he noticed that Norton had brought in several new discs of data to be played on the satellite link video equipment.

"Oh good, there are more movies to watch," yelled out Daniel.

"No, young man, these are some special Digital Video Discs sent to us from the Space Link," replied Michael Norton trying to correct the child's thinking.

"Daddy, can I watch these movies from the Spacer Link?" asked little Daniel.

Raboy did not respond to his son's question as he looked on with concern. The videos revealed mankind at his worst. Everyone watched the clips for about twenty minutes that showed several major cities of India and China being complete obliterated from the nuclear blasts. Japan, Mongolia, Vietnam, Thailand, Iran, Pakistan, Cambodia, Siberia,

Afghanistan, and Korea were the first countries inundated with massive amounts of radioactive fallout.

The nuclear radioactive dust clouds blanketed entire nations blackening their skies, eradicating life instantly where the poison nuclear dust overtook the normal atmosphere. The last clip showed a five thousand mile long cloud of dust and debris hovering over a large section of the Pacific Ocean that appeared to be heading toward the Hawaii Islands. Mr. Norton informed the group that Hawaii Islands would most likely be engulfed by the lethal clouds.

Raboy walked over to little Daniel and squatted down in front of him. He put his arm around him and told him he was sorry that men could live and peace. He then attempted to explain to his son what had and was taking place. Raboy rambled on trying to explain to his son how humans throughout time have resorted to war to resolve their disagreements and disputes. Then he stopped speaking to his son realizing he did not have enough experience with life to understand what had just taken place. Raboy slowly got up and walked over to the oval table, and then proceeded to address the well protected government elite.

"You can see that these videos were not really created for children to view. But since it is reality, in which, not only my child but all children must live with for the rest of their lives these films need to be preserved. It would only make sense that all children living Mother Earth would benefit by seeing these clips over, and over again about what just happened to Mother Earth. Whether their lives are short or long it must be made mandatory worldwide for every child obliterated by this nightmare to learn about this day and never forget the horror unleashed on Mother Earth by man's arrogance. If the Earth ever recovers from this Asian T-War, we must make provisions to prevent this insanity from ever happening again. If there is a planet left for us to live on," said Raboy filled with grief by the massive death and destruction he had witnessed.

Little Daniel turned his head toward his father and yelled as he pointed to the giant monitor that displayed a humongous thermonuclear explosion. Abigail had seen enough of man's hateful ways so she quickly picked up her son and took him out of the room. She. Her heart burned with sorry knowing that she may never be able to see Israel again. Emotionally confused she sat there and cried her heart out. She asked Raboy if they could leave so she could be with her Arizona Native American family, the Begays.

David and Abigail Raboy immediately decided to leave the compound and return to the Hopi reservation to be with Danny and Sarah Begay. The President and the top brass of the White House, Congress, and Pentagon pleaded with them to stay at the shelter, but they refused. As far as Raboy was concerned, nothing the government told him had any merit or foundation.

They left the environmental protected area provided by the Black Mountain II Colorado Subterranean shelter and headed for the four corner region of the United States. Raboy had been educated by the Marine Nuclear Rescue Colonel that the Presidential shelter had been designed to accommodate about a hundred people to survive a nuclear war for two to three years. Since he knew many secrets about the shelter, he had to swear to secrecy the shelter's location to anyone outside of the Black Mountain II compound. President Cleghorn took the time to explain to Raboy that there had to be a secret place designed to protect federal government leaders from any disaster being nuclear war or otherwise that would keep the government functioning. He explained this was done so that law and order would prevail and there would be someone to turn off the war. After being briefed, Raboy trekked back to Northern Arizona.

Upon arriving at the Begay's humble home, Rabbi David rushed in and told them to immediately gather up their most important belongings and prepare for the worst. In light of what was happening to Mother Earth, he explained that they would have to forego their home and animals. Sarah and Danny hurried once they understood exactly what had taken place in Asia.

Three hundred and forty two Native Americans had originally believed Sarah and Raboy's report. The alarm was sent out by each person calling two others to leave what they were doing and run for safety. Those fleeing to the shelter were mostly Native Americans of the Havasupai, Navajo, Apache, Pima, Hopi, and Sioux tribes accompanied by twelve Jews, fourteen White Mormons, and twenty one members of the Page, Arizona Christian Church. Approximately four hundred souls quickly entered the shelters carved deep into the Arizona section of the Rocky Mountains.

One of the shelters was constructed in one of the caves near the San Francisco Peaks mountain range north of Flagstaff, Arizona. The shelter's air was filtered by an organic material made from the Ponderosa Pine trees and some US Army nuclear dust filters. A hand pump had been fitted to a natural spring for fresh water. A portable windmill was cleverly hidden on the mountain top to supply power for their personal electrical needs, short wave radio, and satellite uplink. It took twenty-two hours for everyone to reach the shelters and seal them off. They were kept informed by the federal subterranean presidential shelter via a stellar band radio signal when the radioactive clouds would reach the Western portion of North America continent. Many scientists feared, it would engulf the entire west coasts of Mexico, Canada, and USA states first then continue on through Arizona, Nevada, and then the entire North American continent.

"What do we do now?" asked the Hopi Chief.

"Wait and pray. Maybe the Lord of all creation might have mercy on us," replied Rabbi Raboy.

"The mountains will protect us from any disaster man has brought upon himself," said Sarah.

"Do you think the Whiteman is being paid back for disturbing the spirits of our fathers?" asked Miguel.

"No," she replied.

"Why do you say no?" asked Miguel.

"Because all mankind has forgotten how to respect Mother Earth. We have been blessed for thousands of years because our ancestors protected the environment. Now we are being tested by our creator. Hopefully, he will give us a chance to redeem ourselves if we live through this 'Purification'. Hopefully we can rebuild and repopulate Mother Earth after the last day of her purification. Out of ashes we will have to rebuild and learn from our mistakes. What once was will never be again," said Sarah knowing that the world would never be the same again.

"Does anyone know what to do when the storm arrives?" asked Ronnie.

"Yes, there is nothing to do but wait it out. We have hundreds of videos, musical tapes, and video games for entertainment. Plus, we have to prepare food by the schedule everyone agreed on," said Chief Blackcloud.

"Where is Abel and his family?" asked Rabbi Raboy.

"They are stuck in the road that was washed out. His truck does not have four-wheel drive like your all terrain vehicle," said Danny Begay.

"Then I'll have to go get him," said the Rabbi.

"I can go," said Ronnie.

"No, the insurance on the rented vehicle only covers me as the driver. I must be the one," replied the Rabbi.

"Insurance, ha, ha. What insurance company will give you thermonuclear waste coverage?" asked Ronnie laughing at Raboy.

"Sweetie, please be careful?" asked Abigail.

"Sweetheart, don't worry. The clouds are still a few hours away. I should be Abel to make it down the road and back in a few minutes," replied David.

The Rabbi had only left for a few minutes seeking Abel when he encountered a blinding thunder storm. The powerful storm confused the Rabbi to such an extent that he could not tell which road to take. The washed out muddy roads were void of road signs because they had been swept away by the flood waters caused by the severe torrential rain. He drove around for about two hours and then decided to call Abel using his cell phone. Abel told him he had already made it to the shelter. Lost, Raboy asked for directions to the shelter. At the moment he panicked when a major nuclear dust cloud hit Arizona sooner than the experts had predicted.

His surprise encounter with a possible lethal situation caused the Rabbi to start shaking from head to toe. He stopped the vehicle to put on a radiation suit that had been issued to him by the US Army along with some other nuclear fallout safety supplies. He looked like an astronaut dressed in a cream-colored protection gear. As he zipped up the last part of the suit the deadly cloud completely encompassed him, raining large hot radioactive drops of water everywhere. Raboy started yelling, calling the moisture killer rain. Every raindrop was a mixture of water and radioactive nuclear dust. He jumped around foolishly trying to dodge the rain drops.

As the Rabbi jumped back inside the all terrain vehicle, he grabbed a Geiger counter that was given to him by General Freetag before he left Cheyenne Mountain II. When he turned on the Geiger counter, it started singing louder and louder as the nuclear dust cloud thickened and the radioactive fallout intensified. David Raboy spotted a cave near the road and decided to make a run for it to minimize his exposure to the radioactive storm. Frantically he tried to call his wife and Abel on the cell phone, but all of the signals were knocked out due to the magnetic field created by the black clouds. He became a nervous wreck as he thought about dying from the effects of the nuclear fallout mixed with rain he started calling it Killer Rain.

He stopped running once he entered the mouth of the cave. His heart pounded from the fear the had overtaken his senses. It pounded even more thinking about what creatures he might encounter in the cave. He prayed to the Lord for his safety before ventured any deeper into the cave. He tightly gripped the survival kit in his left hand and a flashlight in his right. He took off running in such haste he had forgotten about the car keys which would haunt him later.

It was so dark outside and in the cave he could not tell if was day and night. The thick clouds smothered the sun and totally blacked out the moon and stars. He sat in the cave, intermittently using his flashlight for several hours trying to safe the power supply while waiting for the dust cloud and stormy weather to clear up. The Killer Rain had virtually paralyzed him. He sat there helplessly praying as he waited for Mother Earth to break free from the bonds of the thermonuclear dust cloud.

A day later, the life threatening clouds continued to mask the sun to the point that it appeared to be a dim red ball. Night was even more frightening to Raboy because the radioactive clouds tinted the night skies pitch black.

On the third day of the killer rain, a coyote stumbled into the cave and lay down on the cave floor only twenty feet away from him. Raboy could not help but notice that the coyote was completely covered by the thermonuclear radioactive dust. It appeared to him that the coyote was already sick from eating, drinking, and breathing radioactive particles that had engulfed everything. Raboy decided to nurse the weakened animal, although he knew the coyote would die very soon from some form of nuclear disease created by the Indo-China T-War.

He walked near the coyote and pitched him some of the beef jerky that was part of his survival kit supplies. Then he poured him some fresh water in a rock shaped like a cup near the coyote's head. "Hey little fellow, this isn't much, but I am willing to share it with you since you are my only companion in this desolate place," said the worried Rabbi.

The coyote watched him as he lay the food down and backed off. The coyote sniffed the food and water before picking up a piece of the beef jerky to chew on. Raboy repeated his actions three times that day. Each time the coyote took a drink of water, ate the morsel of food, and then lay down back on the sandy cave floor to rest.

After a couple of days for no logical reason Raboy decided tied the coyote outside to a tree next to the cave. Raboy felt it was cruel but deemed it necessary to warn to warn him if any other predator came around. After he tied up the coyote he tried to call his family again on the satellite cell phone. He figured since the killer rain cloud had subsided to some degree he could get through to the shelter. The cell phone did not work this time because the battery was dead. The Rabbi left the cave toward his vehicle when he realized the phone had to be charged. He figured he could plug the phone into the cigarette lighter adapter for a few moments and it would work again. Since the Geiger counter's intense beeping had decreased, Raboy felt safe wearing his radiation suit on his trek back to the truck. He was please to find that the sky looked nothing like it did when the black cloud first filled the air with nuclear charged particles that had completely engulfed Mother Earth. "What is this? What do I see? It looks like the stars. No!

It can't be! I must be hallucinating from the foul stench in the air. Hell, I'm not sure what day it is or where I am at. I can see trees and grass dimly lit, but that must be from starlight because objects contaminated by nuclear radiation don't glow in the dark. Yes, I know what stars look like. It's only been one week since the killer rain came over the land. Maybe, just maybe, Mother Earth has cooled off because these intense clouds appear to have broken up," said David talking to the coyote.

He then started talking to himself. For some strange reason that he did not understand, he kept the coyote tied to the tree next to his campfire. Although he felt it was not the right thing to do, he did it anyway. His first thought was that the coyote would, hopefully, keep other animals away from his camp, but then again he thought it odd that he had not seen any other animals. The Rabbi started repeatedly conversing and singing to himself in an attempt to curb his boredom and ease his fears.

"Alright, I've had enough of this talking to an animal. I might as well be talking to a rock or tree. I think I am going crazy, but there is no one around to tell me. Does not there have to be someone to tell you if you are crazy or not? Oh Lord, I can still feel the Earth shaking under my feet or is it that my feet shaking while I stand in fear on Mother Earth? Who cares? I cannot remember seeing the sun for the last time. I cannot really recall what took place because it scared me so much my memory is blank. Oh, I am lying to you. I damn well know what happened. You cannot lie to a survivor. Only the dead can be fooled or those idiots that live in large cities," said David, as he burst out into a mad laughter, falling to the ground.

He tried to get back on his feet but was so grieved it was like watching someone too intoxicated to stand upright. Then he turned his head and looked into the sky and closed his eyes to block out the bright sunrays. It was hard for him to look into the sky because his eyes were swollen from crying so much. He cried often thinking that he would never see his family again.

"God Almighty, I'm not ready to give up and die. I'm your child and you are my father, Lord, am I not your representative here on Mother Earth? If this is so, where is my protector? Why have you abandoned me? Yes, there are stars shining tonight. Okay, not a sky full but there are a few to let me know the universe is still alive. What do the stars have to with Mother Earth being alive anyway? The real question that I must ask you, Mr. Coyote is, what is life and what is death? Do not answer me. I do not want to know at this particular point. Why you ask? Well, because it really does not matter," said David being distraught from his dire situation.

Then, out of nowhere, Raboy heard a voice of someone crying out.

"Hello, Hello! I am Mark James of Pocatello, Idaho," screamed a distant voice.

It sounded like a human voice that came from someone struggling. David's heart rushed with joy thinking it may be a survivor that was familiar with this part of the Coconino National Forest. He figured if it were so, he could help him find his bearing to get back to the shelter.

Rabbi David Raboy ran over to see who the survivor was that endured the Killer Rain. As the Rabbi approached the stranger, he shouted vehemently one more time, and then found the most comfortable place he could find on Mother Earth lay down. He groaned one more time and gave up his ghost. Raboy peered at the lifeless body knowing that all of his earthly possessions were of no use to him anymore. Raboy did what he felt was right and buried Mark James with some tree branches and rocks. Being overcome with fear that he may die soon after burying the dead man, Raboy sat on the ground silently.

David was so emotionally upset and exhausted from the whole ordeal he fell asleep near the dead man's grave. Only moments after he had closed his eyes, the coyote he had tied to the tree cried out with an ear piercing howl that rattled the Rabbi. Startled he jumped to his feet looking in all directions trying to grasp the situation. Being only few minutes before dawn he strained his eyes trying to find out why the coyote was howling.

Stilled startled not being able to see anything, he walked over to an opening in the forest and gazed at the heavens. He was happy and surprised to see a few visible stars that dimly lit the smoke filled dawn sky. He jumped with joy as tears ran down his face. He grabbed the nearest pine tree and hugged it like someone would hug a loved one they had not seen for a very long time. Thoughts raced through his head that he was having a nervous breakdown. He immediately fell to the ground, curled up in the fetal position and grabbed his knees with both hands. He lay there motionlessly for a few minutes looking stars that were quickly fading away. Their power was rapidly being overcome by the earth's master light. He lay there, shaking, until the stars had totally disappeared. Before the sun could show its full glory, a black gloomy radioactive cloud swallowed the sky changing brightness of the sun to a mere dim red glow.

After laying on the ground for a couple of hours Rabbi David Raboy hunger pains blocked out his morbid thoughts. His entire body was crying out for some food. He got up and pillaged through the dead mans belongings. His hunger overcame his will power to resist the temptation of eating something forbidden as he grabbed a can of pork and beans. He began his Ultra Orthodox ritual to bless the food and ask for forgiveness while he prepared to nourish his weary body.

As he blessed the can of food, he wiped the can clean with a handful of leaves he had gathered from the ground. Next, he walked over to a small creek filled with nuclear waste floating down the creek. He thought for a moment and starting washing off any contaminates that may have been on the can of life saving nourishment. After dipping the can of food in the contaminated creek he slowly walked back to the place where the dead man had found his final resting place. With the radioactive water dripping off of his protective gloves opened the can of beans. He started to eat the food but hesitated and decided to read it contents.

He carefully read the label of the ingredients printed on the can of beans. After pondering for a moment, he gave thanks to the creator of all things, and then gave half of the can of food to his captured coyote. After giving the coyote the beans, he counted down for quite a few minutes to see if the Coyote would get sick. He waited for a few minutes and sat the can of beans on the ground. Although he was very hungry, his conscientious forbid him from eating the pork and beans.

"Oh Yahweh, creator of all things in heavens and Earth, I know it is forbidden to speak your name out loud, but I am desperate. I pray I can say your name out loud since you are the only one that can hear me. Please, bless this can of pink chicken and beans to nourish my starved body." prayed the Rabbi. He called the pork "pink chicken" since he couldn't bear the fact that he may starve to death or eat the pork and be forever condemned by his fellow man and God. He decided that if he picked the pork fat out of the beans it would lighten the physical and spiritual damage to his body. He had been educated his entire life that pork was a forbidden food ordained by the creator, but his growling stomach was telling him to ignore his teachings.

After he had asked God to bless the food for the third time, he still couldn't force himself to eat it. Being disgusted as to what he was about to do he repented, and then decided to go back to where the hiker had died. He wanted to see if there was something else left in his backpack he could possibly eat. Raboy's body was weak and felt that he desperately needed some nourishment if he was going to stay alive for one more day. Searching through the dead man's backpack one more time he found some cheese crackers with peanut butter filling. He immediately ate the tasty crackers trying to satisfy his hunger. Raboy ate the twelve peanut butter filled cheese crackers praising God with every bite. Thanking the Almighty supply him with some of the best tasting food he had ever eaten. Being satiated he went back over to the coyote's makeshift water bowl and relieved his bladder.

"David, you are becoming a sick man," he said yelling out into the forest.

"Well, Mr. Jensen, I've always wanted to do this but never really had the nerve," said Raboy as he laughed out loud making no sense with his one-sided conversation.

He then fell to his knees and started to cry out to the Lord. He then turned to the coyote and told him it wasn't his fault but he had to test his body fluids somehow. The coyote paid no attention to David and ate the rest of the can of beans. David then turned to the coyote and tried to explain why he didn't give him any fresh water because it had been contaminated by the Killer Rain. He slowly walked away from the coyote back toward the direction of the dead man.

"Well, do I bury you deep into the ground or let the coyotes eat your corpse before I trek back to the safety of the caves? Really all I want is to be where my loved ones are, hopefully, they are safe and sound. You don't have to understand what I am telling you. I know no one particularly gives a damn what is going on out here. Oh, if you don't mind, I would like to take your backpack with me to take it inside the cave. I am asking you earnest dignity so you won't think I am trying to steal your property without permission. I am not a thief by any means." He picked up the dead man's belongings and went back inside the cave.

He plundered the backpack by dumping its contents out on the cave's rocky soil. He discovered two cans of drinking water, three packages of dehydrated foods, and seven milk chocolate chip cookies. Raboy smiled looking at all of the eatable foods. Then at once he picked up a pine tree branch and approached the coyote.

He raised the stick very carefully to strike the coyote if it attempted to attack. The coyote just lay there looking at the Rabbi, as if to say kill me or let me go free because I really don't care. David loosened the snare to set the coyote free. He slowly backed away from the coyote with the stick raised up ready for defense against any attack.

The coyote slowly got up and bowed his head toward David as if he was showing his respect to the Rabbi. Nervous, David didn't take any chances holding the stick ready to hit the wild canine. The coyote walked about ten feet away from it was tied to the tree, turned his head slowly to look at Raboy, and then turned to walk away. All at once the coyote turned into a brilliant light and vanished into thin air. The Rabbi was in shock thinking had finally went over the edge. He was not sure if he was starting to hallucinate or it was real. He walked over to the tree where he had tied up the coyote and found some of the coyote's hair on the rope. This was too much for him to take. Now he was confused without boundaries.

He shook his head in disbelief and ran to the Tahoe he had abandoned earlier. After opening the door and getting inside of the truck he noticed another problem. While running to find some shelter from the radioactive dust clouds he had left the ignition turned on. Although the battery was nearly dead he immediately turned off the ignition. He then tried to make a cell phone call but the phone needed a charged battery. He started searching for the his spare phone batteries. There they were in the glove box. Still in shock he wondered if they had kept their charge after being exposed to the magnetic field created by the radioactive clouds. He prayed out loud that they still charged enough to make a phone call. He searched throughout the truck but couldn't find his phone.

Rabbi David stood there confused and upset as what to do next. His mind was now so jumbled up he couldn't think as what to do. It was apparent to Rabbi Raboy that he would never find his family again. He sat in the Tahoe seat for a couple of hours thinking about his purpose for being on earth. He figured, since the hell fire and brimstone didn't take his life, then the Lord must have other plans for him. After crying out to the Lord for mercy, the Rabbi got up and decided to go back to the cave. Then, he heard his cell phone ring. He yelled out Hallelujah several times before he found his phone lying on the passenger's floor board. Picking up the phone he answered it as he had done all of his life.

"Hello, Shalom," said the Rabbi.

"Sweetie, is that you?" asked the beautiful voice muffled by static.

"Sweetheart, you are alive," he replied crying.

"Sweetie, you are alive," she replied crying.

"Is Daniel alright?" asked the Rabbi, feeling a warm rush throughout his body.

"We are all fine. Abel said that...We thought you were... oh, I'm so glad to hear your wonderful voice," she said with a sigh of relief. Then the signal dropped and they lost contact.

The Rabbi desperately tried to start the truck to charge the cell phone, but the truck battery was too weak. Not being able to start the truck he decided to lift the hood and see if there was something he could do. That moment the hood opened a big smile gripped his face. He looked to the heavens and praised Yahweh many times. He knew it was a miracle that some engineer at General Motors had designed this particular truck with a spare battery. All Raboy had to do was figure out how to exchange it for the dead one. He looked around for a moment and went back to the driver's seat and sat down. He then praised God again for another miracle because he found the switch from one battery source to the other. Raboy jumped for joy and praised the Lord over since the spare battery was fully charged.

This time when he pushed the switch, the engine started. He left not looking back as to what he may have left behind. He drove around aimlessly searching for the road to take him back to the shelter. After finding his way he decided to stop and take off the radiation suit. As he took off the suit he noticed that his arms had some red spots. This made him very nervous because he realized at that moment that may have had suffered some from of radiation exposure. He was frightened to think that the rest of his body might not have been protected enough by the twenty-five pound radiation suit.

Rabbi Raboy started thinking about his past experiences over that last few months. What struck him the most was that the being of light that he had encountered during his supernatural experience never mentioned anything about him having to experience any personal hardships. But here he was having one extreme situation after another. He then recalled how the coyote disappeared as a flash of light, the stranger with food and water, and the spare truck battery. At that very moment, Raboy knew that he had been protected by the Almighty, but for what purpose when millions humans were dead or dying throughout the world due to the Asian T-war.

He got back into the truck and drove to the fallout shelter. He was thankful that much of the landscape hadn't changed from the storm, except it was covered with grayish dust. The washed out roads had the markings made by Abel to guide him to the shelter. He finally made it to the fallout shelter built carved into the mountain side. He felt a sigh of relief when he saw Abigail's face knowing his family and friends had been protected from the killer rain, too.

"Oh my Sweetie, you are alive and well," cried out Abigail, as she ran to hug her beloved husband.

"Stay back, Abigail, until we have decontaminated your husband," ordered the Marine Colonel. Raboy motioned for her to keep away until he had removed the rest of the contaminated radiation suit and washed off any lethal debris.

"I must hug him, and kiss him, and hold him, I must," she cried.

"Abigail, my dear friend, come with me until your husband has been made safe for all of us to give him a big hug," said Sarah Begay.

About two hours later, Raboy entered the living quarters of the shelter. Abigail grabbed hold of him and wouldn't let go. He would go here and she was there. He would go there and she would still be glued to his side.

"Sweetheart, may I please sit down and rest for a moment? I am exhausted and my nerves are fried from fear. Please, let me rest for a couple of hours," pleaded the Rabbi.

"Sweetie, I am never going to let you go anywhere again by yourself," she said as she sat next to him. She watched him fall asleep in seconds since he was totally exhausted from his unique experience. Rabbi Raboy smiled as he went into a deep sleep knowing that he had tried and tested beyond his endurance and survived.

The next morning the communication system hooked up to one of the satellite networks that kept broadcasting death and destruction throughout the world. The network showed video tapes of China and India being blasted by numerous thermonuclear explosions. It showed destruction upon destruction of cities instantly laid to waste. One could only imagine the many multi-trillions of dollars of collateral damage and billions of lives lost.

It was horrifying to see the millions upon millions of people dead while others were dying because of serious radiation burns. Thousands of victims where being treated in makeshift trauma areas. The suffering of innumerable innocent humans as a result of man's greediness and distorted actions was gruesome. Every communication network had been disrupted except for the space linked news station that kept airing the same story over and over again.

"Abel, this radiation should die out in another two weeks, yes? I don't think we really should leave this shelter until then, but one of us needs to drive to Flagstaff, Tuba City, or Page to find out what actually happened to Arizona," said Daniel the Hopi Chief.

"Chief, you do understand that the one that leaves should come back here in secret. If there is a food shortage or crazy people seeking shelter, we might be attacked. This might be a one way mission for the one that leaves here," said Abel.

"Who cares? We have enough food here to last a thousand people for about two years. Plus, we have the US Marines to guard us," said Ronnie.

"Ronnie, do you really want to stay in this cave for two years?" asked Rabbi Raboy.

"No, but where else in the world can we go?" asked Ronnie.

"If this is only the beginning of Mother Earth's sorrows, we'll need a place to hide out. I am sad to say that greater disasters than this will come upon the Earth if the Aborigine, Hopi, and Hebrew prophecies are correct," replied the Rabbi.

"What do we do?" asked the Chief.

"We shall stay here, but someone has to find out what is going on throughout the world. This television broadcast is only confusing us more. We need to find out the truth about the state of Mother Earth," said Abigail.

As Abigail spoke three black military helicopters landed near the shelter. Six, heavily armed marines were aboard each helicopter. The jumped out and ran to the shelter along with the same US Marine Colonel that had previously gone shopping with Abigail, and Ronnie in Tuba City, Arizona.

"Rabbi Raboy, and Ambassador Raboy, I am here to take you and your families to the Colorado Subterranean Shelter immediately," the Colonel barked out his orders.

"Colonel, how did you find this place?" asked Ambassador Raboy.

"Ambassador, please stop all of that childish questioning. Now get your belongings and get in the choppers pronto!" commanded the Colonel.

"How do we know the air is safe to breath?" asked the Rabbi.

"We don't, but that is not a problem because you will be wearing suits designed to protect you in these types of situations. Now, please, get dressed and get aboard immediately," ordered the Colonel.

"Chief Blackcloud, don't let anyone leave this shelter until I come back. I will come back with the proper information to let you know when it is safe to go home.," said Mario Martinez, the US Marine general in charge of the operation.

"We will assign two men that are equipped with military satellite radio space links along with an array of weapons, to protect everyone in this shelter," said the Colonel.

Rabbi and Ambassador Raboy, along with their respective families, suited up to be taken to the United States Federal Nuclear Fallout Subterranean Shelter. They were briefed during the trip about the death tolls and collateral damage caused by the Indo-China nuclear T-War. Japan had over sixty million dead and Korea had twenty million dead from the radioactive killer rain that had completely engulfed both nations.

It had been calculated by the Department of Defense that over six hundred million Indian and one billion Chinese people were affected by the thermonuclear exchange while millions around the world were suffering from consequences by the blasts or radiation trauma. Raboy was informed that both nations were in total chaos as their people desperately attempted to find food and medical care. It was reported that many nations offered medical care for the sick and injured people but had a difficult time getting the much needed supplies to their destinations.

The ISL had videoed the entire nuclear theater as it occurred. It was surreal to look at what man had done to himself in only a few hours. The Ambassador of Israel tried to contact the Prime Minister of Israel but could not because of the extensive damage to the world wide communication systems. After the craft arrived and landed safely, the Raboys were taken directly to the secret S.T.B. White House.

"Mr. President, what are we here for this time?" asked the Rabbi.

"I was going to ask you the same question," replied the President.

"I have no idea of what to tell you. I'm confused as you are," responded the Rabbi.

"Rabbi, we really need for Sarah Begay, Yirawala, and you to communicate amongst one another to see if the supernatural has any answers for us," said Harry.

"You must be kidding? I can only give you information that the Almighty wants you to have. This mess was created by mankind, so the way I figure it, we will have to live with this and fix it ourselves. All we can do now is ask the Lord for his blessed mercy," replied Raboy.

"Do you have any information that may help us prepare for the future?" asked the President.

"No Sir, I don't. Are we able to go back to Israel yet?" asked the Rabbi.

"Rabbi, we aren't certain of anything yet, but you'll be the first to know. You can return to your Hopi friends for now. You must stay put," insisted General Freetag.

"Why can't we return to Israel?" asked the Ambassador.

"We need the Rabbi to advise us on what to do next," said General Freetag.

"Advise you on what?" asked Raboy.

"Rabbi, you are free to go or stay. We hoped you had some spiritual answers for us," said the President.

"Mr. President, we want to go to Israel," replied Raboy.

"Rabbi, that isn't possible for the moment, because no one is traveling anywhere at the present," barked out General Freetag.

The Raboy's were persuaded by the President to stay at the government shelter until it was deemed safe for them to travel. Everyone agreed that was the best thing to do.

CHAPTER NINE:

MAGNETIC WAVES

"Dr. Keller, what do you make of the eerie sounds that keep whistling through the air? These sounds are really starting to bother me. They are on every frequency of our communication matrix," said General Freetag as he tapped his pen on the desk.

"What sounds are you referring too?" he asked.

"You know what he's talking about. The sounds that have been irritating everyone ever since the Indo-China thermonuclear cloud blanketed the planet. It is driving everyone bonkers," replied the Officer of the Day, Colonel Bigwell.

"How on earth would I know that? I am just a scientist that has lost his world to a bunch of arrogant greedy idiotic war mongers. I'd like to find the idiots that created nuclear fission and fusion and nuke them," cursed Dr. Keller.

"That would be us. We detonated the first atomic bomb first," replied Colonel Bigwell.

"I don't mean those that created the bombs that will be used to give rise for the abomination of desolation. I mean the dumb-ass that told everyone and his brother how to build and acquire them. What the hell were they thinking?" asked Dr. Keller.

"Doctor, regardless of your emotional challenges, we need to find out what the whistling sound is and soon. There may be other serious side affects of the nuclear war besides death and destruction. What if the world's delicate balance has been disrupted?" said General Freetag.

In walked, President Cleghorn.

"Mr. President, good morning. We face a weird problem. A rather disturbing high frequency noise is disrupting our com devices. We need your authorization to check it out," explained General Freetag.

"Don't bother yourselves. I know what it is," said President Cleghorn.

"Can you find a place in the bottom of your heart to tell the rest of us who are running the national defense systems what's going on?" asked the angry General.

"General Freetag, why are you being so irate?" asked the President.

"Mr. President, the world is not only glowing from the nuclear radiation dust and killer rain, but now it is singing to us. It would be comforting to know who or what is causing these eerie sounds, sir."

"General Freetag, what you are hearing is the over charged cosmic particles affecting the earth's magnetic flux lines. The magnetic flux that touches the Earth is generated by the A & B Plasma belts that protect Earth from solar wind and dust. No one knows the extent of damage that has been done or what affects it will have now or later or when it will end. So with that knowledge, what do you suggest? How do we defend ourselves and our nation against it?" asked Dr. Khari, a tall thin physicist that had briefed the president earlier.

"Commander, our military jets are dropping out of the sky as if they are being poisoned," said the radar technetium.

"What the hell are you talking about?" asked the General.

"General, our jets become dysfunctional above twenty thousand feet. Our pilots say that their electronic instruments freeze up and the engines loose power and stall. They have reported that the electronic systems and controls go berserk making the aircraft uncontrollable. Most of the pilots say that at fifteen thousand feet everything still works fine. After that, they have no alternative but to bail out," replied the radar technetium.

"What about the commercial airlines?" asked the General.

"General Freetag, the FAA grounded all commercial and private aircraft days ago," replied the duty officer.

"Damn it to hell, what is going on? Why am I the last to know?" asked the General.

"General Freetag, there appears to be an abnormal magnetic disturbance due to the massive thermonuclear blasts," said Dr. Keller.

"How do we fix it?" asked the General.

"Waiting. We don't have any control over these new phenomena."

"Where is that Rabbi? His maps and visions foretold the future. Maybe the answer lies with him," said Dr. Keller.

"He is in the war room discussing his maps and notes with the secretary of defense at this very moment. He was watching the latest video report on the space link big screen," replied the Officer of the Day.

"Damn it! Find him so he can tell us what the hell is happening!" blasted the General.

The stressed, confused group marched to the communication center and started quizzing the Rabbi. It appeared to Raboy that the world's premier experts were now relying on the supernatural instead of their sophisticated technology to make logical decisions. It made Raboy nervous that the world leaders were depending on him too much for advice. He feared they might start making illogical executive decisions as how to protect what was left of Mother Earth.

"Rabbi, Ole buddy and pal, we have some questions. I hope you have some answers for us," burst out General Freetag.

"Excuse me, General," replied the Rabbi wondering what matter the general was referring to.

"Rabbi, we now have weird noises on every communication frequency channel. Plus, our high altitude aircraft are falling out of the sky. We would like to know if you can help us find a solution," he said.

President Cleghorn looked at Freetag square in the eyes.

"General, knock it off. What the hell are you doing? This Rabbi has given us every bit of information he has. He has forewarned us the best he could as to what was coming. Even General Wentworth from the Royal Navy told us this might happen. He is a guest here, not a member of the military or scientific staff. You act as though it is his fault that India and China nuked it out," said the President.

"Sorry, sir, and I do apologize. Hopefully, you understand that I am weary. I believe this could have been prevented, if the Americans would have intervened," he replied.

"How could we have prevented this mess? What should we have done? Nuke India or China first so the amount of damage would have been greater? General, we have been diligently studying the messages, maps, and notes. If you would stop trying to bully everyone around, you might learn something if you would take the time to listen for a single moment. We think this is only the beginning. After studying the supernatural messages in more detail, it appears that this is only a taste of the woes to come," responded the physics psychologist.

"Mr. President, are these idiots saying more nations are going to nuke it out? Oh hell, no one knows what is going on here. We are now depending on a bunch of psychic nitwits to answer our logical problems," said General Freetag throwing his hands in the air above his head as he left the room.

"Mr. President, why did you bring us here. Why didn't you just call us?" asked the Israeli Ambassador.

"I had you and your families brought here for your immediate safety," he replied.

"Aren't you somewhat late for that, Mr. President?" asked the Ambassador.

"No, I am not. Besides we really need the Rabbi's help with our worldwide management decision making. The Aborigine's drawings of the mushroom clouds that covered India and China were accurate. Needless to say, if we would have been more cunning and understood the situation, just maybe, the world would not be suffering today. No one ever has or had figured a thermonuclear war would ever start like this. Now we are worried about the aftermath and how it will all end. I hope this is not the beginning of our sorrows, but the climax of it all," said the President.

After they were escorted to their private rooms, he took the time to explain to his staff why they were brought to the top secret Colorado

Subterranean Shelter. The explanation stunned everyone there without any exceptions.

"Mr. President, the United States is still in one piece. If I recall, it has not dissolved yet. I feel safe to say that these maps and notes could be telling us something that is symbolic or an event that will take place far into future," said Dr. Keller.

"That is an interesting concept, but what you are not saying is what disturbs me the most, Dr. Keller. The predictions, prophecies, warnings, or whatever you want to call them, are not facts yet, but if this information is correct, how do we plan for what may come. How and when will the next phase take place is a question. A question no one can rightly answer yet, but we must consider what to do with the information that has been given to us," said the President.

"Two hundred top military, scientific, and political leaders have been huddled here for two months trying to decipher the data with no results," replied Dr. Keller.

General Freetag rushed in interrupting the Presidential meeting.

"We have received an urgent message from Professor Greenbaum. He says he needs to talk to Dr. Keller immediately," said Freetag.

Dr. Keller picked up the phone and turned on the speaker so the conversation would be heard by everyone at the meeting.

"Dr. Keller, it appears the death toll is still rising in Asia. At first, we thought it was leveling off, but we guessed wrong. You need to tell those government guys to come out of their holes and stop hiding like rats," said Dr. Greenbaum.

"People may still die from the fallout. With that in mind you still think they should return to their normal lives. Professor Greenbaum what you are saying is rather ridiculous," replied Dr. Keller as he hung up the phone. President Cleghorn left the room to find Raboy.

"Rabbi and Ambassador Raboy, we have been given the all clear signal to return to our homes and jobs. It appears the worst is over, except for the squelching in the lines of our communication systems. If you want to leave, it is up to you. We will escort or physically take you to anywhere you want to go in the United States," said the President.

"Mr. President, I would like to return to the Hopi reservation, so I can tell the Begay household what is going on. After a short stay in Arizona, I would like to return to my homeland, if that is possible?" requested the Rabbi.

Thus, the Raboy families went their separate ways. Colonel Bigwell took the Rabbi and his family to the same fallout shelter he had picked them up from two weeks prior. The Colonel. He was informed that not a single incident had taken place, except that everyone kept asking Mrs. Begay to make her delicious Indian Frye Bread.

"Danny, Sarah, Abel, Ronnie, and everybody, it is wonderful to find you all in good health," said Abigail hugging Sarah.

"We have prayed for your safety, as well as the Rabbi's," said one of the Christian leaders from Page, Arizona.

"Everyone, the most dangerous stage of the nuclear fallout has passed America and Europe. But there are still many nations with people sick and dying from the direct and indirect exposure to the nuclear fallout. I personally feel everyone here must take action to help those less fortunate. We have been blessed during this massive assault on Mother Earth," said the Rabbi.

Everyone held hands and gave thanks to the Lord for preparing them for what had came upon the earth so suddenly. Raboy and Sarah looked at one another for the edification. They both knew that this was only the beginning of the ancient prophecies that forewarned mankind what life would be like on Mother Earth for the next several years.

"Rabbi, we want you to join us in one last farewell. We would like to have a Pow-wow in your honor before you leave and head for your native land," said Ronnie Begay.

Ronnie never thought in his lifetime he would love another race like he loved the Raboy family. He felt as if they were blood kinfolks. Since the first day that Ronnie had met Raboy he become fond of the Rabbi. He felt that Raboy was not so different from himself. The feeling was mutual since the entire Begay and Raboy families had found a place in their hearts to love, cherish and adore one another since the killer rain.

The Pow-wow did not turn out to be as exciting as Ronnie Begay had hoped it would be because some of his mother's precious sheep had been killed by the killer rain. Plus, the Begay household had been broken into and ransacked while they hid from the radioactive dust clouds. Ronnie could not fathom who would tear up his mother's house and not take one item. He called Hopi Chief Blackcloud to start an investigation, but the Chief refused, because he was swamped with far worse complaints. The chief was overwhelmed by the hordes of domestic problems caused by the fallout.

In spite of the damage, the Raboys and Begays had a grand feast prepared by Abigail. She made chicken swarmas, matzo ball soup, fresh kosher vegetables, and Hopi sacred corn-onthe-cob that the children roasted over the campfire. Sarah Begay was so worn out by all of the hoopla that she decided to lay down on her sofa to rest for awhile. She drifted into a deep sleep. She smiled and talked to herself in her dreams as the rest of the family hooted it up outside. All of a sudden, she let out in a deadly scream. Everyone came rushing in the house to see what had happened.

"Rabbi Raboy," she said, crying with the look of fear in her eyes.

"Yes, Sarah," he replied as she sat down near her.

"I will never see you again after tonight, but my son's son and little Daniel will make a worldwide peace treaty among all nations and peoples in the next world to come," she said, as tears ran down her cheeks.

"Sarah, we will be back to visit you again, before you or anyone dies," he said being concerned with her statement.

"I saw a vision of my grandson and your son holding up a flag with a tall, skinny, black man proclaiming a new beginning for human beings. I saw Mother Earth in a form I did not recognize. My dream disturbed my soul because I did not recognize my own land."

"Mrs. Begay, I think the stress of all that has happened the last two weeks may have disturbed your sleep. Maybe you were having a nightmare?" said Abigail.

"Abigail, you are the little daughter I always wanted. I will miss you sorely because you have become a major part of my life. I hope you do call and write me as a daughter should speak to her mother," said Sarah shedding tears.

"Of course, I will. Sarah, you are my American mother. I will always keep in touch with all of you. How can I ever forget you? You are my family as much as those we left in Israel," said Abigail.

The Pow-wow ended and the Raboy's prepared to go home. They had experienced a lifetime of excitement in Arizona, but now it was time to say farewell.

The next morning they packed up and headed for Phoenix, Arizona, to turn in the vehicle they had rented and to catch an aircraft to return home. There was one major problem the Raboys did not think about. Phoenix had lost over two hundred and fifty thousand people due to the fallout from the killer rain. Many other thousands were suffering from radiation poisoning.

The Phoenix metropolitan leaders had police officers stationed on foot at every major street intersection. There were Red Cross first aid stations and numerous radiation signs warning the public to be aware of the dangers throughout the largest desert city in the world. What shocked Raboy even more was the fact that the Sky Harbor International Airport was open, but it did not have any flights departing or arriving. They were told that some unusual magnetic air waves affected the aircraft's electronics grounding all of the jets. It was a spooky feeling to look at this city disabled when only two months ago it was thriving with activity.

"Sweetie, it appears the rental car people do not care if we pay or just leave the truck in its tracks," said Abigail.

"Yes, this is a very strange situation indeed. I think we better call my brother Jeremiah to see if the President can get us home."

It took the Rabbi three days to get in touch with his brother in D.C. because of massive communication failures. The Raboys were glad that hey did not have any problems finding suitable hotel rooms to stay at until arrangements were made for them to go home. Colonel Bigwell was once again called upon to ferry them to Luke Air Force Base, Arizona, on the US Marine Golden Eagle hydrogen fueled helicopter. He unloaded them near a military jet that had been assigned to General Freetag.

General Freetag had direct orders from the President to take the Raboys to Andrews Air Force Base. The flight took approximately eight hours because the magnetically charged air had created chaos for all communication devices. Raboy asked the captain why the military jets could fly and not the civilian ones. The captain's reply was that the craft was built with fiber optic controls and instrumentation. Raboy had no idea what the captain had told him. Upon landing, the President had the Raboys brought directly to the White House. This time the President did not have any questions, but rather just wanted to say good-bye before the Rabbi permanently left to live the rest of his life in Israel.

"Rabbi, we are giving you this military satellite phone so you can communicate with the Aborigine elder Yirawala, the White House, Israeli government, and the Hopi Native American Sarah. We are doing this because, well, who knows," said the President.

"That is nice gesture and very respectful statement, Mr. President, but I do not think I will ever be leaving Israel again for a long time to come," replied the Rabbi.

"I understand that your wife wants to take a luxury liner and stay out of the air for your return trip back to Israel," said the President.

"That is correct. She feels with all of the nuclear particles floating about in the skies that the ocean would be the safest way to travel home," he replied.

"So be it, Rabbi, so be it. We have an aircraft carrier headed that way if you want to travel on a military ship," suggested the President.

"No, and no thanks. We have had enough of the American military to last us a lifetime," said Abigail interjecting into the conversation, "The luxury liner will be quite sufficient."

Ambassador Jeremiah Raboy took his brother and family to New York City, New York to board a Scandinavian ocean liner headed for the Mediterranean Sea. Everyone said their good-byes with long, quiet embraces as though they would never see each other again. Abigail requested two first-class rooms because she figured that while Daniel was playing with his toys she could spend some quality time with her husband. They boarded the ship and steamed eastward for home to see how the Asian T-war had affected their homeland.

"Sweetie, tomorrow Daniel will be five years old. Can we wait until we reach home to celebrate his birthday?" asked Abigail.

"Yes, Sweetheart," he replied nonchalantly.

"David, do not yes me. I am not spoiled like other insecure women that want their husbands to be yes men all of the time. I want a loving answer with some honest down to Earth feelings attached to what you are saying."

"Yes, my most beautiful and loving wife," he replied with a sexy tone of voice.

"That was much better, my Tiger Muffin."

"Ahh, Abigail, when did you start calling me Tiger Muffin?" asked the Rabbi.

"That is what Miriam Cleghorn calls her husband. He is the President of American and she has the same desires as me when it comes to feeling cherished and adorned. The fact is that we women need to feel emotionally loved to feel good about ourselves. Understand?" she asked.

"I suppose you do, but sweetheart that does not answer my question," he replied, as he laughed at her playfulness.

"Have you been thinking about what I have been thinking about?" asked Abigail.

"I am not sure since you know men do not think or listen much."

"You know exactly what I am thinking. Yes, you do and you are correct if you are thinking about making Atlantic Ocean love for the next week or so. You know, David, we might be Abel to create another beautiful human being." She said as she began to gently kiss him.

After three days of making Atlantic Ocean love, Raboy finally got to rest. He enjoyed the peace and quiet so much that he had forgotten about his experience with the Killer Rain. As they relaxed, their inquisitive son ran everywhere on the ship, making new friends by asking everyone he saw questions about this and about that, except one crabby lady stopped him in his tracks.

"Why are you asking so many questions?" she said with a grumpy tone of voice.

"I do not know. Why?" Daniel responded.

"I think I hear your mother calling you," said the grumpy elderly lady.

"No, she is not," he replied.

"Young man, I think I hear your mother calling you," said the lady again trying to get rid of little Daniel.

"No, my mother is not calling me because she making Atlantic Ocean love to my daddy," laughed Daniel.

"Oh my God! You need to run along now and bother someone else," said the lady.

Daniel ran back over to his parents who were enjoying the nice day on the upper deck of the ship about twenty feet away from the elderly lady. The lady looked at the couple and came over to talk to them.

"Rabbi, you need to scold your grandson. He told me his mother was making Ocean love while he was running about the deck asking too many questions."

"Excuse me, that is my son and as you can see we are lounging here," said Abigail as she smiled at the lady. The old lady shook her head and walked away from them.

The next evening, they were invited to the Captain's table for dinner. Abigail wore a bright red silk dress that matched her purse and high heel shoes. The Rabbi dressed in his Cohen Ultra-orthodox Rabbi Jewish attire. After they were seated at the Captain's table, Rabbi Raboy noticed there was a pig head stuffed with an apple on the center table. He took Abigail's hand immediately got up and rushed out of the dining room. The Captain sent his first mate to the Raboy's room to find out what was wrong, but they were not to be found. After searching the ship for a few minutes he noticed that David and Abigail were on the upper deck looking out across the moonlit ocean.

"Rabbi, the Captain has expressed his apologies for having food that was not kosher at the dining table. We feed hundreds of mouths daily and simply forgot that you were an Ultra-Orthodox Jewish Rabbi. He would like to have a special dinner, in your honor, in his stateroom tomorrow night. He wants to know if you will accept his apology and invitation," said the messenger.

"I would, but there must be a kosher cook on staff to prepare the meal by the standards that I am accustomed to," replied Rabbi Raboy.

Abigail and Raboy sat there silently thinking at what had been said while looking around at the mysterious night sky. It was a strange sight to see the skies filled with glowing orange clouds due to the charged radioactive particles swirling high in the troposphere. The full moon looked strange shedding a blue green ring around about it. Having been calmed down, the Raboy's asked the messenger if were possible for him to bring them some snacks to their room. The first messenger told it would be no problem. He left immediately. Raboy and Abigail decided to head back to their cabin. The messenger had been gone for about thirty minutes when a chef knocked on the Raboy's cabin door.

"Rabbi, I have brought you and the Mrs. a kosher meal, in which, I personally supervised the preparation procedures. My father is a Russian Jewish Rabbi and I know what you can and cannot eat. Notice there is no milk or cheese. You will be eating fresh smoked herring served with matzo ball soup along with some other Middle Eastern fruits and vegetables. I am sure this will keep you satiated until tomorrow night. Tomorrow, everyone in the stateroom will be eating kosher because I will be in charge," said the Chef speaking English with a Russian accent.

"Thank you, for your respect," replied Raboy.

"It is my honor to serve the one that have prophesied the end of the world," said the Chef.

"Sir, I have not prophesied any such thing. I had a visitation from a supernatural being that told me to write down various scriptures and then tell the world what had already been prophesied," he remarked.

"Nevertheless, Sir, I am glad you are on my ship because I know the Lord is with you. I know that if I am around you I will be protected by the Almighty's sweet tender mercy," said the chef smiling, as he left the Raboy's cabin.

"Champagne, sir? I mean, kosher wine, Rabbi?" asked one of captain's servants.

"Boys, you can leave now. The Rabbi and I have some things to talk about that don't include either of you," said Abigail, as she handed them a handsome tip.

Rabbi Raboy drank half a bottle of the fine kosher wine that evening which was about half a bottle more than he ever had drank before at any one time in his life. He was tipsy and feeling no pain when Abigail went into the bedroom. She put on some new hot pink lacey sleepwear she had been saving for a special occasion like this to give Raboy the thrill of his life.

"Are you ready for a special surprise?" asked Abigail with sweet soft voice.

"Yes, Sweetheart," said David smiling.

Rabbi Raboy was lost for words when she walked into his view. Abigail smiled as she passionately lay next to her husband that she loved without measure. The night seemed to never end for either of them and for Abigail it was a true pleasure to treat her man with unconditional love and admiration. The night did end and to their surprise the captain of the ship was requesting Raboy's presents.

Five days into the journey, the ships chronometer, compass, and electronics went haywire. Thankfully, the Captain had anticipated that something like this might happen by assessing the aircrafts troubles with their electronic equipment. He had hired the best seamen he could if a similar malfunction were to occur out at sea. He had improvised several antique navigation procedures as a precautionary measure before he left New York City's Port of Call. By employing several experienced sailors familiar with the Atlantic Ocean, he felt secure and prepared for the journey. He knew that the stars were like city roadmaps to these experienced seamen, but hoped voyage would be trouble free.

The captain soon found out that his had picked elite crew could not maintain nor solve the problems the ship was now encountering. His preparedness became null and void when all of the ships engines failed at once. He started to unraveled to some degree when the electrical systems started malfunctioning. Next, the backup generators failed, which negated the use of the shops entire communication systems. To put it plainly, the ship was doomed.

"Can you summon that Jewish Rabbi to the bridge?" asked the Captain.

"Yes, sir, I will attend to it immediately," said the first mate.

It did not take him long to find David and Abigail. They were lounging on the upper deck playing with their son. Raboy did not know what to think when the Captain requested his presence on the bridge of the liner. Nevertheless, he proceeded with the first mate, leaving Abigail behind to attend to Daniel.

"Captain, did you want to speak with me?" asked Raboy.

"Rabbi, we have a serious problem. My ship does not work," replied the Captain. Are not exactly stranded because the ocean currents are."

"Captain, are you saying that this ship is malfunctioning and we are stranded?" asked Raboy.

"Not exactly because we are caught in a special ocean current. It is pushing us at seven knots in the direction we want to go. But on the other hand, my passengers will be in the dark when nightfall arrives," he replied.

"In the dark. Why?" asked Raboy.

"The electrical power generators are not working, so I summoned you," said the captain.

"Sir, I cannot figure out why you would want me on the bridge? I don't know anything about ships," said Raboy.

"Rabbi, I have an entire ship full of innocent people stranded in the middle of the Atlantic Ocean. I desperately need your help to get them to safety," cried out the Captain.

"Captain, I am sure you know that Israeli Jewish Rabbis aren't navigators, so what are you trying to achieve by bringing me to your bridge?" asked Raboy.

"I wanted to tell you about a dream I had last night. The Earth broke up into a thousand pieces and no one could put it back together again," said the Captain nervously, "I am afraid to tell anyone, except you, because I've had this dream over and over for two years."

"Why have you chosen this moment to tell me about your dream?" asked Raboy.

"Because I know who you are a great prophet and everyone has been seeking you out for information," said the captain.

"Where did you come up with these ideas?" asked Raboy.

"The word is out that you are the one that the United Nations has turned to for counseling from the beginning of this nuclear nightmare," said the captain revealing his inner thoughts.

"Well, if the words of the book of the prophets, the Dead Sea Scrolls' book of Isaiah, the Aborigine Rebirth, and the Hopi Native Americans Meha legends are correct, your dream was rightfully in line," said the Rabbi in one breath.

"Do you have any idea what is going to happen to this world?" asked the Captain.

"Captain, I cannot answer you question. I can only tell you what the top scientists of the world have told me about what may happen to Mother Earth," said Raboy.

"Anything would help, Rabbi," said the Captain.

"If you have any doubt what I am about to say, please try to keep the perspective that this is not my theory. In contrary, it is the best guess of the world's top scientist's," explained Raboy.

"I am all ears and no lips," said the Captain.

"Earth has many different magnetic cycles that are both a blessing and a curse. The duration of a cycle is usually about one million years. Ever so often, the magnetic fields reverse or shift poles that can cause many different changes in the way that Mother Earth supports life. When the compass points to what we call north, life on Mother Earth decreases in many ways. Plant and animal species die out and no new species generates itself from existing species. Volcano's stop erupting reducing the spread of highly enriched soil The oceans warm up releasing methane which kills out the ocean life, and finally the methane heats up the atmosphere that kills most of the animals and vegetation. Thank the Lord the cycles reverse themselves so that when the south magnetic pole attracts the compass, life increases. I understand that an entire new species of plants and animals will evolve—like the dinosaurs disappearing and mammals appearing during the first five live cycles of Mother Earth."

"Are we pointed north or south? I don't know because my compass does not work. Is life dying out?" asked the confused captain.

"Captain, I am not sure. All I heard was that we get many new species generated due to the pole shifts, from simple viruses to complex mammals. The theory hasn't been proven yet, but many scientists postulate that a southern dominant magnetic field supports larger and many different forms of plants and animals. In contrast, when the force is reversed and the dominant force is toward the north, plants and animals become smaller and weaker as many die out leaving the world with fewer species," said the Rabbi.

"That is really a complex and interesting theory," said the Captain somewhat bewildered.

"Believe it or not, that is only part of the theories out there. Presently, we are suffering from severe electromagnetic pollution. If the surface of Mother Earth was shocked by the pounding of the hydrogen bombs, the Earth's fragile magnetic field must have been shocked, too. The scariest part of the scenario is the Aborigines believe the Earth's tectonic plates are indeed held together by magnetic lines of force that are perpendicular to all of the fault lines of the continental plates. If this is true, the magnetic grid patterns over the entire face of the Earth may have been altered," said the Rabbi.

"Damn, Rabbi, you make more sense than most of the scientists that think they got it all figured out," said the captain.

"Captain, I have not figured anything out. I heard the educated ones discuss this. My personal beliefs are such that, if we have altered the natural magnetic cycles with the thermonuclear devices in Indo-China T-War, we are doomed. Even more disturbing, if the book of the prophets, the Aborigine Dreamtime Rebirth and the Hopi Meha purification prophecies are correct, life as we know it will cease to exist."

"Why are not you scared, upset, or telling the world what lies ahead for mankind?"

"Captain, if I were to tell the world what I have told you, they would lock me in a padded cell."

"No offense Rabbi, but let's pray that these prophecies will not come about for another thousand years," said the Captain, being alarmed as to what he had just heard.

"Rabbi, did they mention what would happen if the magnetic continental plates decided to reverse their attractions?" asked the first officer.

"No, they did not. If you are through asking me questions, I would like to spend some quality time with my wife and son."

"I do not want to ask you anything else," said the Captain. He then took his orange, digitally enhanced binoculars and looked around the ocean to see if any other crafts were nearby or stranded. For three days, the ship helplessly drifted in the Atlantic Ocean, mysteriously being pushed toward the southern part of the European continent. The ship had been adrift for almost five hundred kilometers when the ship's electrical systems started functioning again. The magnetic zone that caused the ship's systems to malfunction was weakening by the minute.

When the main boiler electrical and electronic instruments all started to function, the captain praised God Almighty for his intervention to rescue his ship. The captain pushed the crew to make the craft run at full speed. He wanted to reach the European coast before some other bizarre event took place. The captain took the ship directly to the Port of Israel, bypassing his original first port of call. He disembarked the Raboys and then steamed off toward Athens, Greece.

"Rabbi Sweetie, I must tell you that since meeting you, my life has been anything but boring. The messenger must have been Holy," said Abigail, as she lay down on her own bed in Israel for the first time in many weeks.

"Sweetheart, I too, must confess that I never imagined this. Since the brilliant light appeared in the secret scrolls room and gave us a direct message, my life has changed beyond the limits of my imagination," said Raboy.

"Before I met you, I did not have a life," laughed Abigail. "I often wonder why over two billion people were killed in such an ugly way. We have been at odds with the Palestinians for such a long time it's ridiculous. Their suicide bombers have had zero effect on the Israeli people's resolve to stay and never leave the land of our forefathers. It seems like child's play compared to what India and China have done simply because they could not agree," he said softly.

He then turned and looked out the south window at the thousands of new Israeli and Palestinian names etched on a limestone wall. A monument that memorialized all the people who had recently died from the radioactive fallout. Raboy was awed by the beautiful and terrible site.

"Will there finally be an end to this?" asked Abigail.

"If the Aborigine, the Hopi, and our book of prophets are correct, we are going to experience even more Earth changes until the Messiah comes and saves the few that are left on Mother Earth's surface, as promised by the prophets," said the Rabbi.

"What will become of Sarah Begay? She was such a wonderful person. I will miss her forever. My only hope is that we get to see her again before she is taken by the Great Spirit that oversees all," said Abigail, with a heavy heart.

"If it is God's will, then so be it." He hugged his dedicated lovely wife.

"David, this may sound selfish but..." she said stopping in the middle of her sentence.

"What may sound selfish?" he asked frankly.

"Well, it's that we never made love one time during the thermonuclear times. I was thinking about what kind of a story we could tell our children about making thermonuclear love," said Abigail.

"Sweetheart, that is a ridiculous request. Is that all you ever think about?" he asked.

"No, I think about eating, sleeping, shopping, my friends, and family. I think about your career, our safety, my child's future world if there will be one, and I think...," said Abigail as the Rabbi interrupted her.

"Sweetheart, I am sorry I ever asked you such a silly question. Can you find a place in the bottom of your heart to forgive me?"

"If you put it that way, yes I can, but you will have to make Middle Eastern love to me tonight before I can completely put it out of mind," she said.

One year passed without any more earth shattering events. As the nations throughout the world worked feverishly to recover from the Asian T-war, Abigail and David had a daughter. Raboy felt that mankind would never fully recover from the massive destruction caused by the first T-War. As promised, the Raboys kept in close touch with Yirawala and Sarah via the United States government satellite phones.

Mother Earth was quiet, but millions still suffered from radioactive diseases caused by the massive thermonuclear exchange. China and India buried the dead by the millions. Some cities were not feasible for the Chinese or Indian governments to enter due to the risk of contracting many different types of illnesses due to germs that had been genetically altered by the massive radiation clouds. The United Nations sent thousands of bulldozers and heavy construction equipment to various nations to tear down the desolate buildings and dig massive graves.

Safe drinking water became a worldwide issue since the thermonuclear exchange. Everyone in the world used Geiger counters to check their water before they drank it. Mother Earth became an unsafe place to live for all plants and animals that who survived the first Asian T-war.

Raboy returned to his studies in the secret scroll room at the university. Abigail was happy to stay home and take care of the children. The Raboy were finally at rest knowing that Mother Earth would take time to heal from her wounds created by man's foolishness. But deep down inside Rabbi Raboy knew that this was only the beginning of man's sorrows.

CHAPTER TEN:

THE BIG ONE

"**I**s this Dr. Keller from M.I.T?" asked the caller.

"No, this is his assistant. He has gone to Japan to study the recent tremors that have damaged much of their nation's transportation system. He should return next month," said Dr. Greenbaum.

"I'm Professor Clemens at the University of California Berkeley. Please tell him we need to talk immediately."

"I'll try to get a hold of him," said Dr. Greenbaum.

"No, Dr. Greenbaum, you are not listening to me. I said I need to talk him immediately. There is an urgent situation that needs to be addressed and I mean urgent," said Dr. Clemens.

"You Californians think you are the Gods of America. Let me tell you something my fellow citizen, we at M.I.T. are the supreme beings when it comes to technology," said Dr. Greenbaum, as Dr. Clemens interrupted him.

"Professor, are you insane or crazy? I don't give a damn about who is who. In a few days there might not be any land for who's who to stand on. Stop your useless nonsense and get Dr. Keller to call me, and I mean now!" shouted Dr. Clemens, slamming the phone down so hard it broke in half. Dr. Greenbaum called Dr. Clemens back.

"Dr. Clemens, the audacity of it all. I forbid you to speak to me in that manner. I will not try to contact Dr. Keller unless you apologize. Meanwhile you need to learn how to talk to the elite of the education system. You westerners don't even know how to spell education much less know what it means," continued the stiff-necked professor, unaware that his speaker phone was connected to the entire schools public address system.

Dr. Clemens decided to call Cal Tech University to find out how to get in touch with Dr. Keller on assignment in Japan. He wanted to discuss with him about any future anomalies that may come since Mother Earth had received her first worldwide, systemic earthquake. A quake that paralyzed the Cal-Berkeley seismographs. Dr. Clemens had discovered that the magnetic shifts below the lithosphere were causing the tectonic plates to quiver constantly. With the entire world's crust constantly shaking Dr. Clemens started to panic knowing that something astronomical was about to happen to Mother Earth.

Where, when, and how much damage to the Earth's surface would occur. He started thinking about the massive amounts of hot magma oozing through the fault lines, which would, in turn, create carbonic acid rain that would eat up Mother Earth's surface. He knew if it were to happen life on Mother Earth's surface would seize to exist.

Five days later Dr. Clemens had not calmed down. He sat in his office constantly watching the instruments and meters radically move all over the charts. Being emotionally drained from it all he knew he needed his post graduate research partner to confirm or deny his findings. By sheer luck, Dr. Keller called Dr. Clemens for some Pacific Rim geological data.

"Dr. Keller, I have been frantically trying to reach you for days, but your lame brain associate professor has a severe case of cranial pelvic disease," said Dr. Clemens.

"I apologize for Dr. Greenbaum. He is a genius, but his relationship to human beings is rather a weird one to say the least. What is so urgent that you need to talk to me about you findings?" asked Dr. Keller.

"Sam, those subterranean fallout shelters the government has are going to be crushed if the seismic readings I have been calculating are correct," expressed Dr. Clemens.

"Steve, you only know half of the situation. Did you know Mother Earth has reversed her internal charge from north to south?" asked Dr. Keller.

"No!" replied Dr. Clemens.

"That's why I am in Japan to see if I can find a clue as to why this happening. Ever since Japan lost 80 million people thanks to the Indians and Chinese T-war, it has been very difficult to get anything done here. I need your help desperately to calculate my lithosphere magnetic values," said Dr. Keller.

"Sure, but aren't you worried about my problem? California is about to have the Big One. I mean a major earthquake that has been predicted for scores of decades. Are you concerned or not?" asked Dr. Clemens using a very strong tone of voice.

"Dr. Clemens, aren't you in the San Francisco, California area?" asked Dr. Keller as he peered out the window to look at the skyline of San Francisco.

"Actually. I am across the bay from San Francisco in the East Bay area that is directly in line with the Golden Gate Bridge" replied Clemens.

"According your hypothesis, if Mother Earth does not calm down, you are going to be part of the San Francisco Bay," laughed Dr. Keller.

"Be serious, because I really need your help to figure out what's going on here."

"Yes, I will be serious. I will call you when we have completed our task over here. It should take a couple of weeks to finish my report. Ahh, better yet, I'll stop by San Francisco on my way back to Washington, D.C., Let's do lunch," suggested Keller.

"Fine. We have some real nice nuclear burgers or maybe you'd like some radioactive organic foods. I thought you would like to know that our organic farms were treated with radioactive fallout," remarked Clemens.

"Knock it off Doctor. Nuclear organic farms. You know the whole world is covered with fallout from the Asian Twar. I'll meet with you when I get to the States," said Keller, as he hung up the phone.

Dr. Keller didn't have any idea that he had received the most important phone call of his life. Clemens had asked about an event that would geologically change the world. All he had to do was converse with Dr. Clemens for a couple more minutes and he would be able to save thousands upon thousands of lives. But he was too engrossed with his studies that morning in Japan. His stubbornness to converse with Dr. Clemens about what was happening would be costly mistake for many thousands of Americans safety.

Dr. Clemens figured Keller would contact him if the situation became worse. He really believed that the world would soon become a very unsafe place. He tried many different things to calm down, but it was futile for him. He knew Mother Earth was about to make some major geographical changes, but did not know how to alert the government or public.

Being bored he decided to read daily journal. One story caught his attention was that the United Nations had decided to reduce the voting power allocated to India and China. The journal explains that this was done because India and China did not have the required population or infrastructure to categorize them as major world voting powers. Dr. Clemens laughed out loud at the rational thinking of the worldwide leader's logic.

"These idiotic restructuring agendas for the United Nations are ridiculous. I wonder if they know about the weird geological problems Mother Earth is having. I cannot understand why our political leaders are so blind. Of course, I have not told them yet what changes that might occur to the earth's terra firma," thought Dr Clemens as he threw the journal into the waste basket.

In fact, many of the elite scientists did not bother to investigate internal problems Mother Earth was having due to the extreme atmospheric disturbances in the troposphere and ionosphere. They totally ignored Dr. Clemens report about the earth quivers. As the investigation scientist he had taken an oath that forbid to warn the public. He sat there shaking his head as he watched the seismic graphs jump around, wondering when hell on earth would arrive.

Exactly one month, three days, five hours, ten minutes, twenty one seconds later Mother Earth started to show her first signs of degradation. Dr. Clemens just happened to be eating dinner with Dr. Keller at the Fish Grotto in San Francisco, California when the first shaker hit.

Dr. Keller actually mocked him as the little tremor rocked their wine glasses. Dr. Clemens politely put his glass of wine down, got up, and left the building, leaving Dr. Keller alone to enjoy his insults. Prior to the meeting, Dr. Clemens had not spoken to Dr.

Keller since he wanted to forge government documents to gain access to federal grant monies years ago. At the time, Dr. Clemens had wanted to through him out the window, but he did not because he respected the J. Edgar Hoover proclamation. Those in government circles should find the truth, lie about the truth, then tell the truth, then lie about the lie to make the truth obscure. This was used to blackmail the guilty to get them to do what the government wanted them to.

Moments after Dr. Clemens left the dinner, the Cal Berkeley seismograph labs called him about unusual activity on the graphs. Dr. Clemens still burning with anger with Dr. Keller because he laughed at his theory that the earth would start producing twisting motions in the near future. As he traveled across the Bay Bridge, he beat his hands on the steering wheel keeping time with his favorite song. He drove back to California-Berkeley knowing that he had given him enough sufficient information to justify his theoretical model and support his fault line hypothesis.

The destruction of the lithosphere would proved his hypothesis, but Dr. Clemens was hoping for that not to happen any time soon. His only mistake was that he did not realize that the situation was far worse than he had calculated. Little did he know that it would not be long before the entire world would be affected by the worldwide systemic lithosphere aberrations. A change that was never considered by a single scientist. An impossibility that the entire earth's plate tetonics could ever move or behave in that manner to the slightest degree. Although Dr. Clemens could see the massive destruction of the magnetic lines of force, he could not warn the world because of federal regulations that may creat public panic. Then two days later Mother Earth started to show signs of unstability.

"Cal Poly, this is Cal Berkeley seismic labs. Are you guys reading what we are reading?" asked Rhonda Begay, the daughter of Ronnie Begay of the Hopi Native American tribe located in Arizona.

"Yes, but we thought it was nothing more than an electronic anomaly, an aberration caused by the magnetic imbalances resulting from the Indo-China T-War. Please tell me what you are reading right now, Rhonda," requested Dr. Clemens. Rhonda was an aide that had worked with Dr. Clemens, at Cal Berkeley before he had transferred to Cal Poly Institute in Los Angeles .

"There seem to be over seventy earthquakes happening simultaneously around the world. What's more disturbing—they register between 5.0 and 7.0," replied Rhonda Begay holding onto the communicator.

"I'd like to see Dr. Keller's fat, ugly face admitting he was wrong. He constantly told me I was on a witch-hunt," replied Dr. Clemens.

"What was that last statement, Doctor?" asked Rhonda.

"It was nothing important. Let's get the facts over to the Pentagon so our defense ministers can evaluate the unfolding situation. Do not contact the newsmedia they will cause the public panic. We do not need their hyped up theatrical version of the facts right now."

"Ahh, excuse me doctor, but it is a little too late for the government to make any evaluations. I think it would be best if they..."

"Rhonda, I know you are an excellent technician, but you do not have the experience or education to make any judgment calls," said the snooty professor.

"Listen here, Dr. Know-it-all, we have a worldwide disaster in the makings. Look at what is taking place and... Oh God, help me." She screamed as a 7.8 quake hit the San Francisco Bay area. The nearly two and a half minute quake ripped land apart everywhere. Rhonda ran outside of the building. Twenty minutes later, a 7.9 quake hit the Sylmar region of Los Angeles County. The skyscrapers swayed back and forth like palm trees in a hurricane. Most of the newly constructed high-rise buildings incurred minor damage due to strict earthquake building codes. Unfortunately, many of the older buildings crumbled and fell to the ground, producing massive dust clouds and piles of building debris.

At Berkeley, Rhonda's building had cracks throughout the walls but since it was built for 9.0;pl earthquakes. Since her lab was equipped with an alternative power supply for the lab's sensitive equipment, she reentered the weakened structure out curiosity to read the latest data. She quickly read the graphs trying to analyze the readings as the building creaked and crackled. As she decided to leave the lab's satellite phone rang.

"Hello. Yes, this is she," said Rhonda.

"Rhonda, I am truly sorry for what I said. Can you forgive my arrogance so we can proceed analyzing the quakes multiple epicenters?" asked Dr. Clemens starting to panic.

Rhonda could tell by his voice she was talking to a man that just had the holy hell scared out of him. Rhonda could hardly hear Dr. Clemens speak since thousands of sirens started screaming at once. Rhonda decided to look out the second floor's window. She frozen in her footsteps and lost her breath. All she could see was smoke and fire everyway she looked. San Francisco looked like a giant bonfire, and Berkeley looked like someone had plowed a field into dirt mounds. Oakland looked like it had just been bombed. Smoke billowed up in all directions.

"I can barely hear you, but I do not think it really matters," replied Rhonda.

"Which major cities were direct hits?" he asked.

"It appears to be Cairo, Egypt; Mexico City; St. Louis, Mo; Los Angeles and San Francisco, CA; Salt Lake City, UT; Detroit, MI; Atlanta, GA; London, England; Helsinki, Finland; Moscow, Russia; Athens, Greece; Genoa, Italy—damn, I cannot count them all. It appears there were over twenty-seven earthquakes between: 6.0 to 8.0," said Rhonda.

"Rhonda that is the whole world. Are you reading the graphs correctly?" he asked.

"Do you think that Mother Earth is coming to an end?" asked Rhonda.

"I would hope not. I do not know," said Dr. Clemens being confused.

"I'm getting out of here," said Rhonda. She hung up the communicator and ran out of the building that was ready to fall down any moment.

Rhonda hastily left the building and walked to her home. Once a once beautiful street that was instantly littered with debris. Within eye sight she saw that her building was in shambles. She approached the building and went inside anyway to grab some of her belongings. Since the communication systems were down or jammed by the masses trying to make calls Rhonda could not call her grandmother. Even those with satellite cell phones could not make calls. Only the governmental emergency GPS communicators engineered by a composite of elite scientists were functioning.

Being confused she stopped for moment to look with awe at the burning cities and wept. After a few moments she regained her composure and noticed that the streets were torn apart and traffic was jammed up worse than anyone could have imagined. It did not matter much to Rhonda because the collapsed building had smashed her car. Rhonda ran over to her boyfriend's house to see if he was safe. He was outside calmly sitting on his motorcycle smoking a cigarette. Rhonda came up to him shaking. He put his arms around her and held her tightly in his arms not saying a word.

Crying she asked him to drive her to her native Arizona Hopi reservation. He did not say yes or no. He started up the motorcycle and left Berkeley instantly without any clothes, except what they were wearing. Her boyfriend dodged in and out of traffic as most of the cars along the 580 freeway were moving less than five miles per hour.

After driving through Altamont Pass, they had to make an unexpected, emergency stop. Rhonda's boyfriend laid the motorcycle down on its left side at forty miles per hour. Rhonda was screaming, crying and shaking at the same time. As it slid along the road's gravel shoulder, Rhonda and her boyfriend were able to avoid injury by sitting on top of the left side of the motorcycle. The cycle slid to an abrupt stop when it plowed into the grassy embankment. They both got up slowly and brushed the gravel off of the themselves and the cycle.

"Why are you trying to kill me?" screamed Rhonda.

"Look at the road! Do you notice something wrong with it?" he asked yelling at her.

"Holy smokes! What caused this? Where is the other side of the road?" asked Rhonda still shook up from the motorcycle crash.

"The road had been sliced up like a pie. The freeway looks like a mini canyon," exclaimed her boyfriend as he looked at the Interstate 205 and Interstate 580 junction.

An 9.8 earthquake had hit the western half of the San Joaquin Valley at the same time San Francisco had been hit by the 8.8 quake. It caused the land to slide on the eastern half of the fault line northward about a thousand feet, leaving a gap over a hundred wide. The once super highways now lay broken up into jagged pieces.

Rhonda turned her head in every direction and as far as she could see the land was ripped apart like a jigsaw puzzle. The buildings in the immediate area were shredded to pieces like a F5 tornado had ripped into them. She then looked at the distant landscape. It upset her to see how everything was disturbed beyond recognition. Adam grabbed Rhonda by the arm and pointed to his motorcycle. They picked the motorcycle and checked it for any damage and took off.

"I see the other half of the road," said Adam, Rhonda's boyfriend.

"We'll have to find a place where we can cross. I need to get to Arizona. I can't believe this California nightmare," said Rhonda, biting her fingernails.

They drove about twenty miles until they came to a place where the gap was only inches wide. After they crossed the crevice, they drove on Interstate 205 toward Interstate Highway 5. They traveled north on I-5 until they came to Sacramento where the buildings were decimated. Traffic and highways twisted together with automobile wreckage slung along the collapsed freeways and intersections.

Rhonda and her boyfriend picked their way through the metal jungle to Grass Valley. At that point, they got back on Interstate 80. There were thousands of cracks and crevices all along the way to Salt Lake City, Utah. They then headed south on Interstate to Las Vegas where giant neon signs lay everywhere smashing cars, plants and what ever they landed on. People were screaming as the buildings that lay in ruins burned. You could feel the panic throughout the city.

They had to drive across the desert to reach Hoover Dam since the Henderson Highway and other freeways were impassable. It was a rough ride on the 250 horsepower mountain bike traveling across the desert dirt bike trails. When they finally made it within eye shot of Hoover Dam, Rhonda was awed by the water boiling violently over the top of the dam. It looked like a manmade giant seven hundred foot waterfall as tons of water fell to the Colorado River below.

"What the hell is going on here?" asked Rhonda the man in a police uniform.

"Glen Canyon Dam broke yesterday during the massive earthquakes. This is not the worst of it," said the Hoover Dam Officer.

"Officer, I am Rhonda Begay, a scientist from the seismic labs in Berkeley, California. Are there any other scientists or earthquake specialists around?"

"Yes, I think that group over there is from Los Angeles," said the officer, as he pointed to a group with cameras that were taking pictures of the event.

"Excuse me. Do any of you scientists work in the Los Angeles seismic labs?"

"Yes. I do. Why do you ask?" asked Dr. Garcia.

"I am Rhonda Begay of the Berkeley seismic labs. I am wondering if anyone here is from Cal Poly and knows what happened to Dr. Clemens?"

"Rhonda, Rhonda Begay, here I am," said Dr. Clemens. They stared at one another for a moment.

"How did you get here?" asked Rhonda surprised he was there.

"I have connections. What are you doing here?" asked the Clemens.

"My family lives in Arizona on the Hopi Reservation. I am trying to get home to see them. What are you doing here?" she asked him the second time.

"I was going to Arizona to assess the damage in the Phoenix Metropolitan Area, but the Glenn Canyon Dam burst from a quake that started at the west end of the Grand Canyon National Park Colorado River basin. The rift went the complete distance of the Colorado River across Utah into Colorado. We figured the Hoover Dam will be the next to fail and come to see it would come crashing down. This may sound ridiculous, but I cannot help myself to say that I admire the beautiful waterfall. I love the hundreds of rainbows the water is making as it is spills over the dam," he said.

"Right Doctor. Why did not you cross at Blythe or Needles, California?" she asked

"Isn't that obvious? The Colorado River basin is flooded to such an extent that all the bridges and roadways have been washed out, all the way to the Sea of Cortez. This is the only way for anyone from Utah, Nevada, or California to get into Arizona," he said.

"Professor, not to spoil your hopes and dreams, but isn't there a thirty foot wall of water pouring over the dam right now?" Rhonda asked.

"That is true for now, but in time, after the water drops, we should be able to cross," said Dr. Clemens.

"I know the Army Corps of Engineers will eventually let officials cross, but I can't wait for the Feds. I need to speak to my grandmother now," expressed Rhonda.

"Speaking about the federal government. Our military is presently building camps to house the millions of possible refugees near Blythe and Needles to keep the masses from overtaking Arizona and New Mexico and of course, give Californians a place to live."

"I am going to cross with you as soon as they let us go. I must see my grandmother to ask about Maasaw," she replied staring straight into Dr. Clemens eyes.

"Well, Rhonda that is interesting because the truth of the matter is that I am taking Dr. Keller to Tuba City, Arizona, located right in the middle Navajo Nations to meet Sarah Begay to introduce us to Maasaw," said Dr. Clemens.

"Dr. Clemens, Maasaw is a spirit. He is the great caretaker spirit of our Hopi people and Sarah Begay is my grandmother," said Rhonda.

"Well then, let's travel together. I can get you across the dam with me since I have federal and state priority. I do not know if we will be the first to cross, but we will get to cross before the general public," he replied.

It took most of the day before the flood waters receded enough to let the Hoover Dam engineers declare the roadway safe. Rhonda Begay and Adam loaded up the mountain bike on one of Dr. Clemens's group's vehicles and took off to the Arizona Hopi Reservation.

When Rhonda and Adam arrived at her grandparent's ranch house, they encountered over three thousand people held at bay by a barbed wire fence near the entrance gate. Chief Blackcloud was accompanied by several Arizona Highway Patrolmen, Federal Police, and six US Marines with M-16s with a Blackhawk gunship all stationed there by the order of the US President to protect Sarah Begay.

"Chief Blackcloud, what's going on here?" asked Rhonda.

"Rhonda, my little darling, come this way so I can let you in," said the Hopi Chief.

"Rhonda, are you going to allow us to join you?" asked Dr. Clemens.

"Please, wait here until I get permission from my grandfather. Don't worry, I'll be back for you," she said walking, toward the humble home made of Adobe brick.

"Rhonda! Oh Rhonda!" cried out Rhonda's mother, Ronnie Begay's wife.

The two embraced and kissed one another. Sarah motioned for Rhonda to come inside so she could fix her something to drink to calm her spirit. Ronnie Begay didn't notice his favorite daughter since he was busy helping Abel tend to their mother's precious sheep.

"Grandmother, can I bring my boyfriend and some fellow workers into your house?" asked Rhonda.

"Yes, but they must act civilized Human Beings," replied Sarah's grandfather.

"They will, grandfather and grandmother, I promise with my Hopi word of honor."

Rhonda returned to the front gate to invite her boyfriend, her old boss, and a couple other scientists into the front yard. She was surprised to find Mr. Kent standing next to Dr. Clemens. Dr. Clemens pleaded with Rhonda to let Mr. Kent on her grandfather's property. Against all of her judgment, she agreed to let Mr. Kent come along. As Rhonda escorted the three government workers and her boyfriend near the front porch, she noticed her father tending the sheep.

"Daddy," yelled Rhonda as she ran and hugged her father, "I have come with my boyfriend, Running Bear, Dr. Clemens, Dr. Keller, and Mr. Kent. They wanted to talk to Grandma. I made them promise to respect our ways and not act like a bunch of wild animals," said Rhonda.

"Alright, but they must sit outside on the petrified wood logs," said Ronnie.

Everyone picked a stone tree stump to sit on to wait to hear from Sarah. Sarah moved very slowly since she was tired from all of the raucous. She had spoken to Rabbi Raboy and Yirawala earlier that morning using the government three-way satellite phone system. Sarah was heavily burdened after learning what had occurred throughout the world. Although she was saddened to hear about the worldwide destruction, she was relieved to know that what Maasaw had revealed to her was the truth. Emotionally drained she thought deep while approaching the group setting on the petrified wood foreboding what they wanted to talk about.

"I am not going to say anything, except the President of the United States has asked Yirawala and the Rabbi to meet here with me. My ranch was chosen as the most appropriate place since I am afraid of flying in those metal birds," said Sarah.

"Sarah, will the world get to see the Rabbi's notes and maps of the three spiritual encounters—the Aborigine Dreamtime message, the Hebrew angelic visitations, and your Hopi Maasaw revelation about the New Meha?" asked Mr. Kent.

"I am not sure who will get to know what. There won't be any secrets kept from the public by us. Originally the government feared to let the public know the facts because they felt the masses would panic. We all know now it's far too late for that," said Sarah.

"When will that be?" asked Mr. Kent dressed in all black.

"Not until after the three of us have met and not a moment sooner. I know everyone wants to know what to expect next or where they can find a safe place to live. I really don't know what to tell you. It will be up to the government to let the people know what to plan for. Bye for now. I must rest since I am tired. I'm a little older than yesterday, so I need my rest."

The earthquake damaged to America was massive. Many in California's cities were left without power, water, fuel, or food. Thousands fled to Blythe, and military convoys escorted many more of those in the worst areas to the Colorado River Basin. National Guard units immediately had taken over Los Angeles, so there was not much looting or shooting by the wayward individuals taking a chance to ravage an unprotected city.

After several weeks of government negotiations, the Raboy's and Yirawala's families agreed to meet at the Begay's ranch. The Feds had the US Army Corps of Engineers install new septic tanks and a pump for running water. Two new houses were constructed for Raboy's and Yirawala's families. A special ops building was set up for the military, the President, and staff to be housed in if it became necessary. The US government gave Danny and Sarah Begay the deeds to each building to show "in good faith" they were not trying to take over their farm. Abel directed the building in an area so it would not interfere with his mother's precious sheep or the land utilized to grow the Begay's sacred corn.

They little ranch was converted into a top secret facility where one needed an identification card to enter. The Hopi Chief thought the US government had gone overboard in their attempt to make this a top priority governmental center. He understood the why but did not understand the reason for setting up a military camp. After the camp had been completed Raboy and Yirawala arrived with their respective families.

"Yirawala, this is Danny and Sarah Begay," said Raboy.

"It is my pleasure to be able to walk about your sacred ancestral lands," said Yirawala.

"It is our pleasure to welcome fellow human beings from the other side of the world who honor and respect Mother Earth," replied Danny Begay.

In all their were ten Aborigines that came from Australia, including Yirawala's wife, daughter, two granddaughters, and Manandjiwala. Yirawala requested Manandjiwala to come along since he was accustomed to working with the whites. Three tribal elders who were the best Didgeridoo players of all northern Australia made up the final ten members. They were housed in a third, multi-bedroom dwelling that were assigned to the Australian government. They were given warm clothes to protect them from the strong cold winter winds that crisscrossed the mile high Northern Arizona plateaus this time of year.

Yirawala rebelled at first because he did not want to wear the heavy clothing, but then decided it would be best to respect the Hopi people's customs. He put on a black western hat, lizard skin boots, some loosely fitting Denim pants, and a flashy multi-colored striped cowboy shirt. He chose a long tailed black leather cowboy overcoat with a fleece lining to keep warm. Abigail kept saying "Howdy Partner" to Yirawala, which Manandjiwala was not able to translate into Aborigine, so he told Yirawala a comparable Aborigine term.

Rabbi Raboy brought his wife Abigail, son Daniel Jeremiah, daughter Rachel Sarah, and Rabbi Klein as his scribe for the triad conference. Rabbi Raboy's brother Jeremiah told David that they would visit them in Arizona if they got a chance. After settling in and adjusting to the situation, the three supernatural spiritual leaders sat down to enjoy some freshly brewed tea together. Yirawala thought the tea was a special gift from the ancient ancestral spirits to the Hopi people. He enjoyed it so much that he drank three cups.

The first night was more exciting than a fireworks show. Aborigines, Hebrews, and Native Americans huddled around a huge camp fire while they watched Abel and Manandjiwala barbeque an entire calf using Arizona mesquite logs. They chose the calf as the main course of the meal because it was a common food to the Hopi, Aborigine, and Hebrew. All agreed it was a kosher, natural, and rather tasty choice. Approximately sixty people had plate and fork in hand to be served the first Native American international kosher meal prepared on Hopi Native American reservation soil. Who would have ever thought that Aborigine, Israeli nationals, Hopi Native Americans, US Marines, world renowned scientists, etc., would be gathered together to have a barbeque a mist the high plateaus of a secluded Native American reservation. Here in Northern Arizona they began to discuss various prophecies regarding the future of Mother Earth.

After the dinner, Yirawala held up some dirt of Mother Earth in his hand and asked everyone to thank the Great Spirit that had created the perfect ancestral mother for all mankind to live on. Ronnie Begay was excited to see another race of people respect Mother Earth like Native Americans. Before the Australian contingency had arrived Ronnie studied the Aborigine. He had learned that the Aborigine were a regulated people, prisoners in their own land as the Hopi had been. He felt that the Aborigine was treated just as evil and disrespectfully as the Native Americans had been.

Yirawala and Ronnie had many conversations together. He agreed with Yirawala's belief that the white invaders did their very best to destroy most of the natural habitats and animals that lived freely on Mother Earth for thousands of years. Ronnie laughed when Yirawala said he felt like a wild animal now housed in the concrete pen like the animals housed at many zoos.

Rhonda helped the newest members of her family—Daniel Jeremiah and Ester Sarah Rachel Raboy roast their Hopi corn sticks. Yirawala asked Rhonda to fix him one because it looked very appetizing to him. It was a special time for the Hopi nation having three visionaries located in one spot on Mother Earth. As they sat there talking, an 8.0

earthquake hit south eastern Utah and the western Colorado border that rocked and rattled everyone at the Begay barbeque.

Everyone around the campfire could feel the ground roll like ocean waves for two minutes. You could only hear the fire crackle as everyone stared at one another with their eyes wide open and mouths shut. Ten minutes later when they had just started to converse again the earth started rolling again, for approximately thirty seconds, but at a lesser magnitude.

After the excitement ended, Yirawala, Sarah, and Rabbi Raboy decided to privately convene in Sarah's living room. The nonverbal communication between them was so self explanatory that no one had to say a word. As each on spoke out you could feel the spiritual bond growing between them. The bond grew stronger by the minute as they discussed their experiences. Although each of their supernatural experiences was unique, they all felt even more concerned about Mother Earth, knowing they had been told some secret hidden from the begging of time what was the faith of Mother Earth and all of her children.

Sarah told Yirawala she often wondered how terrible things would become for human beings before Mother Earth completed her Sixth Purification. Yirawala spoke out about his fears as to how the Sixth Rebirth would affect his people. Rabbi Raboy was taught throughout his education to not to recognize the book of Daniel as prophetic words, but he had studied it any secretly. He took this opportunity to discuss the chapters about the Abomination of Desolation with his colleagues. He explained to Yirawala and Sarah that the Prophet Daniel had told mankind what to expect over two millenniums ago, as the Meha had proclaimed over three millenniums ago. Yirawala explained how the Aborigine Dreamtime had been instructing the Native Australians since the beginning of time how Mother Earth periodically regenerates herself. They discussed among themselves if it was it truly indeed time for Mother Earth to undergo climatic changes and geological land mass disturbances.

"Sarah and Yirawala, our world governments have brought us together, at the same time, in the same place to discuss our supernatural awakenings. I know that they have no clue what will happen next to Mother Earth. We have been given spiritual guidance that has been extremely limited. Should we, or should we not, try to make sense out of the question at hand? I know Jewish Rabbis across the world think it's an abomination for me to discuss the book of our prophets with gentiles. I know your people think it's not proper to discuss their most holy spiritual ways with strangers, too," said Raboy.

"We agree with you, Raboy, but what do we do to protect our families?" asked Sarah.

"I feel that the Great Spirit has chosen us to represent His future plans for Mother Earth. I feel that God is using people from different regions of the world to create a diversity of information which everyone around the world can clearly see that the Creator has no favorites. He does what he wants; it's His prerogative, no matter what we may think. Those that disagree with the Lord, the only Holy Being in the universe, are only wasting their valuable time on Earth and putting their lives in jeopardy. We must be clear, considerate, correct, concrete, concise, and certain as to what we say so that we are not charged with blasphemy," said Raboy.

"I do not understand what constitutes blasphemy, but I do know that those of the Dreamtime are kind to those that obey. The Dreamtime Rainbow Serpent will punish those that are disrespectful to Mother Earth and lie about the truth," expressed Yirawala.

"I know our cultures are extremely different, but we share the belief that the Great Spirit created all things. Thus, it is up to mankind to take care of His personal things, including our own lives. This gives us unity and strength to help those that want to believe our report," said Sarah emotionally as tears ran down her cheeks.

"My friends, I think we are gathered today on Mother Earth because the Great Spirit has chosen us, according to His plans, to announce His will. We appear to be the ones to warn the world at large His future plans for earth. Those that are chosen by the Great Spirit of truth are obligated to do His Divine Will. We must do as He has asked in a humble manner, giving Him all of the glory at all times, and must never ask for any monetary gain. With honor and respect we must be never put ourselves above any other human beings living on Mother Earth. If we were to create an organization using our name as being Divine, then we would be guilty of blasphemy and our Creator would judge us so. It is our duty to inform all mankind what the voice of the Dreamtime has revealed. If a person does not believe our report, it is a conflict between him or her and the Great Spirit," said Yirawala.

"My special friends, I do not understand why the Great Spirit in the sky would send His messenger Maasaw to me. There are others far greater me but I know what I saw and feel that it belongs to all mankind, not just to a certain group that proclaims they are the only ones chosen out of all of mankind to know the truth about the creator's will. I think those that feel they are the only ones with living prophets are blinded by their own ambitions. The Great Spirit has created all of the plants, animals, and all things made of Mother Earth for the benefits of mankind. Some religious leaders cause their followers to live in a world of doctrines filled with darkness and deceit. I will do my best to tell anyone and everyone that is thirsty and needs a drink of the truth that comes from the Great Spirit of truth that this knowledge is a gift to all his children who live on Mother Earth," said Sarah Begay.

The three agreed that the Creator of all that was living on Mother Earth was indeed the ruler and creator of the Universe and the one and only Most High Holy Being. They felt He had chosen them for one of His Divine purposes. They agreed to tell anyone that had an ear about what He intends to do with Mother Earth and they decided to freely disseminate any information that had been given to them without adding or deleting any part of the message. They agreed to plan no defense against those who would mock their message. To believe or disbelieve their report was a choice given to each and every individual. It was unanimous decision that they just simply turn away from those that chose to judge or mock them.

As they finished their meeting, a news alert came over the satellite television station from Salt Lake City, Utah. Many old respected buildings had crumbled into dust as the epicenter of the earthquake hit at Fifth Street and State Avenue next to the original Mormon Temple. Tens of thousands were killed or trapped in their dwellings as the quake caused the thunderous collapse of the entire city. Fires burned out of control and 34,500 volt power lines whipped around through the air causing electrical black outs in many cities.

As the power poles snapped in half hundreds of transformer banks blew up creating a wild fireworks display. Waterlines spewed geysers along twisted streets. Tons of unrecognizable building parts covered the asphalt and concrete. People ran out of their homes half dressed and scared out of their wits. Many did not have time to take anything with them, except the undergarments they were sleeping in. Some feared it was the end of the world, while others died from fright, worry and panic from the destructive power overcoming Mother Earth.

Thousands died while still asleep as the weight of the buildings crushed and pinned them right where they had lain down to sleep. Throughout Salt Lake City, Provo, and Ogden, so many massive fires were burning out of control that the firefighters stood watching and wondering which building to save. Many Utah cities literally burned to the ground before anyone since no one could save them.

Those watching the satellite television at Sarah Begay's house were petrified from the horror they had witnessed. Sarah told them not to worry about where they were standing because they were on protected ground. She explained that what had been done had been done by the Lord because it was His right to do whatever He wanted to do with His property. Everyone was rather shocked as they listened to her. Some returned to roasting the Hopi sweet corn as others conversed about what had just happened. As Sarah turned away, a man dressed in black stood up by the campfire.

"Hello, I am Mr. Kent. I represent the pisonic groups of the United States. I have come to address everyone here to let you know what the United States government is doing about the end of the world, or perhaps, I should say that the radical earth changes around the world, or whatever you want to call it. There are so many groups, be it religious, atheist, political, sacrilegious, or whatever have their own set of predictions or prophecies," as Ronnie yelled at him at the top of his voice.

"Who made you the authority here?" exclaimed Ronnie.

"Please, listen for a moment. We have studied story after story about the world coming to an end. With that in mind, our present leaders from around the world believe that these three people are the most authentic. We have studied their maps, stories, predictions, and prophecies that are not available to the public yet, because they are classified government documents. So we have asked them to compare their visitations or visions to hopefully help mankind survive this desolation, rebirth, purification, or whatever you want to call it," Yelled back Mr. Kent.

"Good, I have many questions for you?" spouted off Ronnie again.

"I will not answer any questions. The President of the United States has asked me to tell each and every one of you to keep what you hear to yourselves until the government has had a chance to decipher what should be released to the general public. Am I making myself clear?" he asked, after making an unusually long statement that literally shocked everyone.

"Who do we report to or speak to if something develops?" asked Abigail.

Mr. Kent stopped and looked at her. He was lost for words. She literally stunned him by her beauty and grace. She looked prettier than the most glamorous movie star to him. He looked around and thought for a moment after having his breath taken away by her natural lovely smile and long shimmering golden waist length hair that was pulled back by a Hopi headband.

"Well, my dear, you apparently know that Rabbi Raboy, Sarah Begay, and Yirawala are the ones to report to. Simply tell them first and they will be Abel to get in touch with those that need to know," he said softly.

"Thank you for telling me something I already knew," replied Abigail as Raboy looked at her wondering what point she was trying to make.

Yirawala, Sarah, and Raboy took three weeks to discuss the information they had been shown by the supernatural beings. Mr. Kent made it clear that the Federal government was not there to protect the three but rather to gather data from those that had received supernatural information. Raboy was convinced that Sarah's, Yirawala's, and his messages were from the same Divine source to warn mankind what would happen. Sarah was tired from all of the commotion, so everyone agreed that she should go back to tending her precious sheep with Abel to ease her tension.

Yirawala's wife helped Sarah and Abel because she dearly loved animals. It was relaxing for her to help another race that respected Mother Earth as hers had done for millennia. She had been taught all her life, by her ancestors, to respect Mother Earth. She felt it was a blessing to help Sarah.

After tending to the sheep Sarah joined Yirawala and Raboy. They made their final conclusions as to what may lie ahead for those living on Mother Earth based on their supernatural experiences. All of them knew they had no real evidence, but still concluded God was giving them a message. A message that every human being on Mother Earth should be made aware of.

The next morning about four o'clock in the morning, Mountain Standard Time, the Begay land started swaying back and forth five or six times like a serpent moving about. Yirawala called it a sign of the serpent that was stalking its prey waiting for the right time to strike. Later in the day, those at the Begay ranch watched an International Space Link video report showing the Mississippi River from New Orleans, Louisiana, to Gary, Indiana twisting and stretching out of shape, creating a rift ninety miles wide.

The earthquake separated the United States in half leaving every road, bridge, and waterway destroyed from Lake Michigan to the Gulf of Mexico. Death and destruction was immeasurable as the 10.91 earthquake was felt from New York City to Winnipeg, Canada, to Havana, Cuba, to Los Angeles, California. No other earthquakes hit anywhere on Mother Earth that day, not even a tiny tremor.

"Yirawala and Sarah, I think we have done all we can here. I really believe we should return to our native lands before something worse occurs. The maps we have marked up denote places that we think are too dangerous to reside in but again, we know we are only guessing. We haven't had any visitations or visions to support our decisions. Maybe we should keep our discussion to ourselves. Of course, this is my assessment," said Rabbi Raboy.

"Rabbi, I agree with you. We have been here for three weeks and the 10.9 Missouri earthquake may be only another sign of Mother Earth's fury to come upon us all," said Yirawala wanting to return to his homeland.

"Yes, I am very tired from this constant invasion of my privacy. I am worn out and can't take any more of this crowd. It would be a true pleasure for Danny and me to have some peace and quiet. We really need to be alone with our family for awhile. I know this is only the beginning of the sorrows that will happen during the Sixth Purification of Mother Earth. It is in the hands of the Great Spirit Caretaker to do as He wishes. We can keep in touch with each other through these CGPS satellite phones," said Sarah, resting her head on a beautifully designed Native American woven wool blanket.

Everyone decided to leave the Begay ranch. Yirawala hugged Sarah and Danny Begay calling them his sister and brother from the other side of the world. After the massive crowds of people and those that came with Yirawala left, the Raboys stayed with Danny and Sarah for a few more days.

"I am going to miss you, Grandpa and Grandma Begay," said Daniel Jeremiah as he hugged two of the people he loved very much.

"Rabbi, you have made my life worth living. I will never forget Abigail, Danny, Little Sarah, and you even after I become a spirit in the sky with my ancestors. I have helped my father carve these Hopi Kachina dolls for you. It is our way of saying how much we love you. Our love for you will never die out. Who would have ever thought a Cohen Ultra Orthodox Jewish Rabbi from Israel would have made such a big difference in my life. I will more than miss you, my brother from afar," said Ronnie Begay as he hugged Raboy, crying silently in his heart.

At that moment, a Super Blackhawk bio-fueled helicopter approached the Begay Ranch making a swishing sound. When it landed, Colonel Bigwell of the US Marines disembarked while the rotor blades were still turning.

"Rabbi Raboy," barked out the Colonel.

"Oh, no," said Abigail, "you aren't going with him again?"

"I assure you I'm not going anywhere without you," replied Raboy.

"Rabbi, Abigail, I am here to fly you to Edwards Air Force Base. From there, you will be flown directly to Israel and thought it would be appropriate for them to say thank you for all you have done for the American people," said the Colonel.

"Well, Abigail, the show goes on," said the Rabbi.

"That is the truth, but must we be displayed like celebrities?" asked Abigail wanting some personal quiet time.

"Sweetheart, let's get aboard. Maybe we can make some Super Blackhawk Helicopter Love before we land in California. That is, if the Colonel and crew don't mind," said David Raboy teasing her.

"Sweetie, this time I will pass, but well... maybe, no, not this time," said Abigail as the helicopter took off to take the Raboys to Palmdale, California.

When they arrived at Edwards Air Force Base there were thousands upon thousands of people to see them. Some cursed the Rabbi, telling him it was his fault they suffered so much pain while other praised him for his warnings. Still others cheered him, treating him like a celebrity. Abigail became frightened as the many thousands upon thousands pushed their way closer to watch her every move. She was glad when they were escorted to the Presidential Boeing 24B ramjet that would be taking them home via the Space Link.

Rabbi Raboy waved good-bye, as Daniel Jeremiah joined his father, while Abigail held Ester Sarah Rachel in her arms. Little Sarah was a little Abigail with long golden blonde hair and sparkling big blue eyes. They were all relieved to know they were going home.

"Mr. President, why did Utah get the most damage from the Missouri-badlands earthquake?" asked Mr. Kent, "It wasn't anywhere near the epicenter."

"I don't know. Ask God Almighty," replied Joshua.

The ram jet made a right bank and blasted to 75 miles high in space before heading toward Washington, D.C.

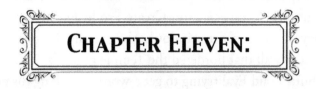

CHAPTER ELEVEN:

FIRST EARTH CHANGES

"At last, home sweet home," said Abigail kissing the front door. "I need to rest. This trip was...," said Rabbi Raboy watching Abigail dash from room to room interrupting him as looked for his favorite spot to sit down and rest.

"Sweetie, I am home at last. Home sweet home. Oh! Yeah! My home," she said.

Half awake, Raboy tried to listen to Abigail but tuned her out and flopped down in his favorite spot, his rocking chair. He rocked slowly closing his eyes while dozing off. Ring, ring, ring sounded the phone. Raboy in stuper got up, stumbled toward the phone answering it. It was Eyal, his best friend, calling to say he was tired of worrying about his family's safety.

"Eyal, we are all tired of worrying. Our world is doing exactly what the prophets have forewarned for thousands of years. We cannot tell God what to do. We cannot say the Lord forgot to warn us over and over. We Jews have disobeyed the Lord's will so many times that it is ridiculous. We have been literally kicked out of the Promised Land several times—once for seventy years and then again for one thousand eight hundred seventy eight years—when will we obey the Lord?"

"Yes, but...but...we were allowed to live in peace in the land of milk and honey for a few hundred years while the Judges ruled Israel, and then again during King David's reign."

"Yes but! Hey listen up! We have constantly disobeyed and were in constant war for hundreds of years and became slaves to the Babylonians before that we were slaves to the Egytians. Yeah, we were redeemed for

235

four hundred years during the time of Persian and Greek empires, but we rebelled against the Lord again, so the Romans were allowed tear us apart because we disrespected our Creator, so he let the Romans tear it down. They did not only tear it down; they totally destroyed it to only leave the outer wall that bordered the Temple grounds."

"Yes, but..." said Eyal trying to get a word in making his point.

"Our prophets starting with Moses have told us over and over and over again to knock off our disobedience and serve the Lord, not man's ideas. I ask you, have we listened? The answer is no and no. We are mere animals that can talk. Of course, that is an insult to animals because they obey God without complaining once. Our world is getting its just due. Hopefully, when we get a chance to build the third Temple, we might obey the Lord for once and keep our homeland. Why are you so worried about something you have no control over? Maybe this Yahshua was the messiah and maybe he will return again with the power and glory we expected from the messiah the first time."

"Yes, David, but I..." said Eyal again trying to get his point across.

"I do know that he was a Jew and a prophet because what he said came true. Regardless of who the Messiah is, we need to rebuild the Temple. To do this we must obey. It is our main goal to build a Temple with all of the splendor and glory that King Solomon gave it. This Temple is not for man, but a house of prayer for all people."

"David, David can I speak!" yelled out Eyal not phasing David in the least.

"I do know that, if we do not obey the Lord, he will destroy us any way he so desires and that is a quote from Moses. I am not condoning what the Christians believe or turning my back on my fellow Jews, but I am telling you the Torah and book of prophets has warned us to not make the Lord angry with our disobedience. A remnant of our people has returned to the land of milk and honey as prophesied by our forefathers. What will befall us if this time we do not obey the Lord? The only thing you need to worry about is obeying the Lord so he will have mercy on your soul," said Rabbi Raboy.

"Thank you, for the sermon. Am I not worried anymore," replied Rabbi Klein.

"Does worrying about something change its outcome?" asked Rabbi Raboy.

"Of course not. Rabbi the answer is no, but is being scared the same thing as being worried?" asked Klein.

"Now that is a question for those psychos that deal with the brain's thinking process. I personally feel the Lord gave us the feelings of hate, lust, worry, fear, depression, love, etc. so we can experience them. Use your emotions, but do not let your emotions use you," said Rabbi Raboy making a sincere recommendation.

"Yeah, I understand what you are saying, but how do you know if you are using the right emotion at the right time?" asked Rabbi Klein.

"I reckon that is why it is called mixed emotions, my friend. Maybe the human body is designed to respond with the proper emotion to protect itself. Then again, it could be part of our design to teach us the universe is not just about us. Contrary to what you or I think, it appears God favors those that demonstrate their compassion and show mercy toward their fellow man. He who has learned the most from our educational process during our short stay on Mother Earth wins," said Rabbi Raboy.

"Rabbi, you said Mother Earth. What do you mean by that?" asked Klein.

"I mean if God Almighty is the father, then Earth must be the mother of mankind since we were made from her dust by the Creator," said Rabbi Raboy.

"Well, if you put it that way, maybe there is merit to what you saying," replied Rabbi Klein somewhat confused with Raboy's philosophy.

"Nevertheless, Rabbi, we are now living in a very unstable world and nobody rich or poor can do one thing to change it. It will run its course and everyone on earth will have to deal with it in their own personal way. Our emotions could possibly be tested beyond their designed limit. When the Creator of all things is angry with us, prayer, belief, and obedience will soothe His anger. What can you do to persuade Him to curtail some of the destruction?" asked Raboy.

"Are we to ask God to stop what he has told us would be through by His prophets? Are we to ask God to stop what He is doing to earth? I say yes, like Moses did on Mount Sinai when the Lord was so angry with Aaron for casting a golden bull to worship. God was so angry he was ready to kill everyone, save Moses," replied Rabbi Klein.

"Rabbi, the Lord has destroyed all of mankind before. Many believe in evolution, but it does not make any sense to me because the universe is too organized. Life started by accident is a better terminology than evolution. Those that think two rocks falling off of cliff were able to reproduce and replenish the Earth are mental midgets," replied Raboy.

"Well, the Lord did use Mother Earth to make mankind, you know," replied Klein.

"I personally think the Lord has made His mind up before the world was created to carry out His will, regardless. I figure that he knew before He instituted Ten Commandments mankind would fail. Since the time of Moses, we have not been obedient. We have repetitively broken His laws written to protect us from one another," explained Rabbi Raboy.

"So you are saying we are all doomed," responded Klein.

"I do not think we are doomed, but we are paying for our mistakes. The Lord will do what he thinks is necessary to control man's disobedience and lust for power. He will destroy the entire planet if need be. The bottom line is that we must stop making our God angry with us. The earth has a very complex, organized, but fragile environment that has been delicately designed to ensure us life. I feel man has impeded the natural flow of things to the point that all of the natural laws that govern the ecological system are such that we are going to have to pay for it with our lives," said Raboy speaking with a heavy heart.

"Rabbi, you are way too deep for me, philosophically speaking," said Klein.

"And so is the Torah for me, Rabbi Klein. I know that the Lord will do what he says and when he gets angry at us, it's time to ask for mercy.

If we keep ignoring the will of God, we are asking for His chastisement," replied Raboy.

"I think obeying our Creator is the most important thing a human being can do, because we are gods in the infancy stage. Our Father knows that we are aware of the difference between right and wrong, because of what we did in the Garden of Eden. He has made it our responsibility to do what is right and His responsibility to correct us when we are disobedient. I know the Lord knows the fate of Mother Earth and outcome of every individual He has created, but He still lets man run around like wild animals. He has forewarned us by several prophets throughout time what will be, and I know we cannot claim ignorance," replied Klein.

"It is unnerving how nature becomes more unbalanced every time mankind tries to improve the natural way of things for human beings to live more comfortably?"

"Yeah. Maybe. You mean we are killing the planet."

"Do we really make life better for mankind?"

"Yes and no, but I mean some things are better."

"Is it really worth all of the trouble for the price we have to pay?"

"Of course, it is. I do not want to live in cave."

"Our rivers, air, soil, and the very fabric that gives all plants and animals life have been infected by our progressive ignorance. We have hid our heads in the sand saying we rule this planet and it will obey our commands. Guess what Rabbi?"

"What?"

"Mother Earth has just let us know, we don't rule squat. We've been like little piss ants running about this planet tearing the living hell out of it. Now it's tearing the holy hell out of us. Oh yes, we think about tomorrow, but with a selfish attitude, not accepting the responsibility we have been given by God to take care of Mother Earth. We are irresponsible—yes, we are!" said Raboy.

"Noah would lower his head to see what we have done. Maybe the plants and animals are crying out for mercy to stop man's abuse, and God is listening to them," said Rabbi Klein.

"What amazes me the most is that the Lord destroys the plants and animals at the same time he destroys man. I wonder what He is thinking?" asked Raboy.

"Noah, born circumcised out of the womb, was given the divine right to preserve the world and take care of those animals he felt could survive in the new earth as its sins were washed away by the great flood. The Lord has watched us constantly destroy His earth because of our selfish ways. Will he have it in his heart to forgive man who is simply an animal who can talk but not think? His thoughts are above our thinking," replied Rabbi Klein.

"Rabbi, now you are getting too deep for me. Our bodies may be made of clay and we have animal instincts, but our souls are spirits like God is," said Raboy.

"Are you referring to what King David said in Psalms that 'Ye are Gods' when he was talking about humans," said Klein.

"I can only speak for myself when I say we must do our best to survive during Mother Earth's purification. We must show our courage during these times. You know the Lord does not like cowards." said Raboy.

"Remember those that were afraid to fight when Moses said God had commanded them so. Only Joshua and Caleb stood fast, ready to do as God had commanded. Since the rest were cowards, our forefathers had to live in the wilderness for forty years and paid for their disbelief," replied Klein being facetious.

"You can be a stiffed neck," replied Raboy.

"They were not allowed to enter into the Promised Land. It wasn't until all of those that opposed God's will had died off in the wilderness, before the Israelites were allowed to enter the Promised Land," replied Klein.

"That must tell you something about God's Will," said Raboy.

"It tells me He is the one in control and we are supposed to listen to His every command. We aren't supposed to make up our own laws that are contrary to His," remarked Klein.

"Gentlemen my little darlings need to go to sleep," said Abigail softly.

"Sweetheart, it's only eight o'clock," said Raboy

"Duh! Do you have any idea what I am saying?" asked Abigail.

"Get what?" asked David.

"Good evening, Rabbi," replied Raboy as he walked Klein to the outer gate.

Abigail stared at him until her face started turning red. She planned to have a surprise birthday party for Daniel the next day. She wanted Daniel in bed early so she could make the cake and decorate it. Rabbi Raboy was told three months ago about her surprise party, but had forgotten her plans. Abigail was an intelligent and reasonable woman, but she couldn't tolerate stupidity. David was acting stupid as far as she was concerned. She started to boil within from her anger.

"Sweetie, what part of stupid don't you understand, the 'stu' part or the 'pid'? Is your last living brain cell starting to function, or do I have to spell it out?" said Abigail being upset.

The light came on as a single spark cascaded through David's memory. He understood why Abigail was upset, and what she was saying. He did not want to live with a disgruntled wife for the next few days, so he changed his attitude immediately.

"Rabbi, I think it's time for me to leave," said Klein almost whispering.

"Good Evening my friend," said Raboy as he hugged his friend.

Raboy went into the kitchen and did something he had never done before. He mixed some cookie dough for Abigail as she mixed enough cake batter to make a seven layer cake. The cookies were to be soft chocolate chip covered with chipped almonds and decorated with smiley faces of various colors. Her plan was to grill Hebrew kosher franks to make American style hot dogs type of party served with kosher snacks and pomegranate juice to drink.

She hired an artist to paint faces on the children and another to make animals out of balloons. She chose traditional Israeli dance tunes for the music so everyone could have fun. Abigail made her own version of a Mexican Piñata she had seen in Arizona, so the children could enjoy the ways of the Arizona Mexican-American traditions. She wanted everyone to enjoy some of her experiences she encountered in the American Southwest.

Working hard through most of the night the preparations were completed. All that was needed was some family and friends to enjoy a day of fun and excitement. Abigail and Raboy managed to get a couple hours of rest. Next thing Raboy knew, there several children running about in the courtyard. They were taking turns being blindfolded swinging a small bat trying to break the Piñata apart to get to the surprise inside, which was various types of hard candy.

The party was a success with fun and games with everyone singing and laughing throughout the day. Abigail finally got to have some peace in her life. Raboy forgot all about the misery he had encountered over the past years.

"Abigail, it has been over eight years since I first met you. Time has raced by so fast that the months seem more like days and the days more like hours. I will be sixty years old soon and you will be only twenty-nine. I know our lives have been anything but normal, but having you by my side has been a blessing that only the Lord could have planned. The earth has been calm now for almost a year since the Mississippi River earthquake ripped America apart. Yirawala and Sarah have not seen any new visions or visitations since we last saw with them. This is the time for us to enjoy ourselves and live the rest of our lives in peace," said Rabbi Raboy, contented.

"Sweetie, we have been through so much I cannot remember it all. I just keep wondering why we have been kept alive while billions of people have died since the Indo-China TWar. I wish it would of never had happened in the first place. I am so sad inside for the millions o f innocent people that have suffered so much from man's own idiotic methods of killing one another. Sweetheart, one of my most kept secrets is that I love you so much that I cry at night while you are asleep. David, I need you and love you more and more everyday," said Abigail, starting to become teary eyed as the words flowed with great passion from deep within her heart. "Sweetheart," graciously replied the Rabbi as he wrapped his arms around Abigail, "I love you more everyday. You become more beautiful every time I look at you. I love you so much it scares me to think what I would be doing without you. As I thank God Almighty for you my heart melts thinking how much I have been blessed by your presence," said

Raboy holding Abigail so tenderly in his arms.

As he passionately embraced Abigail he kissed her ever so gently as he spoke, "I love you with all of my heart. You mean more to me than you will ever imagine."

"Sweetie, have you forgotten something?" asked Abigail.

"I do not think so," he hesitantly replied.

"Sweetie, tonight we must make Birthday Love because that is what gave us our beautiful son of seven years today. I want to make Birthday Love to remember all of the wonderful years we have spent together," she said smiling and giggling like a teenage.

"What are these medicines for?" he asked.

"Sweetie, I bought them for you," she replied, laughing out loud.

"I thought you might need them to satisfy your sexy, loving wife?"

"I am not that far gone yet," he said, laughing at her craziness.

The Raboys made Birthday Love until the full moon rose high into the sky lighting up their new villa. The new villa had four bedrooms and three bathrooms with one of the most dynamic kitchens throughout the land of Israel.

The next morning Abigail started crying for no particular reason. Raboy held her in his arms not saying a word. After she felt better he started cleaning one of his beloved Kachina dolls he had received from Danny Begay. A few moments later she started crying again.

"Why are you crying?' asked David with a sweet tender voice.

"I do not know. It is feeling that has laid a heavy burden on my shoulders. I just feel very sad inside. It is as if something terrible has happened. Do you think I am going through menopause already?" asked Abigail.

"I think you are a bit too young for that to happen. Lean on me, Sweetheart. I will hold you in my arms until you feel better," said Rabbi Raboy worrying about his precious Abigail.

A couple of hours later, the satellite cell phone starting ringing. Rabbi Raboy answered the phone while Abigail had curled up on the new sofa to rest. It was a very sad time. Ronnie Begay informed him that his mother Sarah had passed away that morning. After David heard the sad news, he started crying. It was extremely hard for him to explain to Abigail what had happened. Raboy had to leave the house for a short walk to talk to the Lord.

When he came back home, he found Abigail weeping. Ronnie had called while Raboy was away and told Abigail about the Hopi burial ceremony planned for Sarah. Abigail went numb thinking about one of the most special ladies God had ever placed on Mother Earth had died. Raboy started to weep when he saw his little Rachel crying holding on to her mother. She cried not knowing what was wrong with her mother. Daniel Jeremiah silently watched as mother curled up on the sofa holding Rachel in her arms. Raboy knew that this was one of the saddest days of Abigail's life and did not speak to anyone throughout the day. He was in disbelief that Sarah had died. In shock he did his very best to comfort Abigail during their time of great loss. He spent the rest of the day reminiscing the first time he had met the Begays and all the life changing event that they had been through.

The next day Raboy picked up the satellite cell phone and slowly dialed the Begay's phone number. Abel answered the phone. With broken speech, he told the Rabbi what had happened to his wonderful mother. Raboy could feel how empty Abel's heart was. Raboy started shaking as he listened to Abel explain what would happen at the Native American burial ceremony. He told him every detail since he knew the Raboy's would not be able to attend the funeral. Raboy asked Abel to be the link between the two families. Abel agreed. Both of them wept and said no more as they both hung up their respected phones.

Raboy thanked the Lord for the chance to meet Sarah Begay. A lady that never yelled or acted in any violent way toward her children, family, or for that matter anyone she had ever met. She was the type of person that would always talk to someone and explain what they did wrong and how to improve themselves with a loving care. She had taught her children and children's children that life was a precious gift from the Great Spirit. She had continually taught them that the Great Spirit wanted all human beings to love one another in the worst circumstances. Her children were taught to give their love and love their children with the same amount of affection when they were at their best and worst. Raboy felt that this gentle lady was one chosen by God to give His knowledge, in regards, to the future plans of Mother Earth. Raboy knew that this was an honor very few humans were ever blessed with. No one could have been more gentle, caring, and loving than this wonderful lady. He wept as he thought about this Hopi Native American, who spent her final days loving her family and precious sheep in northeastern Arizona.

"I was blessed to know this woman. Abigail we must visit Arizona again and pay our due respect and see how Danny Begay is doing," said Raboy holding Abigail in his arms.

"I agree. We must go back," she replied and then went a sat in Raboy's rocking chair.

Raboy decided to call Yirawala and tell him the news about Sarah.

"Hi, Yirawala, it is a pleasure to hear your voice. I called to let you know that Sarah died," said Rabbi Raboy.

"My Rabbi friend, last night I was caught up in the Dreamtime. I saw Sarah become like the speed of light. She came to tell me what was to come. She showed me Mother Earth being broken up into many pieces. The earth was carved up into five big slices. Each slice seemed to be in a different location but Australia was saved from this devastation. Although, I was not shown anything happening to my ancestral lands during this Dreamtime, but I know we will be affected by the Sixth Rebirth as the whole earth must go through her cleansing."

"Do you have any idea exactly when or where this might take place?" asked the Rabbi.

"No, except the vision was a powerful one. It made me feel so upset that I have been not been able to rest. I am glad you have called me," said Yirawala.

"Thank you, my friend. I will let the authorities know. I am not sure they can prepare for this. I hope they will believe me when I tell them Mother Earth has started her Rebirth," said David Raboy.

"I am truly sorry Sarah died. She was such a wonderful woman that God was glad to have taken her into His bosom. I really loved the sincerity she had for the safety of her children and respect for Mother Earth. Other than that I do not know what to say," replied Yirawala.

Raboy decided to call his brother at the Israeli Embassy in Washington, D.C. so he could inform the newly elected President Krueger of the USA know what might happen to the world at large. He was aware that the world was a dangerous place to live since over two billion; five hundred million people had died due to the Asian T-War, but had not been briefed about Raboy, Sarah, and Yirawala spiritual knowledge. Being an atheist, the President shunned the information as nonsensical and went about his Oval Office business neglecting what he had been told.

Ninety-two days after Sarah's death the television flashed an alert that there had been a massive earthquake in South America along the Amazon River. The earthquake was so strong that it changed the course of the river by two hundred and seventy-three miles. There was damage to almost every building within five hundred miles of the earthquake epicenter. Villages were inundated by flood waters while others saw the Amazon River dry up overnight. It scared everyone in the world to think that Mother Earth could geographically change again.

This was the second earthquake that took a major slice out of the tectonic plates. It had only been months since the original Missouri earthquake that spread throughout the Mississippi River Valley. Since that quake, the Mississippi Valley kept spreading apart. It was now over three hundred feet deep and sixteen hundred miles long. The water was rapidly became a mixture of sea water and fresh water along the many tributaries along the mighty Mississippi River Bay. The state of Illinois was split in half by the Missouri Earthquake. It separation ended only fifty-three miles from Lake Michigan. Interstate 80 along the southern tip of Lake Michigan was the only gateway between the East and Midwest other than some Mississippi Bay ferry boats. The overburdened US Army Corps of Engineers built multiple, temporary Mississippi crossings from New Orleans to Gary, Indiana.

The most shocking event was that New Orleans did not have one building collapse. The old French settlement escaped without any harm as the city's ground rose up from the earthquake about one hundred and twenty feet high above sea level. New Orleans bobbed up and down like a ship on rough seas. Some of the streets were ripped apart leaving one side fifty feet higher than those living on the other side. Back in Brazil the Amazon River had been diverted and blocked off at hundreds of places along the River for over two thousand miles. Thousands of villages were flooded so fast that many settlements instantly lay in ruins. Millions were caught in bed asleep as it had hit at 3:23 am. New cliffs were created by the land lifted over a thousand feet higher. The Andes Mountain Range slid twenty-two hundred out to sea and twenty-seven feet northward creating new islands near southern Colombia. Everyone on the South America continent felt the land ripping apart right under their feet.

For five months, Mother Earth lay dormant. Most of the dead had been buried in South America. Millions of healthy people were left to rebuild their respective nations. The ancient rivers of the United States and Brazil had developed into small bays. The Mississippi Bay was twelve hundred miles long and ninety miles wide. The Amazon Bay was twenty-one hundred miles long and one hundred and ten miles wide at the largest area.

Tranquility ended when several earthquakes hit the same day in Africa, India, and along the Danube River in Europe. One was 12.8 in Africa, 14.2 in India, and 12.7 in Europe. The Danube River basin was sliced open for hundreds of miles, leaving a gap over sixty-four miles wide in places. Every village, town, and city was affected with thousands of human beings killed or trapped in buildings. Many were injured as the river bottom dropped almost two hundred meters while spreading apart. Africa was sliced south of the Lake Sahara region. The quake carved out a slice of that was over two hundred sixty miles wide and close to three thousand miles long. Its deepest point was five hundred feet. The newly formed Congo slice started filling up with water from the Congo River at one end and Lake Sahara from the northern end.

The last quake occurred along the China-India border in the Himalaya Mountain Range. It cut from Bangladesh to China up through northeastern India into southwestern China across to Pakistan. It was a two thousand mile slice that cut Mount Everest in half. The Earthquake created a sheer cliff that was over twenty-six thousand feet high along the highest point of the mountain range. The rift started along the Brahmaputra River and continued into the Himalayas. It turned and spread down the Indus River all the way to the sea, thus making part of Pakistan and India many islands. The gap was over two hundred and ninety miles wide and a thousand feet below sea level. The Indian Ocean immediately rushed in to fill the gash with a three hundred foot wall of seawater.

Thousands of dead were swallowed up by the gigantic tsunami caused by the massive Indian Ocean sea floor earthquakes. Entire villages were swept away. The rich and poor were treated with the same terror as three giant waves crushed the life out of them. What once were well organized cities and villages instantly turned into waste lands. Millions were left homeless and some their entire families were carried out to sea to never be seen again. Many would not eat the fish caught at sea fearing they might be eating fish that had just consumed their loved ones.

Two weeks later after the earth had stopped moving about, many different African nations started to fight over the Lake Sahara and Congo Bay water rights. The Sudanese wanted all of the water of the Nile River that entered into Lake Sahara. They wanted the lake completely filled with fresh water, giving thousands of African people new farmlands that would be irrigated by the newly formed Lake Sahara. The Egyptians were ready for all-out war since their fresh water supply had been cut off. Saudi Arabia stepped in and offered a compromise in the name of peace. Each nation was given the necessary water they needed to survive on and the rest ran freely into the Sahara abyss. The Congo River now drained into the Congo Rift.

The leader of the UIP peoples (India, Bangladesh, Pakistan, India, Kashmir, and Sri Lanka declared the five mile high cliff national park for all people. This was done so that everyone on earth could see the marvel that had been created in three days. Sri Lanka was not an island any more since it had been lifted up to make it join the Indian continent and part of (UIP). With over eight hundred million killed in the Indo-China T-War the countries of Indian origins decided to unite peacefully unite so they could rebuild their lands.

The world now had five rifts carved into it in less than two years. It was miraculous that only a few million people died from the massive earthquakes that literally moved real estate borders and national boundaries over night. Mother Earth had geographically changed the way she looked. Sarah Begay's dream had come true.

"Rabbi Raboy, those that live in the Sahara Desert want you to visit them," said Dr. Einstein.

"Dr Einstein, are they Cohen Orthodox Jews or those Reformed Jews that ignore most of the true interpretations of the Torah?" asked Rabbi Raboy.

"No Sir, they are Islamic brothers and sisters that pray to Allah,"

"But . . ."

"Hold your tongue. This is not about religion or any religious war. They merely want to meet the great prophet from their father Abraham. They are not going to harm or worship you. They want to meet the prophet that restored life into the desert lands."

"Dr. Einstein, what are you trying to do? I do not want to hear any guff, lies, or nonsense. Exactly what will be achieved by me visiting this land of, whatever you call it? What is your motive?"

"I want to continue my studies of the different layers of sentiment before the rift is completely filled with water. Who knows what artifacts could be found?" said the Dr.

"If he would be granted permission, in turn, it would also bless me with a commission of watching these people," explained the chief ISP agent.

"Watching these people? Dr. Einstein, I am not a Prophet, a Blessed One, or a Saint. I am merely a son of Abraham, as you are. This would be deceiving the complete world population to say the "Blessed One" has come to bless you. How many different governments or people would you lie to for your own benefit? Never mind I do not want to hear your lie about my question. What is the point?" asked the Rabbi.

"That is the point. You are someone that has told the world the truth. There has not been a major prophet in the world for hundreds upon hundreds of years. You are the first prophet from Israel in over two thousand years," said the Dr. trying to use Raboy.

"Dr. Einstein, do I have to hit you over the head with a brick to knock some sense in your brain? I would like to see the results of the Sahara Desert earthquake but not under false pretenses. I will only go as a tourist to see with my own eyes what God has done to Mother Earth. You see, Professor, there are great gulfs between the way that you believe life started and how the earth was created. The time for purity has expired between Jewish scientists and religious Jews. Plus, that fact that there is a great gulf that exists between me, a Cohen ultra orthodox Jew, and those that believe in Islam." said the Rabbi.

"Rabbi, strange as it may seem those believers of Islam believe that Mother Earth was created by the Lord in six days, too, as you do. This makes the gulf between them and you much smaller now, does it not?"

"Professor, is that like saying sea water and fresh water are both water and should be considered a good source to obtain drinking water? I think not. I will visit this area for the sake of our nation, Israel, so hopefully the Temple can be built without any remorse from those that oppose its location. So do you're exploring or whatever you call it," said Rabbi Raboy being disgusted with Dr. Einstein's cunning ways.

Arrangements were made for the Rabbi to see those that were Christians, Jews, and Moslems that lived along the newly created Sahara Lake that stretched from Sudan to Morocco to Zaire. Those that worked the ancient salt mines of Timbuktu and the nations of Mali to Niger, Zaire, Algeria, Chad, to western Sudan were ready to attend a celebration of the prophet. They had to meet the man that asked God Almighty to cause the great and terrible miracle that brought the Sahara Desert alive again. They wanted to honor the one chosen by the Lord to shower them with His many blessings. "Are you ready for this?" asked David directing his comment to Abigail.

"Sweetie, after what we have been through, this is child's play," replied Abigail.

"Woman, if Sarah, Abraham's wife, was anything like you, no wonder he is the father of many great and diverse nations. Of course, I could compare you to Noah's wife, the second mother of all present human beings living on Mother Earth. What I am really saying, sweetheart, is that you are the most remarkable lady on the planet. The Lord must have put a lot of thought into creating you," said Rabbi Raboy, feeling the most unique lady living on Mother Earth standing by his side.

"Flattery will get you everything you want, sweetie," said Abigail.

"I understand that we will be escorted and protected by the United States Air Force, Marines, and a contingency of police from many nations," said Ambassador Raboy.

The Ambassador had constructed many political alliances with many nations before his brother, Raboy was to fly over and visit the Sahara nations. The Israeli government thought this would be an excellent opportunity to open some new political doors and trade negotiations. Raboy had no idea he was being used as the go between for international political agreements.

The Raboys were taken aboard a large helicopter that flew low to the ground so the people could see the Prophet—Rabbi Raboy. As they approached the Nile River in southern Egypt, they could see thousands of people wearing white garments and shouting along the riverbanks, waving their arms at the air parade. Abigail was the first to notice the giant gash across the Sahara Desert as far as she could see. It looked like the Grand Canyon in Arizona to her.

"Has the Sahara Rift filled up with that much water from the Nile River already?" asked Raboy.

"No and yes," said the commander of the mission.

"A geologist on the International Space Link has located several giant fissures spewing water into the rift from underground rivers located only eighty feet below the Sahara Desert surface. It has helped the rift fill with water much faster than anticipated by our scientists," said the commander.

"Remarkable," said Abigail.

They flew along the length of the rift for hours until they made their first stop in the middle of the northern African nation, Chad. Thousands upon thousands of desert dwellers were yelling out "Holy One, Holy One." They cheered Raboy like he was the one responsible for all the remarkable changes that had occurred in the desert. After a short rest, they traveled on to Nigeria near southern Algeria where thousands had encamped at the rest station to praise the Rabbi.

After another short stay, they traveled on to Timbuktu, Mali, where the salt mines had supplied the fuel to support the economy of the Mediterranean Sea Empires for thousands of years. The salt mines finally had easy access to the Nile River via Lake Sahara. The salt slabs were still a valuable commodity even in the modern markets. Though salt is easily mined throughout the world, this special type of salt was not available anywhere else. The three thousand year old salt mining continued producing the perfect salt for human consumption.

"Sweetie, this is marvelous. These people think you are a hero," said Abigail laughing.

"Maybe they do, but it is for the wrong reason. I have done nothing other than make people aware what Isaiah and the other prophets had prophesied hundreds of years ago. If it weren't for the Jewish businessmen and political sharp edged movers that support the Hebrew University, which supports my career, I'd tell them all where they could go, and Hades would not be my first choice," said Rabbi Raboy.

"Calm down, David. This lake is going to change their world so let's help them celebrate," said Abigail.

"Abigail, this is not the end of the disasters that have been foretold concerning earth and you know it. Aren't you a bit weary of the fact that this lake may not even be here in the near future?"

"Sweetie, God has chosen you for that very reason," said Abigail.

"And what would that be for, my little Honey Dew?"

"Ahh, that excites me. When did you come up with that name? I like it. Now, the reason I chose you because you are serious, meek, and humble. This makes you the most likely candidate in the world. Pride and greediness is what causes grief and all wars," replied Abigail.

"I know what you are talking about," he replied.

"Not to change the subject, but I suppose now you will want to make Lake Sahara Love in the middle of the desert," remarked the Rabbi.

"I was thinking more on the line of Sahara Desert Love, but Lake Sahara Love will do just fine, my Tiger Muffin," said Abigail, as she kissed him in front of the thousands attending the jubilee.

As Raboy looked upon the thousands of souls that lined up for miles and miles along the Sahara miracle, he became speechless from her kiss. He knew it was God that had changed the Sahara Desert forever, but he did not know why. His biggest fear was the fact that the Abomination of Desolation that Daniel the prophet spoke of had not occurred yet. He wondered what the people would shout when the desolation would occur.

"David, what do think about running for Prime Minister of Israel?" asked the Ambassador.

"Brother, brother, brother, where have you been all of my life, locked in a closet? I am not a political leader, I am a spiritual leader. I know Israel was never supposed to have a king, President, Prime Minister, or whatever in the first place. It was always to be judged by the Levites known as Judges described in the books of the Torah. The People of Judah and Benjamin decided they wanted a King. After they got a king, the other ten tribes were absorbed while the others started migrating to Europe, the Mediterranean Sea lands, and to the outer regions of the Middle East. We lost being ruled or judged by the Lord's ways. Our secret scrolls have revealed these facts. Israel is not a small nation along the Mediterranean Sea, but on the contrary, it includes most of what we call European nations," said Rabbi Raboy.

"David, I did not need an education, sermon, or serenade. I only was making a suggestion."

"Dear brother, why did you think I would want to become the ruler of Israel when it is not in my blood? Furthermore, every nation that readily accepts the Ten Commandments as their basic laws are rightfully sons of Abraham. I believe they are the ten lost tribes of Israel. I think it amazing that all European, Northern Mediterranean Sea, and most Middle Eastern nations use the Ten Commandments as the fundamental foundation in constructing all of their laws? The secret scrolls have recorded the truth that the ten lost tribes were never lost in the first place. We knew where they were all the time and still do, today as we speak," said Raboy.

"Dear brother, I am sorry I mentioned it. I will tell the leaders of our country they do not have to worry about their jobs being whisked away by you," said Jeremiah.

The ceremonies were to be a grand event for Israel because they could make more political headway with the Islamic nations that it had done for hundreds of years. Even with many praising him, Rabbi Raboy was to be given the highest security possible during the celebration. They did this because they felt Raboy would be a target for the malcontent. Even Dr. Einstein figure that what constituted a blessing for one person or group people could spell disaster for the other so she personally supervised the protection plan for Raboy.

Rabbi Raboy looked the Sahara rift over one last time before the aircraft made its landing. He knew that Yahweh worked in mysterious ways, but this was a spectacle beyond Raboy's imagination.

"Sweetie, do you know what is coming up next month?" asked Abigail. He knew she had something planned for the near future, and was obviously giving him a hint, but he had no clue.

"Yes," he replied quickly.

"Yes, what?" she asked.

"Yes, to your question,"

"What was my question? I bet you were not listening to me," she replied.

"Yes, I was. I even know how to read your mind intelligently."

"What am I thinking right now?" She asked getting angry with him.

"You are thinking that I do not know that you want to celebrate Sarah's birthday. How's that for reading your mind?" asked Rabbi Raboy.

"Well, maybe you're right, but I will never admit it," she replied wondering if he could really read her mind.

The Sahara Lake ceremonies started at a lake that had died years before ending the means to earn a living for many Africans. Now it was full of water. A miracle for the desert dwellers of northwestern Africa.

CHAPTER TWELVE:

THE SECRET OATH

Raboy was shocked, awed, and bewildered by the millions that wanted to see and touch him. Some even wanted to kiss his feet. The African desert dwellers marveled by the great wonder of the world had been formed by the creation of Lake Sahara. Many chanted Raboy over and over again as he tried to tell them it was Gods work and he had nothing to do with the lake filling up with fresh water.

They boarded a aircraft that was escorted by three American F-51ZT class fighter crafts, which had three engines and four wings for total air and space supremacy. Raboy was told that these crafts could fly Mach 18;pl during engagements. A pilot could fly at Mach 8;pl and turn in any direction instantly at this speed with the aide of a suppression gravitation monitor. This would keep the pilot only feeling 1-2Gs during three hundred and sixty degree turns. Plus the crafts could fly at a mere eighty miles per hour and land like a helicopter. What amazed Raboy the most was that these lightening fast, shiny silver-grey triangular fighters could fly for seven days at a time without refueling. Dr. Einstein disclosed secret military information to Raboy that many people had mistaken them for UFOs back in the twentieth century during a time of development when they were under flight tests.

"Captain Johnston, I noticed you are using the Space Link to navigate this ionosphere class fighter," remarked Dr. Einstein.

"Yeah, our Commander-in-Chief wanted to take this opportunity to let the world leaders know that America still has air superiority, although our nation has been torn apart by the Mississippi Earthquake we still can protect our nation," replied the captain.

"Why list them as Mach 18;pl when every secret agency throughout the world knows they can fly faster than the speed of light?" asked Dr. Einstein irritating the captain.

"Dr. Einstein I remember that one of your ancestor's say that we will never be able to fly faster than Light Speed?" asked the captain snapping back at Einstein.

"Captain please. I have been told by our military spies that these triangular anti-gravity crafts can fly about 1.4 times faster than the speed of light. You can be there before the sun can send its lambda waves through the solar system," replied the cunning Einstein.

"Yes, the sound barrier was broken in the mid-twentieth century and the light speed barrier was broken in the late twentieth century, but it had to be kept secret. Can you imagine what would have happened to the economy if the world did not have to depend on oil?" asked the captain.

"Yeah, I know. We would not be in this mess we are in now if the economy was less dependent on a product that kills Mother Earth. That's what it is all about—greed and power. The Asian T-war would have never happened, and Mother Earth would still be in tact if it weren't for the lust for power. Now we have a planet that dying from over use and abuse, because America's military kept the zero green house power supply a secret so their military could manipulate the world into their way of thinking. Which might I add is merely a ploy to control the world's economy, just as the Romans did with military might, and then with religious doctrines," said the angry Einstein.

"Einstein, any other nation would have done the same thing. At least, America keeps rough nations from making slaves out of everyone. And might I add, we have kept Israel from being overrun many times. Not that we are against the Arabic nations, in contrary, we are for the freedom of every race and their political and religious methodologies. So that is why the Space Link crafts using heavy metals as fuels have been kept secret," said the captain.

"What are you mighty Americans going to do about the magnetic fields in the earth's core from tearing the earth's surface apart?" asked Einstein.

"Absolutely nothing because we have the wait and see approach," remarked the captain.

"Yeah, wait and see if anything is left to salvage. I know that you may know this, but just in case your have forgotten, this is the only planet in our Solar System that we can live on. Your light speed space link craft cannot fly fast enough to take us to a planet that has what Mother Earth has to offer humans," replied Einstein.

The captain and Einstein then laughed out loud at each other knowing that Mother Earth was is trouble and there was nowhere for humans to go. They even laughed harder when they started discussing how man's secret weapons were useless against powers of the universe. Einstein rejoined the Raboy's since they had flown across the Nile River near the Sudan and Egyptian borders.

Raboy had listened to the captain and Einstein as they flew over millions and millions of people standing along the banks of the three thousand mile Sahara Lake. Ironic as it may seem, the newly created lake was a direct result of the worst earthquake in African history.

The Sahara Lake ceremonies ended with the Raboy's returning home to a big welcome from a group of his fellow countrymen that were Moslems, Christians, and Jews. Rabbi Raboy shook his head and waved at the screaming crowd, wondering when it would all end. He never really wanted all of this attention, because he truly felt a great prophet or special one chosen by the Lord should be humble at all times. In his heart he knew it was not appropriate to receive glory and praise. He knew that praise and glory always belonged to the Lord of Hosts and never to any mortal man. He silently asked the Creator to have tender mercy on those that did not understand the ways of the Almighty.

Raboy reluctantly helped Dr. Einstein achieve his goals of exploring the Sahara Rift. Raboy persuaded the African nations to let Dr. Einstein gather data that might help substantiate the three prophecies. Of course, Raboy did not know that the new world order really were the ones that put Einstein in charge of the exploration. They were looking for a to disprove the Bible and its contents and context. If the Rabbi would have known the facts, it would not have mattered. He was a puppet of man's evilness and a saint of God's Holiness. A multitude of earthquakes continuously rattled the newly formed Sahara Lake region during the months of extensive digging and exploration. Dr. Einstein did not submit to the warnings Mother Earth was giving him because of his arrogance. He wanted to find out if there were any ancient artifacts relating to the Hebrew people ever living in Egypt. He employed over twenty thousand scientists and laborers to sift through the thousands of miles of the newly exposed layers of ancient earth. His findings were interesting, but unfortunately nothing was discovered that would explain man's prehistoric past or disprove the existence of early Biblical history.

"Rabbi Raboy, we need to talk secretly," said Rabbi Blumenthal.

"That would be fine with me," replied Raboy over the phone.

"Did you finish your report about the Aborigine circumcisions?" asked the elder Rabbi.

"Yes, about six years ago." He was irritated by the elder rabbi's question.

"Oh, good then, I will be Abel to assign you a new project to research," joyfully responded the elder Rabbi.

"Rabbi, why would you want to assign me another project?"

"Raboy, when you were younger, you would never question me. Now that I am on my deathbed, are you testing me? I thought I taught you something about respect? I thought you were taught to respect those that know the truth about the Torah. Why are you abandoning me? Why do you forsake me so? You know I have always loved you the most of all the Cohen sect. Please, can you fulfill my last dying request?" asked the elder Rabbi, lying supine on his hospice bed with IVs hooked to his arm and oxygen plugged into his nose.

"Of course, my brother, it would be an honor to fulfill your request."

"Rabbi, I must tell you a secret that can never leave your lips. Promise me. You must promise me or the Lord will curse Israel another two thousand years."

"I am committed to my promise the conceal the Cohen oath until death."

"Good, then I will continue. I am one of the sixteen and my successor died an untimely death due to a heart aliment. I need to pass on the secret name to another and I wanted you to be the one."

"I cannot accept your offer, Rabbi Blumenthal."

"You cannot accept my offer? It's your obligation to honor the true pronunciation of the Name of God," sternly replied the elder Rabbi.

"Rabbi, I cannot accept your last requests before you die."

"Why? You must honor your God, the nation of Israel, and your Cohen brotherhood?" asked the weakened Rabbi breathing harder to gain his strength.

"Rabbi, I am seventh of the sixteen and cannot take another position. Now you must not tell the others of my position and find another before it is too late."

Dead silence came from the other end of the phone. Rabbi Blumenthal was lost for words after hearing the truth from Raboy. He breathed many sighs.

"Well, that creates a secret problem, my Cohen brother. I did not know. I am not supposed to know that either, am I? I will have to find another in days or even hours according to my physician. What fate has the Lord left me with? You do know all sixteen secret names have no specific value given to them individually, but the seventh name out of the sixteen happens to be the pronunciation used by Elijah. You are a blessed man," replied the elder Rabbi.

"I did not know that, Rabbi. But you say that you have the first of the sixteen pronunciations. The one spoken by Moses which he heard during his encountered with the Holy of Holies at the burning bush. Is that true?" asked Raboy.

"I have been sworn to secrecy, Rabbi, but since I know your secret I will expose mine only once by agreeing," said the elder Rabbi as he passed out.

"Rabbi. Rabbi! Rabbi!" yelled Raboy.

Rabbi Raboy held the phone in his hand for five minutes, wondering what to do. He thought that one of sixteen had died without passing on the pronunciation of Yahweh that Moses personally had passed down from generation to generation for thousands of years. He wondered if the first pronunciation of the name of Yahweh would be lost forever as he slowly hung up the phone.

"Abigail, where is Daniel?"

"He is in school. Why do you ask?"

"I must fetch him at once and take him to the room of secret scrolls," he hastily replied while running out the door.

Rabbi Raboy ran to the school and yanked his blue eyed, red curly haired son out of school. He grabbed his arm tightly as he hastily ran to the room of secret scrolls. Raboy explained the secret ways of the elite Cohen theology to his son and ran out the door. He quickly dragged his son to Rabbi Blumenthal's deathbed chambers. Upon hearing the news of his grave illness, many dignitaries from around the world had gathered outside the elder's chambers. Raboy was mystified how so many knew about his condition and he didn't. Upon entering the cottage, two other Hebrew Cohen High Priests and one Catholic Priest looked at the beads of sweat running down Raboy's face as he tightly gripped his son's hand and pulled him along.

"What is the matter?" asked a Conservative Rabbi having tea with the Catholic Priest.

"It's Blumenthal. Has he died?" asked Raboy.

"No, he is fine," replied the Priest.

"Why has everyone gathered about his dwelling then?" asked Raboy.

"Dr. Einstein has reported that he may have found a tablet with writing about Joseph that was exposed by the Sahara earthquake. He thinks it was buried in the Sahara Desert thousands of years ago along the Egyptian-Sudan Nile River border. He was to expose it after meeting with Rabbi Blumenthal," replied the Rabbi.

"Oh my God, I thought Rabbi Blumenthal was dead, dying, or something of that nature," said Raboy.

"Well, he is dying, but are we not all dying?" replied the Reformed Jewish Rabbi.

Raboy had enough of the small talk and the gossip spewing from the mouths of the dignitaries. He demanded an immediate private audience with Rabbi Blumenthal. The door opened so Raboy rushed to his bedside, dragging his son along.

"Rabbi, here is my son. You can trust him with the first secret pronunciation of the Lord's Holy Name," said Raboy hastily.

"I'm not sure it is kosher to let two secret names be in one family, especially father and son," said the weakened Rabbi.

"The Name of God has nothing to do with being kosher, Rabbi. If my son is not acceptable, then I have no other way to help you. I am not sure how to recruit anyone else for you while upholding the secrecy of the Code. You know the pronunciation of the Name must not be lost. Samuel anointed King David when he was a child and gave him the second secret pronunciation," replied Rabbi Raboy.

"What assurance will I have that he will become one of the chosen of the Cohen Ultra Orthodox Rabbi of the Secret Sect that Moses started at Mount Sinai?" asked Rabbi Blumenthal in his last breaths.

"Rabbi, we haven't time to spare. What do you want to do?" asked Rabbi Raboy. He worried that the ancient of all ancient pronunciation of the name Yahweh would be lost forever. He knew that his great grandfather, the patriarch

Abraham, was the only one that ever pronounced the Name of God like Adam did until Noah. This pronunciation was almost lost when Joseph was sold by his brothers into slavery since he was the barer of the Holy Name. When Joseph became the great financial advisor of Egypt, a great famine struck the Middle East. Joseph had no one to pass down the one of sixteen pronunciation of the Lord's sacred name. Later, after Jacob joined him in Egypt, the name was handed down through the tribe of Levi. That's how Moses became the one who knew the real pronunciation of the Lord's Holy Name. It was apparent to Raboy that his son Daniel would inherit the secret pronunciation of the Lord's Holy Name. They way Moses had pronounced it over thousands a years ago.

"Rabbi Blumenthal, you know that the fifth pronunciation of the Lord's Name is the way the prophets Daniel and Jeremiah pronounced the name when the second Temple was built. All sixteen pronunciations must be preserved just as the original Ten Commandments have been over the last four thousand years. From the time the Commandments were entrusted to Moses to govern men on earth, we have never lost them, save once to the Philistines. I will help my son remember the pronunciation without hearing it myself," argued Rabbi Raboy as his colleague gasped for his last few breaths of air.

"Let it be done. I must speak to the young man alone first so he knows exactly how it shall be pronounced. He must speak it to himself at least ten times a day for the rest of his life without anyone else hearing his voice. I expect that you will take care of everything necessary in this regard. When he becomes of age, he must enter the Cohen secret brotherhood. According to ancient Hebrew unwritten laws Moses handed down to Aaron, Joshua, and etc. He must utter the oath and keep it secret throughout his life," said the elderly Rabbi gasping for air.

These sudden change of events did not rock or shock Rabbi Raboy much. Since his first encounter with Abigail at the fresh fish market his life had been anything but normal. He knew God was running the show on Earth, not Satan or man as many disillusioned human beings tried to proclaim. Raboy walked outside the room and wondered what Yahweh thought as He watched mankind needlessly kill his fellow man to gain a false sense of power, which eventually ran out as time ran out on each leader's legacy. Raboy had never once questioned the Lord's authority during his many years as a Cohen. From the time he had taken the secret oath to preserve the secret scrolls and the records of Moses, Raboy had never loosened his tongue, save this one time. He knew the truth about how the twelve tribes of Israel crossed the Red Sea into the Promised Land, and then migrated throughout Asia, Africa and Europe.

Now his son would become one of the sacred sixteen that held the secrets of the holy sect handed down from Moses to Aaron to a very few hand selected Levi tribal members. It often bewildered Raboy why the High Priests of Israel were called Jews, when Moses, Aaron, and all other High Priests were not members of the Judean tribe, but rather were Levites. Raboy was upset in his heart with the Maccabee's decision to allow the other ten tribes that worshiped the God of Abraham, Isaac, and Jacob to be called Jews, when it was not the truth.

Nevertheless, King Solomon built the first Holy Temple for man's atonement to the Living God of Abraham, Isaac, and Jacob. It was to house the original Ten Commandments written by Yahweh Himself. The Cohen Jews knew it was proper by the laws of the Torah for the Levites to be the High Priests and judges of the land. The Judeans now called Jews, tried many time to take command of the Holy High Priesthood ordained by Yahweh and rule the land with one man. As the people wished, the end of Judges ruling Israel came to and end when King Saul was inaugurated as the first king. The most perplexing issue known to the Cohen's was that Yahshua's (Jesus) father, Joseph, was a Judean and his mother, Mary was a Levite. None of the past or modern Sanhedrin would ever admit that Jesus was the only spiritual leader in centuries that was a rightful heir to both the kinghood and priesthood. They even forbade his name to be used or any children to be given the name Yahshua (Joshua) from the seventieth century A.D. until this very day.

The new deal between the Sanhedrin and the Cohen Rabbis was to built the Temple and then see what the Lord will do. They made it clear that their number one goal of all Cohen's and members of the modern day Sanhedrin was to build the Temple under any circumstances. If thermonuclear weapons were necessary to protect the Temple, then so be it, but, since the Asian T-war, their rock hard approach had softened. But now any thermonuclear weapon would destroy the very fiber that held Mother Earth's magnetic field in tact. With all of these variables, the Cohen group that Raboy belonged to felt that the Hebrew University should do blood tests and DNA scans to ascertain who was a Levite and who was not. The object was to use only Levites of the original twelve tribes of Isaac to be the High Priests of the Temple. They wanted only them to carry out the rituals and atonements in the Temple so the lineage had been kept secret and sacred. Some cried out against this act because it was too familiar to the Hitler's Aryan race scam that brutally murdered millions of human beings.

He knew the sixteen sacred pronunciations of Yahweh were left in the hands of the original Levites and that only a handful of Jews really ever knew the truth. Since the Levites had never considered themselves Jews, but rather sons of Isaac, they rarely let their Judean brothers into the realm of secrets contained within the Holy Scrolls written by Aaron and Moses.

His son had now heard the words that Moses had heard upon Mount Sinai. They were the very words handed down to Aaron, Moses brother, when he became the High Priest of the first Chosen People to bring the Lord's laws of obedience to mankind. It now became the responsibility of his son to hold the first of sixteen secret pronunciations of the Lord's Holy Name and preserve it for all time. After thinking about what had just happened, he took his son by the arm and told him the truth about the Cohen society that dated back to Moses.

After returning his son to school, Raboy returned home to sit in his easy chair and relax from the turmoil that had invaded his peaceful life. Abigail tried to pry out of him what was so secret, but David did not budge. He lodged his tongue to the roof of his mouth to control his speech. She did not like the blank stare on his face but figured this wasn't something she had the right to know. He told her to drop the fifty questions. As she walked away in disgust, Mother Earth started shaking and rocking the in many directions. Abigail immediately dropped what she had in hand and prepared run for cover. She picked up her beautiful daughter with both arms.

Dust rose throughout their house as pictures were thrown off the walls onto the floor. Abigail's eyes became big as saucers when she discovered that she was unable to move her body in any direction. As the earthquake grew in intensity the floor became just like a boat twisting and turning upon the rough seas as wave after wave tossed them about the room.

"David, do something! David, do something, please," screamed Abigail as loud as she could while bracing herself and holding on to little Sarah with one arm.

"It's out of my control, dear!" He yelled back at her.

They both rode out the 8.1 earthquake for three minutes that felt like an eternity. The quake ended with the two of them frozen in place waiting for something even more drastic to happen. The room was filled with dust, and the floors were covered with the Raboy's personal belongings. The house looked like a thief had rummaged through it desperately looking for something valuable to steal.

"Abigail, I must call my brother the Ambassador. I must know if this happened around the world," he said wearily, as he hugged Abigail and his daughter. They were all shaking as they clutched one another too afraid to let go.

"Yes, that would be the right thing to do," said Abigail not wanting to let her husband out of her grip.

"Hello is Ambassador Raboy available?" asked Raboy.

"Yes, may I tell him who is calling?" said the secretary.

"It is his brother, David from Tel Aviv. I urgently need to talk to him right away."

A few moments went by that seemed like an eternity to Raboy.

"David, what is the urgency?" asked his brother.

"We have just had an enormous earthquake. I think the prophecies should be considered again. This may be the beginning of the end."

"Beginning of the end of what?"

"The end of Mother Earth."

"David, you are overreacting," replied the Ambassador.

"Brother, I do not think you understand. You must contact the President of the United States at once and set up a meeting with him," ordered David.

"Brother, brother, I know they are not going to jump because Israel had an earthquake. Hold on a minute, I am being summoned on another matter." Ambassador Raboy put David on hold. Rabbi Raboy was on hold for over five minutes, but he did not dare hang up.

"David, the President of the United States will see you right away along with six other world leaders," said the Ambassador.

"What did you say? Only a moment ago you scorned me, and now six nation's leaders would like to meet with me. Why the change in attitude?"

"Seventy earthquakes occurred around the world at the same time," said his brother.

"Seventy earthquakes! How severe were they?" asked David.

"From the message I recently received, the quakes ranged from 6.0 through 8.2 on the Richter scale. Many cities, buildings, dams, and other structures have been severely damaged causing immeasurable death and destruction. Many nations want to convene to discuss the damage," said the Ambassador, saddened by the news.

"What do they want to do? No one can stop the earth from releasing its fury and inflicting damage to the inhabitants of Mother Earth."

David was stressed with what he had heard but at the same time felt that the Torah, Dreamtime, and Meha prophecies were starting to unfold. He remembered what had been written in a book titled Revelation by a rough Jew named John the revelator who had told what would happen to those living on earth during the end of time," explained Rabbi Raboy to his brother, "Woe to the inhabitants that dwell on Mother Earth, proclaimed John the revelator seven times."

"Brother, the survivors of the Asian T-War hope you are wrong," said Jeremiah as he abruptly hung up the phone.

Rabbi Raboy turned to Abigail and asked her to turn to a news broadcast on the television to find out what was going on worldwide. Seventy earthquakes had rocked Mother Earth at the same time causing massive worldwide destruction.

The scientists said it was impossible, but this was before the discovery of the tectonic plate's magnetic lines of Vibra Force holding Mother Earth's fragile existence together. Now the scientists searched for answers so they could fix it. Their only problem was to understand the

Vibra Force of equilibrium and develop a counter measure or synthetic reproduction. Raboy had heard them speak of this before in the map cellar of the White House.

CHAPTER THIRTEEN:

PACIFIC RIFT

"Abigail, are you looking at what I am looking at?" asked the Rabbi.

"What do you mean? We are both watching the same news broadcast," she said, breaking out into tears.

"Sweetheart, I mean...do you understand what is taking place as we speak?" he said thinking about the original message he had received from the being of light.

"All I can see is more death and destruction caused by mankind's lust for power. I feel God didn't have anything to do with man's animalistic behavior. Mankind has done all this by himself. The Lord has simply told us beforehand what we would do to destroy Mother Earth," she cried, caressing her children.

"Sweetheart, you have a point. The Lord has used his servants to reveal what lies ahead for those that live on Mother Earth through prophesy. You have been very perceptive in your statement that the Lord didn't have to do a thing to eliminate humans from the face of the earth. Oh, my God, look at that!" cried out Raboy watching the news broadcast. The broadcast showed millions of people overtaken by a gigantic tidal wave. Possessions and bodies were churned up and mixed with the sand along the sea shore. Buildings and vehicles were swept out to sea as the two hundred foot waves wiped out everything in their paths. Hundreds of dead bodies and coconut palm trees lined the beaches mingled together among the mixture of debris.

"I think He knows He will eventually have to step in to stop the destruction or else no one will be left alive on earth. Exactly when He will step in to stop this nightmare is a good question for all of us to ponder. Know one knows but Him. Why are intelligent human beings so evil? Man is paying for his disobedient ways. I wonder what it was like in the days of Noah when man's every thought was seen as evil in the eyes of the Lord," as Raboy spoke out he looked toward the heavens.

The international news stations continued to televise city after city as each was churned into rubble. Journalists cried out as they witnessed Mother Earth destroying thousands of the millions of Asians who had survived the Asian T-War. One reporter tried to encourage those who were seeking good news to hear his report out. He announced that it was good news that only 340,000 people were killed during the day of the seventy quakes. He tried to convince the survivors it could have been far worse. His attempt was in vain since the maltitude of tsunamis smashed the coastal Asian homes and infrastructures into bits and pieces. One international journalist showed thousands of cities destroyed throughout East Asia just hours after the seventy earthquakes caused the numerous tsunamis worldwide.

Two weeks later the Rabbi was asked to address the U S Congress and International Consortium. Abigail was initially upset about Raboy leaving their home, but decided it would be best for him to meet the worldwide political leaders in Washington, D. C. In Israel, he was grilled by fifty hungry reporters anxious to get an insight of what would happen next. Raboy laughed at all of them until his sides hurt. He explained in depth how the Lord's agenda could not be controlled by any form of intervention created by man, except prayer and obedience.

Raboy decided that a conversation with Yirawala and Sarah Begay's eldest son before attending the meeting could help him. He hoped they had some valuable information that would help the world leaders make some sound decisions for their people. After three days of meeting with the world leaders, which was a waste of time, he decided to visit Australia once again to meet his Aborigine friend in person.

Landing in Queensland, Raboy was met by a host of Rabbis and officials from the Australian government. Abigail put on a million dollar smile as she play acted for the general public. In reality, she was foreboding as to what Yirawala might reveal from his latest Dreamtime experience.

A fairly young man wearing conservative Jewish Rabbi attire approached Raboy. "Rabbi, how was your trip? Did you receive any angelic visitations on your way from America or Israel?"

"No, Rabbi Simone, we saved that event until you were present so you could experience the Lord's messengers first hand," retorted Rabbi Raboy.

"Rabbi, what did your brother, the Ambassador, have to say about the devastation caused by the seventy quakes?" asked an elder statesman from the Australian Government.

"He stated that only 340,000 lives were lost throughout the world from the abomination, but I personally view this number as a significant, tragic loss. I'm telling you that if one of your loved ones had been killed, then it would have been tragic experience for you, too. I do not understand how some human being think. If it happens to them it's God-awful, but if happens to someone else, it seems to be alright," replied Rabbi Raboy.

"Rabbi, you seem somewhat bitter," remarked a parliament member.

"Not bitter, but rather concerned that everyone seems to be discounting the fact that this could be only the mere beginning. The prophetic words given to us by our heavenly father are being ignored by the so-called expert theologians. The prophetic messages given to our ancient prophets are Divine words of knowledge. Discounting the prophetic Holy Words given directly to the prophet by the Holy Spirit is blasphemy. Our present day wisdom is simply an insult to the intelligence of the Lord. Our understanding of the Lord is a mystery to all of us."

"It appears to me that the Lord predetermined what would transpire on Mother Earth long before she was created," said Rabbi Fellerman.

"Brother, the Lord has chosen whom He has chosen and man cannot change that, but we can change how we live on Mother Earth, and the way humans think about how to live our lives," said Raboy.

"I think I know what you mean," replied Rabbi Cohen.

"You might think you know what I mean, but you do not have any idea, because I have no clue as to what I mean," said Raboy.

"God Almighty wants us to love one another like ourselves, but we cannot do that, can we? No, we cannot. He does not want to destroy us or Mother Earth," boldly said Rabbi Cohen.

"Are you talking to me or yourself?" asked Raboy.

"I am talking to you and myself at the same time," replied Cohen.

"Alright and maybe, but I somewhat agree with your point, but what does the Lord really want from us? My opinion, from mere observation, is this. If humans do not know what they want out of life, how could they comprehend what the Lord wants them to do with their life?" asked Rabbi Raboy.

"Enough with all of this guessing about what we think the Lord wants. It's time to get on with the finer things in life like, ahh, like having a kosher dinner with some fine wine," suggested Rabbi Cohen.

"Rabbi, you just do not get it, do you?" replied Raboy vehemently.

"No, Rabbi, you do not get it! We were put on this planet to live and die, and that is about it. You have very little power other than to eat, sleep, and die. Since we are not dead, let us eat, and then take a nap," replied Rabbi Cohen.

"I am beginning to believe that the people down under are upside down in their thinking. I do not want to eat with you or sleep near you. I am leaving here and going directly to the Aborigine to have some wild lizard meat, freshly cooked over an open fire pit, along with a cup of fresh spring water. I am going to mingle with those that have taken care of Mother Earth," said Raboy, walking away.

In their first contact together, this same Rabbi had tried to get Raboy to divulge secret Cohen information to him regarding the sixteen secret pronunciations of Yahweh. Raboy got word that he was going to attempt to persuade him to surrender knowledge about the four thousand year old secret scrolls. This secret Cohen knowledge had been entrusted to Rabbi Raboy until the next Cohen Ultra-Orthodox Rabbi could step forward to continue to care for the ancient Holy Secrets. Raboy felt it was blasphemy for the Rabbi to ask him these type questions. With in mind he decided to leave immediately. Raboy requested to be taken away from all the massive confusion at Sydney and taken to Alice Springs, so he could meet up with Manandjiwala who could take him to Yirawala.

"I see you have returned just as Yirawala had envisioned in the Dreamtime," said Manandjiwala, while loading Raboy's luggage into his Land Rover.

"Of course, we have returned. Your father is one of my closest friends. Plus, I am fascinated with his ability to use the Dreamtime as his link between the physical and spiritual worlds," replied Rabbi Raboy.

"And we love him and your people," added Abigail.

"We are especially glad to know both of you are alive considering all that has happened to Mother Earth over the last six years," said Rabbi in a softer voice.

"Yes, it is remarkabel who has survived. My father has known from the beginning what would become of his people. Rabbi, the Dreamtime messages are part of our secret ceremonies given to us by the spirits of the Aborigine people that lived thousands of years ago. I am amazed that my father has even told you anything at all. It is unbelievable how he has revealed the secrets about the Aborigine to you. The people from my tribe love the both of you. You came to learn and accept our ways, in contrast with the white invaders that came to destroy our customs along with our lives," said Manandjiwala.

"It is an honor to be accepted by your people," said Raboy.

Manandjiwala was frank. "I cannot tell you anything about Aborigine tribal ceremonial ritual secrets. Only my grandfather can do that since he has been chosen by Ngaljod to expose this knowledge. He determines who is permitted to have access to our spiritual knowledge about how Mother Earth will cleanse herself in preparation for the next generation to come."

"I understand," replied Raboy knowing his culture had the same secrecy.

"Truly, the Lord works in mysterious ways," thought Abigail. She had quietly listened to them discuss information and ideas for almost five hours while riding down the dusty Australian Outback roads. Abigail took the time to reminisce about the first time they had met the Aborigine. Learning about the sacred birds that protected the people and the ways that the Aborigine had survived on Mother Earth for thousands of years fascinated her. She laughed within her heart as she thought about how she had to expose herself while participating in the circumcision ceremony. It tickled her soul that she had to keep the whole thing secret.

Upon arriving at the tribal grounds, the Raboys couldn't believe the grand feast that had been prepared for them. What really amazed Raboy was the fact that the Aborigine had prepared a Judean kosher style cuisine. He said nothing as he ate the perfect kosher meal that had been prepared to honor his family. Yirawala was present but never whispered a word, not even as to say hello to Raboy.

The Rabbi did not attempt to speak to Yirawala either. He knew any attempt to pry information out of him would be an insult. Raboy had been told before the ceremonies that every Aborigine was afraid to find out what knowledge had been given to Yirawala during his last Dreamtime experience. It was well known throughout the Aborigine tribes that Mother Earth had started her Sixth Rebirth, but it was not known when and how it would affect the Aborigine people.

"Rabbi, are you well rested?" asked one of the tribal leaders.

"No, I am still very tired from my journey."

"Good. The more tired the flesh is, the more acceptable the spirit is. We will escort you and Yirawala to the secret caves of Ngaljod so the Dreamtime messages may begin," said a tall thin elder with a snow white beard.

David Raboy hugged his son and daughter and kissed his lovely wife before he walked off with a group of ten elders. This would be a challenge for Raboy, being out of shape, because he would have to walk approximately five miles to get to the secret ceremonial caves. The Rabbi had been there only one other time and that was six years ago when he got the chance to study the Aborigine circumcision ceremony.

Raboy could feel the heat from the twenty foot bonfire was intense as they walked into the camp. He heard four Aborigines playing some ceremonial tunes. The sparks sprayed so high in the sky it appeared as though they could reach heaven and touch the Lord's toes. Raboy laid his feeble body down in the sand as the elders started to pranced around the bonfire. One elder brought out some special drink prepared for the Dreamtime ceremony. When it was given to Rabbi Raboy, he drank his fair share. Being somewhat drugged by the ceremonial drink he sat there in silence for hours as he listened to the repetitious sounds of the horns.

The early morning sun broke over the horizon as a cool breeze gently rattled the leaves of the Eucalyptus trees. Mother Earth was awakened by the gift of warmth and nourishment as the sun poured out upon the land. Blinded by the intense morning sunlight, Raboy's eyes immediately shut and he was not able to reopen them. Due to the physical stress his body had endured over the last three days and partaking of the toxic Aborigine ceremonial drink, he was beyond exhaustion. Since he did not even get a couple of hours of sleep his body was numb. One elder came and handed him some cool fresh spring water to splash on his face. Hoping it might soothe the Rabbi's painful eyes, but it did not help him much.

"Where is Yirawala?" asked Raboy. He tried squinting his eyes and putting his hand up to block out the sun's bright rays tyring to see what was going on around the camp.

"He is in the Dreamtime. We are not sure if he will ever return," said one of the younger elders.

"What do you mean you're not sure if he will ever return?" asked Raboy frantically.

"Rabbi, we are not sure if he will return. How else can we say it?" asked the young elder.

"Is he dead, going to die, or what?" cried out Raboy.

"Rabbi, when one enters the Dreamtime, we are never sure if they will return. He may decide to stay in the spirit world," said the tall thin elder.

"I have traveled thousands of miles to speak with Yirawala at his request. Now you are telling me I don't get to say hello or good-bye. Is this some secret ceremonial test or initiation? I really don't have time for your tribal secret nonsense," said Raboy, thinking Yirawala had died that evening while he had been sleeping on a sand pile.

"Rabbi, I think you need some more rest. You are not acting like the person we met six years ago," said Manandjiwala.

"Manandjiwala, Mother Earth is not the same she was six years ago either. Billions of people have died and millions more are suffering and are confused, including me. What will happen to my children and their families in this uncertain times? No one is the same anymore," said Raboy being very upset with Manandjiwala's calm Aborigine disposition.

"Rabbi, are you asking me what will happen to your family? I am sure your God, Yahweh will take care of them in the spirit world."

"Shhhh! Do not speak alound the Lord's name. Do not say the Lord's Holy Name out loud. That is forbidden!" screamed Raboy.

"Sorry, if I have disrespected one of your idiosyncrasies. Like I was saying no one dies or disappears. The Creator of all life takes care of His children. You are one of His children, are you not?" asked Manandjiwala.

Rabbi Raboy sat back down on the sand pile shaking his head. He started to rock his body back and forth like he had done many times at the Wailing Wall in Jerusalem. As he rocked and moved his head back and forth the Aborigine tribesmen seemed puzzled. When Raboy saw everyone staring at him he stopped rocking. He sat there motionless as he looked around and patiently waited to find out what had happened to Yirawala. Yirawala sat there for hours not moving a muscle.

After three more days and nights of eating Aborigine cuisine and drinking fresh spring water, Raboy noticed Yirawala come out of his trance. Raboy sighed, and then yelled out so loudly that those playing the horns stopped to see what was going on. The ceremony continued as one of the elders restarted another monstrous bonfire. A few minutes later, Yirawala slowly started to move about.

"Yirawala, you are alive! I am glad you have decided to rejoin those living in the flesh. I am so glad to see you," said Raboy jubilantly.

Yirawala looked at him and walked over to the bubbling, fresh spring water and drank two handfuls of water. Then he walked back over to the elders and motioned for them to leave Raboy and him alone. For almost two hours, Yirawala stared at Raboy not saying a word. The Rabbi was so tired that all he could do was stare back wondering what Yirawala was doing.

"If he would just speak one word, I would be happy," Raboy thought to himself. Suddenly, Yirawala began to speak.

"Brother, our land is going to be magnetically torn apart. The great magnetic lines that hold Mother Earth together will break up into thousands of pieces. Some pieces will be small and others will be large. Those that decided to annihilate one another have upset the very foundations where Mother Earth gets her strength. Even the ancients of the Dreamtime are worried that the Aborigine people won't survive the Sixth Rebirth. It will take the next ten days to explain what I have seen," said Yirawala. He got up, lowered his head, and then started walking toward his outstation leaving Raboy and the others behind.

"Wait a minute!" yelled out Raboy, "Please wait a minute! I need more information than that. I have not traveled this distance to see you just so I might sleep on rocks using weeds for my pillow."

"Sit down on these fallen trees destroyed by the White Devils that have tired to change Mother Earth to their likings. We are guests of Mother Earth and when she is tired of her guests she simply gets rid of them," said Yirawala, slowly and calmly.

"Yirawala, what is causing Mother Earth to be torn apart?" asked Raboy.

"Since the Sixth Rebirth cannot be stopped by any human being, whether dead or alive, I will tell you some of our oldest ceremonial secrets" replied Yirawala.

"Can I get my notebook first so I can write them down? My memory seems to have decreased over the last three years," requested Raboy. He knew if he did not write it down, he would forget something that could be the crux from those that live at the speed of light.

"The Aborigine believes that Mother Earth is held together with lines of magnetic force and if this force is disturbed in any fashion she will become unstable and break apart. I have seen, in the Dreamtime, Mother Earth breaking apart just like the clay bed that has dried up after the rain storms," said Yirawala.

"What will spark the Sixth Rebirth and cause this to happen?" asked Raboy for the third time.

"I have already told you that the T-War between India and China has already done that," replied Yirawala slowly.

"You are saying it is too late to prevent what will happen to Mother Earth?" asked Raboy.

"Rabbi, you are not stupid! You know exactly what I am saying, and yet you refuse to believe what has been said. I have read the prophecies of your Torah, in which you were instructed by your Angels from the Master Spirit of all life to tell mankind about the pending desolation. I have studied your Holy Book and know that thousands of years ago four of your prophets told you that Mother Earth would go through some devastating changes. Why do you keep acting like a child?" asked Yirawala.

"Alright my friend. So man has started the destruction of earth, which is exactly what the Lord revealed to our ancient prophets concerning what would come upon the earth. What are we going to do now?" asked Raboy.

"We are going to have to ride it out. Hopefully, some human beings will live through the desolation to propagate our race. If not, we will vanish like the dinosaurs forever and ever. That means our species will never dwell on Mother Earth again. We will simply become fossils like the dinosaurs," said Yirawala. He held his speech as the tears started running down his withered face.

"We are going to have to stop this insanity," replied Raboy.

"We are not going to stop anything. You and I will watch Mother Earth rebel until she has finished her temper tantrum. Maybe our ancestors will be here when she starts her Seventh Rebirth. That will be the final rebirth to end Mother Earth's life cycle as a life producing planet. She will ultimately end up like Mars did billions of years ago. Our history will turn into dust, whereon no future life forms will be able to make sense out of what transpired during our reign of the planet," replied Yirawala.

"You make it sound so final. Some of my ancestors have said there will be a new heaven and new Earth where man will live in peace and harmony. I am not sure what they were talking about, but I am sure this is only the beginning of our lives. I mean there must be something for our spirits to go to after the flesh dies out," replied Raboy.

"Rabbi, the Aborigine knows that life continues after the flesh dies," he replied.

The two got up from the old stumps and walked the last two miles back to Yirawala's outstation in silence. After they returned to Yirawala's village, Raboy and his wife stayed with his tribe for ten more days so that he could write down Yirawala's Dreamtime message. Their children got to experience the Aborigine's culture which was extremely different from that of a Cohen Orthodox Jewish belief.

One hour before they were due to drive back to Alice Springs, the Earth started screaming with high-pitched sounds, like owls screeching in the night. Some of the tribal dogs cried out while others tried to bury their heads to block out the high-pitched sounds. Yirawala looked over at Rabbi Raboy one last time before his grandson Manandjiwala put the Land Rover in gear and drove off. Raboy and Yirawala did not tell anyone what they had discussed about the Dreamtime. Abigail kept quiet knowing better than to ask her husband about the time he spent in the Outback; she knew he would tell her if she needed to know.

Five hours later they arrived at Alice Springs. Manandjiwala gave David and Abigail a boomerang carved by Yirawala for protection against the Sixth Rebirth. Yirawala did this hoping that Raboy's seed would help replenish Mother Earth after the Sixth Rebirth. At that time, Manandjiwala shocked them by mentioning that Yirawala was going to die soon and that he wanted them to always remember the ways of the Aborigine. Since they had experienced his culture firsthand with open arms, Manandjiwala told them that Yirawala loved the Raboys with all of his heart and soul. He told Raboy that Yirawala saw visions of his son becoming an important and greatly loved ruler after the Rebirth.

Abigail started to cry and wanted to go back to say goodbye, but Manandjiwala told them that it was best to remember his grandfather the way he wanted. The Raboys were picked up at Alice Springs by several Australian and Israeli government officials. An Ultra-Orthodox Jewish team wanted to escort the Raboys to Brisbane for a day of meetings with a worldwide Jewish council to find out what had been revealed. Raboy declined the offer knowing that the Jewish group just wanted to question him about the Aborigine and Cohen secrets.

Rabbi Raboy kept quiet. Some Jewish leaders were furious with Raboy, but kept their silence knowing Raboy. He sealed up what Yirawala had told in the outback as to what was going to take place within the geological earth. The Raboy's left the next morning for Israel.

"Dr. Einstein, what a coincidence meeting you here boarding the same plane that we are taking to leave Australia for Israel," said Abigail knowing his waywardness.

"Well, yes, and no, my beautiful lady," replied Einstein.

"Yes and no. What does that mean, Doc?" asked Raboy.

"Well, the truth is, I was put on this plane to gather any information that you may have. Since you totally shut down during the debriefings and such, I was selected to work on you," replied the professor.

"I have not said anything because I do not know anything, except what Yirawala saw in his Dreamtime. The fact of the matter is, I am not sure what he said, so there you have it. Since I am not sure what I could say about what he said as being fact, fiction, or fantasy, I have remained silent. Is that clear enough for your spying efforts, professor?" rattled off the Rabbi.

"Why did you say that? Rabbi, I am not a professor, or a spy, and my real name is not even Einstein. How does that settle with you?" replied Agent Simon. Raboy became upset as he listened to the obnoxious fat man grinning from ear to ear.

"Why are you following us around? Are you some kind of international secret agent? Are you here to keep me from revealing any secrets to the wrong side of someone's government?" asked Raboy.

"The answer is no to all of your questions. I am here to make sure you are protected at any cost. This plane is filled with security agents from over sixteen different nations that want you kept safe. That is why I am around you. Whether you believe it or not, I am assigned to protect you. So relax and enjoy your flight," said Dr. Einstein (aka Agent Simon).

"The world is getting ready to be torn apart from within and you think you can keep me safe, ha, ha to you," said Raboy getting into Einstein's face.

"I am just doing my job," said Einstein lying to Raboy.

"Since you are a man with many talents and names, maybe, just maybe you can answer some questions I have. These magnetic tectonic plates that hold Mother earth together are they real or theory. Have I found a real geologist to answer my questions or are you a complete liar at everything you do?" asked Raboy being angry with Einstein.

"Well, the truth is no one knows anything about your Aborigine beliefs," he replied.

"Thanks for putting my life in chaos as all life on this tiny planet that may end any day now," replied Raboy knowing Dr. Einstein was still lying.

"You do not need to find a real geologist. All I have to do is relay any question or problem to our top scientists, and I will have an answer for you in minutes, if you have a logical and reasonable question that can be answered."

"When we land in Tel Aviv, I want to have a complete chart of any information about the magnetic tectonic plate lines of force that hold Mother Earth together. And I mean drawings from an artist, a quack professor, freaky scientist, or normal educated scientific person's work. It will help me immensely," replied Raboy.

"I will find out what I can, but the Americans, Soviets, and British will have to help including the German, French, and Japanese scientists.

You are the one that can motivate them to assist you, but I will try to have a comprehensive report for you in two or three weeks."

"That would be the most helpful thing you have ever done," replied Raboy.

"What are you going to do with such information, if it exists?" asked Agent Simon.

"I have no idea. But the sooner I gather some data, the sooner I will know." Raboy started to stare down Dr. Einstein. Dr. Einstein laughed at him.

All of a sudden the Jumbo Jet started falling out of the sky. The flight attendants were thrown around the fuselage along with the notebooks, magazines, and drinks. Numerous high-pitched, ear piercing screams shot throughout the aircraft. Raboy looked at his beautiful Abigail to say good-bye as the aircraft began to shake very hard. As everyone prepared for the worst the pilot regained control of his craft. He immediately announced over the public address system that they had just encountered a fifteen hundred foot drop caused by a wind shear. Dr. Einstein's face was white as snow and his eyeballs looked like they were popping out of his head. A hush fell over the plane as the flight attendants calmed the passengers down.

Everyone went back to the personal agendas as their jumbo jetliner continued to Tel Aviv, Israel. About an hour before their arrival time, the aircraft pitched and dropped another thousand feet causing one engine to fail which caused the other jet engine to scream as it took over the aircraft's entire load. The captain let the air traffic controller know the craft was in trouble. He told the controllers he should be able to land according to the manufacture's parameters governing the emergency landing procedures for that particular aircraft. The cockpit door swung open for a moment and the captain took a good look at everyone's disposition. The passengers were motionless as the flight attendants did their best to keep everyone calm. As the captain glanced around looking at the passengers the other jet engine stalled out.

"Oh, my God! Everyone, we have lost both engines. Thank God Almighty we are on a glide path that will hopefully take us directly into Tel Aviv's International Airport runway TwoNiner. Nevertheless, flight attendants prepare everyone for a crash landing!" barked out the Captain, as he jumped back into the cockpit.

The jet was flying about thirty-two thousand feet when the captain started to glide it down. Abigail started crying. Raboy held her hand as he looked out the fuselage window to see if he could get a glimpse of what was happening to the plane. Sweat started beading up on his forehead. The passengers were prepared by the flight attendants for the worst when the captain made another horrifying announcement.

"Ladies and Gentlemen, this is your captain. We have another major problem with our aircraft. All of the electrical systems have all failed except for the oxygen generators and cabin pressure controls. We are going to try to gently take the plane down to ten thousand feet. We are presently attempting to crank down the auxiliary generator propeller. This will enable a small generator to supply enough power to hopefully keep the electrical navigational circuits energized. At this time, we do not have any radio contact with the ground. Please, sit in your seats quietly," he said calmly. Dr. Einstein's started sweating blood as his hand froze around his glass of scotch and water. Abigail and Raboy looked at each other wondering why the Lord would let them be killed this way after all they had been through. All of a sudden a brilliant light appeared inside the plane. Everyone thought the craft was exploding as they ducked and screamed out for mercy.

"Rabbi Raboy, do not fear for Yahweh has sent me with this message," said a voice coming from the mist of the brilliant golden light.

"Who are you? Is this a message that we are about to perish?" asked the Rabbi.

"Fear not, for I, Michael the Archangel have been given authority to take control of the plane and land it safely. Yahweh's message is thus: He, the Alpha and Omega, is controlling everything on earth, not man. He still has many works for you to do. Those left on earth need to read our Father's Holy words of truth written in the books of the Law, Prophets, and Revelation," said the thunderous voice as the light instantly vanished from their sight.

The craft engines were dead quiet and the electrical systems that navigated the craft were still not functioning properly. If the flight had not been during day, the passenger section of the aircraft would have been in complete darkness. A tall lanky man dressed in an expensive suit suddenly spoke up. He was one of three Russian Jewish secret agents there to protect Raboy.

"Please, Rabbi, forgive me and bless me for I am a terrible person that has done many wrongs in my life. I do not want to die, but if this my hour, please asked the Lord to forgive me," As Rabbi Raboy was about to reply to his request, the bright light appeared again.

"Fear God Almighty and trust in Him, not man," said Michael the Archangel, as he appeared and vanished from the aircraft leaving everyone dead silent.

Out of the silence, Raboy's son started singing his grade school theme song. Most the passengers looked at him if he were insane or had a serious mental problem.

"Hush up Daniel, so your daddy can speak," said Abigail.

"Everyone, I have no idea what is taking place. How this plane will land is a complete mystery to me. I believe the angelic messenger sent from the Lord has control of this craft. So you might as well sit back, relax, and enjoy your flight," said Raboy, being nervous.

"Hello, this is your Captain. Everyone, please take your seat and fasten your seatbelt. We are now on our final approach to Tel Aviv International Airport. Our navigation controls and engines are dead. We have no way of telling the air traffic controller of our problem. Rabbi Raboy, please pray for a safe landing," requested the Captain, trying to control his aircraft.

The plane glided gently to the ground in a textbook landing mode. There were hundreds of firefighters and rescue teams all along the tarmac. Then just as the plane was about to touch down both engines fired up and all electrical navigation worked as if nothing had happened. The Captain and First Officer both scurried about adjusting the controls to land the plane. They taxied over to the appropriate gate and stopped twenty feet short of it as many military, federal, and airport police surrounded the craft.

A drive-up gate was locked onto the door next to the cockpit. The flight attendant opened the craft's doors to let the officers on board. When they looked around, they could see that almost everyone on the plane were fellow colleagues in government law enforcement. Then again the brilliant light spoke as one could make out the image of an Archangel. All of the law officers ducked and hid their faces as the light blinded them, except for Dr. Einstein.

"Yahweh and the Messiah rule the universe. Worship no other God and only trust in Him and His messiah forever and ever." His voice echoed like thunder throughout the plane, as he vanished into the unknown.

"Abigail, I love you with all my heart and soul," said Raboy embracing his wife, son, and daughter in his arms. Out of the corner of his eye he could see Dr. Einstein approaching him.

"Rabbi, Rabbi, you must immediately tell everyone what the visitation from the Lord means," cried out Einstein.

"I do not know what you are talking about. Can you accomplish what I have asked you to do regarding the lines of demarcation via the magnetic tectonic plates?" asked Raboy.

"Yes, we can," said about thirty agents at once.

Raboy turned and looked at the passengers, and then peered back at Dr. Einstein who was the devious secret agent of the Israeli Secret Police. Raboy then turned to exit the plane when a man wearing a white shirt and black tie came bursting into the belly of the plane. He frantically yelled at the captain of the airliner.

"I lost you after your last communication. You said you lost both engines and then poof just like that you disappeared off of my radar. Then moments just before you landed, you reappeared on my screens out of nowhere. I figured you had crashed somewhere near Mount Sinai. Next thing I know, you are landing without a runway clearance or assignment. What the hell is going on here?"

"Jehovah was just showing us who is running things in this world, that's all," remarked Dr. Einstein. He spoke right into the Air Traffic Controller's face while pushing him back away from the crew.

Raboy immediately turned and looked at Einstein and smiled. Abigail grabbed the children and told Raboy to get the carry on luggage. They walked down the steps not commenting about the flight. Still frightened from the ordeal, everyone looked like mannequins to Abigail. She could not reason if they were safe or if she was dreaming.

Three days later there was a knock at the Raboy's home. Abigail rolled her eyes back when she looked at her husband as Daniel Jeremiah rushed to open the door.

"Mama, the fat man that keeps irritating father is at the door," said Daniel, now the official holder of the first pronunciation of sixteen secret pronunciations of Yahweh.

"Isula! Can you ever leave us alone? We would like a week of peace and quiet, especially after the chaos we encountered from our last trip!" demanded Abigail.

"Sorry, but we need your husband more than ever," said Dr. Einstein.

"What is so urgent that you must come to our house in the middle of the night?" asked Abigail.

"We have the plate tectonic maps with some futuristic illustrated drawing of magnetic lines of force composed by Dr. Johan Larsson. Hopefully, it will help your husband interpret Yirawala's Dreamtime message. You must hurry because the Jet Propulsion Laboratory in Southern California has recorded some very unusual magnetic disturbances near the Greenland/Canadian Arctic Circle border."

"Simon, we have to go back to the States and speak with our Arizona Hopi Native American friends first before any interpretation will be presented to any government officials," said Raboy.

"What do those Native Americans have to do with magnetic disturbances in Canada?" asked Einstein.

"I have no idea, except the Meha may give me a clue as how to unravel the mysteries. I am not sure if it will be useful or have some sort of a significance that will answer some of my questions. But since I feel the need to know your concerns will have to wait," said Raboy.

"Maybe, maybe not. I will simply inform the rest of the world that you are too busy to help us. Don't you realize that we are scared so much that no one think straight, much less sleep at night because of these weird earth changes? Here you are procrastinating without any regards to the rest of the human race. It must be nice to know that you are personally protected by the Lord," said Einstein.

"How am I protected? Why are you such a rude person? The Lord does what he wants. I do not have the power to tell Him what to do. He has His own timetable—no idiotic human being can control His schedule. I am a servant of the Most High and must obey His words and commandments. I am not subservient to man's silly dreams based on extremely little knowledge as to how the universe really works," said Raboy.

"Alright already, I apologize, except my family is at risk. You ask me to get this information and now you are scolding me. What is a simple man like me to do? I saw the angel appear on the aircraft that told us how God is running the world, not some evil spirit or man. If the Lord is in complete control of the universe, why is He allowing this desolation to happen to innocent human beings?" barked back Einstein.

"Einstein, there are not any innocent people living on earth. We have all sinned from the beginning. When Adam and Eve sinned, it became part of our genome. So no one is innocent in the eyes of the Lord. I say to you, trust and obey the Lord for there is no other way," said Raboy.

"I am scared Rabbi, and so is the rest of mankind. Have you been asleep the last few years? We need some sort of answers so we can sleep at night," said Einstein.

"I know your fears, but I am at the Lord's mercy just like you are," said Raboy.

"Rabbi, I think it is a little too late to do anything since half of the earth's population is dead already," replied Einstein being upset with the earth falling apart.

"Give me two days to mill over the information you've given me," replied Raboy.

"Goodnight, Dr. Einstein," said Abigail ready to push Einstein out the door.

"Please come back in a couple of days. I must talk with my wife and colleagues before I address your request," said the Rabbi.

Dr. Einstein shook his head and left without making any more comments to the Raboys. David knew they had to address the situation, but he wanted to leave on his own terms, not the term of some character that seemed to have no concern about his family's welfare. After two days had passed, Einstein decided to visit the Raboy's home again.

Einstein used his fist to pound on the door several times. He knocked and knocked for almost two hours, calling out to Raboy. As he pounded for the umpteenth time an Israeli military police stopped to see what all the fuss was about. Einstein immediately pulled out his ISP badge and showed it to the officer.

"Why are you yelling and calling out their names, as if they can hear you, Doctor?" asked the Israeli Army Major.

"I told them I would be back in two days. Well, that's not true. I was told they would let me know their decision in two days. Since I didn't hear from them I came over in person to find out why," replied Simon.

"How long have you been pounding on the door, Doctor?" asked the officer.

"For about two hours."

"Two hours. For God sakes, why so long? It should seem apparent to you that they aren't home. Or they don't want to talk to you," suggested the officer.

"They must talk to me. Our world is going to explode, and the government needs to know when and how. This is Rabbi Raboy's house. He has been instructed by the Lord's Holy Angels. Surely you must know who he is?" asked Simon.

"Yes, indeed, I know who he is because he is my cousin," said the officer.

"Then you will help me find him?" asked Simon.

"No, I will not help you find him because he isn't in Israel," replied the officer.

"What do you mean he is not in Israel? How do you know such information?"

"Because he was taken to a special jet at midnight to leave for the States. He requested that you would not be included," said the officer with a stiff lip.

"I am not included? I am the man that discovered him and protected him. Now I am not included in Israel's secret government operations? How can I be left out when I am the man in charge of all operations?" asked Simon.

"As you have said, you apparently don't know everything about every operation your office provides for its citizens. Please, stop beating the door down and go home, sir," said the officer.

"Stop beating the door down and go home! Stop beating the door down and go home!"

You idiot, I am not beating the door down! I am trying to help save as many people as I can. I need Rabbi Raboy to interpret the damn Dreamtime, Meha, and Torah messages for the Israeli government," said Dr. Einstein. His face had become bright red.

"Sir, I was told they would contact you through the Israeli Embassy in the United States when they needed you or had some significant information," said the officer.

"I suppose they will," said Einstein. Dr. Einstein walked away from their house with his head lowered. As he kicked the ground, he did not wonder why the Raboys had abandoned him, but rather why his own government and staff had played him for a fool. Nevertheless, he knew he would have to get to Arizona as soon as possible in order to push the Rabbi to decipher the information he had gathered about the tectonic magnetic fault lines.

He asked the American CIA agents to give him a lift to Washington, D.C. via Andrews Air Force Base. He needed to convince the Americans that he had to contact Raboy to deliver some information he had gathered from Manandjiwala in Alice Springs from the Aborigine tribal leaders.

"Ambassador Raboy, it is my pleasure to present the Israeli scientific documents on magnetic flux lines and the information you had me gather from the Aborigine," said Dr. Einstein.

"Without question you have done an excellent job. Does my brother have any idea that he has been spied on for the last two years?" asked the Ambassador.

"Not really. I think he knows something but has no idea his own brother has had the Israeli government pry into his private life. I know he isn't aware that you gave the order to place him under twenty-four hour surveillance over the last two years."

"Unfortunately, it was necessary since he hides so much of his mystical information. We need to know the truth about his fantasies involving visitations from angels and such. Mother Earth is falling apart at the seams and it is essential that we need to know why and where."

"With all due respect, Ambassador Raboy, your brother is not making up any stories in regards to his visitations from angelic-like beings," quickly responded Einstein.

"Why do you say that, Dr. Einstein?"

"Because I have been involved in one experience with these angelic visitations and let me tell you one thing. If you have ever experienced one, you will stop talking like an idiot, sir." Everyone got quiet and stared at Dr. Einstein. As he looked back he shook his head grinning ear to ear thinking about how ignorant humans can be. He gave Ambassador Raboy a copy of some phony Aborigine information and left the Embassy. He knew he had to find a way to the Hopi Native American Reservation located in northern Arizona.

As he walked out of the Embassy gates, Simon could hear the Earth make an ear piercing annoying sound. The dogs started howling throughout the area. You could see Mother Earth's atmosphere bend into strange bluish-green and reddish patterns. His hair stood straight up all over his body as the earth started shaking in all directions. Einstein fell to the ground and plugged his ears to block out the highpitched sound.

He looked around to see if the buildings and trees were still standing when he noticed that they seemed be twisting around like the limbs of a diamond willow tree.

It lasted for about ten minutes and then it stopped. Dr. Einstein could sense something had just happened to Mother Earth that was irreversible. Walking to his car he could see people gathering in the streets talking about what had just happened. One lady yelled out that her watch was running backwards. Einstein looked at his very expensive Swissmade watch to see what time it was when he noticed his was also running backwards. At that point, he knew he had to get to Arizona somehow, someway, even if he had to crawl on his knees there. He held fast that he was not going to miss out on any new information that Raboy discovered.

After a day of haggling with several transportation companies, he was able to persuade a private jet owner to fly him to Arizona. They landed just moments before a blinding snowstorm created blizzard-like weather conditions for hundreds of miles. The pilot told Einstein that he could not take the plane back up. Einstein had no choice but to drive the rest of the way. The storm was so powerful Dr. Einstein had to pull off the road at the nearest exit of Interstate 40. He had to find a motel to ride out the storm. If he knew that the storm was only producing light snow flurries at the Begay ranch house, he would have driven on. The Raboys were at the Begays's ranch house when the weather changed for the worse.

"Mr. Begay, it is such a pleasure to see you again and visit your cozy home," said Abigail as she hugged Danny Begay, Sarah's true and faithful husband for over fifty years.

"I have prayed to the Great Spirits in the sky to please have you return because Sarah left me with a special message to be deliver to you. Since the day she left me, it has been the secret cry in my heart to prepare a place for the two of us in the hereafter. But I knew I could not leave until I had delivered her last message to you," he said as his eyes filled with tears.

Abigail immediately hugged Danny as the two began to cry vehemently missing the lady they loved so and the gentle lady Abigail called mother. Raboy took their children outside so that Abigail and Danny could freely share their loving memories of Sarah. As Raboy walked outside Ronnie Begay drove up. He slammed his truck into park while it was still rolling and jumped out. He ran over to David Raboy and hugged him, and then picked up his son, Danny, and spun him around like a whirlwind. Little Sarah was wide-eyed as he spoke the native Hopi tongue talking too little Danny spinning him around.

"Daddy, what is wrong with this man? Is he crazy?" asked Sarah as she screamed at the top of her voice.

"No, my little darling, he is overjoyed. Before you were born, he told me I would return with a daughter and son that would rule the world." Sarah looked at her father wondering what he was talking about.

Moments later, Abel Begay drove up in a new four wheel drive truck with several vehicles following him. The new Chief of the Hopi and Navajo Native Americans came with their families and various other tribal leaders. Everyone got out of their vehicles at the same time. Little Sarah was frightened by the stampede of people that were shaking her father's hand and hugging him. Jeremiah ran over and grabbed Abel by the arm.

"Yatehay!" yelled out Daniel Jeremiah.

"Yatehay!" yelled out Chief Mac, Jr. of the Navajo Native American contingency.

Danny Begay and Abigail rushed outside onto the porch to see what all of the commotion was about. Abel reached into his truck bed and pulled out a staff made of ironwood. He held it to the sky, crying out to his ancestral spirits in his Hopi language, thanking the God of Heaven for the safe return of the Raboys. After his cries, he quickly stepped over to Abigail and handed her the staff made of ironwood.

"What is this, Abel?" asked Abigail. "My mother's last wish," he answered.

"Okay, thank you very much," she responded not knowing what to say.

"I will tell you more after we have a powwow with our friends and relatives. After we start the evening bonfire, I will explain about the staff."

"Rabbi, Rabbi, how are you?" asked Benjamin, the new Hopi tribal leader.

"Chief, I am fine and your people are?" asked Rabbi Raboy.

"We are waiting to hear the news you have brought us. And hoping it will answer our questions about the New Meha," replied the Chieftain.

"Then let's get down to business and exchange ideas," said Raboy hastily.

"Not tonight, Rabbi. Tonight we must celebrate you and your families' return. Our world has changed much since you first came to us. We figure that since you have returned we must rejoice together as a family. We know the Sixth Purification has just began is not completed yet throughout Mother Earth. She still needs to cleanse herself from the filth and destruction modern man has plagued her with," said Chief Benjamin.

"You seem bitter about man's modern society," replied Raboy .

"I am bitter. Those that speak with the forked tongue have plagued the world to such an extent that she now has turned her back on us. Our ancestors knew this day would come. We knew the white strangers would cause our present world to end," said the new Chieftain.

"Chief, it was the Asian T-War that started most of these Mother Earth terra firma changes," replied Raboy.

"Maybe so, but if the white strangers would have not been so blind, they would not have created the modern weapons that have literally destroyed the foundations of our Mother Earth. That is why we are in this predicament," said the Chief being upset with the current dilemma.

"Chief Benjamin, you know very well that Mother Earth has cleansed herself five times before and there were not any white strangers in the land to blame. The Purification runs in cycles and this was the time for it to happen. Why are you blaming those that had nothing to do with it?" asked Danny Begay with a soft voice.

Everyone stopped what they were doing to listen to him. Danny was well respected since his wife Sarah had been the caretaker of the New Meha. Being the husband of the one chosen to bring forth wisdom to all Hopi was an honor, but Danny remained humble.

"I apologize, Danny," said Chief Benjamin, "I am scared for my family because every time this Rabbi returns to our sacred land something terrible happens. He is here again so I know something is about to happen in a grand way that will change our lives," cried out the chief.

"Chief, we did not come here to curse or cast a plague upon your land or people. We came here to, hopefully, find some answers that might help us solve some of the riddles hidden from the foundations of Mother Earth," replied Rabbi Raboy.

"Rabbi, could your son and you join me and my sons to pick out a fatted calf for this evening's festival to celebrate your return? The Chief means you no harm. He is scared like everyone else. Our population is dwindling because so few of our tribesmen have survived the changes that have occurred on Mother Earth. You are the one my people call the prophet of Meha. Chief Benjamin knows that what you say will come to be and fears every word that comes out of your mouth," said Abel. Raboy and his son accompanied by Danny and Abel walked along the Lone Wolf trail to the outer pen where the cattle were grazing.

"I did not know that so many Hopi people know who I am; much less respect me as some sort of prophet. I know the Torah has had many prophets, but I am only telling what I was told to tell everyone. Please, tell everyone that I am not a prophet," replied Raboy.

"You crack me up, Rabbi," said Abel.

"What do mean by that statement?" asked Raboy.

"Rabbi, that is exactly what a prophet is—one that delivers God Almighty's word to the people in short statements that have not been added to or changed to suit the peoples expectations," said Abel.

"If that is true, I am still only reiterating what other prophets have already told the people," said Raboy.

"Rabbi, your prophets only told your people what was to come. You are telling the whole world what is going to happen which makes you a prophet. Some of my people are calling you the Meha and Dreamtime interpreter. What matters is that you are the one delivering God Almighty's message to his children," replied Abel.

"What about your mother? How was she looked upon?" asked Raboy.

"She was the New Meha, but you were the one chosen by our Great Spirit to reveal its meaning to the world. Have not you noticed how you have been protected throughout the many different catastrophes that have taken place during the past seven years?" asked Abel.

"Now that you have mentioned it; it seems as though I was always in the right place at the right time. I mean timing is everything, is it not?" asked Raboy.

"Raboy, what about the coyote that turned into a bright light and disappeared during the killer rain generated by the first T-War in Asia?" asked Abel.

"Was it luck that a spiritual being shaped like a coyote would be there. Was it?" asked Raboy. He really did not want to hear an answer, fearing the truth.

As they walked down Lone Wolf trail, several cattle walked up to the wooden fence.

"Hey boys, what about this calf?" asked Abel laughing out loud.

"Daddy, it would be an excellent choice to have as a pet," said Daniel Jeremiah.

"Father, it is honorable that the guest choose, is it not?" asked Abel's son.

"Not in this case, son, but we can ask Raboy what he thinks," replied Abel.

"I will leave this up to Daniel to make the best choice," quickly spoke up Raboy.

"So be it then. The one you have chosen shall be prepared for the feast of our brother who has returned from a land far away," said Abel as they lassoed the black and white heifer.

After they had walked the calf back to the front yard, Danny motioned to his son and Raboy to come over to him. Both of them hastily walked over to see what Grandpa Begay wanted.

"Rabbi, I must talk to you alone. Can you drive me to Coyote Creek?" asked Danny.

"Yes sir, I can, but I am not sure where Coyote Creek is," replied Raboy.

"Rabbi, I will show you. I am not blind, just unable to drive like I used to," replied Danny.

"When did you want to go?" asked David Raboy.

"Now, if you would take me," responded Danny.

"What the snowy roads? Are we to go alone in this weather?" asked Raboy.

"We must go alone for what I have to tell you must be in person without any interruption from anyone, be it from my sons, friends, or any of your family members," replied Danny.

The two got into Abel's new truck and drove north the muddy road for about two and half miles to Coyote Creek. They arrived at a place where a Hopi tribal marker was sticking out of the ground. Danny slowly got out of the truck and walked over to the marker and kissed it on the top of its most vertical point. Many tears started to run down his cheeks as he grieved silently thinking about Sarah.

"Is this where Sarah is buried, my friend?" softly asked Raboy.

"No, this is where we first met and I fell in love with the most beautiful lady the Lord has ever created. When she died, my heart died. My body and soul lives on but my heart is buried here along with every emotion a man could have for the woman he loves," said Danny speaking softly as he wiped the tears from his eyes with a handkerchief Sarah had made for him over twenty years earlier.

"I must confess that before Abigail, I had a wife that died. It broke my will to live and my heart. If Abigail had not entered into my life, I do not know what would happen to me," said Raboy with a wavering voice.

"I had to visit the place where I met my love before I could utter her last request. I never knew if you would ever come back. My heart is sad, but my soul rejoices that I can fulfill my precious love's last wishes," said Danny.

"What would that message be, my friend?" asked Raboy.

"I can't tell you yet, for it must be at a time when you have found your most comfortable place on my farm and then I will tell you," replied Danny.

"How will I know where that is?" asked Raboy.

"I will know, and then I will tell you, my friend."

The two then got in the truck and drove back to the Begay farm. Raboy was puzzled by Danny's comments. Raboy kept silent as they got back into the truck to drive back to Danny's ranch house. The truck would not start. The two got out of the truck and opened the hood to look over the engine. Rabbi Raboy looked at his watch to see what time it was and noticed that it was running backwards. As they opened the hood, they could hear a high-pitched hissing sound coming from the battery.

The both looked at one another, and then looked at the sky and surrounding landscape. Both noticed some orange flashes that resembled the Aurora Borealis, except that it was during the mid-afternoon in Arizona. After Danny looked under the hood for a few moments he concluded that the battery was dead. Rabbi Raboy looked at his watch again to see what time it was and noticed it was not working.

"Danny, let us try to start the vehicle again," suggested Raboy.

"Okay, I do not see anything wrong, except maybe the battery is dead," said Danny.

The two got back inside the truck, and this time it started right up. Raboy quickly sped down the two and half mile dirt road leaving a massive dust cloud behind. He pulled into the driveway and slid to a quick stop. Everyone rushed out to see what was going on.

"Did you guys see it? Did you guys see it?" asked Raboy.

"Did we see what?" asked Ronnie Begay.

"The sky turning orange and clocks running backwards!" exclaimed Raboy.

"Yes, we did!" said someone in the background.

"I know that voice but it couldn't be who I think it is, could it?" asked Raboy.

"Yes, it could and yes it is. You can't escape me. My watch started running backwards last week. To be exact, it was at the same morning you left Israel without notifying me," said Dr. Einstein.

"We did not leave without telling you. The Americans came and whisked us away. We were told it would be safer to fly at night on their new triangular military space link craft, so we left immediately," replied Abigail, shaking her fist at Einstein.

"Alright, I get the picture, but I still need to be here to protect you," pleaded Einstein.

"Protect them from what?" asked Abel.

"From anyone trying to harm you," he replied.

"Harm us from what?" asked Ronnie.

"You would not understand if I were to tell you," blurted out Einstein.

"Okay, that is enough of this bickering which won't resolve anything. We are all here for the same reason and everyone knows what that reason is, I hope," said Raboy calmly.

"What about the orange sky and your watch running backwards? Do you have any idea what is going, Rabbi?" asked Abel.

"It was Mother Earth giving us a warning. After the powwow, we need to concentrate on what knowledge we have. Please, everyone take a seat on the fallen tree stumps that Mother Earth has provided for our weary souls to sit upon," said Danny Begay with an old but stern voice.

Everyone agreed to celebrate the rejoining of their friends that had been through hell during the Asian T-war. The fatted calf was prepared according to the kosher standards of the Cohen Jewish sect. It was placed on the grill and slowly barbequed over an open pit lined with lava rocks and hot Mesquite coals. The children roasted Hopi candy corn on the ends of ironwood sticks until the corn shucks caught on fire. As the Mesquite coals crackled, the distant creek rumbled from the melting snow runoff.

Earlier that day, it had rained upstream, and the creek where Sarah had originally begun her purification was running over its banks. The full moon lit up the desert so one could see as if it were early dawn. Everyone was quiet during the opening rituals of the powwow to remember and respect their beloved Sarah. The next morning Danny woke Raboy, and they drove near Sarah's grave. Danny knew the Rabbi was forbidden to come into contact with any dead person or walk on or near a grave. Danny kept Raboy always back from the grave site.

"This lady stole my heart when I was young, and now she has stolen my soul when I am old. I don't know how much longer I can live without her. I did make her a promise before she passed into the land of the spirits of my fathers," said Danny Begay softly.

"Have you brought me here for that reason?" asked Raboy.

"Yes, I have."

All of a sudden, the earth started shaking. Raboy grabbed Danny as Danny grabbed onto Raboy since they were both standing in an open field. The type of shaking was nothing that any human being had ever witnessed or experience on Mother Earth before. They let go of each other after a couple of moments. Danny motioned for them to go back to the ranch house to see if everyone was alright. Upon returning to the ranch, they found everyone fast asleep.

"Abel, Ronnie, Abigail did you guys feel that tremor?" said Raboy.

"David, we didn't feel anything. It must have been in your imagination," said Abigail, turning on her side and readjusting her pillow as she went back to sleep.

"Abel, Ronnie, did either of you feel anything at all?" asked Danny.

"Father, we felt nothing," they both replied.

"Let's get a cup of coffee and return to where I had taken you," suggested Danny.

"I suppose we might as well since everyone here seems to be still sleeping," replied Raboy.

The two grabbed a cup of hot coffee and left again for Sarah's grave site to finish their conversation.

"Do you think that was Sarah communicating with us?" asked Danny.

"Danny, I am not sure what we experienced. It appears no one else felt it. I don't think that both of us were hallucinating," replied Raboy.

"This is where Sarah lies. She is dressed in her Hopi ceremonial garments. I wanted her to be dressed appropriately when she appeared in the land of our ancestral fathers," said Danny.

Raboy broke down and started to cry. Danny said nothing until Raboy had regained his composure. Begay put his arm around him and embraced his friend.

"I loved her so, Danny. I love her so much. I miss her dearly. She was such a wonderful lady. Oh, I miss her, and I know Abigail would like to visit this site," replied Raboy.

"She loved Abigail and you as if you were her children. We all miss her," replied Danny. They got back into the truck and drove off slowly.

CHAPTER FOURTEEN:

TERRA FIRMA ROCKS AND REELS

They drove down one of the dusty reservation roads for a couple hours until Danny had Raboy stop by an ancient Hopi sacred mountain area. Danny got out of the truck and walked over to a jagged monolith. The orange-red cliff went straight up for over a thousand feet. To Raboy this was one of the most beautiful places he had ever seen. Staring at the windswept reddish orange monument he lost track of where Danny had walked off to. He had to look around for a moment before he noticed Danny sitting down on a strange looking rock that was a section of a petrified tree. Danny waved at him to join him on a section of the petrified tree. Raboy slowly walked toward Danny being taken back by the awesome sight. Danny did not say a word until he had finally stopped looking around at the landscape and sat down on one of the petrified tree stumps.

"Sarah, my beloved darling, told me two things would happen when you returned and set foot on our land. She told me to tell you to find a safe place for your family so they can be protected," said Danny in reticent voice.

"Is my family in immediate danger? How much time do we have to prepare for what you are about to tell me?" asked the Rabbi frantically.

"Sarah told me to tell you in secret because she knew you would panic," replied Danny.

"I beg to differ with you. Nothing you say would rattle me," replied Raboy.

"Mother Earth will be a dangerous place during the sixth purification," explained Danny.

"Danny, I am not panicking. I am just anxious. Can you go on, please?" asked Raboy.

"Rabbi, chaos will abound and fear will overtake every human being left living on Mother Earth. You are the one that must keep calm and listen to every word the Great Spirit has told her. She told me to keep this from you until the time was right. Now I feel the time is right to utter her unspoken words. Please, listen to all of the words before making a decision or coming to any conclusion?" asked Danny calmly looking at Raboy's disposition.

"I promise, I will listen and be calm," said Raboy giving Danny his complete attention.

"No, Rabbi, you do not have to promise me anything. If you are not spiritually ready, I will wait to reveal her message," said Danny watching Condor float through the air.

"Mr. Begay, you must tell me Sarah's message now or I will not be able to sleep. Now I am wondering more than ever what is so important that I had to be told in person and in secret. Why did I have to return to the American Hopi lands to receive this message? A message so important you cannot tell when you are to tell me. What is going on here?" asked Raboy.

"Rabbi, I can see that you must purify yourself the way my father's fathers have done for centuries before I can go on. If you are not cleansed properly, I w ill not be able to tell you the message. Your ancient forefathers have given you ceremonies and rituals to cleanse yourself. We have our ancient ceremonies and rituals to cleanse ourselves, as well. You will have to make yourself worthy to receive Sarah's last words by purifying your spirit. I do not take it lightly to give you a message from our ancestors. When you have been purified, then you will be ready to hear the last words of my darling Sarah. What must be done must be done," replied Danny.

"Where and how must I do this purification that will cleanse me to be presentable to receive Sarah's last message?" asked Raboy.

"You are in the right place, here on Hopi sacred land. No one knows what I am about to tell you, so until you are purified I will patiently wait. You must keep silent like the great mountains where the Spirits of my fathers live in love and peace," said Danny.

"Do you have any idea how I am going purify myself?" asked Raboy.

"It is simple. You must touch the ground you walk on and discover how it feels, and then you must feel the creek bed soil and its life giving water. You must become one with Mother Earth. Observe the animals and understand their oneness with Mother Earth. Learn about every plant and listen while they talk to you. After all of this, you will know who Mother Earth is and how she nourishes all life with her earth, fire, water, and four winds," he said.

"How will I know if I am purified?" asked Raboy.

"We will both know when your purification is complete. Once you understand Mother Earth, you will understand your purification. She must shed her poisons soon. When you understand her ways, you will become wise as to why she must purify all that dwells on the face of the Earth from time to time. It will take you twenty-one days to complete the purification. Once your purification is complete, I will give you Sarah's message. Oh, my lovely Sarah. I miss you so," said Danny, as tears ran down his weathered cheeks. He got up and started walking back to the truck.

"Danny, where are you going? I need to talk about this some more," yelled out Raboy.

Danny did not turn or acknowledge Rabbi Raboy in any fashion. After he got into the truck on the passenger side, he rolled down the window. He patiently sat there and waited for Raboy to drive him back to his little Arizona Native American farm. Rabbi Raboy walked about for a couple of minutes bewildered. Finally, he got back into the truck and drove Danny home not saying one word. His mind was running in circles wondering what Sarah last words were. Raboy got lost in his thoughts that day pondering what was to be. Abigail became frustrated with him by the evening had come since he had totally ignored her and his children.

"Good Morning, sweetheart. Did you sleep well?" asked Rabbi Raboy.

"Sweetie, I always sleep well. Why do you keep asking me the same question over and over for the ten thousandth time? You already know the answer."

"We must discuss what I need to do for the next twentyone days. What I am going to do will affect you but not involve you."

"What must you do for twenty-one days without me? Huh! Do you mean to say what our family will be doing for the next twenty-one days?" she asked trying to include the family.

"No, it is what I must do. I need to purify myself in the ways of the Hopi so I will be able to receive Sarah's last message. It will instruct me to do something about something," he said.

"Something about something. We flew thousands miles for you to learn to do something about something. That is ridiculous," she said feeling she would be left out his life.

"Listen, we can go home right away or stay and find out what Danny feels is so important for you safety. To do this I must be here to purify myself in the way of the Hopi," he uttered.

"Sweetie, I understand, but do you understand that I need you to make Reservation Love to me in order for me to maintain my feeling of well being" she said with a smile on her face.

"Not tonight, because I need to think about becoming one with Mother Earth. Please understand that I need to focus on learning about Mother Earth's earth, fire, water, four winds, her plants, and animals? That basically leaves all other activities out of the question for the next twenty-one days," he said sternly.

"Okay, I understand. But since your purification start tomorrow, it would be best if you would make a gallant effort to satisfy your damsel in distress," she said with sweet passion.

"Sweetie, is that all you ever think about—sex?" he asked.

"Of course not. Although, I do think about a lot when you are alone with me, sweetie pie," she said kissing and hugging him.

That evening they made passionate love throughout the night because Raboy knew he would not rest until she was satisfied. Abigail knew she needed his tender loving to help her emotionally endure the next twenty one days of her husband's sacred quest. Raboy was more passionate than he had ever been before. Abigail feel asleep holding him in her arms. He finally dosed off just before dawn. With only three hours of sleep, he got out of bed and got dressed.

He looked out the window and saw the distant mountain range that had protected him form the killer rain. He could see the snowcapped San Francisco Peaks glisten as the sun shinned bright across the vast regions of the Hopi ancestral lands. He walked to the kitchen and got a cup of hot coffee and returned to the bedroom and sat down next to Abigail.

"We have traveled quite a distance to find out what the Lord is trying to tell us. It is wise for you to do as Sarah has asked, and then spend the evening with your family," she said wiping the tears from her eyes.

"Abigail, I am not entering a prison camp or isolating myself on some tiny island in the middle of the Pacific Ocean. I am just taking time to get to know Mother Earth and all the life that God permits her to support up close. You know this is Sarah's last request."

"David, I know and somewhat understand. But this is hard for me because we have always done everything together. I feel left out. I am feeling empty and lonely deep within my heart," she said with broken words.

"Abigail, what is a man to do when his sweetheart is shedding such tears? I will be around the farm where you can constantly see me. Please, stop breaking my heart," he said, as he gently hugged her to support her emotional out burst.

"Okay sweetie, but I want a daily report, as to what you experience, so I can be part of you experience. Well, vicariously," she replied.

"My love, you know I would never leave you out of any part of my life. You are the most important person and priority of my life. Please, don't cry so I can start the task set before me," he said, hugging her good-bye.

Raboy walked out the door and walked to the first site Danny had taken him to. Along the way he tried to understand why Danny would carry his grief of Sarah's death in the manner that he did. Near the site he stopped about ten feet away from the marker and prayed to the Lord to help Danny with his burden. Then he walked closer to the site where Danny first met Sarah and bent down and kissed Danny's Hopi burial marker. A marker that represented not a grave site, but the place where Danny had met his true love and lost his heart and soul. This is the only way Raboy knew how to say good-bye to the lady he missed and loved so much.

He stood there and shed many tears while thinking about how his missed Sarah. He then rubbed his hands on Danny's marker and bent down picked up a hand full of dirt. Grabbing a small handful of the sacred Hopi soil he rubbed it between his fingers. He put it to his nose and took a sniff, and then threw it up into the air. After thinking about the many experiences he had with Sarah he proceeded to accomplish her last wish.

He walked along the creek bed listening to it sing out to him as it traveled down to the to empty into the mighty Colorado River. When stopped to look at the mid-morning sun, he noticed a hawk chasing another bird. After a few minutes, the hawk circled over him and landed in a nearby tree. He decided to sneak up to the tree to get a closer look at this bird of prey. On a single tree limb about twenty feet up was a nest with two little ones chirping as their desert hawk mother fed and protected them. As he stared at the hawks for a few minutes, he wondered who taught the mother hawk what to feed her babies. Raboy then thought about human beings as the only species that has actually altered the natural life sustaining properties of Mother Earth.

"Truly Adonai, you created a paradise for us called Mother Earth. Why human beings are doing their best to destroy her is beyond my imagination. You must be very angry with us. Will you forgive mankind's abusive, careless behavior that has forsaken your special creation? I am remorseful for how we have been so selfish. We only worry about our own needs, not paying attention to the other creatures that live among us. It is pitiful for my species to change Mother Earth to make our lives easier without considering our fellow inhabitants. Adonai, we have sinned and need atonement, but we cannot obtain it until the Temple has been built in Jerusalem. Destroying your creations with our ridiculous technology is pathetic. I am ashamed of us all," said Raboy out loud. The hawk stared at him as if she knew what he was saying.

The Rabbi then took his hat off and bent down to scoop up some of the creek water to drink. Before he took a sip of the water, he studied the creek up and down stream for a moment. As the water touched his lips he gave thanks to the Lord for creating the creek to nourish life on earth. As he swallowed some of the ice cold water, he decided to pour a portion of the water onto his hands. He wanted to feel the ice cold water run through his finger tips. After few moments his hands they started to hurt and turn red. Immediately he wiped his hands on his pants and grabbed the gloves out his left coat pocket.

After his hands stop hurting from being cold, he felt his first day of being in touch with Mother Earth was enough for one day. He looked at the landscape in all directions for one last time before returning to the Begay farm house. Slowly walking back down the dusty road observing the rustic fence he wondered if he had actually accomplished anything the first day.

"How is my little lady doing?" asked Raboy, giving his daughter a loving hug.

"Daddy, I missed you. Where did you go? Did you miss me daddy? Mommy took a shower and is combing her hair. She already combed mine. Is it beautiful?" asked little Sarah.

"Of course, I missed you. Yes, you are lovelier than a bed of roses. Sweetheart, I do know the words to describe how beautiful you," said Raboy, as he kissed his little angel.

"Dad, did you learn the ways of the Hopi ancestors today?" asked Daniel Jeremiah.

"Son, I am not sure what I learned today, but it was an interesting experience."

"Grandpa Danny said you will become one with Mother Earth to understand the ways of the Hopi people. I want to become one with the Hopi people like you. Dad, can I join you?" asked Daniel.

"Son, if that is your wish, I will do my best to help you when you become a man," replied Raboy.

"Dad, I am already a man. I want to become one with the Hopi land," replied Daniel, then he ran out the door to continue playing with Abram, the Begay's pet goat.

"Sweetheart, I'm back," said Raboy, softly speaking to Abigail.

"Yes, and the children are wide awake, too, but we can close the bathroom door," she replied in a very sexy voice.

"Sweetheart, you know the rules while being guests in other's homes. It's not kosher to meddle with others' belongings and in this case in their shower," replied Raboy.

"Who's meddling? I'm playing with my husband, which is an order given from the Lord to all mankind that started with Adam and Eve. Which, might I add, the command was to be fruitful and multiply, which was handed down to all humans. The only way I know to comply with His command is to do what Adam and Eve did. Do I have to teach you what the Torah states so we can meet the requirements the Lord has commanded all of us to do?"

"Abigail, you know I have studied every word of the Torah and clearly understand what it says. What am I going to do with you? You seem to have a one-track mind," said Raboy.

"Yes, I do. Loving you with all of my heart and soul."

"I really do not know what I would do without you," said Raboy, as he left the bathroom. Noticing Danny walking out on the porch, Raboy was egger to talk to him.

"Danny, I must talk to you right away," yelled out Raboy.

"Then come over here and speak your mind," replied the elder Danny.

"I want to find out how I did on my first day of purification. I am hoping you can help me understand if I am making positive progress," said Raboy.

"Rabbi, I will not be able to help you."

"Why not?" asked Raboy.

"I have not purified myself before. I know nothing about how the process works. I am not a Medicine Man. You'll have to ask one to get the answer you seek," replied Danny not really telling him the truth. He outright lied to Raboy so he would not disrupt his purification process.

"I thought," paused Raboy, "Is there one nearby?" asked Raboy being upset with Danny.

"I do not know, but maybe Ronnie or Abel might be able to assist you," replied Danny.

"Well, if you do not know anything about the purification process how will you know or better yet, how will I know when or if I am or ever will be purified?" asked Raboy bewildered with Danny answer.

"I do not know that either," replied Danny not to interfere with Raboy's quest.

"So, in twenty-one days I can say I am purified, and you will believe me not knowing if I am really purified?" asked Raboy.

"Yes, your word is good enough for me. If God Almighty will judge you based on your word, then why cannot I? Your spoken word is how I will make my decision as to fulfill Sarah's request. The forked tongue is the most lethal weapon a man can have. A man's tongue that tells the truth never has to keep changing his words. A man is only good as his word."

"You have made your point, but I do not know if my word has any merit. Since I do not have any idea what I am doing, I would not know if I was telling the truth or not," said Raboy looking toward the heavens, noticing a lone, dark gray nimbus cloud slowly move about in the wide open blue Arizona sky.

"Rabbi, you are a man of God, and it mystifies me that you do not know what purity is."

"Danny, I am doing my best to understand the ways of the Hopi people, but I really do need some guidance to get through this purification process properly," said Raboy.

"We shall discuss it when the time comes my friend," replied Danny.

"That is your response?" asked Raboy.

"That is my only response, now can you help me milk this goat?" asked Danny.

"I do not know how to milk a goat," replied Raboy.

Danny just looked at him and smiled. After Danny had milked the goat they sat down and discussed Sarah's legacy. Danny talked about his loneliness until it was time to retire for the evening. Danny went to his room that was full of cardboard boxes filled with Sarah's personal belongings. He sat on the edge of the bed that evening feeling numb quietly staring at a picture of Sarah that was in a unique wooden frame that he had whittled from a Cottonwood tree root. On the other hand, Raboy went to his room puzzled about as how to get purified and how to deal with Abigail's stubborn attitude as to how their relationship should be.

The next morning Raboy walked to the west since the day before he had walked to the east. He thought that walking in the opposite direction might help him figure out what he needed to do to accomplish his Hopi Native American purification process. As he walked along, he heard a flutter in some nearby juniper trees. He paused for a moment, and then decided to investigate. He slowly approached the small Arizona high plateau shrub. As he got closer to bush he heard the rustling intensify, and then, all at once, he heard a shrieking, high-pitched cry. Almost on top of the juniper tree a coyote jumped out of the thicket toward Raboy. Caught off guard, he jumped back about three feet. His body rushed with adrenalin freezing his body in place and causing his heart to pound so hard he could not breathe.

"You cannot be the same coyote I fed nuclear waste water to! That was years ago."

The coyote darted away leaving Raboy and his prey behind. Raboy could still hear High-pitched sounds coming from under the tree. After taking a moment to regain control of his emotions he decided to investigate the situation further. Slowly approaching the brush glanced into the thicket to see what was causing all of the commotion. He got to see a once in a lifetime sight.

There was a baby cottontail rabbit half swallowed by a very large Diamondback rattlesnake. What stunned Raboy was the fact that the head of the snake was detached from its body, and it was still trying to swallow the wounded rabbit. Raboy watched this unusual event for a few moments, wondering what to do. Deciding to pick up the little baby cottontail rabbit and take it back to the Begays' rustic barn, Raboy took off his overcoat. Ever so cautiously he wrapped his overcoat around the baby cottontail rabbit with the snake's head still trying swallowing it. Hastily walking back to the ranch he met Abel driving along the road headed to his father's outer pasture.

"Rabbi, what do you have wrapped up in your cloak?" asked Abel.

"You would not believe me unless you saw it with your own eyes! Can you take me to your barn? I need a place that will not disturb any of your farm animals," requested Raboy.

"Yes, of course, Rabbi. Hop in the truck," said Abel.

"Thank you, but will this impede my purification?" asked Raboy.

"Not at all. What purification?" asked Abel.

"I will tell you later. Now I need to shelter this injured baby," replied Raboy.

After parking the truck near the barn, Abel took Raboy to a work bench. Raboy opened his cloak and then took out the most amazing thing Abel had ever seen.

"Wait here right here. I will be back in a second," replied Abel. He ran to the front porch, grabbed the door and slung it open. Entering the house he called out to his father. Talking to his father in Navajo they both immediately went to the barn. Abigail followed hot on their heels to see what Abel had told his father in his Navajo tongue.

"Sweetie, what is wrong?" asked Abigail.

"Nothing, sweetheart. Danny, while I was purifying myself this morning I came across an unfamiliar sight that I wanted you to see. Maybe you can explain to me what this might mean," he replied.

All four of them went to the south end of the barn so Raboy could open his cloak. As he began to open it the baby rabbit started jumping around moving his cloak in an attempt to escape. Raboy quickly opened the cloak so that everyone could see a true mystery of nature. It was a gruesome sight for Abigail to see that a rattlesnake was trying to eat a baby cottontail after being beheaded by the coyote. It was a shocking sight for all of them to experience one of the mysteries of survival on Mother Earth.

"Don't just stand there. Set the poor little creature free from its bondage. The Lord has given you a chance to make a difference. Now, please do it at once," said Abigail, feeling pity for the bloodstained little baby rabbit trying to escape from harm.

"What does this mean?" asked Raboy.

"I do not know. Sarah saved a grown jackrabbit from the clutches of an eagle, and now you have saved a baby cottontail from the clutches of a Diamondback rattlesnake," said Danny as tears filled his eyes. He lowered his head as he reminisced about Sarah's experience.

"I did not save the baby rabbit, a coyote did," replied Raboy.

Daniel Jeremiah came running up and saw the bunny with the snake head around his abdomen. His eyes opened wide. Amazingly, the cottontail stared back at Jeremiah as though he wanted his help. Daniel responded. "Father, I would like to take care of this little baby rabbit. Can I, mother? I will be very gentle and do what Grandpa Danny wants me to do. Can I, Daddy? Please let me take care of him," pleaded little Daniel, as everyone stood silent.

"Well, ahh, Danny, Abigail, ahh, Abel what do you think?" asked Rabbi Raboy.

"It would be a pleasure to let my grandson take care of this little creature. The Great Spirits of my ancestors would be pleased. It would be good for him to learn how to take care of one of Mother Earth's children," replied Danny.

"Yes, it may teach and expose him to what his great grandfather, Noah, went through while living on the Ark," said Abigail, hugging her son. Everyone looked at Abigail and wondered what she meant by the statement.

Abel removed the snake's head from the frightened rabbit while Daniel Jeremiah watched. Everyone else left the barn. Little Daniel petted the rabbit while Abel used some diagonal pliers to cut the snakes head into pieces. The cottontail sat there motionless after the snake had been completely removed.

"Uncle Abel, what do I feed Bambi? Do you think she is thirsty? Can we give her a bath to wash the blood off? When does she sleep? Will you help me make her a house to live in?" asked little Daniel.

"Daniel, you asked far too many questions. In due time, I will answer you," replied Abel. He placed the rabbit in a small cage and set it on the workbench tabletop.

Later that day Raboy started questioning Danny again about the snake head attached to the baby rabbit. He asked him so many questions Danny was starting to get angry.

"Rabbi, that is enough questions," burst out Danny trying to get Raboy to hush up without any results.

"Danny, what does this mean? Do you have any idea?" asked Raboy.

"I know nothing of the purification process, if that is where you are going. I admit it is a strange thing to find what you did today, but that is all there is to it," replied Danny.

"I do not really understand what you are saying. I think it is time for me to stop asking questions that does not have answers to them. I think it best for me to move on and leave it at that," said Raboy finally catching on that Danny was not to answer one of his questions.

"I will tell you about Sarah's experience with a jackrabbit tomorrow morning after I am Abel to walk back in time and remember her experience. Since it was long ago, I will have to reach deep down into the past I have tried to forget. After I have walked back through time, I will tell you about her wonderful experience with Mother Earth's living spirits," replied Danny.

Raboy was had reach the point where he was not restless anymore. He told everyone good night and retired to the tiny bedroom hoping to get some rest after the second day of his purification process. Raboy closed his eyes and within seconds he was fast asleep.

The next morning, Raboy headed south walking along the sheep bend trail. He spoke out freely to the plants while feeling their leaves and stroking their branches. As he walked along, his emotions increased every step of the way. He was getting a natural high from experiencing the wild animals as if they were communicating to him when he spoke to them. Then it hit him that he had just strolled passed the first place on the farm he had encountered Sarah Begay. He looked around and noticed a cattle guard with three white stripes. Then he stopped and looked around to see if anyone could see or hear him. No one was in sight in every direction so he spoke to Sarah as if she were by his side.

"Sarah, I have no idea what I am doing, but since it was one of your last requests before your death, I will do my best to honor you," said Rabbi Raboy, as tears started to run down his cheeks. He cried so hard that his tears started dropping onto his shoes. He walked about for a few moments to regain his composure and then spoke out again.

"Sarah, I hope you can hear me in the spirit world. I miss you so much I can't express my feelings enough. You were a very kind lady. Lord Almighty, I hope you can hear me, because if anyone ever deserved to be in your bosom, this lady must have passed your test."

He then walked down the trail for about two miles until he decided to head back home to talk to Danny about Sarah's experience with the jackrabbit. After much thought, he was now more confused than ever as to what his assignment was in order to become purified. Stressed out from worrying what he was trying to do, he headed for his temporary Arizona home.

It was raining the next morning, but that was not a concern for Raboy, because he was determined to finish his task He got dressed, ate a light breakfast, and strolled out the front door.

"Good morning, Rabbi," said Danny, sitting on the front porch swing.

"Yatehay, Danny. Are you ready to tell me about Sarah's experience, yet?"

"Yes, it is a good morning to have a good cup of coffee. Whatever the Great Spirit has decided for me today I will accept. Another good day to be alive in Arizona."

Danny got up from his favorite chair and walked away from him. Raboy followed him as he walked toward the barn. Danny took a minute to check on the baby rabbit. It was cuddled up in the straw next to a blue water bowl. Raboy didn't say a word as he waited for Danny to tell him his about his wife's experience with one of Mother Earth's offspring. Both of them noticed that the rabbit watched every move they made. After milling around in the barn for about ten minutes, Danny spoke.

"Having this rabbit here gives me a strange feeling. It is hard for me to get involved since Sarah had a similar situation, except with a different set of circumstances," said Danny slowly.

"Yes, and that would be?" asked Raboy not knowing when to be quiet.

Danny did not reply to Raboy's question as he quietly continued his rounds. Starting to understand Danny somewhat better Raboy followed keeping quiet. They left the barn and walked to the pasture that had Sarah's precious sheep fenced in, and then Danny went to the front porch and sat down. He took out his knife and started to whittle on a Cottonwood tree root. Raboy did not dare ask him what he was doing. He went to the other chair made of Ponderosa tree wood and sat there thinking about day three of his purification. After a few minutes Danny spoke out.

"It was during the beginning of her purification. She brought a wounded jackrabbit right here to this very same spot and nursed it until it was healthy enough to return to the wild. I noticed on a few occasions that every time she fed the creature it would stare at her as if it could understand what she was saying. I had never seen any animal like that before in my life. I am talking about every domestic farm animal or pet I have dealt with during my entire life," said Danny with a soft tone of voice.

"Do you think this is a sign that I am doing what has been requested of me?" asked Rabbi Raboy.

"I do not know. You are doing what you doing and she did what she did. That is all I know about this purification process. I wished I could tell you more, but I cannot."

"Does that include the two things you were to tell me once I am purified?" asked Raboy.

"No. What I have to tell you is what Sarah has entrusted with me to reveal to you when it is time. I will tell you exactly what she had requested when you are ready," replied Danny.

After that Danny and Raboy went into the house and ate some Indian Fry Bread Abigail had prepared. Day after day, Raboy did his best to experience the ways of the Hopi and got closer to Mother Earth. Nothing eventful happened after the rabbit incident.

Although Raboy had not idea what he was doing he still struggled to purify his spirit by the ways of the Hopi. He continued his quest for twenty days feeling the soil and water with his bare hands. He would splash water on his face from time to time from the creek where Sarah has first encountered Maasaw. While listening to the animals make their unique distinct sounds, he did his very best to understand Mother Earth.

Finally, the last day. His last chance to get it right and be one with Mother Earth. This would be the day he would complete his purification. Being emotionally empty, he drank three cups of coffee in an attempt to fire up some enthusiasm to complete his twenty-first day of purification. He was very discouraged that the spirit world had not contacted him but figured it was not meant to be.

Raboy had woken up earlier than usual this morning to complete his mission. To start the last day of his journey, he hastily walked over to the rabbit cage to see if anything strange or unusual had taken place with the baby Cottontail rabbit. He did not feel any significant spiritual connection had transpired between him and the rabbit, except his son had put his heart and should into taking care of the bunny.

The rabbit quietly ate his lettuce and drink from his blue clay bowl crafted by Abel Begay's daughter in her Hopi Native American culture class. Raboy being not sure upset about his purification process stood there quietly and studied the beautiful Hopi art work on the water blue bowl. After a few minutes of observation, he decided to exit the barn and marched toward Sarah's grave site. He knew that he would not be able to touch any part or walk to close to her grave because his religious rules forbid such an act because he would become unclean. Still he wanted to be near Sarah, and this was the only way he felt he could.

Along the way, he looked at the sky in all directions waiting for something to happen but there was nothing significant. Raboy kept looking over his shoulders first this way and then that way. He even went to the point of grabbing up handfuls of dirt, rubbing it between his hands, and then throwing it over his right shoulder hoping for something to happen.

When he approached the grave, he immediately lifted his hand and looked high into the sky. He praised the Lord and then thanked Him for creating such a wonderful human being. After a few minutes of praising Yahweh for his goodness, he looked down at the east end of Sarah's grave site and noticed a black ring-tailed rattlesnake skin with the rattler still attached.

Raboy bent over and picked up a stick to poke the skin to see if any living reptile was still attached to it in one form or another. He figured the skin had been abandoned by its owner when it had molted but wasn't completely sure. Rabbi poked at the skin several times with an ocotillo cactus branch. Then he decided to pick it up and carry it back to Danny, being curious to know if it had any significance in Hopi mythology. Upon returning to the Begay ranch, he saw Danny sitting on the porch whittling on a cottonwood tree root, carving out a Tawa Kachina Doll.

"What do have there on your stick?" asked Danny.

"I think it is some sort of snake skin," he replied.

"You are thinking correctly. Did you know that you are holding one of the skins of the deadliest rattlesnakes in Arizona?" continued Danny.

"It is not deadly poisonous now being just a skin is it?" asked Raboy, being a bit alarmed.

"No, it is harmless now, but if it were alive it would be mighty dangerous."

"Glad to hear that," replied Raboy.

"Where did you come across this black ringtail rattler's skin?"

"I found it on the east side of Sarah's grave site," said Raboy reluctantly.

"On the east side you say, Hummm. That is very interesting indeed. Are you sure it was on the east side not on the north side?" asked Danny.

"I am sure it was on the east side, Mr. Begay," replied Raboy.

"That is good."

"What do you mean by saying that is good?" asked Raboy.

"Well, it was good the snake did not live in this skin anymore or else you may have had a poor experience while saying good-bye to Sarah," said Danny, as he kept whittling on the cottonwood root.

"There is no significance whatsoever having a snake skin lying next to Sarah' grave?" asked Raboy, hoping for an answer that would signify his completion of the purification process.

"Today is your twenty-first day of Sarah's request?" asked Danny.

"Yes, this is the final day of my purification process," he replied.

"Good. Tomorrow morning we must have coffee together so I can tell you my sweethearts' last request," said Danny laying down the root getting up and walking over to his wooden outhouse. Abigail called out to Danny and Raboy from the farm house kitchen.

"David, I have prepared your favorite breakfast this morning. Bacon, scrambled eggs, melba toast and black coffee," said Abigail smiling knowing Cohen's not eating pork.

"Abigail, we do not eat pork, or melba toast," said Rabbi Raboy with a stern face.

"Okay, do you want some pink chicken instead?" asked Abigail, laughing at her husband.

"Pink chicken! You have been listening to Sheldon Chernoff, the white Russian Jew that was at the Seminar during my Jewish inquisition," said Raboy, smiling back at his Miss America.

"Oh! You are no fun," said Abigail happy that his purification was over.

"Sweetheart, will you ever grow up?" asked Raboy.

"You grown-ups never have any fun! Do you know that the little girl in me is always waiting to get out and play? Can we play before the children awaken?" asked Abigail.

"What is a man to do with a woman like you? You are too much to handle at times," said Raboy, laughing as he spoke.

"I bet there are millions and billions of men wishing they had a woman half as good as I am," she replied.

"Yes, sweetheart, you are one among billions. The Lord must have taken a rest, and then broke the mold after creating you," he said, laughing.

"You told me after the Lord created Eve He broke the mold from whence she was created. And then He proclaimed 'Woe to men because the female gender will never let a man have peace again'," said Abigail.

"I do not think I said it quite that way. Eve was unique because she is the mother to all human beings born of the flesh, although she was never a infant or was born. But might I add, she was the first human being to commit the first sin—" Abigail interrupted him.

"Alright, I have heard enough of that Eve disobeyed the Lord first story. You know man wandered around aimlessly, lonely with nothing to do with his time until the Lord created Eve as a help mate. A human being that is to be equal to man not his subservient. So as your equal we have merely given man purpose to live his life at its fullest and help him do something with his idle time."

"Okay, you win. I should have remembered to never argue with a woman. If I were to get you to agree that I am right, you would just hound me until I asked for you to forgive me for being so rude and unloving," said Raboy.

"You are right because women are always thinking how to improve their family's life and make it a happier experience. Regardless of what men think, woman are the caretakers of humans," replied Abigail.

"What about breakfast?" asked Raboy, changing the topic.

"Duh! It has been ready and waiting for you," said Abigail The two walked into the Begay's kitchen where Abigail had prepared eggs over easy, Hopi fry bread and coffee the same way Sarah had prepared the meal for Danny. Abigail wanted to show her love for Sarah and Danny, so she made an extra effort to prepare him the perfect breakfast. Abigail went out of her way to express her respect for Danny and show her love for the Begays was special. Danny said nothing and sat there with an expressionless face as he ate his perfectly cooked eggs. As Abigail watched him eat breakfast tears started running down her cheeks. She grabbed Raboy's left hand under the table and tightly clung onto it.

Later that day, Danny had Raboy drive him to a place along the creek bed that he had never taken before. Danny slowly got out of the truck and walked over to an old mesquite tree stump and sat down. Raboy got out of the truck and walked over next to Danny trying to figure out what Danny was doing. It was futile for Raboy to understand because he was whispering in Navajo—his native tongue.

"Rabbi, Sarah told me that when the sun starts to rise from the west and sets in the east man would start to become one family," said Danny.

"That is a very remarkable and confusing statement indeed, Mr. Begay," replied Raboy.

"That is not all my friend. She told me that as Mother Earth starts to purify herself, many nations will disappear and many new lands will rise from the depths of the ocean floor. She said our ancestors have left us a message to read if we had survived the fifth purification. They left this message for us over five thousand years ago," said Danny, as he looked at Raboy for some type of response.

"I am speechless and awed by Sarah's message, but I am not sure why I had to go through the Hopi Native American purification process before you would tell me this," said Raboy exhausted from the ordeal that was extremely confusing to him.

"Sarah merely wanted you to take the time to enjoy Mother Earth as she did before the earth becomes a violent place for man to live on. She said when Mother Earth starts to cleanse herself, to rid the poisons that are destroying her, there will not be any peaceful place on Mother

Earth for man to hid from the destruction that will occur during the purification," said Danny.

"How will I know when this will happen?" asked Raboy.

"Only the Creator knows the time of the time since he has created all things to his liking and not to man's. The rich and poor will suffer the same fate. I am sure the angels that have visited you have been instructed by the Creator as how to take care of you. Sarah said your son is special and will help many to live as the Great Spirit had intended us to from the beginning of time," said Danny.

"That is an awful lot of information to digest. I know the Lord has been man's caretaker from the beginning of time, but now ever the more I feel the need to pray for the Lord's tender mercy for every plant, animal and human beings' safety," said Raboy.

"That is all any man can do. Pray and wait on our Great Spirit to take care of us with His arms open so we can hide under them," said Danny, as he got up from the stump.

"I assume we are finished?" asked Raboy.

"Never assume anything, Rabbi, because it will lead you down the wrong path. Assume is another word for hearsay. We all know that if someone makes a decision based on hearsay they are an idiot. Most of the time hearsay is information that has no basis as to being the truth. So beware of those that make their decisions using hearsay as evidence. They are evil by nature and do not want to hear or live by the truth," expressed Danny.

David felt his journey was finally over and knew it was time to tell Abigail they needed to go home. Abigail and David retired to the front porch that evening to discuss their voyage back to Israel. They talked about the journey until it was about three in the morning. As the sun was losing its power and night was gaining her strength you could the nearby creek and in the far distance cry of a coyote packs howling.

"Wow, what was that?" said David Raboy.

"I am not sure but look at the moon. It appears to be moving about," responded Abigail

They watched the moon dance in the sky for over two hours until daybreak. As the sun rose they could hear the distant sounds of several helicopters thundering in the south. They could visibly see that the helicopters were headed straight for them. Within moments, three Marine helicopters landed and unloaded several Marines in full battle attire with their M-16s in their arms ready for combat.

"Rabbi Raboy," called out a familiar voice.

"Yes, I am here. Is that Dr. Einstein?" asked Raboy not being shaken by the situation.

"Yes, it is I, and I have come with General Freetag to take you at once to Washington D.C.," replied Dr. Einstein.

"We are not ready to leave yet. I have promised the children we would see the Grand Canyon National Park first," yelled Abigail, trying to make herself heard over the choppers.

"There is not enough time for that. We need to apprehend Rabbi Raboy immediately," said the General Freetag.

"What is it with you military men? Always treating people like they are dogs or cattle being rounded up for the slaughter," angrily remarked Abigail.

"Madam, I am only doing what I am told to do," remarked the General.

"We are not going until we see the Grand Canyon!" yelled Abigail angry with it all.

"General, can you fly over the damn Grand Canyon on the way to Winslow, Arizona International Airport?" asked Dr. Einstein.

"It is against my orders, but what the hell, if that is what it takes to get these people to Washington D.C., I will damn well do it. So let us get a move on," barked the General.

"What is so urgent, General?" asked Rabbi Raboy.

"The Langley experts have some scientific information that we would like to consult with you about. We need your spiritual side of the equation in order to make out why the moon is moving about in the sky," said the General.

322

"Oh, malarkey, the moon is not moving to and fro—Mother Earth is—and the whole educated world is scared to death what will happen next," said Dr. Einstein, being honest for the first time in his career.

The Raboys reluctantly packed up their belongings and said good-bye to Danny Begay's family as they boarded the choppers.

"Madam, we will fly right over the top of the Canyon breaking every rule ever written about military protocol, but I said you would get to see it. So let it be," said General Freetag.

The three choppers broke many laws and flew right down into the Grand Canyon as the visitors above and below the rim were awed by the three gun ships flying in formation up and down through the Canyon where they should not have ever been. General Freetag was tired of being the caretaker of the Raboys, but knew it was necessary to complete his mission. He figured the Grand Canyon excursion would end his command, but he did not care anymore.

"Dr. Einstein, we have two F-54 from the Air Force flying cover for your safety," said the General.

"That will be not necessary flying with the Rabbi. He has protection you would not understand nor believe coming from a place you would not think possible," remarked Dr. Einstein.

"What are you saying, Dr. Einstein?" said the puzzled General.

"Never mind what I said, General. Do what ever you want," said Dr. Einstein.

The group flew over the Grand Canyon and then took a special aircraft to Washington, D.C.

Chapter Fifteen:

Mother Earth Turns Upside Down

"David, Abigail, it is always so nice to see you. I am glad to see that you are all in good health," said Ambassador Jeremiah Raboy.

"Jeri, stop all of the kibitzing and get down to business. I am whisked away once more to a meeting that is so secret know one knows what it is about. We were amongst our friends in the Arizona high desert plateau Hopi reservation and out of nowhere comes a military high jacking," replied David being irate with it all.

"You seem a bit disturbed this afternoon. I think you need to find a place to rest before dinner is served," said the Ambassador.

"I am sorry to act up, but I am worn out. Mother Earth is bending and twisting in ways our top scientists thought impossible only a few years ago," said Raboy.

"About the scientists, ahh, well, ahh, I have been informed by the American CIA that several M.I.T. scientists want to meet with you tomorrow. It is my understanding that they want to attempt to apply your spiritual knowledge and their applied psychics to form some sort of logical explanation to why the cosmos is rapidly changing," replied Ambassador Raboy.

"These guys have always been skeptical about the spirit world. I really wonder what they want. Am I to be one of their experiments? I will cooperate, but only because you pleaded with me to help these evolutionist," said Raboy.

"David, they are wise men that merely want to meet with you. Some of them are Jewish scientists that believe in the Lord as much as you do. Why are you so rebellious and negative?" replied Jeri.

"I suppose they are still trying to get me to solve the problems that they have created. It is not something they can control. As far as I am concerned, man is doomed by his own hand," countered Raboy.

That evening Raboy rested his worn out body by sitting in a reclining chair. He elevated his legs to help the swelling in his feet go down and to ease his left knee pain. When dinner was served, Ambassador Raboy was nowhere to be found. Raboy and his family ate peacefully with the Ambassador's immediate family, talking about old times. It was peculiar to Raboy that no one seemed to miss the Ambassador's presence. It was fifteen after eight o'clock when five men dressed identically in black attire came to ask Rabbi Raboy to accompany them to Langley Air Force Base for a special meeting.

"Rabbi Raboy, the society of Mensa scientist have decided to reveal our top secret discovery of an unique magnetic force that holds the universe together," said a tall man with long, curly, dark hair. He was wearing a red tie instead of black one like the others. The tall scientist sat down and let an older gentleman with an unshaven face and a raggedy suit take the lead. He walked up to Raboy and shuffled through several papers.

"Rabbi, I am not sure why we are telling you this, but here it goes. There are four known force to physicists: weak nuclear, strong nuclear, magnetic and gravity. A magnet has two well known magnetic forces—a positive field or charge and a negative field or charge. The third part of a magnet has a mysterious force that holds separates the positive from the negative fields. Now we have discovered a fifth force that hold all matter together which we have named Vibranic Force. We feel this is the force that really holds the universe together. It is the galactic cement we have been searching for. It is the most stable and destructive force throughout the universe. If it looses the power to hold negative and positive forces at bay equally, then the two forces of magnetic attraction become imbalanced. It appears that Mother Earth has lost her Vibranic

Force. We have concluded that earth's delicate Vibra force has been obliterated by the Asian T-War," said the scraggly looking gentleman.

"We would have never looked for it where we found it, if it had not been for you," said the tall, lanky gentleman wearing black attire.

"You have unraveled one of Mother Earth's biggest scientific secrets because of me. Why am I here? I know it is not to reveal data about your newly discovered scientific theorems," said Raboy.

"Yes, that is true, but if you would hear us out and just listen, maybe you will understand why you have been invited here," said the CIA agent.

"Are you the one I spoke to at Ayers Rock in Australia?" asked Raboy.

"Please, listen and stop interrupting," said the straggly professor being annoyed with the Rabbi's questions.

"Sorry to interrupt, but I need some rest, so cut to the chase," barked out General Freetag.

"Scientists have been looking for this missing force for centuries. After intensive investigation, the top astronomers and physicists concluded that the unknown force that holds the universe together is not gravity but this neutral magnetic force, a gravitational modifier that holds the tiniest molecules together. Basic physics has always missed the possibility that a force that could allow matter to emit neutral energy could exist throughout the universe including Mother Earth. Accepting the fact that it was not antimatter, we should have said it was a phenomenon without any explanation, but we arrogant scientists could not do that. We have dug deep trying to identify the secret force and right theorem. Here you come along and open up the doors for us," said the professor.

"This vibranic force allows negative and positive magnetic lines of force to coexist without any lines of demarcation or stress upon one another. Some of us have been mystified while others had guessed this was happening but didn't have an explanation to solidify or prove our theorems. Now we know the force exists, but we do not have the means to explore or measure how it works. It is something that is there that has no beginning or ending. Our Mother Earth is literally being torn apart at the seams because this force is decaying. We are puzzled and perplexed as what to do, except to ride it out and see how Mother Earth will react. We do know that the magnetic iron core charges of Mother Earth are reversing themselves by re-establishing new grids and lines of demarcation. The most frightening aspect of the magnetic realignment is that the direction of the earth's rotation appears to be changing," said the other professor.

"Again, gentlemen, why am I here?" asked Raboy. "Sir, can we finish?" asked the professor.

"Yes, of course," replied Raboy.

"Good, then hear us out. The magnetic tectonic plates have started to unravel. I believe this vibranic force field is neither magnetic nor nuclear but an element of the gravitational force that holds the universe together. The universe would have unraveled billions of years ago if it were not for the Vibra force that controls its expansion or collapse. The newly discovered vibranic force causes magnetic lines of force to shift in the form of waves due to disruption of the movement of atoms away from their basic directions, which tears atoms apart," said the professor.

"Gentlemen, I have no clue what you are talking about. I simply asked my Israeli government to give me a map of the world indicating where the tectonic plates of Mother Earth were. No more, no less. Do you have this type of information or not?" asked Raboy rudely.

"As a matter of fact, we have many different sets of maps," said General Freetag, sitting in a unique eight-legged chair.

"Can we do this tomorrow? I want to get some rest so my mind can function. My entire body is dysfunctional. Can I get some rest?" asked Raboy.

"You are here because I would like to know, what you know," demanded Dr. Einstein.

"I suppose you would," remarked Raboy.

"Gentlemen, please, let us keep our focus to the matter at hand," said the professor.

Everyone looked at the professor. Three men dressed in the same black attire appeared from the shadows to hastily escorted Rabbi Raboy away. He was driven back to the Israeli Embassy grounds where three Israeli guards escorted him to the foyer of the exquisite building. When Raboy entered the embassy, he stopped to take off his shoes. Not paying attention to what he had done since this was routine at his home in Israel, he walked around the embassy barefoot. Raboy could feel the cool floor covered with black Italian marble start to crackle under his feet. The high chandeliers started swaying in many directions.

Raboy became weak as fear over took his body. He tried to figure out if he should run or duck for cover, but he was frozen in place. His heart started pounding like a bass drum as his blood veins beating throughout of his body. Sweat was dripping off his forehead as he clutched onto a nearby beam. The swirling motion stopped as the floor continued to creak and pop. His brother came running down the staircase looking sheepish and shaking out of control.

"What was that David? What the hell was that?" yelled the Ambassador.

"An earthquake, I suppose, my brother," replied Raboy quickly.

"That was not an earthquake. It was something far worse," remarked the Ambassador.

"I do not know what to tell you. Where is my wife?" asked Raboy.

"Brother, please relax. They are all safe and sound," said Simeon, Raboy's youngest brother.

"Relax! Did you feel this building twisting and turning like a pretzel?" asked the Ambassador.

"Simeon why are you so calm?" asked Raboy.

"You are in denial or insane," remarked the Ambassador.

"Neither," remarked Simeon Raboy.

"You have to put things into prospective. We do not have any control over certain things that happen in life, and this simply is one of those events. So grow up and take the heat."

"Simon, can you please take me to Abigail?" asked Rabbi Raboy.

"Yes, but you need to calm down and pull yourself together," said Simon.

"What are you talking about? Take it easy and calm down?" asked Raboy.

"David, you do not want your family to think that you are scared or weak do you?" asked Simon.

"What are you talking about?" asked the Ambassador.

"If you guys go to your family shaking and trembling, how are you going to comfort them? Think about it. You must be strong and resilient to handle their fears," replied Simon.

"Whatever. Take me to my family now, please," commanded Raboy.

Then the building started swaying even worse than the first time. This time Simon ducked under the table in the great hall while the Ambassador and the Rabbi hung onto a nearby pillar. The earth swayed and twisted for over a minute and a half.

"Simon, you coward, you can come out now," yelled Raboy, making fun of his younger brother.

"Alright, alright, I was scared, too. Knock it off. I was scared. Please do not let my wife and children hear about this. Can you guys work with me on this one?" asked Simon.

"Brave one, lead us to our families," said Raboy, still chastising him.

Before they had taken one step, Abigail came running down the spiral stair case wearing a pink negligee. She was in sheer panic running for her life. Everyone stared at her, forgetting about Mother Earth's twisting tremblers.

"Abigail, what's wrong with you? It is only the Mother Earth dancing about," remarked Raboy, trying to calm his wife down as he clutched her in his arms.

"David, I saw him. He said this was the end of the period. I am so scared I do not know what to do. I saw him, and he talked directly to me. What do we do?" said Abigail frantically.

"Who did you see?" asked Simon.

"I saw Michael, the Archangel. He was beautiful and big, and so powerful. He was so sweet and gentle, but he still scared me so much I could not breathe. I was already scared out of my wits from the building shaking and all, and then a brilliant light appeared. He said this was the beginning of the end. Oh, David, it is all over," cried out Abigail.

"Honey, you have experienced several angelic visitations before. Why are you so upset?"

"This was my first experience with a messenger from the Holy of Holies. A messenger that spoke directly to me. It was frightening, especially when Mother Earth started shaking. I thought it was already all over," said Abigail, breathing hard clutching onto David.

"Sweetheart, where are the children?" asked Raboy.

"Oh my God, oh my God, oh my God, the children, I forgot about them," she said as she ran upstairs. David pursued Abigail. The children were fast asleep as if nothing had happened. Abigail and the Rabbi held one another with such a tight embrace that it have would taken a pry bar to pull them apart. They kissed and hugged one another for a few moments. While they were holding each other tenderly, an earth twister hit. The earth started swaying, twisting, and rocking more violently than the prior episode. They both grabbed a child and ran to the doorway for protection. Raboy cried out to the Lord praying for His sweet love, tender mercy and protection all at the same time for he feared the worst.

Dust stirred up everywhere as the glass windows broke apart and fell out of their window frames. Daniel Jeremiah woke up and started laughing like he was on an amusement park ride. The building swayed one way and then twisted the other way. This was nothing like any earthquake anyone had ever experienced on Mother Earth since the beginning of time. The horrible event stopped after a few seconds.

"David, we have got to get out of this place if it is the last thing we ever do on earth," said Abigail, grinding her teeth from being so scared.

"It does not do any good to hide from this sort of terror," said Raboy.

"I know, but it is just that I am scared for the first time in my life. This is worse than the killer rain we experienced after the Asian T-war that started because of greed to have exclusive rights to some stupid glacier water," responded Abigail.

Abigail and the Ambassador's wife gathered up personal belongings necessary for all of the children to sleep outside of the building. They spread out some blankets on the lawn so everyone could try to sleep within the embassy yard. The Ambassador, Simon, and David Raboy sat on the front porch just staring at the half crescent moon that seemed to be dancing in the night sky. David and the others could feel the mysterious static electrical charge that filled the air. You could sense something was about to change on Mother Earth. All of them sat there quietly pondering what would happen next. The Raboys did not know if they would still be alive by sunrise.

After spending the entire night outside, Abigail looked up and secretly thanked the Lord for the tender mercies. She had reached both arms high into the sky while lifting up her head praising the Most High. She wanted to say Yahweh out loud but refrained knowing it was forbidden to say the Lord's name with the spoken tongue. Abigail praised the Lord that David was the seventh secret name keeper of the sixteen unspoken pronunciations of Yahweh, but she had no idea that David Jeremiah was the first secret name keeper of the sixteen pronunciations.

As the sun broke over the horizon, you could see the Raboy's children sleeping on the lawn. Blinded by the early morning sun, Abigail put on her sunglasses to shield her eyes. At that very moment several black trucks sped into the Israeli Embassy courtyard.

"Rabbi Raboy, you need to come with us immediately!" yelled out one of the agents riding in the forward vehicle.

"What do you want with me now? I have told you guys everything that I knew last night. There is no more information, visitations, or otherwise, so leave me alone," he replied.

"Rabbi, something unusual has happened. We need your assistance to figure this out. Please, come with us without any delay. Come peacefully or we will drag you into the vehicle with brute force," said the general.

"Let us see now, come along peacefully on my own free will or shackled and taken against my will. I guess that means I am going with you, regardless of my personal decision," said Raboy wondering what the government was up to now.

"No time for humor, Rabbi. Get your butt in the truck right now. Move it! Move it!" barked the general.

Raboy kissed his wife and told her not to worry. He would be right back. The trucks sped off not stopping for traffic signals or stop signs. Raboy was tossed about in the truck as it rambled along the highway headed for Langley Air Force Base. When the trucks got to the main entrance, they did not take the time to stop or even salute the main guard. They drove through the gates straight into a secret elevator chamber camouflaged as a wall.

Inside of the building, they exited the elevator and walked into an oval room furnished with a large oak table and several chairs. Video screens made out of glass that you could see through encircled the entire room. Raboy could see a digital panoramic view of Mother Earth. Mother Earth was highlighted with grids that measured the earth in square meters. Each square meter was numbered and named according to each different geographical location. Raboy had seen government screens before but nothing near the magnitude of this awesome sight.

"Mother Earth's magnetic field has been jumping around in all directions and now appears to be sideways. Our GPS satellites are being jammed by the magnetic configurations expanding into the A and B plasma zones. Presently they are useless. We are screwed. Rabbi Raboy, you better have some answers or else," commanded the six foot six inch tall General.

"Or else what, General? Are you going insane or something? The Rabbi does not control the universe. General Ravers, I think you need a butt kicking, and I am the man to do it," said Dr. Einstein.

"Who is this idiot?" yelled out the General.

"An idiot that is right in this case," said the President. "Mr. President, pardon me for my outburst, but we are stumped with this one and."

"General, please be quiet," commanded the President of the United States.

"Rabbi, so we meet again. I am sorry I keep demanding your presence but this time we meet under a totally different set of circumstances.

Before it was nuclear fallout, and today it is only God Almighty knows what," said the President putting forth his hand to the Rabbi.

"Mr. President, I have told you everything I know. I studied the magnetic tectonic plate charts but have no clue what is going on. My understanding about the tectonic plates is a blur to me. I cannot give you any foresight or knowledge about this topic," responded Raboy.

"I think you can. That is why you have been brought to this location. Our top scientists worked hard all night long preparing what you seek. Shortly it will be displayed on these silicon crystal video screens. I know you will help us make sense out of this nightmare," said the President being confident the Rabbi could interpret the information.

"Mr. President, gentlemen, and Rabbi, I am ready to start my presentation. This display will reveal what the Rabbi has requested," said the professor.

After his brief comment, the professor had the computer graphics technician fill the giant screens with Mother Earth's tectonic plate grid patterns. The professor pointed out that the Aborigine may be right in their thinking when they say earth is held together by those that race about at the speed of light and lines of magnetic force. There are magnetic lines upon lines crisscrossing everywhere. Raboy looked at the maze and remembered what Yirawala had told him in secret. He knew Yirawala would be able to pick them out, but he also knew that Yirawala would not break his tribal secrets about the Dreamtime to outsiders. This was a perplexing situation for the Rabbi, who knew that several billion people's lives were at risk. Here he stood with several dignitaries looking over his shoulders hoping for a solution. He put his left hand to his head and quietly stared at the screens trying to figure out how to expose secret Aborigine information to those that had tried to genocide their race.

"Professor, what I am about to disclose to you cannot leave this room. Can everyone agree with that?" asked Raboy.

"Rabbi, rabbi, what kind of jerks do you think we are?" answered Dr. Einstein.

"Okay, here goes nothing. I told you the Aborigine and Hopi Native Americans believe that Mother Earth is going to have a sixth purification and/or sixth rebirth. She will turn upside down according to what Isaiah and other prophets have told us. Upside down can have many different connotations, so let us be frank about this. I have no idea what Isaiah meant. I have given my word I would not reveal any Aborigine or Hopi secret tribal knowledge to anyone and that is final. They have been ridiculed enough, so stop pestering me," said Raboy.

"Rabbi, Mother Earth is falling apart, and you are worried about an oath of secrecy with the Aborigines? What the hell is wrong with you? Can you just tell us what you know? That is, if you know anything," said the professor.

At that very second, the building started twisting and turning in all directions. Some of the people started screaming and yelling while others stood still, frozen in a catatonic state. Then it stopped. Everyone looked at Raboy waiting for some answers.

"Alright, here it goes. You should already know that the Aborigine have a spiritual experience called the Dreamtime. They believe their spiritual creators live on this world unlike Jews, Christians, Moslems and many other religions that believe their Creator lives in a dimension hidden from the flesh somewhere in the universe. The Aborigine hand down information from generation to generation that tells about the several rebirths of Mother Earth. They believe much of their present knowledge has been revealed to them the Dreamtime by the Rainbow Serpent. They have been told that our planet will go through a sixth rebirth, wherein she will cleanse herself. Their forefathers have told them, through the Dreamtime, all about the fragile magnetic plates that hold Mother Earth together. I was shown several cliff paintings how this all is put together. I could not tell the difference between what was fantasy and reality, so I looked at the carving and paintings as works of art and made sketches to study at a later date," explained Raboy.

"Rabbi, we already know that," said the professor.

"I know, but please let me finish. The next group I encountered was the Hopi Native Americans which believe Mother Earth will go through a process called the sixth purification. Please note the similarities both spiritual groups have in common. Both believe earth has gone through this five times before. Please note that their worlds are ten thousands of miles apart, divided by the great gulf called the Pacific Ocean. I would like to point out they do not have any cultural similarities, except they both respect the earth's creatures and elements," said the Rabbi.

"We already know about the Aborigine and Hopi cultural beliefs. We want to know more about the Aborigine secrets about the forces controlling the tectonic plates that hold Mother Earth together," said the General.

"May I continue?" interjected the Rabbi.

"Yes, by all means Rabbi, be our guest," replied the straggly professor.

"According to their ancient beliefs, man has experienced magnetic pole shifts many times, but reversal tectonic magnetic lines has only happened five times since earth began to produce life forms. It means Mother Earth has had five major life cycles. The Hebrew Torah has deemed that Mother Earth was created about six thousand years ago, and there is only one recorded event in which Mother Earth purified herself. By studying the book of the prophets, my guess is the fifth rebirth was the great flood during the time of Noah. I have interpreted the book of the prophets as suggesting the sixth purification is the time of times when the abomination of desolation strikes Mother Earth. At that time, our present age comes to an end so a new age of creation may begin. It does not tell us where, when, why, or exactly how, but only that it will happen," said Rabbi.

"Rabbi, please elaborate," said the President.

"I thought this prophecy may have already taken place or was a symbolic notion. In the small scale of things, Mother Earth has had several catastrophes that have disrupted life on our planet. The only problem I have is that I have been visited by several messengers from the Lord in the form of angelic beings. These beings came to me to forewarn the people as our prophets have proclaimed thousands of years ago," said Raboy.

"Okay, so we are believers. What in God's green earth do we do now other than pray for His divine mercy," said Dr. Einstein.

"I have been desperately trying to make sense out of the various prophecies. I believe the Aborigines when they say that Mother Earth is held together by lines of magnetic force that reverse every so many millenniums. If the lines of force reverse and start to twist out of their present shape the continents will be pulled into positions forming a different Mother Earth," said the Rabbi holding on his beard with his left hand.

"I am impressed with your theory. Are you able to recognize any of these lines on our maps the Aborigines have shown you?" asked the professor.

"Yes, every one you have pinpointed on your maps looks almost exactly like the ones Yirawala painted on the sacred caves in Australia," said the Rabbi.

"So, man is doomed," said Dr. Einstein.

"I hope what you say is not so, because if you are correct many will die and few will be left. The book of the prophets has declared these events thousands of years ago. Of course, that is my opinion. Of course, everyone has their own interpretation," replied the Rabbi.

"Those damn Indian and Chinese arrogant bastards started this whole mess because of their greed," barked General Freetag.

"What are you going to do, kill them?" asked the professor.

"Funny professor, you know almost everyone in China and India is already dead or dying. So man's demise has been created by his own carelessness through his destructive creations designed to destroy rather than preserve Mother Earth. God Almighty does not have to do a thing to destroy the earth or mankind. We have done an excellent job on our own," said the President.

"Do you have any idea if there is a safe place to live?" asked the professor.

"The Hopi Native Reservation, New Mexico, Nebraska, and north central Texas will be the safest places. Other than that, I have no idea where anyone will be safe," replied the Rabbi.

"Everyone let us go home. It is evident that the massive amount of thermonuclear bombs used during the Asian Twar have given rise to many magnetic aberrations within the tectonic plates. Mother Earth is going to break apart into a millions pieces like a muddy lake bed that has dried out. We will have to live in an obliterated earth that will change every earthly inhabitant's way of life. I mean every plant, animal, and even the elements will be affected," summarized the professor of applied physics from MIT.

"Sorry, Rabbi, if we have interrupted your vacation," said the President.

Everyone put their heads down knowing there was nothing any man living on Earth could do to stop the massive global destruction set in motion by the Asian T-war. The scientists knew that time would answer the question whether the human race would survive the sixth purification and rebirth of Mother Earth. Rabbi Raboy was driven back to the Israeli Embassy. He got out of the car and looked at the sun move in very unusual patterns in the morning sky, wondering what was going to happen next.

"David, kiss me," begged Abigail, as she hugged and kissed Raboy if she had not seen him in a long time.

"Okay, Sweetheart what is wrong?" asked Raboy very calmly.

"I am packed, and we are going home before this world falls apart. Enough is enough. If God Almighty is going to destroy us or let us live, I do not care anymore. I am tired of traveling around like vagabonds," said Abigail.

"Sweetheart, Are you pregnant again?" asked Raboy.

"I am not sure, but your third child could be on the way," she replied.

"How could that happen? We have not been making love," said Raboy.

"Tiger muffin, I think it was Hopi Reservation Love that might have set the life creating process in motion," she replied.

"The high altitude of the Arizona plateau seems to make you fertile or something. Maybe you are more comfortable there than any other place on Mother Earth. Do you think?"

"David, does it really matter?" she asked, whispering in his ear.

"Are you really packed and ready to go home?" asked Raboy.

"I told you earlier. I am ready to go. Have you noticed the sun moving about like it was dancing in the sky? Everyone in America is moving about blind. They must be living in complete denial, because it appears to me it is business as usual for most of them. Something is terribly wrong with Mother Earth, or the sun, or the moon, or the universe. Let us go home. I want my children to be born, live their life, and die in Israel." Abigail stopped when the Ambassador walked out on the front porch.

"David, arrangements have been made for you to be taken to Andrews Air Force Base so that you may once again be flown back to Israel. The US government would like to thank you for your assistance. Will you be available if they have any questions or need your help?" asked his brother.

"Yes, that would be fine," replied David Raboy.

Then it hit. Mother Earth started wobbling to the point the Raboys could now feel the earth move back and forth under their feet. Abigail froze in place. The Ambassador hung onto a nearby tree limb to keep his balance. Rabbi Raboy was knocked off balance and fell to the ground. Then Mother Earth stopped, but the sun appeared to be dancing around in the sky.

"It is time to go home," said Raboy, as he got back on his feet.

"I will get the children," said Abigail.

"Dear brother, where is the vehicle that will be taking us to the Air Base you had spoken about earlier?" asked Raboy.

"Hell with them. I will take you myself. I want to talk to the pilot that will be flying you home," said the Ambassador.

"Why would you want to do that?" asked Raboy.

"I want to see if there is space for me and my family, too," replied the Ambassador.

"You want to come home, too?" asked Raboy.

"Well, if I am going to die, it might as well be on my home soil," replied the Ambassador.

"That is a very bleak outlook on life, brother. How do you know you are not standing at the safest place on Mother Earth?" uttered the Rabbi.

"Where does one hide when the earth moves? The Lord did not start this global abomination, but will He intervene to stop this cosmic collapse?"

"Brother, I wonder if human beings really started these earth changes or if happens to be timing that Mother Earth started her rebirth right after the Asian T-War. Do you think human beings have really put themselves in this predicament?" asked Raboy.

"If your thinking is correct, then why does the Lord let things like this happen?" asked the Ambassador.

"Brother I cannot speak for the Lord, nor do I have the power to influence Him to change His will. I am sure it all has a purpose that will make sense sooner or later," replied Raboy.

"What is His will?" asked the Ambassador.

"You should have read the book of the prophets and the laws of the Torah. Maybe, just maybe you would have some idea what He requires man to do," replied Raboy.

Six US Air Force black Powerstars drove up and parked on the driveway. Several armed guards stepped out. It was the convoy sent by the president to escort the Raboys to Andrews Air Force Base safely. They boarded an US Air Force transport aircraft that immediately took off for Israel.

"David, sweetie, I have a problem. I have wanted to discuss this with you for a long time now and I feel that the time is right," said Abigail.

"What is that, sweetheart?" asked Raboy.

"I am afraid to fly," she replied.

"You must be joking with me," he answered with a smile on his face.

"No, I am serious. Every time I get into one of these metal containers, I am scared to death. I have always wanted to tell you since our first trip to Australia, but held back because I wanted to be with you so much," Abigail uttered softly.

"I am puzzled and shocked at what you just have said. What can I say or do now? We are half way between Europe and North America," he replied.

"I know there is nothing that can be done at the present moment, but in the future you will have to travel by yourself. I love you and will miss you every second you are gone, but I cannot do this anymore," she said.

"I am stunned. The amount of sacrifice you had to do for me in secret. I thought you always enjoyed our trips together. Abigail I am lost for words to say, except I love and cherish you even more," he replied.

"Thank you, I needed to hear that. Now, I have enjoyed our trips immensely. It is just getting there on all of these helicopters, jets, and planes. Can we take a train instead? It would make it easier on my nerves."

"Of course, my sweetheart, we can. I am not sure what trips or traveling we will do in the future, but I will remember what you have spoken this day for eternity. I cannot express how much I adore you," said Raboy, embracing his wife tenderly.

The US Air Force aircraft landed safely at an Israeli military installation. The Raboys and were greeted by a host of Israeli officials including Dr. Einstein. Raboy said nothing to those that wanted to know what was going on with Mother Earth. He waved at a few and shook a few hands as his family boarded a private bus headed for his humble home in the rocky formations near an old well that was dug over three thousands years ago.

Thinking about what Abigail had told him, he decided to walk up to the three thousand year old well and get a drink of water. He needed the time to digest all that the world had thrown at him. With Abigail's confession about the fear of flying Raboy wondered what other secrets she held in heart to be with him.

In the past, Rabbi Raboy had often walked up to this well encased with sandstone thinking about the many different generations of people that had taken a drink from this well. Many times he tried to envision who and when did his ancestors take a drink of water standing exactly where he stood. Although, the water had sustained many of his ancient Israeli ancestor's lives, it did not seem to matter to him anymore.

He often looked around at the landscape thinking about the people that had lived in this arid area, but not today. Today was different than the many other times he had walked back to his home throughout the years. Mother Earth was doing the unbelievable and unimaginable. At first, he thought he was imagining something strange happening, but it was real. He looked this way and that way watching the rocks twist out of shape. The sky started to change to a strange bluegreen just like the color emitted from fireworks when they explode. He was knocked off his feet and fell to the ground. All he could think about was the safety of his family. He started to cry out for Abigail, but he knew she could not hear him. He managed to get back on his feet only to experience a tremendous earth twister. He felt like he was sliding around on wet ice as he fell to the ground again. A high-pitched, deafening sound seemed to come from everywhere as the sun appeared to become stationary.

Rabbi Raboy tried to get up, but the gravitational force pull on his body was too great. His head felt like it was being crushed and twisted out of shape. His bones felt like they were turning inside out throughout his body. Suddenly it stopped. Rabbi Raboy got back on his feet again to find that his eyesight was distorted. He kept rubbing his eyes until he could see good enough to get back to his house.

"Abigail, Abigail, where are you? Abigail, Abigail, where are you? Are you alright? Did you feel and experience what I just felt? Abigail—" said Raboy, as Abigail interrupted him.

"David, what is wrong? Why are you yelling and puffing so hard? What is wrong?"

"Did you feel it!" he replied still shaken from his experience.

"Yes, David, I felt it," she said, looking at him if he was insane.

"Okay, never mind, everything is fine. Everything is wonderful and fine," he said, as he sat down into his favorite chair. It was apparent to him that Abigail had not experienced what he had just gone through.

Later that month, Mother Earth started making eerie sounds that could be heard throughout the world. They made a sound like a screeching, tearing, ripping, and grinding all at the same time. Raboy plugged his ears with cotton balls to block out the sound to keep from going crazy. Animals of all sorts cried and howled throughout the night. The eerie sounds did not stop until the next morning when the sun started to set at nine o'clock in the morning. Raboy ran out the door to witness what he thought was a solar eclipse. He was highly mistaken.

"Abigail, there appears to be a very unusual solar eclipse taking place. The sun appears to be setting at nine o'clock. Does that happen during an eclipse?"

"I do not think so. Why not call the weather station and ask them what is going on?" she replied not being aware of the situation.

Then the sun started to rise against, and then later on it began to set again at approximately noon. Knowing something beyond logic was happening Raboy called the news stations and weather service to find out what they had to say. One newscaster told him the sky was falling. Another told him it was a normal phenomenon. He knew they were lying to him. After listening to the bogus information, Raboy decided to call Dr. Einstein, to see if he knew what was taking place.

"Is Dr. Einstein available?" asked Raboy.

"I will have to ask Dr. Einstein. Can you please hold for a moment?" said the operator.

"Rabbi, I knew you would eventually need me. I knew it. How can I assist my fellow countryman?" asked Dr. Einstein.

"Why is the sun going down at nine o'clock, and then it rose and set again at noon?" asked Raboy.

"Since you are the great prophet of Israel I think you should be telling me, rather than asking me this," smartly replied Dr. Einstein.

"Simon, this is why I avoid you. Can you tell me without all of the drama?" demanded Raboy.

"It appears Mother Earth has changed her axis relative to how it used to be positioned to the sun. It appears that the rotation in the southern hemisphere is stuck with constant sunlight and the northern hemisphere in a state of constant darkness. I saying that the earth has flipped or repositioned so that the South Pole is constantly facing the sun," replied Dr. Einstein.

"That is impossible. The northern hemisphere would freeze and the southern one would burn up," replied Raboy thinking that Einstein was not being truthful.

"If that is true, I have no idea what will happen to life as we know it. Rabbi, you knew this was going to happen all along. Since your original prophetic research paper that hit my desk years ago I knew you knew the future of our planet," remarked Dr. Einstein.

"How many times do I have to repeat myself! It was not my prophecy! That paper was the summation of a message given to me by a supernatural being. I am going to have to study it over and over again until I understand what my forefathers were trying to tell us. Talk to you later, Dr. Einstein," said Raboy, as he hung up the phone.

He scurried out of his house and headed for his office building where he had pinned the original angelic message to his bulletin board. He wanted to read it one more time to see if he had missed something it proclaimed. Methodically he scoured over the verses, message and interpretation his colleagues had given him.

After three days of cross referencing and studying the ancient Hebrew phrases, he could not find any connotations that changed the original verses' meanings. Next, he carefully compared it to some of his colleague's modern interpretations of the ancient text of Isaiah. Again, he could not find any differences in the text's meanings. Even with all of his painstaking research, he could not find any differences in the interpretation from that of his colleagues.

It burdened his heart to think about whether Mother Earth was literally going to turn upside down or if this was a prophecy that had another symbolic meaning. Having a prophecy right in front of you and figuring how it should be applied to what was happening to Mother Earth troubled Raboy.

As he sat there thinking about the meaning of the angelic visitation the building started to shake in a very peculiar fashion. The stone blocks twisted out of their natural form without breaking. Raboy watched the building twist inside out. After being in the building for a few moments, he decided to go outside and see what was going on. He stepped out on the mezzanine and noticed it was still dusk, as the sun had drastically changed its position in the sky. He looked at his watch to see what time it was. It was three o'clock in the afternoon.

Reluctantly, Raboy decided to call Dr. Einstein one more time. It burned his soul to ask Einstein anything, especially what was physically happening to Mother Earth, but his curiosity was getting the best of him. He picked up the phone and started to dial when a massive golden bright light appeared in his office. Raboy did not duck, although he was scared. He covered his face and blocked the fear that usually overcame him as he stood there in awe.

"Rabbi, this is the beginning of men's sorrows for they have not believed the truth. Fear not for our Father is with you," said the gigantic angelic being, disappearing as fast as it had appeared.

"Well, well, well. What does that supposed to mean? I am sure this visitation has an outlying message I am suppose to decipher, but what would that be? I am going to call Dr. Einstein against my better judgment. Maybe, I should not. Yes, I am going to call him and find out what he knows about what is happening to my planet," said Raboy out loud.

He picked up the phone and attempted to call Einstein, but was unable because he was still trembling from the unsuspected visitation. He sat the phone down and then picked it up again several times before dialing. It rang seven times with no answer. Raboy knew Dr. Einstein was there but did not choose to answer his phone. He tried dialing several different times, getting the same results. Frustrated he decided to go home.

He locked up the secret room with his Cohen departmental R&D key. He strolled down the street, thinking about the supernatural visitation when a strong wind started blowing against his face. His hat blew off. He picked it up, dusted it off, put it back on his head, and continued strolling home thinking about what was, what is, and what will be. As he approached his street, a green German automobile rushed passed him, and then came to a sliding stop. Dr. Einstein jumped out of his car along with three other secret police.

"Rabbi Raboy, is that you?" asked Dr. Einstein.

"Yes, you know it is."

"Were you trying to call me just a few moments ago?" he asked suspiciously.

"You know I was trying to call you."

"Good then," answered Dr. Einstein, as he jumped back into his car and sped away.

Rabbi Raboy shook his head back and forth wondering what kind of a psycho Einstein was. He walked up to his front door, took the keys out of his pocket and opened the door. Upon entering the house, he noticed there weren't any lights burning save the porch light. He entered the foyer, reaching for the light switch, and then all of a sudden all of the lights came on throughout the house. Over a hundred people started coming out of the woodwork yelling at the top of their lungs.

Rabbi Raboy jumped back, his heart started racing, and his eyes popped wide open. Stunned, he noticed Abigail heading his direction with a two layer German Chocolate cake with many candles burning bright. He stood frozen in his footsteps. He couldn't speak a word. Everything seemed in slow motion. He couldn't fathom what was going on.

"Surprise!" yelled everyone at the same time.

Then Abigail placed the cake in front of him as Jeremiah kept yelling at his father, "Blow them out, blow out the candles, father."

"Sweetie, happy birthday," said Abigail.

Then everyone joined in and started singing "For He Is A Jolly Good Fellow" for a few times until Abigail got everyone to sing, "Happy Birthday." As Raboy realized what was happening, he started smile from ear to ear.

"What is this all about?" he asked knowing what was going on.

"Your sister decided to celebrate your birthday, so we all agreed that when we came back from America we would have a family gathering to surprise you. Were you surprised?"

"Oh, yes, I was surprised. I was scared out of my mind. This is a wonderful and frightening experience at the same time. I am lost for words," he replied.

"Blow out the candles father, before it's too, late," cried out Jeremiah.

Rabbi Raboy took a moment to blow out the candles as everyone cheered him on. His eldest sister hugged him and then grabbed his arm to force him to dance with her. The musicians started playing Israeli traditional folk music. Everyone joined in to dance around anywhere they could in the overly crowded house. No sooner did Raboy start to enjoy the party and forget about the earth changes when Dr. Einstein yelled out for the Rabbi.

"Rabbi Raboy, Rabbi Raboy! I need to talk to you immediately," cried Dr. Einstein.

"Have a piece of cake, and then I will talk with you, Simon the Pest," replied Raboy.

"We need to talk now," yelled out Dr. Einstein over the noise produced by the crowd.

"Not until you have a piece of cake. With all of the craziness I have been through today, I am going to take the time to sit down and enjoy my life for a moment. Relax, your questions can wait and no other answer is acceptable," said Raboy, smiling at Dr. Einstein.

"The world is coming to an end, and all you want to do is celebrate your birthday by eating cake. I do not know what to make of this, Raboy," said Dr. Einstein.

"I know you do not. That is why I insist you must sit down and have a piece of cake with me before I will hear you out," replied Raboy.

Einstein got angry with Raboy's nonsensical answers so he politely got up and left the party. Abigail smiled as she watched Dr. Einstein scurry out the front door with his three body guards. The Raboy's did not hear from Einstein again for several weeks.

For three months now, Mother Earth remained tilted at a ninety degree angle that prohibited the sun from shedding her light on the northern hemisphere. With this positional configuration of earth, the sun neither rose nor set. An ice age was starting to develop in the northern hemisphere while a boiling mess ensued at the South Pole. The gases from the boiling oceans formed massive clouds that saturated the atmosphere. The saturated with moisture raced to the northern hemisphere through the swirling jet streams caused the ninety degree angle of the earth's rotation. The massive clouds caused one continuous snow and ice storm north of the Tropic of Cancer. Ice layers were building up daily throughout Canada and Russia while Argentina, South Africa, and Australia turned into unbearable instant deserts. In the northern hemisphere, millions of green plants were instantly frozen by the frigid temperatures. Innumerable numbers of humans and animals marched south, abandoning their frozen habitats in the northern hemisphere. At the same time, millions of humans and animals in the southern hemisphere headed north to find relief from the extreme heat.

Throughout most of the planet humans were either burning up or freezing to death. Only those living between the Tropic of Cancer and Capricorn had any semblance of normal weather patterns, except for the constant daylight/darkness mix. It appeared to be either constant dawn or dusk to the Raboy household. The sun did not quite rise but never quite set either.

"Rabbi Raboy, do you want to talk to me, yet?" asked Dr. Einstein in a muffled voice over the phone.

"What would we talk about? Mother Earth has started her purification and rebirth process," replied Raboy.

"For your information the Antarctic land mass has melted away enough ice to flood the world, but since the arctic has balanced the problem with the massive amounts of ice being formed has stabilized our sea shores," said Dr. Einstein.

"I already know that from the newsreels," replied Raboy.

"Do you know about the ancient village recently discovered in Antarctica? Some paleontologists are saying this is the first civilization of man or the lost continent of Atlantis," smartly remarked Dr. Einstein.

"You say that the melting ice in the Antarctica has exposed an ancient civilization," replied Raboy now closely listening to Einstein.

"This is something you need to see with your own eyes. I assure you that will be astounded to hear what I know," replied Dr. Einstein.

"You really think I will be astounded after what I have been through," remarked Raboy.

"Yes, you will be flabbergasted. I am not joking around with you Rabbi, you must see this," said Dr. Einstein.

"Come on over and have lunch. We will talk about me taking a trip down there with my wife. That is about me taking a trip to the fiery continent of Antarctica," said Raboy.

"I will come over immediately," said Dr. Einstein, slamming his phone down.

Two hours later, Dr. Einstein, accompanied by two Israeli archeological scientists, knocked on Rabbi Raboy's door. Abigail answered and invited the expected guests in. Although, she had a great disliking for Dr. Einstein, she made him and the others feel welcome by offering them some rare Turkish coffee. Raboy sat outside on an old cedar tree stump that had been carved into a chair.

He sat there drinking some fresh pomegranate juice, listening to the wind make his olive trees sing. He just sat there on purpose to make Dr. Einstein and his scientists wait for over thirty minutes to see if they really wanted to see him. He made sure they were serious before he came in the house to discuss the Antarctic archeological find. As he came up the stairs, Dr. Einstein started to say something rude but held back his tongue knowing Raboy was up to something.

"Rabbi, it is a pleasure to see you this fine afternoon that seems to be drawn out by your absence and lack of concern for my time," said Dr. Einstein.

"Let's cut out the nonsensical chatter, Simon. Rabbi let us get down to the business at hand," said a tall curly haired scientist.

Everyone stopped and peered at him thinking what was wrong with this person. Then Abigail came in and stared directly at the scientist.

"Professor, I know you are some kind of super spy so that archeology nonsense does not go over with me. Why do you want my husband to travel to that hot desolate island continent?" she said firmly.

"Fair question. It's like this, an ancient civilization has been found that has writing similar to ancient Hebrew script. We wanted someone to look at it that knows ancient Hebrew text and experienced with ancient cultural geographical meanings, the architectural designs, and art work's possible connotations. We are hoping Rabbi Raboy was that person that could decipher some of the ancient cryptic writings. The ancient script has an intelligent flow to its contents and context," explained the scientist.

"What you have said so far sounds make sense to me. Please continue," said Abigail.

"We need him to help us understand or give us a clue as to how to understand some of the ancient scripts, that are all," said the tall curly haired scientist.

"Sir, what is your name? You do have a name?" asked Abigail.

"Dr. Paul A. Wiseman, and this is my brother Dr. Paul B. Wiseman," he answered.

"Your jokes will not get far with me, buster. Now if you do not answer me honestly and correctly I am going to throw you both out on your heads. Do you understand me?"

"Without any disrespect madam, these are really our God given names," said the other scientist.

"Dr. Einstein, David is not going on your mission. Is that clear?" sternly remarked Abigail. She then bent over and grabbed her stomach.

"What is wrong, dear?" asked Raboy.

"It is just our little one kicking me," she said moving her hand around her stomach.

"I assure you Abigail their names are as they have stated. Their father was a bit eccentric, and their mother died during the birth of the second twin, so their father named them the best he could under the extreme circumstances," said Dr. Einstein.

"If what you are saying is true, then I apologize. David can go, but only for two weeks. This eerie darkness along with millions of people migrating makes me very weary. The thought of being left all alone makes me nervous. You better take care of him and no funny stuff Einstein. I think, oh, go ahead," she replied with a distraught voice.

"Abigail, I will put a dozen sentries to guard you, your family, and your household twenty-four hours a day while the Rabbi is away with us," said Dr. Einstein.

"Thank you, but he is going because I think it is the Lord's Will," she replied.

Abigail agreed with Einstein, so Raboy started packing right away. Three military vehicles drove up to his front door only ten minutes after Einstein and the two scientists had left the Raboy's home. Abigail cried, knowing this would be the only second time they had ever been apart since they were married. She would have loved to gone but knew she could not take her children and unborn child into a dry, desolate climate that reached temperatures of over one hundred and sixty degrees.

"Boy, they did not take much time to come get you. I know that sneaking Einstein had the trucks waiting around the corner," complained Abigail.

"Sweetheart, you know how Einstein is. If you say you do not, you would be lying," said Raboy trying to make Abigail feel at ease with the situation.

Rabbi Raboy felt weak inside knowing he would be separated from his family for two weeks, but he felt the trip was necessary. He figured if he was able to make something out of the ancient writings, it might be possible to answer some of the questions about Mother Earth's purification and rebirth process. He left on hours from the time he had met with Einstein.

The flight took fourteen hours from Israel to reach the Antarctic colony called Port Thermo. It was located near a Antarctica river eight hundred miles north of the South Pole. The jet landed on the tarmac during an Antarctica dust storm. Many of the scientists were calling Antarctica the Sandy Ice Desert. A rather illogical term since all of the ice had already melted, that exposed the bare soil that made the entire continent a lifeless desert. After Raboy got off the aircraft, he read an airport plaque.

"Who would have ever thought that Antarctica would look like this?"

Raboy thought about the sign remembering what Sarah had seen in her dream. Knowing that she really did see Mother Earth in a way she could not describe.

As soon as he stepped off of the plane, he was shuttled by a military helicopter to the ancient Antarctica settlement. He walked slowly about observing every inch of the civilization feeling like he had walked back in time before Noah built the great Ark. The ancient colony was haven for Raboy to explore the antiquities of early man.

Einstein and the two scientists took Raboy right away to a giant building carved out into the mountain side. It had archways build far superior to those of the Roman and Egyptian architecture.

Then Raboy came upon something that sent a shock wave through his body. He felt like he had been hit right between the eyes by a club. Looking around the building he beheld writings presented in a similar fashion as Moses had written the first five books of the Torah. Rabbi Raboy did not totally understand this method of writing but since he had studied many early forms of written scripts he felt he could translate it.

"Dr. Einstein, do you have a tablet so I can write this down?" asked Raboy.

"Yes, and a video recorder, too," he replied.

"This says or states, if I am interpreting it correctly, due to the different connotations it may have, since it appears to be older than ancient Egypt—"

"Stop the mumbo jumbo and let us have it," said Dr. Einstein interrupting Raboy.

"I am not sure, but here it is. This passage states that the sun started shining one day and kept shining as the trees died out and rivers dried up. Everyone became scared and built boats to flee to the hinder lands," said Raboy not telling Einstein the entire truth.

"Where would these hinder lands be?" asked Dr. Einstein. Rabbi Raboy looked at him shaking his head in disbelief but continued, "This passage states that the sun never disappeared for many years, and it grew hotter and hotter until everyone was dead or had left for the hinder lands. The message was left by people that say they are from the fourth generation of mankind," said Rabbi Raboy.

"Amazing," said one of the scientists.

"Where did you learn how to read this language?" asked one of the American Jewish professors. This professor had studied many ancient Hebrew language types, interpretations and various ancient Hebrew scripts but could not interpret the script.

"It is against my oath as a Cohen to tell you, but since you are Jewish I will tell you this. Certain scripts of our forefather's ancient writings, which are well protected and kept in secret, are similar to this script," explained Raboy.

"That does not satisfy me," said the snotty Hebrew scholar.

"Sir, you are very disrespectful person. I am not a scientist, archeologist, cosmologist, or meteorologist. I am a rabbi that studies ancient Hebrew texts, and that is all."

"I think the Ice Age was caused by Mother Earth turning on its side, and then it turned back during a period of magnetic instability that ended the Ice Age. Presently, the ice in the northern hemisphere is growing at three inches a week, so it will not be long until Canada and Russia will be an uninhabitable ice blanket. How can you tell me such nonsense? We need more scientific information than what you are saying to deal with the present weather phenomena destroying the nations of the northern hemisphere," said the American Hebrew scholar continuing, "Why do you Cohen's always keep the rest of the Jewish sects at bay? We are children of Abraham like you."

"Feel the way you want, but I will tell you one secret. It is far deeper than being a child of Abraham. Deeper than being of the same bloodline of the original tribes of Jacob who Moses referred to as the chosen people," said Raboy.

"What might that be?" asked the American.

"This is the key secret we Cohen's know," replied Raboy knowing that the American Hebrew scholar had figured out Raboy was not telling the truth about what the writings told. The American walked away shaking his head cursing Raboy and the other Israelis.

"Rabbi, you have done well. I have to admit that you are one of the most obstinate people I have ever met," said the twin Israeli scientist.

Raboy shrugged his shoulders and went back to work. After studying the script for some time, he became frustrated. He decided to walk about and look at the various ancient artifacts. Many of them gave him an eerie feeling since they were almost identical to ancient Hebrew designs. He thought that perhaps this was the origin of his ancestors. What caught his eye were the cherubs inscribed onto many objects of pottery, buildings and various artifacts. Every Cherub was covered with a layer fine gold leaf. Raboy asked to take one back with him to study, but his requests were denied. Those in charge wanted to keep the ancient city as they had found it hoping it would them some clues as to how to deal Mother Earth's upheaval. Later that week Raboy was taken to a meeting held in one of the cavernous rooms near the center of the city.

"Rabbi, you must not tell anyone what we are going to tell you. Those of us that are involved with government circles are trained to lie about the truth. You must swear by the Lord's name that you will not tell anyone what you saw here. The public has always been lied to about the truth. So you must swear not reveal what we are about to tell you," said the tall curly haired scientist.

"I am not going to swear to anything using the Lord's name. If you want to tell me, then tell me. If not, then forget about it. I want to go home," replied Raboy.

"You are a tough nut to crack, Rabbi. Nevertheless, we just wanted you to know that the ice sheet in northern Canada and Russia is growing at one inch per day. That is significantly different than our first calculations. We now know the first known Ice Age to man could have been made in only a few years instead of centuries as we had previously calculated," said the second scientist.

"Our planet is a living nightmare and you are worried about an ice age theory. I must go home so I can get out of this insane asylum," said Raboy, shaking his head.

Raboy did not understand the magnitude of what he had just been told to keep secret. If he would have understood what the scientists were saying, he would have understood why the American Hebrew scholar was so upset with him. Raboy did not understand that America and Russian's world power was coming to an end. Raboy did not know how important he was because he could interpret the ancient script. Einstein felt that if Raboy could interpret the writings, Israel could become the next world power, because they would know how to deal with Mother Earth. Raboy told the Israelis, Americans and Russians important parts of the message, but did not tell any of them the true secrets of the ancient civilization rise to power and demise. After convincing the scientists there was nothing left to decipher, he was allowed to go home.

Raboy boarded one of the Israeli military aircraft and was taken home. He waved good bye to Dr. Einstein and his two weird scientists. He returned home without any strange aberrations or occurrences during the flight, which, for Raboy, that was an unusual experience. Abigail, accompanied by two military personnel, picked him up at an Israeli Air Force Base. The base commander attempted to ask Raboy some questions, but Raboy avoided him by acting like he was ill. Abigail was worried at first, but then started to laugh at the play-acting her husband did to get out of the officers grip.

"Did you miss me?" asked Abigail.

"Sweetheart, you were on my mind every second I was gone," Raboy replied, "Did you miss me?"

"No," replied Abigail.

Raboy's head dropped and his heart melted. Abigail felt bad saying what she said, seeing how reacted. She could feel his rejection by the expression on his face.

"David, if you are going to ask a stupid question, then you are going to get a stupid answer," she replied.

"You could have said a simple yes. I am always bothered by the fact that I have to say three times a day I love you and always answer your calls. But you on the other hand you ignore my calls with the excuse that you were busy. Why are you so difficult?" cried out Raboy.

"I am not difficult. I spent so much of my time worrying about you, I am exhausted," she replied holding her emotionally ruffed up sweetheart in her arms.

"What is it about you that makes you so you?" asked Raboy feeling more relaxed.

"Ask the Lord, He made me this way and you made me pregnant," she replied.

"Abigail, I have no more to say," he said, being happy just to be home.

"Tiger Muffin, let's make airport love right now on the top deck of the parking lot?" asked Abigail.

"Abigail, I do not think that would be appropriate since this is a military compound, plus you a bit too pregnant to make love," replied Raboy knowing that Abigail was playing with him.

"I am good for almost four more weeks according to Dr. Swartz," she replied.

"You know it is not good during your pregnancy," rebutted Raboy.

"David, I am just having fun with you. I missed you so much I am angry inside, but filled with so much joy to see you. I just want to hold you in my arms and never let you go. Darling, I love you so much" explained Abigail.

"Sweetie, it is time to go home," he replied hugging her so tenderly.

"I need you to make love to me and you are not going to get out of it, so submit yourself and put a smile on my face," she replied.

"This is insane, but I did promise you during our secret oath between one another to keep a smile on your face," he replied starting to play along with Abigail little girl actions.

Abigail and Raboy held each all through the night. The next morning Raboy noticed that Dr. Einstein had called him six times that morning. Raboy reluctantly decided to see what Einstein wanted so he called him right away.

"Hello, this is he," said Dr. Einstein.

"What is the meaning of calling my house six time this morning?" asked Raboy.

"I urgently needed to talk to you. You must meet me at the Israeli Secret Police Academy at noon in two days. This information is so shocking I wanted you to hear it in person," said Dr. Einstein.

"Are you still in Antarctica?" asked Raboy.

"Yes, but I am on my way back to Israel. I will leave in about two hours."

"Okay, I'll meet with you, but please stop calling every two hours," commanded Raboy.

"I cannot very well call you while I am in flight, can I?"

Two days later, Raboy figured Einstein had made it home, so he got dressed and drove to the ISP headquarters to meet with him. After waiting around in the ISP front office for a couple of hours, Raboy finally asked why Dr. Einstein had not come out to greet him.

"Ahh Miss, I am here to meet up with Dr. Einstein this morning. Can you please call him and let him know I have been waiting for almost two hours now?" asked Raboy.

"I will inquire his whereabouts and let him know you are here," she replied.

After about ten minutes, three gentlemen in identical dark green military attire approached Rabbi Raboy. One stood to his left, one to his right, and the other directly in front of him. They stared at him for a moment.

"Are you Rabbi Raboy?" asked the grey bearded officer.

"Yes, that would be me. Are you here to take me to meet with Dr. Einstein?" asked Raboy.

"Not exactly, Rabbi. We are here to tell you of some very unfortunate news," said the officer.

"So, Dr. Einstein is unavailable to meet with me?" asked Raboy earnestly.

"No, Sir! Sir, Dr. Einstein, will not be able to meet with anyone because his jet went down yesterday over the Indian Ocean. We assume he is dead along with the other passengers. We are very sorry and regret to have to tell you this information," said the grey bearded officer.

"That is very sad news. I guess I will go home now. Thank you for informing me about Dr. Einstein," replied Raboy

Raboy was in shock. He had lost someone that bothered him a great deal, but someone that was close to him, too. Raboy had grown accustomed to Dr. Einstein's dogmatic, overbearing ways. He slouched down in his automobile seat as he drove home thinking about the Israeli government official he had to constantly deal with since his first trip to Australia many years ago.

For months, Mother Earth continued to wobble and jerk about causing several worldwide destructive events. During this time Raboy wondered why he was not approached by the Israeli government to assist them. From the news he learned that the South Pole continued to melt as the northern hemisphere continued to build ice glaciers hundreds of feet high. He never uttered one word to anyone about what he saw or knew about the ancient Antarctic city. Mother Earth constantly rocked and reeled, adjusting herself to the newly forming magnetic tectonic plate alignments.

Earthquakes abound in many regions throughout Mother Earth because of the effects of gravitational forces caused by the moon and sun as the earth rotated in her new position. Temperatures in the Antarctic had climbed above 200 degrees Fahrenheit, causing the thicker ice shelves melt away. Millions of refugees kept traveling to the more favorable climatic regions where the food, water, and the weather were more stable.

"Abigail, did you feel that?" asked Raboy.

"Yes," she answered.

"Did you feel that again?"

"Yes," she answered again.

"What do you think?" Raboy asks.

"I am not sure," she replied staring at Raboy.

"What do you think it was?"

"It feels like something is slipping underneath us," she replied.

357

All of sudden the sun peaked up over the horizon. Strange looking orange clouds started rumbling toward the Raboy's cottage. The storm clouds started twisting and spinning, and then turned a bright shade of royal blue near the storm's vortex. Abigail and David ran into the backyard and grabbed both of their children who were playing. Abigail screamed as she took the children to the cellar. The Rabbi got down on his hands and knees and started praying vehemently.

"Lord God of Israel, the God of Abraham, Isaac, and Jacob please, hear my plea for help. This storm looks too strong for my humble home to withstand. You have sent your mighty angels with many messages to my forefathers and a few to me about the fate of Mother Earth. Now it appears my life will be instantly destroyed by your terrible wrath," cried Raboy.

About that time two, ten foot tall angels appeared before the Rabbi.

"The Lord has heard your prayers and has heeded your call. The Lord God of all creation has sent us to comfort you," said the Angel on the right, then both angels vanished. Raboy then saw his house destroyed by the gamma ray storm by turning it into molecular dust. Then he saw the vortex coming straight toward him turning everything into molecular dust.

"Lord God of Israel am I to die this way after going through so much?" cried out Raboy.

The angle reappeared and said, "God's Will, will be done in heaven and on Earth."

Raboy ducted his head expecting the worst, to be turned into molecular dust.

END OF PART ONE